Permanent October

Cally E. Raduenzel

ISBN-13: 9780692235881

ISBN-10: 0692235884

Library of Congress Control Number: 2014910614

CreateSpace Independent Publishing Platform

North Charleston, South Carolina

Chapter 1

I sat strumming my acoustic Fender on the dusty red velvet covered futon I had inherited from an old roommate who was a sometimes hustler in Boys Town. I rarely used this sun-room but today with the warm light of a winter sun winking in and out of the clouds it gave me hope that spring would some day be here and I wouldn't feel so conflicted about my life.

Joe Jackson was singing about his hometown from my stereo and I was trying to follow along on my guitar. "I want to go back to my hometown, though I know it'll never be the same..." That's exactly how I was feeling today. With those mixed emotions on my mind I still felt I was better off than the poor rabbi attempting to escape from the pant-less drug addict asking him for money while walking down Lunt Street. I checked the INTHEHOOD "app" a digital bulletin board for our neighborhood and a favorite for the busy-bodies and someone had posted they were sending a cop to deal with the *pantless wonder* who was now pacing in front of the bus stop pontificating about God and the Rolling Stones. Thinking better of recording this for YouTube, I got up and placed my guitar back in its case, snapping it shut. Stretching my arms to the ceiling, I mused just another day in Rogers Park, my Chicago neighborhood! Honestly, I wouldn't change a thing but now it was time to get moving I had business in Indiana.

Hohman, Indiana, my hometown, was forty-five minutes and a planet away. I'd called Chicago home for over fifteen years, and I loved it here but today I was feeling squirrely. Still, as I'd grown up and changed in the past years, my hometown had as well. My gut was full of mixed feelings. A small part of me was excited to catch up with my old friend Crystal, but the larger, adult part of me was a mass of anxiety. I wasn't going to

Hohman to do anything fun - I was going to Hohman to meet with a lawyer about my late uncle's will.

Hohman had shaped me, but Chicago made me a woman. To be honest, sometimes I missed Hohman and longed to be a teenager again, walking to Dairy Queen, singing in choir, and watching movies at Crystal's house drinking soda (or cheap beer, if we could get it) until the sun came up. These thoughts churned in my mind as I got into my red VW Beetle and made my way onto 80/94, following the familiar path to Indiana.

Hohman was very much an upscale version of the American dream of the 1980's, trying so hard to be "more than Indiana" with fancy hair salons that served pink champagne and little boutiques selling monogrammed purses and Izod shirts. Many of Hohman High School graduates went to Ivy League schools (or at least to in-state colleges) and Woodmere Country Club reigned supreme as the quiet driving force that propelled Northwest Indiana's upper crust.

It certainly wasn't East Coast sophistication, more Jean Shepherd and letterman jackets, with just a smidge of Cheever-esque middle-class angst. We kids had our share of lazy teenage days at Hohman Mall, the grand bastion of zit-hiding, cosmetic-buying, boy-and-girl watching *mallness*. I hated to admit it, but I loved that mall. I'd spent many quality hours looking over cassette tapes and vinyl in an almost obsessive study of all forms of rock music. This was where my dreams of super-stardom had begun and stewed. Hohman Music was my Mecca, as a rock and roll obsessed teen. Those were the days of planning for fame and fortune in my chosen careers of rock star and writer! I would be the white girl version of Michael Jackson and get the hell out of this boring town, and see my name in lights at The Chicago Theatre or Danceteria in NYC! That was my grand plan.....

Then the prosperity of the 80's ended, and the town changed. Woodmere Country Club became Cabela's Sporting Emporium, and the cute boutiques were taken over by Target and Best Buy. The salons morphed into retail chain hair shops, dotting the area in its urban decline like the zits of those long lost mall kids. Even the mall was torn down, with just one lone major retailer left in its place, the store standing in the concrete parking lot like a lost kid in a Gary police station.

Now, I only came back here to visit my dad and his wife, but the memories still gave it the shadowy feeling of home. We'd go to the Commander Restaurant for lemon-rice soup, buy a cute gift at Maria's Hallmark, and drive past my childhood home to wave to the neighbors. I lived in Chicago now and I was no longer tied to this town. I wasn't like George in "It's A Wonderful Life," I did get to leave Hohman. In Chicago, I was reborn, my business cards listing my status as "Lucy Zwich, #1 Curly Hair Stylist in Chicago." These days, I was just a visitor in Hohman. It didn't keep the place from having an uncomfortably magnetic attraction, like maybe if I stayed, I'd be an idealistic teenager of the 80's again.

But alas, the other joke about Hohman was that no one ever leaves it for long, and I did not want that statement to apply to me!

I was meeting my high school best friend, Crystal, for lunch before a visit to the attorney's office. My favorite thing to come home to was Miner-Dunn, an old- fashioned burger joint that had changed very little since the early 50's. My mushroom burger would still come with a cup of swirly orange sherbet and the best onion rings I'd ever tasted. Parking my Beetle in the lot, I waved to Crystal, who'd found a window seat.

"So, what's the meeting with Functer for?" Crystal asked as I settled into the little booth facing busy Route 41. Crystal's dad used to golf with Mr. Functer, the town attorney, at Woodmere Country Club. As far as I knew, the town power brokers had moved their new martini gulping head quarters to Briar Ridge Country Club, the new and improved command post that had taken over Woodmere. I wondered where Mr. Functer golfed these days.

Crystal repeated the question as I glanced over the menu. "I don't really know why he wants to meet" I replied. "It's something about my Uncle Tavis' will."

Crystal nodded, looking like the young mom she was with her high-lighted hair pulled back into a quick ponytail an a touch of mascara and pink blush on her rosy cheeks. The boys had always loved Crystal, with her button nose, pouty Clara Bow lips and big wide green eyes that always made her seem very interested in what you were saying. Since she'd just finished teaching little kids how to play the piano, she wore her reading glasses that made her look more mature. Even though Crystal had two kids she still kept her figure slim - which I really admired, seeing as I could stand to lose about 25 lbs.

"You look great," Crystal fibbed, while we ate our burgers.

"My hair is the only thing I like these days." I sighed. People always said I must have had great 80's hair, with my huge mane of blond curls. Honestly, though, it either looked like a Little Orphan Annie afro or I straightened it till it sizzled during those years. The upside, back in the day, that fried straight hair made me look older, which came in handy for buying beer when I'd been underage.

"I do like you best with this arctic blond deal," she said, referring to my hair color. I guess she hadn't liked the previous color, a flaming carrot orange-red. "You're so lucky to be tall, Lucy. It means you never look porky. Short as I am, the minute I gain 20 pounds, I look like a balloon." Crystal sighed.

I didn't agree. I might be tall, but I was pushing the voluptuous status, to put it nicely, and I didn't even have the excuse of pregnancy to explain away the extra pounds. There were upsides and downsides to being built like a female Viking. My shape, my hair, my nearly six foot height, all of these factors sealed my fate as being something other than the cookie-cutter dainty little yuppie girl I had longed to be as a kid. The grass is always greener... I wanted to be skinny and petite, and Crystal wanted to be tall and powerful.

We gossiped about the usual suspects from our community. Sometimes it shocked me, how well our little group turned out despite the real life soap operas of our youth. Aside from parental suicides, murders, embezzlements, and a few scandals that made it to Chicago television, the Hohman kids had turned into respectable adults. All I'd heard growing up was that my friends were reprobates - but now they owned companies, managed banks, and ran for Senate instead of running from the law.

Crystal and I often discussed why she had not left Hohman. She and her husband had lived all over the world before the kids were born, so in my eyes, coming back here would be a total let down. Yet as I listened to her talk about dinners with her dad, shopping with her kids and mom, and the block parties they were planning, I could appreciate the insular cocoon-like charm of a small town. Something this star-struck kid could never fathom, when I was listening to Roxy Music at age 13 and counting the days until I could move to the big city.

Crystal finished off her last bite of burger, reminding me, "I really hope you'll come with us to trick or treat with the kids this year. You can bring Combover!" I could just imagine my overweight English Bulldog trotting from house to house, begging for treats. "Sounds cool," I said, grabbing the check before she could.

Walking to the register, Crystal and I hugged, and I promised to call her after the appointment with Functer. Then we parted in the restaurant parking lot with a wave. I'd wanted her to come with me to the appointment, but she was off to pick her two kids up at daycare. After Crystal departed, I found myself feeling scared, alone....and suddenly adult.

Chapter 2

I took a drive past our former high school on the way to the lawyer's office. The grey concrete façade of Hohman High School had gotten bigger, but not much prettier. The high school was a cheap brick and mortar fortress with just a few small windows, capped off with a red dome painted with the worlds "Go Hohman Henchmen." The dome had always reminded me of a crimson flying saucer, like aliens had landed at the high school. Ironically, I felt like the alien now, disguised as a local.

The parking lot of Mr. Functer's law office was right between a funeral home and a Red Lobster. Business was clearly booming at both today, since I was forced to park next to the hearse in back of Bishop Funeral Home. I wasn't relishing the idea of a visit with Mr. Functer, even with the prospect of good financial news. Going to meet an attorney always seemed to me like being called to the Principal's office in grade school. I always felt like I was going to be in trouble.

I walked into a forgettable-looking office building, which smelled of sculpted office carpeting, new paint and stale air. The plants that lined the long, silent hall were dusty and plastic. Nothing real could live in this off-white, laminated mortuary of a workspace.

The secretary who showed me into the office explained that Mr. Functer had just returned from the golf course. She wore an itchy-looking brown brittle tweed suit and had a leathery tan, probably from too many summers in the backyard spent trying to erase the fact that she worked here.

Functer bounded into the reception area in an eye-searingly bright ensemble of fine patchwork trousers and a lime green polo. Did it matter that it was 2006?

Nope, here the dress code was 1980's Preppy Handbook. "Lucy! So sorry for your loss!" Mr. Functer boomed, like a wrecking ball in a public library. He ushered me his office and shut the door. "I miss your uncle *like a son of bitch*. He was the best goddamned golf partner I ever had!" he said, and offered me a cocktail while making his way behind his desk, shuffling some papers.

I declined the drink, but that didn't stop him from pulling a bottle out of his desk and helping himself to a nice three-finger serving of McCallan's.

I stood awkwardly, confused as to why I was here. Mr. Functer had been very cloak and dagger on the phone, and I was curious. The same way Ray Charles would have been curious counting the teeth in the open mouth of a crocodile. "Please, have a seat," he said, than repeated, "have a seat."

I suddenly remembered that Mr. Functer repeated things a lot, like Jimmy Two Times from *Goodfellas* (the movie). Functer clearly hadn't changed at all over the years since I'd met him as a child, aside from a little gray at the temples. Crystal's parents, who knew him well, always joked that Mr. and Mrs. Functer looked like Barbara and George Bush. Mrs. Functer had always acted like her husband's mother, whose better half responded by behaving like a spoiled child whenever allowed to wander away from his wife.

We sat down in the office's overstuffed leather chairs, which sank under our weight. I noted that the chairs made Mr. Functer seem about eleven feet tall. He rubbed his hands together and said "Let's get down to brass tacks." Even his clichés were the same. I nodded in response. Mr. Functer took a sip of scotch and let the bomb drop.

"Your Uncle Tavis, God rest his martini-guzzling soul, left you his hunting lodge in his will." Functer spoke like a machine gun. "He used to invite everyone up - that man loved the great outdoors, a real man's man, we had some great times up here...." he trailed off, clearly savoring the memories. His eyes glazed over and he murmured "Great times up there." Again.

My mouth hung open, lip curled like Stallone, as I attempted to absorb what he had just blurted out so casually. For just a moment, I was stunned into an uncharacteristic silence, but I recovered quickly. "Can you explain a little?" I asked. There had to be more details. Surely there was some explanation as to why my outdoorsman uncle had left a hunting lodge to his city- dwelling hairdresser niece.

"I feel sort of like a game show host!" Functer said, with a grin and another gulp of scotch. "Miss Lucy Zwich, you're the big winner of the day! Hell, of the year!" He was attempting to play the part, but he didn't have the panache to pull it off. Functer rubbed his well- cared-for hands together, and then pointed to me. I was sitting still as a stone, trying to absorb what little information he'd given me. "You can go up to the Northern Territories and check things out," the lawyer said casually, leaning back in his chair. "You'll have to see if you want to live up there or not. There's a guy named Ned Bradshaw who always kept an eye on things for your uncle. Nice enough fellow, so he can show you the place when you go up there."Functer said, taking another slug of scotch. I didn't reply. The term "live there or not" echoed in my ears. Functer, didn't notice my lack of reply, being a rhetorical kind of guy. "You know what a gadget hound your uncle is - or was, I should say," he continued. "The place is loaded with all the modern amenities, so it's no dump. It's got a kind of Tyrolean flair! Tavis left you some money for renovations, since you might need to update it if you want to keep it. Thing is, though, if you don't keep the place, you don't get any money." Functer blinked twice and took yet another sip of his scotch.

"I have to live there permanently? In a hunting lodge?" I stammered.

"That's one of the stipulations of the inheritance." He said pedantically, finishing his drink. Functer's upper lip was beginning to glisten with perspiration, I noted.

I was still trying to get my head around the idea that my deceased uncle thought it was a good idea to leave me an inheritance only if I yanked my life up by the roots and whisked myself off to the middle of nowhere. The money and a cool pad absolutely sounded *kick ass*, but living in the Canadian wilderness?

"Mr. Functer," I said, trying to be polite but to the point, "I hope what I am about to say doesn't offend you, but I am a lesbian hairdresser who's lived in Chicago for the last twenty years. Why would I want to move to the backwoods of Canada?"

He didn't miss a beat. "Two hundred thousand dollars, plus change, after taxes. Oh, and you don't have to pay taxes on the place, there's a trust. It's a rent free situation." He said, smiling like a teenage boy who'd caught a glimpse of a naked lady.

My jaw dropped again. Why would my uncle do this to me? It was a blessing attached to a boulder. I was speechless. I knew my uncle loved me, but there were other kids in the family he probably loved more. It all felt so unreal. This kind of stuff just doesn't happen to the black sheep of the family! It wasn't sinking in. Mr. Functer was talking, and it was like a scene from a Charlie Brown cartoon - the ones where you can't under-stand the teacher, wa-wan-wah. I just let him ramble, and figured I'd let my cousin's attorney husband look over all the technicalities and explain things to me.

"So, *anyhoo*...you let me know your plans and then we'll get this ball rollin'," said Mr. Functer cheerfully. "Paper work and such," he added, nodding and pouring a bit more scotch into his crystal glass. "Sure you don't want to drink?" he asked, as he swirled around the beverage in his glass to accentuate the point.

"I'm in a Twelve Step program." I said flatly.

"Oh," he said, still nodding. "Well, bully for you!" His feelings seemed genuine; he wasn't a bad guy. He was just from another generation, and I didn't feel connected to him or any of this. I was in shock. I'd always felt like I was simply a visitor in the hotel of life. The feeling kind of made me sad, but I also knew I was the only one who had the power to change it. My dad used to say that we are defined by the decisions we make in life - and this was a big one!

I was left in the corridor with the lingering scent of his Old Spice and my head swimming with possibilities. As the leathery secretary began to close the door to the office, she added "You're just too pretty to be a lesbian! See you soon - bye!" Click.

I rolled my eyes. There was something so presumptive and rude about that backhanded compliment, and yet *so very* Hohman, Indiana.

I got into my car and gunned the engine of my Beetle as I backed out of the parking lot and got onto the road.

What a decision for me to make! It would definitely take a few Twelve Step meetings, a talk with my cousin Lauren, and maybe I'd call my sponsor while I was at it.

Excitement and fear felt like a bubbling cauldren in my stomach, or maybe it was that Miner-Dunn burger I had inhaled at lunch. All I knew was I felt different as I rode through my hometown and as usual, I was happy to get back on the highway to Chicago. Chicago...could I leave it for Canada?

Chapter 3

"Soooo, what are you going to do?" My coworker Bradley asked comically. He looked like a cross between Snidely Whiplash and John Waters, right down to the dyed- black toothbrush mustache and tall, thin physique. I'd been dragged out back at work for a smoke, mostly so we could dish about my recent inheritance situation.

Bradley was the only one I'd shared my secret with at work - I didn't really want to talk about it at the salon. The whole situation seemed surreal. If I spoke about it at work, it would be real, and I'd have to explain my decision. I hadn't made a decision yet. I was still reeling with shock, and my Twelve Step sponsor Trudy had advised me to pray about it and let the decision just ride for the moment.

As Bradley and I sat on the picnic benches on the weathered porch facing the back lot of the salon, the landscape looked pretty barren. Unkempt and in desperate need of attention, thick, stubby city-cactus weeds jutted out from the crevices between the buildings, which were old red brick coachhouses. You'd never guess what the back look like, from viewing the front of the posh salon. "Rat Warning" posters were stapled onto telephone poles, reminding us to be on the look out for the creepy rodents. Someone had misspelled "Suk it" with spray paint on the coach house doors, which still could be opened like the old stable doors they'd been a hundred years before.

The mystery and architecture of Nelson Algren's gritty city had always appealed to me. Layers of paint and old crown molding were priceless artifacts I felt very connected to, living in an iPhone world that seemed to drag me into its clutches like tin cans behind a herse.

"God...I, I'm sure I want to keep it. Not just for the cash. I love Canada...I'm just wondering if I should move there...live there." I replied to Brad, pulling my sweater more tightly around my shoulders.

Fall's early fingers were tickling me with their chilly touch. An offer of more from the universe was making me excited, or maybe it was the expectation of the unknown. Maybe it would be cool to get out of this rat race. Maybe I could leave Chicago.

"Are you crazy?" Brad asked sincerely, giving me the stink-eye and crinkling his nose. "Canada? Now if it was South Beach....." He sighed, glowing in his own fantasy for a millisecond.

"No, seriously." I replied. "My ex and I use to fantasize about retiring to Provincetown, or somewhere out east, and this would be even better. I love snow. My uncle use to take me up to Fossil Creek, where the lodge is, when I was a kid and we would go horseback riding, sailing, fishing...it was amazing. He always made me feel very special. The place is only about an hour outside of Montreal. There are high-end ski resorts there - it's not a shack in the woods, Brad."

"Do they speak French?" Brad asked, arching his eyebrows.

"As I recall, yes. Lots of French." I sighed. "I took seven years of it between college and high school and still can't speak it. But I'll learn."

Brad was suddenly a bit more intrigued. Leaning in towards me, he volunteered, "...get Rosetta Stone, you're a talker, you'll learn." he suddenly was changing his tune. "But Lucy, no one's going to pay $75 for a special 'Curly Girl' haircut in the sticks." He crushed out his cigarette and gave me a long look. "I'm just saying."

With that, he sauntered back to work, leaving me alone in the parking lot to listen to the people in the coach-house next door have loud sex. I listened for a few moments, taking the last long drag off my nicotine stick. Yeah, I thought and there's that too. I bet there's no lesbians in Fossil Creek, either.

My Uncle Tavis loved Fossil Creek. It was far away from the city, and the strip joints and sporting goods stores he owned there. Most people had no idea about the strip joints, but I'd overheard my dad arguing with my uncle one night. I couldn't make out too many words, but I did over-hear something about some woman from the Playboy Club. The terms "seedy," "make the right decision," "sell those dumps," and "marry again" also featured heavily in the discussion. Then my dad saw me lurking, and

I got grounded for playing I-Spy. "One of these days, Lucy, you are going to get your fingers snapped in Pandora's Box, and you won't like it!" Dad had warned. He'd added that I wasn't 007, and sent me off to bed.

Years later, my uncle told me about his clubs. It didn't bug me, as long as the women didn't get beat up or treated like shit. For me, part of being a feminist is being able to do what you want to do for a living, and not having people tear you down for your choices.

My Uncle Tavis liked women, he liked me, and I needed someone who made me feel less toad-like as puberty reared its ugly head. On our Canada trips, we always talked about comedy, music, and writers - even spiritual stuff - but never about our personal lives. I'd never come out to him, but I think he knew, and there was just nothing to say about it. I knew he was lonely and sad, and I couldn't figure it out. My uncle always had a pretty women waiting in the wings, and he went to the coolest parties. He seemed to be like me, a thumb on the hand of life. When Tavis died, it felt like I had lost a sibling. It had broken something in me; something I still didn't know how to fix. Tavis had a certain Santa Claus type of joy that he'd brought to every occasion. I didn't know anyone else who made me feel that way, and I was afraid I never would.

Calling my cousin Lauren wasn't the tonic I'd hoped for, since she was more than a little shaken up about the news. She'd always had a fantasy that we would be the city girls, and I would come and hang with her kids, but between her business and my writing, salon commitments, and attempts to record a CD, we had to work hard to see each other once a month. She was a classy, Ann-Taylor- wearing, social-events-attending doctor, who also happened to have two little kids and an attorney husband. Our lives were on radically different time schedules, if nothing else.

"I'm getting burnt out on Chicago full time." I admitted to Lauren. "What about your music and writing?" she asked. I could hear the Cubs game on in the background, and the kids attempting to get her off the phone. "I can do it there." I said. "It's not like these part-time endeavors are making me any real money. I have to face facts - music and writing are hobbies. Believe me, it kills me to say it. You know how hard I've worked."

"Honey? Can you flip the steaks?" she called out to her husband, then apologized and let me ramble on. She listened to the whole thing, like the saint she'd always been in my eyes. She might not always agree with me, but she respected my decisions and even stood up for me. I explained, "I love Chicago Comics, Quimby's, Strange Cargo, Hollywood Mirror and Second Hand Tunes," I said, "plus the Alley, Kopi Café, Sushi Luxe, Fiesta Mexicana, Furama for Dim-Sum and shall we not forget my sanctuary, SHAKE RATTLE AND READ, but how often can I shop and eat? I go to these places all the time, I need new digs - then a few times a year I can come back to Chicago, pig out on pop culture, and stay with you."

I could almost hear her mental gears turning. "I'm just going to bring a few things up," she said finally. "I don't want you to get mad at me for saying them; I just want you to chew on them while you're making this decision. I want you to know you will make the right decision, and that I have great faith in you."

She switched to her professional doctor voice. "This is Canada. It's a foreign country and Lucy, you don't like change, you get lost easily, and you get stressed when denied your pop culture pleasures. You're a spoiled American... just like me," she said, and then giggled. "You need The Annoyance Theatre, The Scooty and Jo-Jo Show with the drag queens at Hamburger Mary's on a Tuesday, you need your opera at the Lyric and dance at The Joffrey Ballet, not to mention Marshall's, yeah, Marshall's and The Brown Elephant, for the best upscale thrifting you could ever flippin' want! They don't have all this in Fossil Creek, so do you think you can live happily there?" Then she got quiet suddenly and asked softly, "Can you just keep it for pleasure? As a vacation house?"

"Unfortunately, no. It's either living up at the lodge, or give it up entirely."

"That is so controlling on Uncle Tavis' part." grumbled Lauren.

"I know," I sighed. "But since he's dead, there's no arguing the point now."

"Whatever you choose, I will support you 100%."

Now that's why Lauren was a saint in my book. But after I got off the phone I felt uneasy. She'd brought up good points. I went to sit on my sun porch, even though the sun was gone. The starry night sparkled, and my iced tea grew lukewarm in my hand. The only deep thought that came to my mind was "shit or get off the pot."

Chapter 4

After our chat, Lauren insisted on coming to see my possible new home.

We used her frequent flyer miles to fly free from O'Hare to Trudeau Airport, where the property caretaker, Ned Bradshaw, picked us up. He couldn't have looked more Canuck in his red flannel shirt and canvas, putty-colored painter pants. His mint green Ford pickup truck was no limo, but it had lots of room for our bags, and the heat worked. It was one of those old sturdy forestry vehicles, like the one my friend Kelly had when she'd lived in Evergreen, Colorado. The seats were covered with woven rag rugs "to cover the holes," Ned explained as he stroked his newly clean-shaven chin. "The Missus hated my beard, and I just got sick of arguing." Ned explained, as we loaded our things into the tarp- covered truck bed. The drive was cozy, in a carnival ride kind of way, considering the cab barely fit three and the shocks felt about as spring-y as a New York City cab. Lauren was unusually quiet.

Ned seemed really nice, and reminded me of Andy Capp in the newspaper's Sunday cartoon section. He was sporting a hat with floppy fur ear protectors, and his fatigue-green galoshes squished and squeaked every time he hit the brake or the gas. His face was weathered with friendly smile lines, like a man who enjoyed laughter and a good pipe by the hearth. "You guys came all the way from Chicago! My son lives in Chicago... actually Evanston. He's an architect." he told us.

"Fantastic! I lived in Evanston for a while," I said, shifting my butt on the hump in the center part of the seat.

"How did you like Evanston?" Ned asked curiously. "Honestly, Ned, it's not my cup of tea. A little too much pretension, but they've got a great library!"

Ned chuckled, "I'm glad to hear you say that, Lucy, because Fossil Creek is not a darn thing like Evanston." Lauren and I cocked our eyebrows at each other.

"So, how do you think Lucy will fit in?" Lauren asked Ned. Ned got quiet for a minute. There was no radio to fill the silence in the truck. Then he gave me a quick sideways glance and smirked. "I have the feeling wherever Lucy goes, she's going to find a home." he said. It was my turn to smile, and I announced "I like you, Ned!"

I noticed Lauren seemed to exhale and relax. She looked really cute in her Ralph Lauren Fall collection, but I had the feeling she would have fit in better in Kennebunkport than Fossil Creek. She was like my classy sister. Ned had commented on my smiling skull and cross bone sweater and there was the obvious difference between Lauren and me. She'd always veered to the right, and I veered to the left, but somehow we managed to meet right in the middle.

The drive took about an hour. As I looked at the panoramic golden and red trees, I could hear their chatty rustle as the wind picked up their leaves like a grass skirt in an autumn hula dance.

The sun's glow peeking over the horizon of the winding road made me feel like God was taking us on a grand tour of his finest artwork. The intoxicating oily pine scent, rich and rustic, mingled with the earthy fragrance of distant chimney smoke, wafting in through the open car window, and there was a sense of ease and comfort that settled over me. It was a long time coming. It made me sad to think I didn't have a partner here to share it with me. I knew I shouldn't be thinking of romance at that particular moment, but that's the story of my life. I don't know if I'd call myself a romantic...more like someone with unrealistic expectations.

"I hoped you two packed some warm gear, because it can get mighty chilly up here." said Ned. "Now you're speaking my language," I told him, "I'm a Nordic girl at heart." I grinned.

Lauren sighed, an asked "Does the heat work...or is there at least a fireplace?"

"Lauren, my dear," said Ned, "you're in luck. The lodge has a furnace, three air conditioners, two fireplaces, a dishwasher, a washer and dryer... all the comforts of home. Problem is that it's been vacant for a few years. The decorating is about twenty years old, so don't get too bent out of shape about the decor. I'm not a maid, just a handy man." He eased the truck down the heavily tree-lined, graveled driveway - we could hear the stone and shell bits crunch under the weight of the tires as we pulled in.

The driveway was in pretty good shape, considering what Ned had just told us. My heartbeat quickened as we approached the lodge. The view was stunning, in an unreal way. I almost expected Hansel and Gretel to come running out of the forest asking for help.

The lodge's design was circa late 19th century, facing out onto the lake. The Swiss-chalet-meets-country- lodge spread seemed almost too fantastic for words. I didn't recall it ever being as picturesque as it looked right now. Maybe I'd just been too spoiled to appreciate it when I was young. The old leaves and webs full of bugs gave it a mysterious flair. The more closely we inspected the property, the more obvious it became that repairs were going to be needed. Shutters were falling off the front windows, the steps were bowing, and the roof looked like a little moss sanctuary had been in residence for the last hundred years. Can anyone say Hobbit-habitat? But all the same, it felt like seeing a long lost friend, and I was immediately in love. So were the mice, raccoons and birds that had made the lodge their home while it had been vacant.

When Ned opened the front door, the first thing Lauren said was "We have a lot of work to do." It wasn't condescending at all, just a statement of fact. My first thought wasn't about the repairs needed, but about the Scooby Doo episode with the ski lodge and the Peter Lorre bellhop char- acter. It looked like a haunted cabin. The great room's walls were cov- ered with mounted heads of long dead animals, nicely draped with thick filmy cobwebs that blew like fairy capes when we opened the front door. Elk, moose, pheasant, deer and other wild game greeted us with silent stares. Rod Sterling's voice was running through my head, "Submitted for your approval." The animal's eyes seemed to be following me, sizing me up. Creepy-cool, I smirked to myself as my eyes took in the whole room. Every surface was shellacked blondish red wood, with a stunning old world richness and dust as thick as a lint trap.

"Was this a hotel at some point?" I asked Ned, who had fallen behind and was standing close to the front door as if hoping for a quick escape. "It's been a lot of things." Ned replied. "But yes…it was a ski lodge, back in 1846." "1846!" I yelped. "Oh my God, I had no idea it was so old. How amazing."

"Some of the fixtures in the hallway leading to the rooms are still gas light." Ned told us, and then led us over by the hallway to the left. He turned a little key on one of the hurricane lamps that screwed into the wall and took out a package of stick matches to light the lamp.

"I'm kind of surprised my uncle didn't tear down the front desk." I said, looking around. "It still looks like it's ready for people to check in."

"Well," Ned said nervously, "there were some strange stipulations in the sale of this place back in the late sixties when Tavis bought it…no tearing down of major structures. The building has some kind of landmark protection."

I wondered how I was supposed to renovate this place. "Do I have to get permission to tear down walls and stuff?" I asked Ned.

"Why would you want to tear down walls?" Ned asked suspiciously.

"I may not…but if I did?" I prodded. "You can go over it with that attorney." Ned said firmly. His cheery manner seemed to have cooled considerably.

"Ned, I love this place. That's one of the reasons I'm considering moving here. But we can't live in the past, and I may need a better bathroom or something. That's all I'm saying." I reassured him. Ned seemed to relax. "We're definitely going to need a cleaning crew," Lauren added, pointing her thumb at the hearth, which had a huge barn spider centered in a trampoline-style web. "I think it's been waiting for us," she said, shuddering. I squinted at the spider. Ned took that as a cue to go over and squish it with a little ash shovel from the hook next to the fireplace.

Lauren wandered off, the explorer spirit drawing her in. "Check out the bedrooms," she called back. "Real fifties type stuff. Norman Bates meets Boy's Life at the Betty Crocker Ranch."

"Lauren, you have a way with words," I called back. I was glad all the furniture was covered with sheets, or we would've had a terrible time cleaning the dust off.

Ned commented. "The house where time stood still." He patted a five-foot statue of a Native American that stood nobly in the long hall.

"How far is town?" I asked Ned from the mouth of the hallway, as we made our way towards Lauren. I admired an old photo of a grizzly-bearded fisherman showing off his five-foot catch. Hooks, fishing rods and old snow shoes lined the pine log walls. It was the most intimate setting that my uncle owned...his other residences had a more hotel-like quality. This was obviously the place he loved the best.

"About ten minutes or so to town." Ned replied.

"I'd be happy to take you there." Ned seemed to enjoy walking around, too. "That would be great." I said. "I want to get some supplies, maybe rent a car."

"You'll notice the kitchen and bathrooms are clean and everything works." Ned said. "My wife and I made sure of it."

"That's really sweet of you." I said.

Ned smiled and blushed. I had the feeling he would be my surrogate family here in Fossil Creek...I just hoped I wasn't misled.

Chapter 5

The town of Fossil Creek was right out of a Bob Seger song. Rustic, friendly and small- town reserved. There was a lot of French being spoken, due to the town being close to Montreal. There were no Menard's, no Target's, and no Chili's Mexican restaurants around. "Was this an old mining town, Ned?" I asked.

"Right-o," he said, parking the Ford up at the general store.

Ned introduced us to Bob, the store's proprietor. He was a huge hulk of a man with a bristly beard, wearing a tie-dyed Harley-Davidson shirt. I was going make some dough on facial hair maintenance here. That was a fact!

Bob pointed outside to his Harley, and regaled us with stories of his amazing road trips from Maine to California. "Then my back and knees went out and I got this dang arthritis, so I took over my dad's store. It was the best thing that could've happened to me, since I was becoming a bit of a burn out."

Bob did resemble Jerry Garcia, furry, jolly immediately likable. He loaded us up with every possible thing we'd need to set up house - including a box with flashlights, knives, and a large assortment of tools. I saw him smirk as he tossed an odd-shaped something on the top of the pile "...and don't forget the Oreos! Je suis mon prefere."

He chuckled, in a mock hillbilly-French accent, as we all carried the groceries and supplies out to the truck.

"If I decide to move up here," I said as we finished loading up, "I'm thinking about getting a horse for travel when the snow is deep. Do you think I'd also need a snowmobile, or maybe a truck?"

"Out where yer at," Bob replied, "I think the horse would be a definite plus. Are you sure you can make it up there on your own? These winters are no joke, Lucy. People die out here."

"Don't know if I can do it, Bob, but I'm pretty sure I want to try."

If the house weren't as up to date as it was - minus the desperate need for housekeeping - I might have had second thoughts. The house was a ten minute drive from town, though, and I had not one but three backup generators. I felt pretty sure that I could survive at least one winter up here.

"Honey," said Bob, "don't think about it, just do it. Things are harsh up here, but it's worth it." He put a few more canned goods in the truck for me. "Chicago is a great city, I know. I played with a band there when I was just a kid, 19 or so - but up here, this is where God lives, you know?"

"I get it, I really do." I said, looking at pocket-knives. They had a mother-of-pearl inlay, just like the one my Gramps had used to teach me to whittle. Bob explained, "We'll try and help ya through, but you got to be prepared. You're comin' in late in the year, and we've already had the first snow."

We all piled into the truck, but before we left, Big Bob invited us down to his favorite bar. "We got karaoke tonight at the Houndstooth, you guys should come. It's the central meeting place, whatever you want to know, whatever you need...you'll find it there."

"Bob, I don't drink anymore. You think the Houndstooth can handle me? "He smirked and got closer to the passenger door, "Friends of Bill meet in the backroom every Thursday night at eight. I'll be there!" he said quietly. "It's a date!" I said, and Bob winked at me. With that, he slapped the truck door and waved us off.

I nodded at a smiling Lauren, and said cheerfully "I think I'm going to like this place."

"Ok, last stop." Ned pointed to a store. "We got to get you a gun, and teach you how to use it."

"A GUN!" Lauren shrieked.

"We're up here in the wild, "Ned said reasonably. "Without a gun, Lucy could wind up dead. We've got bears and other wildlife, and these critters aren't tame. Not to mention, she's going to be alone up there, unless you're planning on moving with her. She needs protection, and her uncle already picked out a gun for her. All she has to do is learn to use it."

"Seriously?" I squeaked. I was shocked.

"Yup." said Ned. "Tavis said that when you were a kid, you used to shoot skeet. The shotgun he chose has very little kick, and you'll feel comfortable with it." I felt a fleeting lump in my throat. Uncle Tav had really thought this all out, right down to protecting me. Lauren, meanwhile, was giving me the stink eye and shaking her head.

"Ned, you seem pretty sure I'm going to stay." I said.

"Let's just say your uncle knew you would," he replied. "Tavis said you were a soulful girl, but you'd never really found your place in the world. He wanted to give you that special place, where you could belong. Where you could be happy."

"God bless him." I said, feeling a lump in my throat. "He was a great guy. Heart of gold."

"Funny," said Ned, "that's what he said about you. Now after the gun, we're going to talk to a man about a horse."

We all chuckled at that one. Honestly, I wouldn't have been buying all this gear if I hadn't already made the decision to stay - but I said nothing out loud, just in case I chickened out. I could always take the stuff home with me to Chicago, I reasoned (everything except the horse).

Back at the lodge, Lauren put her anal-retentive cleaning skills to use. As soon as we walked in the door, she was pulling out the mop buckets, brooms, and the Murphy's Oil Soap. "Lucy, since you stink at cleaning, you take the laundry." she decreed. "Those sheets, bedspreads, towels, they're all pretty musty. Don't be afraid of the bleach."

She sounded like my grade school gym coach. "Lauren," I said gently. "I really appreciate your help. I know you're not thrilled about my moving all the way up here."

She put down the full mop bucket and sighed. "I love you so much." she said. "And I'll be honest; the idea of you moving up here scares the hell out of me. I just don't want anything to happen to you - it would kill me.

You're the sister I never had, and I want you to be happy. Even if being happy means moving to the wilds of Canada."

"Me too." I said. "I want to be happy. And I think I can be happy here." Now I sounded immature. But a little less intensity and a lot more grounded-ness was exactly what I wanted for my life.

"I know. You're funny, positive, hard-working, creative, spiritual, kind, you've got so many great qualities, but I think your uncle knew that you were missing something in here." She circled her heart with her finger-tip. I nodded. I couldn't speak or I'd get teary, because I knew what Lauren was saying was the absolute truth.

I meditated, I went to Twelve Step meetings, I prayed, went to comedy shows, tried to exercise, and had a nice group of healthy friends. I was educated, had published short stories (many of them comedy) and I loved to sing, but I still felt something deep inside me was missing. I didn't know if this change of life would heal that, but I was willing to try. I started in on the laundry and put on my iPod, listening to Spinal Tap. That made me smile.

By the time 10pm rolled around, the Lodge was shaping up. Lauren and I regrouped in the main room on the freshly-Frebreezed couch to discuss our finds. "I found so many cool things in the bedroom drawers," I said. "I have to wonder if my uncle didn't plant these things for me. He loved games - any kind of game, but especially treasure hunts.

"You never talk about your aunt." Lauren said. "What's up with her? I always assumed she was dead." Since Lauren was a relative from my mom's side of the family, she didn't know all the dirt from my dad's family "Oh, it was heartbreaking." I said. Which it was, at least the version of the story I'd been told about my aunt.

Chapter 6

I did my best to recount the story of Aunt Greta for Lauren. The details had always been a little fuzzy.

"My aunt and uncle met in Germany when he was stationed there at an airbase. Greta came to America with him after he left the service, and they got married. Believe it or not, she was a Playboy Bunny. Made a bunch of cash doing it, then quit and went to nursing school. Eventually, she went back to Berlin to visit her mom and dad and when she was coming back...the plane crashed, she was killed. Tavis never remarried. He had some girlfriends, but nothing serious." I thought of Henna, his last one before his death. I'd liked her.

"So...she was a Playboy Bunny!" said Lauren. "That was in the hey-days of the Playboy Club, right? The Sixties?"

"I think so," I said slowly. "I'm not great on details, and you know how elaborate these family tales get." Lauren agreed. Our family had such a "Secret Squirrel Agenda" that it was almost impossible to separate the fact from fiction. Lauren and I had gotten sick of it and did our best not to get caught up in the gossip. Like smoke, the truth always seemed to seep through the cracks, if you were willing to wait long enough.

We kept cleaning until I lost patience and plunked down in the big wingback chair by the fireplace. "Are the beds made?" Lauren asked, sounding like the ultimate mother. She had spoken with her kids at least eight times today. Unfortunately for them, her cell reception was great out here.

"Yes, Drill Sargent." I sighed, and took a swig off my water bottle, staring into the dark fireplace. Soon we'd light the hearth and tell some ghost stories.

"I think tomorrow, since its Thursday and all, we should go hit the Houndstooth." I said. "Terrific," said Lauren, stretching her muscles. "I can't believe Bob's a Twelve Stepper, it's so cool for you to have an instant buddy." I absolutely agreed. The last thing I expected to find in Fossil Creek was an active Twelve Step group, but this place was surprising in a lot of ways.

"You going to sing karaoke?" Lauren teased. "I know you hate it."

"I hate it because I take music too seriously. It's like flashbacks to the State competitions when I was a teenager. Logically, I know I'm singing to a bar full of people who don't give a rat's ass about me or my music, but I hate not pulling out the stops and doing my absolute best when I'm on stage." I replied, trying to negotiate my psyche into being cool and laid back. "I can just sing for fun here, the pressure is off." I didn't even sound convincing to myself.

Lauren was leaning on the front desk, in her green sweats and a pink bandanna.

"Are you really going to buy a horse?"

"Hell yes." I said firmly. "There's a stable out back, and I'm sure I can find a local guy tomorrow to help me clean it out. I just want a sweet natured old galoot. One that Combover will like."

"Your dog is going to love it here, I bet," said Lauren.

"I wish you'd move out here with me." I whined, knowing it was impossible.

"When I retire," Lauren said, "it will be to a hot sunny place with room service and pedicures. Not the northern part of the middle of nowhere in Canada."

"I know." I pouted. "Promise me that you'll come to visit?"

She sighed dramatically, assuming a regal pose. "This lodge will be my summer retreat. Jackie O. had Bar Harbor, I'll have Fossil Creek."

"I wouldn't really compare Fossil Creek and Bar Harbor." I said skeptically.

"And I'm not Jackie O!" Lauren replied, giggling. We squealed with laughter like teenagers. Then the Drill Sergeant tone was back, and

Lauren had the furniture polish in hand. "Ok, I'm turning the music back on, I'll finish the front room by the fire place so we can chill and set up the morning coffee, you get our rooms finished. I want three pillows; this princess doesn't want a pancake for her pillow!"

We slept like babies in the cool air coming off the lake. Lauren had set up two electric heaters around her bed, since she liked her bedroom toasty warm. My bedroom was cold, because I prefer snuggling in with down comforters. Everything smelled fresh and clean.

I recalled sleeping over at my beloved Grandma's, in her attic. The little twin bed folded me in like familiar arms, and the downy goodness of the old pillows felt safe and reassuring, like I would always have a home. Thank God for dry cleaning dryer sheets from Bob's store, otherwise I'd be recalling camping with Grams and how the sleeping bags smelled like spilled milk and garage mold. I chuckled myself to sleep.

The next morning, I padded into the kitchen in my Homer Simpson slippers and flipped on the local classic rock station. To my delight, they were playing one of my favorite Stones songs, "Till The Next Time We Say Good- bye," a slow burning and atmospheric tune, by The Stones. Lauren and I sat in the little breakfast nook off the kitchen, surrounded by windows. I had the sneaking suspicion that the nook had been a newer addition to the house, due to the cooler temperature there and the modern feel of the built-in U-shaped seating around the long table.

I sipped my coffee slowly, taking in the various photos and drawings of different types of indigenous fish and wild game, framed and matted. Each picture had little preparation notes, like gourmet recipe cards, below the fish or fowl in old-fashioned calligraphy. The homemade cheese Danish that Bob had supplied us with the day before was pastry heaven, and Lauren and I munched for a few silent moments. Lauren couldn't help herself, and blurted out, "Your hair looks like Don King this morning."

"You want me to get Mike Tyson on you? I just woke up!" I said. Then I added, "I don't think I'm going to need any of my pine candles up here, because the air actually smells fresh and woodsy. You forget what clean air smells like when you've been in the city for 16 years."

Lauren nodded in agreement. "I have decided to reserve the room I'm in as mine in perpetuity. I'm already nesting, and my room has a great view of the stable and pond," she said, taking our plates to the sink.

"There's a pond?" I asked. "How did I not know there's a pond?"

"There is a pond." Lauren confirmed. "While you were still snoozing away, I walked around with my coffee and the grounds of this place are amazing. I saw two old guys fishing on the lake, drinking beers at 6 in the morning. Got to love that. Then I saw a little trail by the stable, followed it around, and I'll be damned if there wasn't a little pond right there, all green and slimy, but still beautiful. There was a deer just standing there staring at me, like I was interrupting." Lauren's new found enthusiasm reassured me about my decision to stay here.

"There are little shacks around there, too. I could see them in the distance. Plus a tree house - well, probably a hunter's fort, in this area." Lauren continued, bringing me over to the twelve foot windows that looked over the lake. "See, up there to your left."

I saw it immediately. "It's like a look-out loft - neato!"

After breakfast, we changed into our ugly clothes and spent day two doing more cleaning and organizing. By late afternoon we needed a coffee break and a change of activity!

"Let's go scout and check out the shacks...we may find tools and stuff there." I said.

"You can bring your shotgun!" Lauren taunted.

"Whatever!" I said, slightly offended by her mocking tone. "I promised I wouldn't use it until Ned gave me a few lessons. Unless you get outta line!"

She shook her head. "So you really used to go shooting?"

"My dad liked to take us when we were kids," I said. "My uncle, too. All that macho stuff." All the macho stuff, "plus assisting my dad in his gourmet cooking endeavors."

"What about your brother?" Lauren asked. I wondered for a silent moment what Neil was doing in Hauula right this minute.

"What about him?"

"I mean, does he know your Uncle gave you this place?"

"I don't know." I admitted. "He's in Hawaii, and I haven't emailed him yet."

"You get along with him?" Lauren asked.

It was a hard question to answer. Since my brother had moved to Hawaii, he and Jenny, his wife, hadn't really been in communication with much of the extended family. Due to the tug-of-war that my mother and stepmother had tried to set up, my brother and I tended to keep our relationship as a distant, closed loop, not involving anyone other than the two of us. We texted, emailed, and sent out cards occasionally. There were times that I felt like he and I were like some kids in a Civil War family, where some members were on the North and the others were rooting for the South, and everyone was still family but there was still a war on.

There were times when we'd have needed to walk on eggshells around one another if we'd talked about anything personal, so we talked about music, TV and current events. All I knew was when I did spend time with Neil, I was so purely connected and happy...but also afraid I could lose him at a moment's notice. There had been times when we didn't communicate, when I'd had to learn to stand-alone against the crowd. My family was the toughest crowd. I didn't ever want to lose my mom, my brother or my dad again. But I also wasn't going to sacrifice my sanity to try to please everyone...my grown up self knew that couldn't be done.

"Neil and I are close in our own way." I said, and then paused for a minute. "It's difficult to explain. He and I have this weird, unspoken bond. He knows if I need him, and I know when he needs me. He sends me lots of funny email photos, and I write back."

"Um." said Lauren, sounding dubious, "Okay. Will he be jealous?"

"I have no idea." I said honestly. "Maybe because of the money? But he'd never want to move here. He and his wife live in Hawaii, for God's sake. That's where he and I are total opposites. I like it cold and snowy; he likes it warm and beachy."

"Okay, Ranger Rick." Lauren said. "Let's go out and scout around."

I brought a crowbar, some WD-40, and a ring of keys that weighed about 40lbs. It was slightly frosty outside, so we put on our gloves and zipped our coats tight.

"Hey," said Lauren, after we'd been tramping around for a while. "Check out this little building...what is it, a cottage?"

She was right. It was an adorable modern-ish Tyrolean cottage with a seventies A-frame vibe; I could just imagine some shag carpeting and a bottle of *Mogen David* on ice, waiting for me after a day on the slopes. The song "Love Shack" ran through my head as we peeked in through the window.

"It looks like someone lives here!" I said, seeing the pot on the little stove by the fireplace. "Someone does!" A voice bellowed behind us. It wasn't a man's voice - this was an angry-sounding woman.

"Sorry!" I apologized quickly, turning around and walking up to her slowly.

"Who in the hell are you?" The woman demanded. She was tall and bundled up really well, with a knee-length down coat and a stocking cap pulled down tightly over her ears. She looked like someone used to navigating the woods - this woman was no tourist.

"I, um" I stuttered, "My uncle Tavis used to own the lodge up here."

"Oh yes...I know your uncle." said the woman. She was frowning and her tone was condescending.

"He really was a great guy." I said, feeling defensive.

"Did he kick off?" she asked bluntly. Something about her bad-ass demeanor seemed contrived.

Lauren was at my side, bristling like a guard dog. "Lady," she snarled, "that's a rude thing to ask and a ruder way to ask it."

"Oh?" said the stranger. "And who might you be?"

"I'm the goddamned Welcome Wagon." Lauren growled. Lauren was scary when she was pissed off. She might have seemed like a nice, upper middle-class lady doctor from the North Shore, but she'd been in West Point for two years. Some things stay with you.

The stranger twitched, pulling off her stocking cap. A long, thick braid tumbled out, the color of limestone and sand, and her face was revealed.

Without the hat and closely-wrapped scarf, it was easy to see that she was...lovely. Chiseled features, cool blue eyes, and from what I could tell under that down coat, a compact and muscular body.

"This is my place," the stranger said defiantly. "I rent it from Ned."

"We know Ned," I chimed in, trying to smooth over the uncomfortable edge we were all on.

"Good." she said. "He can tell you that I'm not trespassing, and you can just move on."

I got closer to her. She smelled of cedar chips and Dove soap. "I can tell you like to be alone," I said, as gently as I could. I knew we'd surprised her, so she probably wasn't at her best right now. "We won't bug you, but you should probably know that I'm moving up here, into the Lodge. It'd be nice to know a neighbor, and I promise I won't intrude."

"Well," she said, "you already did." Her tone had already softened. Then she looked me straight in the eye and granted me a small smile. "As long as you don't bug me all the time, though, I think we'll be okay."

"Deal." I said, relieved. "We'll be scouting around the property, but I'll try not to get in your way."

She snorted. "I suppose I'm your tenant, since your uncle did own this land."

Lauren was eyeing me as I nodded at my new neighbor. "I'm Lucy Zwich," I said, "and as far as I'm concerned, we'll just keep things like they were with my uncle. Same deal, if that works for you."

She nodded, "Suits me fine," she paused for a minute, "I'm Amanda." she offered. Then she turned and walked quickly away.

Lauren and I took off fast in the opposite direction. We didn't make it far before Lauren pointed out "You've got a mountain woman for your closest neighbor, that's so lovely!" She said sarcastically.

"Don't be like that!" I protested, though I could certainly see her point. I felt somewhat defensive of my new tenant. "Wouldn't you freak out too, if you saw two strangers peeping into your window?" Lauren nodded.

"How old do you think she is?" Lauren asked idly, looking through binoculars, off in to the distance.

"Younger than she wants to look." I replied. "My guess is that she's in her forties."

"Is she your type?" Lauren asked. "I have the feeling she'd be a real ball buster."

"Oh, I don't know who my type is anymore." I said casually. But the mountain woman was pretty cute.

We checked out three sheds. It was mostly just old fishing gear in them, along with some snow shoes and tarps. We did find a canoe, which had obviously been built out of one log, and was still completely solid. Sheltered by the side of a shed, the elements hadn't done any real damage to it. "Let's drag it back home." Lauren suggested, putting her gardening gloves on. Despite the fact that they were totally inappropriate for the weather and the situation, she'd insisted on bringing them from home.

"It's too heavy." I whined. "Quit moaning." Lauren said unsympathetically. "You called it home," I said, and smiled. For that, I'd drag a wooden canoe for a mile. *Reluctantly.*

The ringing of a phone was audible from inside the Lodge by the time we got back. "There's a working phone!"

I yelped, then dropped the canoe on the path and ran inside. The phone call was from Ned - which was unsurprising, since no one else would have the number. He and Bob though they'd found a good horse for me.

Ned explained. "Real sweet-natured, he's a Clydesdale, long story on how we ended up with him. You'll need to feed this horse, since he's been neglected. Lester does rescue horses, so if you want this fella, he's yours."

"I'll have to meet him first." I said, and then added "Can you call that kid about the stables? They'll need cleaning."

"Sure, sure." said Ned. "Todd will cost ya, though."

Oh crap, I thought. Here we go. Here's where the big bucks come in.

"$50. Canadian." "$50!" I repeated dumbly. "That's it?!" "That's a lot of money to most of the people around here." Ned told me, sounding a little defensive.

"No!" I protested. "I just mean that it's so much work for $50! How much would the horse cost me?"

"Bob said he'd give you a real deal - $300 for the horse."

I didn't know if that was good or bad, but it was definitely in my price range. I'd call Mr. Functer and get the money transferred in the morning, so I told Ned to relay my acceptance of Todd's stable-cleaning services and the run-down Clydesdale. It was all very exciting. All those years reading books about boarding schools and horses (too much Judith Krantz, Lace and Lace II), and I was finally getting my horse.

I had completely made up my mind about moving to Fossil Creek. I knew I was leaving the city behind, and it scared the hell out of me. But the driving motivation that had brought me to Chicago had faded the longer I lived there. I'd thought that moving to Chicago was a guaranteed start to a musical career and the great American novel, but it hadn't come to pass.

However unexpected, this was the direction my life was leading me in, and every instinct I had told me that this was the place to be for the next phase of my life.

I think deep down, even Lauren knew that this was the right move for me. Let's face it, I thought, I'd never get a chance like this again. For me it would be like living off the grid, Lucy Zwich style!

Chapter 7

When I got back to my apartment, all was quiet - except for my dog Combover tapping around on the old pine floors like a fat Fred Astaire, his little English bulldog snout bumping my leg in search of petting. The dog walker had left me a note on my circular oak coffee table, and my stomach sank a little. I really liked my dog-walker, who was a grad student. She was an actress, and I had gone to see her in "Co-Ed Prison Sluts" at the Annoyance Theater a few months ago. There were so many great, fun small theaters in Chicago. Was there any theater in Fossil Creek?

In the bedroom, I plunked my suitcase on the bed and looked around, mostly at my black-framed, silver-matted David Bowie and Lou Reed posters. I wondered how this city chick would fit into woodsy surroundings. Maybe the posters could hang in my new writing office, behind the front desk of the lodge. There was a huge manager's office facing Lac d'Lune, which would be the perfect contemplative spot to work on my book.

The lodge was full of empty shelves waiting to be filled with my writing. My music and writing had seemed like an albatross at times, a heavy burden I carried and could never seem to put down. My whole life, I'd been attempting to publish a novel, or record an album of music, but I'd never been able to get it right.

Getting older was making me feel freer, ironically, because I wasn't worried about what was expected of me. Still, I felt that I'd let people down - I'd never achieved the fame and fortune that had been expected for me.

I wished that the expectations of other people didn't weigh so heavily on me, but they did. When I was a kid, I used to watch the TV show "Fantasy Island" with my uncle when he was babysitting. I thought Mr. Roark had the best job in the world - awarding people their fantasies.

I wanted so badly to be just like him, but I'd never even gotten close. On the other hand, therapy had taught me to take care of myself, and then take care of other people. It just seemed like a cop out to take care of myself rather than granting wishes. Maybe that's why I idealized Uncle Tavis - he was able to make so many people happy, and had a rare gift for reading people's hearts and knowing what they needed. Maybe that's why I'd inherited the lodge, weird as it seemed.

Even with the fall light coming through my big vintage windows, and the familiar sight of all of my belongings, it felt like I'd already started leaving.

This wasn't home anymore. My Rogers Park apartment was a place where I'd lived for a while. It was a good place, it had been good to me, but it wasn't home.

I had moved so much over the years, and my gypsy ways were starting to wear on me. I think the reason I never invested in decent furniture was that seemed so permanent, and I knew that sooner or later, lovers and apartments would change. For a long time, I was resigned to that, but I felt differently now. I liked my own company enough that I felt I could make my own nest, with my creature comforts, and be happy. I had learned how to bring the mountain to Lucy, so to speak.

I sat down on top of the accordion-grill radiator that heated my enclosed sun porch. Petting my ever-eager dog, I watched the people scurrying in the windy cold to the El train up the street. Some had laptops and shiny tight work shoes; others carried backpacks and ran sleepy hands through scruffy hair as they made their way to class at Loyola University up the street. I would miss sitting here, watching the urban world go by, but I needed to move forward. I couldn't stay in this holding pattern anymore.

I gave my notice at work and the news went off like a stink bomb. My bosses said they'd miss me, but they'd miss the chunk of income I brought in for them even more. Their resentment was aimed at me daily, which made for an unpleasant few weeks. Most of my coworkers didn't think Canada sounded particularly romantic, or even very exciting, but Bradley had been there when I got the news about the lodge. He'd also seen photos of the place. When the other stylists teased me about "exotic Canada," Bradley told me "Ignore those bitches, they're just jealous."

It did hurt my feelings that my coworkers were so rude about it. I had known these people quite awhile…through false pregnancies, dating drama and even one sex change… I didn't even get a "congratulations" or "Bon Voyage!"

At the end of the day, I knew a job was a job. Co-workers came and went, but as someone who was passionate about my job, it hurt that these people I'd spent so many years with were being so cold. I had taught Brad my curl-cutting technique, so I wasn't leaving my devoted clients high and dry.

The experience with the salon wasn't making me too eager to tell my friends, but I decided to tell Connie first. She was another ex-Chicagoan, having made a big move back to her hometown in Florida. Her Art Institute co-workers hadn't reacted to her decision as she'd expected, so I figured she would understand best.

She was a Southerner with a china doll face, raised by a lovable but self-centered mother obsessed with her job at Cape Canaveral and a bearded father who bore more than a passing resemblance to Kenny Rogers, and worked the impersonator circuit. Both of Connie's parents were hardcore Christians, polite but not overly friendly (with me) for obvious reasons.

Connie had bonded over our eccentric parents and our love of the arts. She had been my first next door neighbor in Chicago. We had met in the laundry room when she and a bunch of her art student friends were filming a class project…in the nude. It was hard to put a load in the dryer when six naked people were doing a Twister game while the director splashed fake blood all over them to the music of Tom Waits.

Ironically, Connie's mom had spent a lot of time trying to get her daughters skinny and married off. She'd hoped to get them all into the Amish community, since she'd grown up with her parents trading citrus fruits to the Amish. By accident, Connie's folks had raised some pretty adventurous daughters. Connie's sister married a French man and moved to Marcilly-Sur-Seine, in France, and Connie was dating a guy in a metal band, plus seeing a lawyer from Tampa whenever he came into town. Connie was a high school art teacher, who was finally finishing her MFA and probably would end up teaching at University of Florida's art department. When she'd moved to Florida, we'd stayed in touch. Even if we weren't as close as we'd been, I still wanted her to be one of the first to know.

"I was wondering when you'd make a big move!" Connie said loudly into her cell phone. She was sitting on the beach after a run for a marathon she was training for in New Smyrna Beach. "My folks have been so awful this year, if they're not ragging on me about marriage, it's the mom and dad tug of war with me as the monkey in the middle. I just need a break. Maybe I'll come and visit you for Christmas. It's been a long time since I've seen snow."

"You'd have to get some cold weather gear. If you thought Chicago was cold, that wasn't shit, compared to Fossil Creek."

When Connie had moved back to her hometown of New Smyrna Beach, she'd gave me some of her great winter wardrobe, pitched the rest, and never looked back.

"J. Crew Catalogue." Connie replied. "I've got it covered. Greg took me skiing in Aspen last year so I think I'll be ok." Greg was the lawyer. I had noticed Connie seemed to care more about experiencing the finer things in life these days. Maybe Greg was the reason.

"So give me details, Lucy-loo," Connie said.

"I got a freakin' horse," I blurted out, excited. "A big ass Clydesdale. The place is totally gorgeous, though it does take a village." I explained about how Lauren had come with me to Canada and all her help, and told her about Big Bob, Todd and Ned.

"Ned's wife Kathy found me work at the Hair Hut, so I'll still be working as a stylist." I told Connie.

"So you'll still be working?" Connie repeated, acting shocked.

"Yeah, girl. I'll need money to live on." I said.

"I thought your uncle left you money."

"Not so much." I replied. "I get the property, and something to take care of it, but I still need to buy my groceries and pay the electric bill."

Word sure travels fast. I had the feeling she'd talked to my cousin Jeff - he was Lauren's brother, and he and Connie had dated for about a minute and a half. They still talked occasionally, mostly via Facebook. Lauren would have told Jeff about my inheritance, of course, and Jeff would have made assumptions.

"Oh...I thought you'd get to be a lady of leisure," Connie replied sounding disappointed.

"My work is my social outlet, anyway, especially considering it would be really easy to become a hermit up there. I do want to get back to writing and music."

"Doing hair will be a good way to integrate you into the community. Jeff didn't give me all the details." Connie divulged.

"Speaking of getting to know the community, I'm throwing a horror movie marathon at the lodge for Halloween. Inviting the whole town. Open house style."

"What?" Connie yelled into the phone - the wind was kicking up on the beach. I could hear her friend Mindy talking to her son in the background. They had been roommates when Connie attended the School of the Art Institute.

"Remember the Music Box Theatre?" I asked. "They used to run a 24 hour monster movie marathon on Halloween, so I want to do the same. Add chili and baked potatoes..." I explained excitedly.

The Music Box was an old historic art-house movie theatre on the north side of Chicago, one that still had a pipe organ, a stage in front of the screen, and twinkling lights in the ceiling that were supposed to look like stars in the sky. I'd spent the last six Halloweens going to this annual movie marathon, where I'd met all kinds of once-famous actors and directors who spoke about their films. My friend Larry would come from Hohman and we'd stay at the Music Box till 4a.m. watching funky old movies like *Rabid*, with Marilyn Chambers (of *Behind the Green Door* fame), the 1970s version of the *Phantom of the Opera* with Paul Williams, and *The Black Cat*, black and white with Bela Lugosi. Most of these movies had never made it onto DVD, so a lot of the time you were seeing movies that had been lost in the vaults for many years.

The movie marathon was also a lot like a horror convention, complete with vendors selling memorabilia, posters, clothes, and books. I wanted to bring the movie part of that fun stuff to my first Halloween in Fossil Creek.

Connie agreed that it would be a good time.

"The food will be on me, so hopefully that will attract people." I said. "Plus the place is a lodge, formerly an old motel. It used to be twelve rooms, but my uncle knocked out a bunch of walls when he bought it, so now there are three suites and big common areas. The foyer is huge, so we can hang a screen there and I'll put some cushions on the floor."

"You did catering long enough, you'll know how to handle it! Makes me wish I was there," said Connie. "Well, call me as much as you need to. I'll see you in a few months, when I come up to visit."

When I hung up, I had the feeling that she'd never be visiting me in Fossil Creek.

Crystal and Brad were supportive about my good fortune and volunteered to help me pack but I could tell Lauren was still a little bummed about losing me as a neighbor. She was my closest relative, and we got together at least every six weeks for haircuts and chat.

Nevertheless, Lauren was the first one to show up at my apartment with bubble wrap and boxes. Moving is always proof of who your real friends are…

Packing is always a chore, but between Brad and my cousin and the extra- large pizza, it was less painful than usual.

"This is so you." Lauren said, with a hint of mixed emotions. "The next adventure! What does your dad say?"

"He isn't 100% wild about it." I replied. "He thinks I'll be bored, but he told me it's going to be a 'real journey'. He's getting philosophical in his old age. Apparently, he argued with Uncle Tavis about leaving it to me. My dad sees me as this helpless little girl, and then he reverses himself and calls me his fearless Commander. I think he's worried we won't see each other that much." Commander was my dad's nickname for me.

My relationship with my mom, Tanya, was a little more strained than the one with my dad, though we loved one another. We tended to ping-pong back and forth between being close and not really speaking. The man she'd married after divorcing my dad had insisted I go to boarding school, so I'd moved in with my dad. When my mom had been diag-nosed with cancer, her husband had left and I'd moved back in. Once the cancer was in remission, she met a doctor at the gym and moved to Los Angles. She went through a bunch of plastic surgery, and then her husband Dr. Tim tried to kill her. Allegedly, he'd been writing himself too many prescriptions, so she never pressed charges. He got help, but Mom said she could never trust him again.

She moved back to our hometown of Hohman, and got really into horseback riding, "I find it so therapeutic." she'd explained. Two months later her new "therapy," also known as her horseback-riding instructor, moved in with her, but that only lasted a year.

At least I'd learned something about horses from him, before they broke up. Then Mom was single for a while, and we became really close when I was in college at Purdue. By the time I graduated, she'd moved on to Gus, who was a restaurant owner. The whole relationship got really awkward, since I'd dated Gus for a while when I was nineteen and still unsure about my sexuality. Gus was very sweet, not to mention good in the sack. But we never got serious, since I knew I wanted to move to Chicago and I had a feeling that men might not be my gender of choice.

I was actually happy for Mom when she hooked up with Gus. He was a really good man, and I knew he'd take care of her. He had a pro-tective nature and a taste for blonds with big boobs, so I'd been pretty sure things would work out. Now that he'd retired, they had moved to his hometown of Athens, Greece. There were times when I thought to myself that it could have been me, married to Gus and living a life of luxury in Greece, but then I'd snap out of it and thank God that I hadn't chosen the wrong direction for my life.

Mom loved Greece, which had surprised me. I could never get her to leave Northwest Indiana after the last divorce, but the sunshine and the beautiful beaches had convinced her that Greece had some things that the Midwestern US lacked. Gus' six sisters took my mom under their wing, so she had shopping pals, and she'd even learned to cook a little. It was the family my mom had always wanted. She had been a black sheep in her own, so the warm Greek lifestyle suited her.

The first Christmas my mom and Gus were together and I brought my girlfriend Diana over, it was awkward. Gus had gotten a little drunk, which was unusual for him and asked me in private if I had been thinking about girls when I was with him. I told him I hadn't, which was true. The person I'm with is the person I'm with, and I don't fantasize about other people when I'm with them. We never spoke of it after that, thankfully.

I'd skipped my mom's wedding to Gus. At the time, I was in stylist school in Chicago and holding down two jobs to pay for living expenses and tuition. My mom was angry with me, because she felt like I was throwing my life away. "You've make your life so hard, getting involved with a woman with kids," she'd grunted, "and you're making foolish decisions. You could have had it all, Lucy, but no, you're going to do hair."

My mother loved her hairstylists, but she didn't want me to be one. I think she felt she'd ordered a Grace Kelly for a daughter...and gotten me instead.

When I'd told her that I was miserable at my public relations job, she'd switched it up. "I know, sweetie." she'd told me. "I do understand. I just love you; I don't want people to be mean to you for the choices you've made. It would be so much easier...if things were different."

I told her not to go there. That had gotten me a lecture on her religious beliefs, and how she couldn't accept or endorse my lifestyle. I wasn't buying it. Her final words to me were "don't bother to come to the wedding."

"No problem," I replied, and then I'd hung up the phone and cried. In my heart of hearts I knew the decisions I was making were right for me, but without a parents approval...I felt rejected.

Ironically, when Diana and I broke up, neither my mom nor dad gloated or had a harsh word to say.

"*Bradley, be careful with the art!*" Lauren directed, snapping me out of my walk down memory lane. She handed him some bubble wrap, since he kept poking himself on the sharp metal-edged frames.

Combover, my pooch, was running around nervously, sensing a big change to come. I tried to reassure him with pets and kisses and he finally settled into the couch, with a huge snort. English Bulldog style.

It took me a few weeks to get everything packed, even after the packing party help...I had a lot of stuff. Also finding a moving compan that didn't charge an arm and a leg to schlep me to remote Canadian town was tricky.

I would take my dog and the electronics in my car, and the moving company could take the rest.

The week prior seemed the longest of my life but finally my car was loaded and I was ready to roll.

I had called Ned before I left when I heard the Montreal (the closest major city) weather report of snow storms mixed with ice.

I asked him to pick up some snow chains for the tires. I had a VW bug, so it would be interesting to see if it would make it. Ned didn't think the car would make it in Canada, but I didn't want to be car-less and I couldn't afford the car payment for anything new at this point, since Mr. Functer hadn't made any deposits in my account yet. There was a heated garage at the lodge, so maybe there was a chance my Bug would survive.

Leaving Chicago on a crisp autumn day made me excited and confused. Autumn was the adventure season for me...but Chicago had been my home...my safety net.

My cousins Jeff and Lauren looked nervous and Brad seemed sad and distracted. Hugs were passed around and I explained my course of action. I was going to try to drive all the way through, but Lauren was concerned. "If you get tired," she said, "then stop. I don't want you falling asleep at the wheel."

"I know," I told her, "but I want to get there."

She and Jeff just shook their heads, since they knew not to argue with me.

Brad was busy checking out Jeff, but took time out to say good-bye. I actually detected a bit of a tear in his eye. He gave me a vibrating seat for the car and told me "it's good for long drives - keeps away restless leg syndrome and hemorrhoids."

As I drove away, it felt like I was just going on a long vacation, I couldn't wrap my mind around the fact that I wasn't going to be living in Chicago anymore. It all seemed too surreal.

After six hours and two stops, my ass was numb, my iPod selections were getting on my nerves and I decided to stop outside of Detroit.

I texted the group, to their collective sighs of relief and chose the little Motel Chateau. It was forty bucks a night with cable, and it was easy to sneak in Combover. We settled in, I took a hot shower, and then put on some David Bowie.

The decor was stuck in the sixties, with a lovely avocado and burnt orange color scheme. The bedspread was dusty, so I pulled it off to make Combover a little bed of his own. The heat was struggling to make it out of the radiator, and I decided to go to the car for the quilt my late Grams had sewn. Maybe I'd stop for a pop on my way back.

The sky had turned a charcoal grey, and the clouds looked dirty and smoky. The wind was whipping up on my way back to the room. As I fed my change into the pop machine, I could hear two guys loudly arguing in the room just beyond. Their door flew open when my pop came slamming out. Shit.

"Being nosy?" asked the young guy in a black leather motorcycle jacket.

"Actually, no." I replied. "I just wanted a pop."

"Traveling alone?" he said in a sleezy way.

"Never." I said flatly.

"Where's your boyfriend?" the other guy asked, smirking. "Oh, the one with big teeth and four legs?" I snapped back. "You got a pit?" Mr. Leather asked.

"English Bulldog." I told him.

"Like the Mack truck." The other guy, who was wearing a brown fur-lined ski jacket, took off his hood and smiled. "Are you freaking serious?" he asked. "Shit, I always wanted one of those."

"Can we see him?" the guy in the leather jacket asked. "Yeah," I said. "I'll bring him down." I'd learned the best way to self-preservation was to trust your instincts and I'd found a mixture of humor, a touch of Mae West seductiveness, and some Fonzi cool with a touch of Divine worked best for me. Relaxed-matter-of-fact seemed to work best. I'd given them a few minutes of time and respect. This was what I'd learned from living in "transitional neighborhoods," where questionable characters loomed and these situations routinely arose.

"Why can't we come to your room?" the other man asked. "I don't think so," I told him, "but I'll buy you a pop." The Mr. Roger's theory applied here - the idea was to be a good neighbor, then get out of the situation as fast as I could. They shot each other that look men get sometimes, the "should we fuck with her or not" look, then they laughed.

I breathed a sign of relief. I went and got my pooch. We talked dogs and drank our pop for a few minutes.

"Okay, boys," I said, "I've got to get some shut eye. Be good and don't let the bed bugs bite."

"My ma used to say that," the one in the leather jacket told me.

"Yeah, yer mom said a lot of shit." Brown-coat-guy said, pushing the other one back into the motel room.

While Comby and I walked back to our room, I realized the temperature had really dropped.

"Combover," I said, "I'm putting your sweater on." Tucking him into his Union Jack sweater I turned out the light and we rested.

I awoke to someone spinning out in the parking lot. The snow was swirling like a crystal-opaque vortex. "We're going to have to take it slow today." I told Combover. He raised his eyebrows like he understood.

The night clerk said they offered coffee and donuts in the morning, so I got suited up and went to get a cup of the hot stuff. A new desk guy was lounging in a ratty old green vinyl La-Z-Boy lounger, watching the early morning news. "Coffee to the left," he said, without looking up. After I got my coffee, I watched the news over his shoulder. "News of two convicted felons," said the anchorman, "considered armed and dangerous." The little TV screen flashed a sketch and a police photo of the two guys I'd spoken with the night before, and my stomach flipped like a wet pancake.

I scooted out of the lobby like a gorilla on a banana peel, quickly packed up the car, and dropped off the key in the motel office.

"We're outta here." I said to an already-snoozing Combover, patting his bulldog butt. The road was desolate. No one with any brains was traveling today. I just hoped I could make it to Fossil Creek by sundown.

As I drove, I kept thinking about the men I'd spoken with last night. It was sad to me, to meet and have an enjoyable conversation with two "bad guys," knowing they had a good side. Why did the bad have to overtake the good? These two men clearly had the potential to be kind, the way they'd loved on Combover and talked about their childhood pets. The whole thing broke my heart.

Living in the "bad" neighborhoods of Chicago had given me a special sense about these things. I recalled the place I had in Wicker Park in the early 90's, $425 a month for a three-bedroom apartment in a gorgeous Greystone.

My roommate Lenny and I couldn't believe our luck, until we'd discovered that the three-flat next door was a crack house. When the police finally raided the place, Lenny and I decided to investigate a day later. We'd found the place strewn with glass pipes, homemade can pipes, needles, old couch cushions and junk food cartons all over the first floor. We didn't go upstairs in case any live leftovers were still in residence.

I had said good morning for a year to all my neighbors, and I'd never realized what was going on there. They'd seemed nice - maybe a little seedy, but it wasn't a particularly good neighborhood.

One of the regulars, a guy called "Hollywood," would keep an eye on my car so no one messed with it. He'd seen me upset one morning because someone had scratched gang graffiti on the passenger side door of my car.

"I don't have insurance cause I'm too broke," I'd said to him.

"Too broke?" he'd asked, eyeballing me from his stoop. "Yeah, man, if this car goes...I'll have to drop out of college. I'm finishing up at the Purdue extension in Hammond, Indiana, and there's not like there's an express train or anything," I blubbered some more tales of woe, and he'd introduced himself.

"Don't worry, sweet thing, I'll keep an eye on it, ok?" "Thanks Hollywood."

"We friends, ain't we?"

"Yes! You're a good neighbor!"

"Just like Mr. Rogers," he'd laughed, and waved me off. "Now get your ass to school."

Those were my first lessons in listening to your gut. Be nice - but don't be stupid.

I crossed the Canadian boarder without too much drama. I figured they'd check out the car, so I tried to keep everything easy to see. I'd even brought Combover's vet papers, though the Mounties didn't seem to really care.

I thought I was really making great time until I realized we'd been on the same highway for far too long. Somewhere back by the boarder, I must have made a wrong turn, or maybe Mapquest had done me wrong. I couldn't get a hold of Ned on my cell phone, so I tried Bob. He picked up his phone right away.

"You're driving that Beetle in this? Good God, girl!" I could hear his dismay over the phone line. He shot off some easy directions, and met me at a little coffee shop.

"My God, if that isn't an ugly mutt." Bob said, petting Comby through my driver's side window.

"Ah, he's my little baby." I told him.

"Not a biter, I see."

"He's never had the occasion to bite." I said, "But he did go after this suspected pedophile in my old neighborhood."

"Good boy." Bob smiled, scratching Combover's ear. "Okay, let's go. It's really gettin' ugly out here." I followed Bob and watched him skid a little, and was grateful that my Beetle was faring pretty well.

It didn't take long to get to my new home. A warm feeling settled in my belly as we pulled up to the lodge. Ned must've left a light on for me, because the front porch glowed invitingly in the slowly creeping darkness.

Bob helped me carry my stuff in and I offered him some coffee, which he declined.

"Getting old," he said, "can't do caffeine after three in the afternoon or I'm up all night. I'll get my son up here with the truck to plow you out - by tomorrow, you're gonna see a real Canadian snow."

"I start work next week," I told Bob, "is it going to be weird to ride the horse in?"

"No, honey." he replied. "In fact, there's a little stable a block away from The Hair Hut. For a small fee, you can hook him up in the barn and they'll even feed him."

Bob left, and then it was just Comby and me. I wished Amanda were friendlier so I could invite her over, but I realized I needed to get used to being alone. It just seemed so quiet up here, after living in a city for so long. I set up my computer in the den facing the lake, plugged in the DSL I'd ordered, and did a little Facebook chatting, telling everyone I had made it safe and sound and recounting the drama with the convicts. I stared out over my computer into the inky night. It was pitch black out there, and suddenly I started hearing Alfred Hitchcock narrating something in my head. I shook off the creeps and went to check on the horse.

The Coleman lantern lit right up, and I ventured outside into the feathery snowfall. It was a bit muddy as I trudged over to the stable. My horse was such a docile and thoughtful creature, and he seemed to have such a wise old soul. I'd named him Tao. I used Taoist meditation to lead me through some very lonely, scary times, and the meditations gave me a plan for how I could guide my days positively. After the neglect this poor creature had endured, he appreciated the bag of oats and soft strokes on his coat. I was amazed he wasn't nippy, or "a biter" as Bob had said earlier. Tao made horsey noises to greet me, and seemed very happy I was there. He'd gained a little weight and didn't look nearly as starved. He also didn't seem scared of Combover at all, but Comby was scared of him and stayed by the barn door, faking a watchdog pose.

Todd had really done a good job with Tao - his mane was nicely brushed and he had a thick quilted blanket strapped over him.

The horse and I talked for a few minutes. "I'm so glad you're liking your new home." I told him. "I'm gonna be your mama and I'll treat you really good." I petted him and put my face to his chest. He dipped down and snorted in my hair. He was one of the friendliest horses I had ever met, not an ounce of nerves. I could feel he just wanted a friend, someone to love him. Me too, I thought. I talk to all my animals like people - they're my buddies.

Wild animals, though, they're a different story. You can't be a fool with wild animals. My dad use to love to tell the story about the time a baby bear had crawled into our cabin in Colorado. I was petting the cub and mama came home and I guess I figured it was like the three bears. I recall the mama getting up on her haunches and I told her I wasn't going to hurt her baby. My dad said he could hear me inside and had gotten the ranger. They had guns. They darted the mom and baby and I cried and tried to explain she was just protecting her baby.

My dad explained, "So am I." That's when my dad had the talk with me about wild things. "Respect them and give them their distance," he told me.

I had carried that message with me all my life, into the city and now into the wild. I was no mountain woman, and I was no gambler. In life, we can take risks, but I always knew planning was the key. But if the planning didn't work, I always trusted my gut instincts.

Back in the house, Comby was curled up by the fireplace getting toasty, when I came in and petted his hunky head. He followed me to the bedroom and I plunked him on my bed. The gun was behind the bedroom door, and I put Mace on my bedside table. Hopefully I'd never need to use it, but one too many Law and Order episodes kept me vigilant. I knew eventually I'd get used to the creaking floors and whistling winds, but tonight the lodge felt big and empty and I felt very alone.

Would I find what I had always longed for in Canada? Or would this be a really messy mistake? Why did I have to think of all this shit before bed? I recalled hearing someone saying the key to happiness was to want what you have. I felt very blessed by what I had, but I wasn't sure what I wanted anymore.

My dog snoring up a storm would be my midnight meditation. I would be fine. I kept repeating that to myself until I fell asleep.

Chapter 8

I woke up to a winter wonderland. Combover was first out of the house and sank up to his pudgy little belly, freezing his nether regions, eliciting a yelp. I checked on Tao and gave him some oats, then walked around the house. I could see a little white cottony swirl coming out of Amanda's chimney.

I needed to talk to Amanda about buying the sleigh Todd had told me about, but I was dreading it. A truck would be my choice for the future, after I looked over my finances, which Mr. Functer had laid out. Up here, I didn't have my little posse of friends to lean on, so I would just have to wing decision-making the best I could on my own. From what everyone here had said, there were times in winter when only a horse would be able to get through.

I decide to go back in the house and see if my coffee was ready. I was wet and cold and ready to warm up and dry off. I'd tackle Amanda after coffee.

I flipped on the stereo, which I'd hooked up to my laptop so I could hear my personal playlists. Uncle Tavis had a nice set up - CD, turntable, cassette. I'd always been a music fanatic, and still owned over three hundred albums, about four hundred cassettes, and countless CDs. That didn't include my three iPods full of musical goodness. My movers had not been very happy with the huge crates of music, but it wasn't like I could leave it behind in Chicago. Even Bradley had complained, "Can't you pitch some of this shit. Who listens to albums anymore?"

I'd snorted. "Sacrilege! Those babies are my treasures...don't even think about pitching them." I'd said much the same thing when my cousin Jeff had helped me move years earlier, when I'd made the glib comment, "I'd rather sleep on a broken futon then pitch my albums."

Unfortunately, fate ended up putting me in that situation. I spent my early twenties absolutely stone- broke. I ate miles of Ramen noodles, peanut butter sandwiches, many a midnight burrito and I had no bed, just a crappy pull out sleeper couch that smelled like feet and dust.

Those were some lean years. Maxing out credit cards, selling all my gold, which amounted to two bracelets and some small rings, to pay for classes, I'd had to sell my guitar to cover a car payment, and pawned my jam box to get the heat turned back on. When my windshield wipers went out driving to Purdue Calumet Extension one day, I'd pulled over and cried. Hohman wasn't that far from Chicago, but it was far enough that I needed a car to commute.

I thought about dropping out of college, or at least transferring to Columbia in the city, but one of my mom's friends talked me into finishing up at Purdue.

I'd refused to ask my parents for help. Those were the silent years. My parents were pissed about the gay thing, mad about me moving up to Chicago, and they disapproved of my "erratic" behavior, which mostly had to do with my becoming an alcoholic. So I refused to communicate with my family - either side.

My stepmom had been so terrible and my dad wouldn't - couldn't - calm her down, so that was one relationship already ended. My relationship with my Dad had been put on hold when I wrote Dad a letter telling him that we weren't going to be able to speak for a year. My therapist had told me it was necessary to focus on my own life and making appropriate choices for myself, without being so enmeshed in my parents' personalities. The therapist was right, as it turned out. The break in communication had been a gamble, but it had worked out for all of us. Our family had survived, and we'd even become close, in our own weird way. It's funny, looking back, how you can long for the past even though it was so imperfect.

My uncle's stereo sounded terrific, which wasn't surprising. Uncle Tavis had loved gadgets and electronics. As old as the lodge looked, it had lots of updated extras. A wine cellar with controlled temperature and humidity, a humidor for cigars, a Japanese rice cooker, a waffle maker from Sweden, a Krupp's coffeemaker - Uncle Tavis had spared no expense on his electronics and cooking goodies. He'd even ordered a washing machine that did dry cleaning, which they'd told me was still on back order. Not that I needed a lot of dry cleaning done. The TV, VCR, and DVD had special attachments for other video and sound equipment, all very state-of-the-art. In the will, Mr. Functer had told me, Tavis had left my brother his Mercedes - the one with all the bells and whistles, including bullet proof glass, and a device that re- inflates tires if you get a flat. Why would he have something like that unless he was doing something illegal? Still, he always was a little too obsessed with James Bond, so maybe that's where his fascination with all the gadgetry came from. If there'd been a bad side to Uncle Tavis, I didn't want to know about it.

During my lean financial years, I'd get cute holiday cards in the mail with checks from Tavis. Not crazy huge, but enough for me to buy groceries. My uncle had respected my decision to support myself, my need to know I could make it on my own. But no one really makes it alone. Whether it's family, bosses, neighbors, food stamps or just a Good Samaritan, life does toss you a bone every so often.

Before Tavis had died, he'd come to visit and we'd gone out on his boat in Chicago.

"Lucy," he'd told me, "I think doing hair is great. You're making a name for yourself."

At the time, I'd been written up in a few industry magazines for my work with curly hair.

"But honey," he continued, "its physical work. I'm getting old and so will you, God willing." He'd nodded, looking like a tired Paul McCartney, with sleepy eyelids and pouty lips, puffing on a Kent cigarette.

"I know, Uncle Tavis," I'd reassured him. "Believe me, that's why I want to have my own salon in five years or so, depending on the kind of financing I can get. I'm already in the process of cleaning up my credit, I've invested a little in money market funds, and I have a Roth IRA."

"Good girl," he'd said approvingly, adjusting his fishing cap and pulling up his socks. He'd seemed fidgety. I'd kept thinking he was going to drop some heavy secret on me during the trip, but he never did.

Uncle Tavis had a sort-of-girlfriend, Henna, a hippie chick about ten years older than me. She wasn't really part of my life, though, as she never attended family events. I often noticed that Tavis still kept pictures of my Aunt Greta around, and he would look at them wistfully when he thought he was alone.

I thought it was sad that he never moved on romantically. He'd gotten really drunk that night and asked me why I had quit drinking. I'd told him the truth. "I was broken, and I thought alcohol would fix me. Then it took me over. All the good stuff in my life just slipped away. All I had was the past and living in my head."

He'd nodded, and I helped him to his bed.

Henna was back on the deck, smoking a joint. I went up to find her. We'd talked a bit that night, and I got the feeling she was an ex-working girl. She knew a lot of sexy inside information about some of my favorite Chicago bands. Things only a groupie girl would know. But obviously, she had moved on.

"How'd you hook up with my uncle?" I'd asked. "I mean, you're like sort of a rocker-hippie chick and he sells sporting goods."

She'd smiled like a Cheshire Cat and evaded the question. "He's good to me, we like being peaceful...he's a funny guy. I was tired of the way I was living. He sort of saved my life."

"Do you love him?" I'd asked.

"Kid, you're only in what, your twenties?" She said hitting the joint again, an inhaling deeply.

"Thirties, actually." I'd responded.

She nudged me with her shoulder playfully, and exhaled. "Lookin' good girl! But, well...what is love? Really think about it. Love in your teens is desperate and lusty, in your twenties you're all jaded and shit, and you think you're real hot stuff, then in your thirties you question it all, and I'm in my forties. Early forties. This is good, this is real. Tavis isn't Robert

Plant or anything, but he's a kind, deep, and sometimes confused guy. But he's good people, you know. Soulful and intelligent. I wouldn't want to live without him."

"That makes sense." I'd said thoughtfully.

"You sleep with women, right?"

"Dang, Henna. You make it sounds like a porno." I'd said, nervously, trying to be comical.

"Sorry," She apologized, but was firm. She had something to say. I'd told her the truth. "I have two step kids, a money-pit of a home and an overworked, underpaid partner. So it's not all hot and passionate on a daily basis."

Henna had turned to me and said, very seriously, "Get out while you can. You're not house wife material."

I'd been offended when she said that, but I'd also known she was right. That night, I decided that if Diana hadn't recovered from her depression by the time her youngest was eighteen, I'd leave. Three years later, I moved out.

And now here I was, living in Tavis' lodge in Quebec with a horse and a bulldog.

I wondered if I'd ever see my youngest stepdaughter, Brandy, whom I was closest too. She was in college now, and that part of my life seemed so long ago.

About 10 a.m., I trudged through the snow with Combover to Amanda's little house. My stomach felt like it was full of anxiety, as opposed to coffee.

I knocked on her door and she shot an annoyed look through the frosty glass. She did open the door, though.

"Sorry to bother you," I said nervously, "but Todd said you might have a sleigh for sale and I'm really going to need one."

"OK." said Amanda grudgingly. "Well, I guess you can come in. Wait - what's that thing?" she exclaimed, pointing to Comby.

"That's my kid," I told her firmly, "he goes everywhere I go."

"Oh Jesus, you city people." Amanda said sounding disgusted.

But she did let us in, and we sat down at her little pine table. The place was homey and very small. One room, really, except she'd sectioned it off with curtains, for the bedroom and toilet. I didn't see a shower, but I was trying not to be too nosy.

"I'm not crazy, you know." Amanda said abruptly. "I just like to be alone."

"I know crazy, and you don't really seem the type." I lied.

"Yes, well, the sleigh, I'll give it to you for three fifty."

"Wow...that's a lot." I said.

"When you see it, you'll know why." Amanda said confidently. "Your horse can pull it. I'll show you how to hook it up as part of the fee."

She was all heart.

I told her I'd have to go to the bank today to get the cash, and she asked if my car was going to make it.

"I think so," I said, "back in Chicago, it could do about six inches..."

"Good you got the horse, then." Amanda snorted. "We get a hell of a lot more than six inches up here."

She was loosening up.

"I guess I should offer you some coffee," she said. "Or are you a tea drinker."

"Coffee, definitely." I replied.

"Good girl." Amanda said, putting a cup before me. "Listen," I said, "I know you're probably not into this sort of thing, but on the Saturday before Halloween, I'm having a monster movie marathon, if you want to come. I've been collecting DVDs for years - mostly the classics, like Boris Karloff, Lon Chaney..."

She shook her head. "I don't think so."

"Ok." She didn't say it in a mean way, and she didn't seem too sure about it, either. I love a challenge.

"You think people will come?" she asked.

"Even if it's only Todd, Ned, Kathy and Big Bob...I'll be happy." I added, "I'll just have a lot of Chili and hotdogs to freeze."

She nodded, and smiled.

"Why did you buy that big old horse? Couldn't Bob get you a better ride?" Amanda asked, topping off my coffee.

"He was a rescue horse and I'm almost six feet tall, so I can get around him. He's skinnier than most, due to the neglect."

"Yeah, I was the one who called it in. People up here don't like to rock the boat, but the horse was starving, wasn't right."

"No, I understand. I had to call the Humane Society on the parents of a friend of mine. Had this Dalmatian on a short chain, swarming with mosquitoes, no water or food, and they were out of town."

"Your friend was an ass." Amanda said firmly. "He should've done something."

"It was his parents' dog. He just couldn't bring himself to turn them in, I guess."

"Well...do you want to see the sleigh?"

"Absolutely." I replied. She took me out back to a makeshift carport and uncovered the most amazing sleigh I'd ever seen. It was like something out of a movie - black lacquer with gold trim and red leather seating. $350 suddenly seemed like a steal.

"You'd make Santa proud!" I said, stunned.

"Took me all summer to fix it up," she told me. "Neil Saunders was just letting this baby rot in his back yard, along with his five toilets, endless old tires and his junk cars."

"I feel bad taking it away from you." I told her.

"I wasn't really going to use it for anything – more a project to keep my mind busy."

"I'm going to go get Tao and we can hook him up." "He should be fine with it," Amanda said, explaining. "Pulling is what Clydesdales were bred for."

"It'll be like a Budweiser commercial," I snickered.

"Oh, brother," she said, rolling her eyes and smiling.

Tao was glad to get moving, and clomped along happily as I led him over to Amanda's place. I decided to leave Comby at home, since I still needed to get used to riding the horse.

"I think I'm going give it a test run." I told Amanda, after we got Tao harnessed to the sleigh.

"Suit yourself," she said, "I'll help you up." She said taking my hand and keeping me steady while I entered the sleigh.

I sat on the cushioned seat with the reigns in my hands "are you ready," Amanda asked as she climbed in next to me. I answered "yup," and away we went. She helped me steer, pulling at the reins every so often. There seemed to be something kind in the gesture.

We slowed down, and she re-harnessed Tao to just be pulling the sleigh while I rode him on a saddle. Her advice to me was, "Just tighten your thighs and go slow." Kinky, I thought wickedly.

Amanda actually followed me on foot. I wasn't going fast, but she kept shouting out, "Keep going!"

By the time I got to town, I realized I shouldn't wear snowmobile boots on horse rides. It made me nervous about sliding off, since they didn't fit very well in the stirrups. Somehow, though, we'd made it. Tao seemed to understand and had gone slowly and carefully.

I hooked up Tao to a post with the sleigh behind him outside Big Bob's Groceries. "You sure know how to make an entrance." he told me. I looked around for Amanda but she had disappeared.

"This is the solution to my transportation problem," I said proudly, "and I give Todd all the credit."

Bob chuckled, and then whispered, "You coming to the meeting tonight?"

He meant the Twelve Step group. "Sure am," I said. "Seven thirty at the Houndstooth in the back room, right?"

"Yup."

Bob filled me up on dog food, coffee and every other conceivable thing I could need. While I was checking out, I reminded him about my idea for a Halloween party.

"Up here in the winter it gets real quiet and people are desperate for entertainment." Bob assured me. "Plus, I'll use my sway...you have Dracula?"

"Do I have Dracula? *Like four versions of it*! Bela, Frank Langella, Christopher Lee and even George Hamilton - oh, and Coppola's version, too!"

"Excellent!"

"I'll need chili fixings for the party, plus lots of potatoes and toppings."

"Sounds delicious." Bob said. "I'll have the wife bring a Texas Sheet cake, and I'll supply the weenies if you want 'em."

"Bring on the weenies!" I giggled.

Tao and I hustled back home for a bite to eat before the meeting. Amanda's house was dark and I was slightly disappointed.

Walking Combover, I got the distinct feeling I was being watched, but I saw no one.

The night was back to bone-chilling cold, so I layered up like The Mummy and got back on Tao to get to the meeting. I was so excited to meet other Twelve Steppers that it was comical.

The meeting was just what I needed, and I was pleasantly surprised to see that there were three women out of the ten people who showed up. When it came time for comments, I felt like the men and women seemed really sweet and were listening. Thank God for Twelve Step, my home away from home.

My first day at Hair Hut was one for the books. These women wanted to know my business and I don't mean my resume. I was chicken feed in the hen house! But I tried to keep things professional.

I had three clients booked for my first day. Kathy, Ned's wife, had warned me that these ladies were the town gossips. They ran the church, the diner, and the roost of Fossil Creek.

My boss, Joelle Nedermeyer, was a bodacious babe in her fifties with a red beehive hairdo, tight pants in emerald green, and a very tight fuzzy yellow sweater. She reminded me of the wife on Married with Children, but a few years older. She was as sweet as I could ever hope for, and I felt immediately that she was on my side.

"I'm so excited to have a city girl like you here," Joelle said as I got settled. "You'll know all the latest styles - this is just fantastique!" She sounded like a complete Anglophone, but later when I heard her get into an argument on the phone her French was flying quite fluently.

Joelle set me up with a station, and the three other stylists stared as I put away all my gear. The place was surprisingly charming (I was worried with a name like Hair Hut it was going to be the pits). Joelle had kept it classy with a black and white scheme. It was the only salon in the town, so the magazines ranged from Vogue to Hot Rods and Chatelaine (French women's magazine).

"I think you're going to have to give us a class - when you're ready, of course!" Joelle told me excitedly.

The other three stylists didn't look too keen about this idea.

"I'm sure you think you're better than us." hissed Pasha, a beautiful Russian girl with long brown hair highlighted in thick chunky streaks. The hairdresser in me was not a fan.

"Oh Pasha," scolded a man with a thick black pompadour, "don't be like that. You were new here once, too." Then he turned to me and introduced himself. "I'm Randy, the town's only queer hairdresser, pleasure to meet you," he said, shaking my hand like a wet noodle and smirking.

Candy, the third stylist, was a little nicer than Pasha. Immediately, I pegged her for the town hootchie. Her boobs were falling out of her gold metallic top, and her ultra-low-rise jeans came to just above her pubic hair zone. Enough of a wiggle and she'd be flashing the public, no matter how tight the jeans were - *and they were skintight*. She was wearing platform Steve Madden heels, and her eye makeup would have looked more appropriate in a dark bar. It was freezing out, so I had to assume she lived close by - nobody would stroll outside in her get up.

I have a fondness for underdogs and her kind smile was naive and hopeful. I extended my hand and she took it cheerfully. "Hi," she chirped, "I'm Candy and I'm kind of new here too."

"But they all know her..." Randy said rolling his eyes.

A thought occurred to me about making one of my Russian stews as an attempt to try and bond with Pasha, but then I remembered my Russian ex-boyfriend Pavel. He'd taught me about never sucking up to Russian women - they don't respect you. If I was going to work with Pasha, I was going to need her respect. I'd just have to hang in there; I'd worked with bitchier stylists.

The town gossips were waiting patiently in their chairs for a look at me. It was time to shine!

Marilyn, who ran the local church office, was my first client. She wanted a roller set. YUCK. I'd done a lot of high styling, but I'd never been famous for my roller sets.

Okay, I told myself, think Margaret Thatcher with a little spice!

"Hi Marilyn," I said cheerfully, "come right over and let's talk about what you want and what you don't."

She explained in detail and I proceeded to shampoo...no assistants here.

I gave her a head massage and I think that's when I won her over.

"If I could only get my husband to do that, I'd be in a better mood every morning!" she giggled like a girl.

We chatted about her kids and grandkids and her secret dream to be a silver screen siren.

"Did anyone tell you, you look like Bette Davis." she said sweetly, smiling kindly.

"Well thank you! She's my fave!" I replied "Dark Victory was my favorite movie of hers. Those women were really stars, back in those days, not like that stupid old' Britney Spears. I saw Crossroads with my granddaughter...just stupid."

"It's no International Velvet," I agreed. "But give Brit a chance - she's a hot mess right now, but maybe she'll get her act together."

"Doubtful." she sighed.

I put Marilyn under the dryer and got her a cup of hot cocoa. Then it was on to Sophie, owner of the local diner.

"So," I said politely, "we have you in for a trim and a touch up."

"The grey is taking me over." Sophie replied. "I don't want to look like some old maid."

"We'll help Mother Nature right along," I assured her.

"Do your stuff, girl," she said, in a totally un- ironic manner. *Girl!* She was quickly winning the prize for bad manners.

As for the old maid comment, wearing a housecoat in public wasn't really a fashion forward statement. Nor did the snow boots add much in the way of chic to her ensemble. The grey hair was just about the last thing anyone would notice about Sophie - her puzzling wardrobe choices would draw the eye before her roots did.

I did Sophie's roots in fifteen minutes, and then let her sit on the couch with her trashy romance novel.

My last client was Olga, who announced "I do not work. And I do not do my own hair. Or my nails."

Well. Okay, I thought, this would be a lot like one of my old Gold Coast clients.

Olga looked good. She had a nice pantsuit on, pale pearl grey accented with a silk pink champagne iridescent scarf that I'd been secretly coveting since she'd walked in.

"Just a simple blow dry." Olga told me. "I don't want it flat. I hate flat... make it full." She explained waving her hands dramatically.

I washed and moussed her espresso colored locks, adding root lifter and rubbing it gently in. "Please look down?" I said as I began the rough dry.

By the time we finished, her hair had a new zip code and she seemed pleased. But she left me a lousy $2 tip. This isn't Chicago, I told myself.

Marilyn's roller set turned out cute, but teasing wasn't my thing. I think it was a little flatter then she'd hoped.

"I hope you like it," I told her, and promised "we'll get it even fuller next time."

"It's prettier then when I came in and that's all that matters." Marilyn replied, and handed me a $10 bill. "I know how to tip," she whispered, "unlike some other people we know."

Sophie was happy with her fresh color and trim. "How'd you get it so shiny?" she asked, looking at her reflection.

"See these drops?" I said, displaying the bottle. "They're magic. Joelle's got them over here." I directed her to the black wrought-iron bakers' rack with hair supplies.

"I'll take it," she said, grabbing the bottle.

"Just remember," I told Sophie, "point your blow dryer down when you're smoothing the hair and hit it with the cool shot at the end."

"Thank you. It looks great." Sophie said and frankly, it did.

Since I needed to bond with Pasha, who'd been quiet all day, I went over to her on break to chat.

"You do a great roller set," I told her, then asked if she could show me some of her magic to help me improve my skills. "Well...maybe...ok." Pasha responded unenthusiastically.

It was a start.

I was really hoping Randy and I could become pals, because I needed an in with whatever passed for a gay community in Fossil Creek, but I was out of luck. He was already gone by the time I punched out.

Joelle walked me to my horse. "You did real good, honey. You got the toughies today and no one cried, so it's good stuff."

Chapter 9

By the time I got home, I had three messages on my answering machine - for all the high tech gadgetry my uncle had installed in this place, he'd kept the *Rockford Files* retro style answering machine. I loved kitsch, so I'd kept it.

Bradley was checking up on me, Bob was using his copier to make flyers for the Halloween Party, and Ned asked if we could do a pumpkin carving for the kids on movie night.

I called Bradley back immediately to tell him all about my first day at work. We started dishing right off the bat and it felt good to talk to a familiar voice. As I sat in my new favorite chair, I looked out of the window at the little glowing light in Amanda's window.

I mentioned her to Brad. "How is Miss Amanda?" Bradley asked, slyly.

"Actually," I said, "I bought a sleigh from her and she was really nice."

"You'll be gettin' busy no time!" he said crudely, making grunting noises.

"Shut up, you big perv." I replied.

"Your cousin Jeff called me." Bradley mentioned. "He's all excited about visiting. I think he was trying to get secret info from me."

"What secret info? There isn't any. Job, horse, lodge, blah blah blah." I sighed, annoyed.

"He probably just wants to know the lay of the land," he assured me, and then snickered. "I told him you had a gun and he almost shit." Brad had cut Jeff's hair a few times, and now Brad was Jeff's resident spy. I loved my cousin, but he was a huge gossip.

"God, I wish you were here." I said suddenly. "I miss you."

"Well, I'll visit you soon, but it probably won't be until after the holiday rush. The boss is giving us a week off end of January when we're slow."

"Excellent for you!" I said. "Oh, I met a gayboy!" "Lemme guess," said Bradley dryly, *"at work."*

"Right-o. His name is Randy."

"Is he handy?" Bradley snickered.

"He has a black pompadour."

"You are kidding me."

"No," I replied, "but it's cute...like that 50's American Crew collection for men a few years back." "Rockabilly queen." said Bradley. "...how wonderful."

"He's the only gay guy I've met so far!"

"Scope him out, let me know," said Bradley.

"I made twenty dollars today."

"God, how are you gonna live?" Bradley asked sounding worried.

"Frugally," *was my answer.*

"I guess you will. Thank God for Uncle Tavis."

"Indeed." I replied. Lingering in the thought for a few moments. There wasn't much else to say, and we hung up with the promise of talking soon.

I left messages for Bob to okay the flyers, and to agree with Ned's idea of pumpkin carving for the kids out front on the picnic bench during the party.

Then I was done with everything I had to do, but it was only ten, and I didn't feel like calling it a night yet. I went into my mostly-unpacked office and sat down in the comfortable iron swiveling desk chair, which was probably older than me. I flipped the switch on my laptop, and a Peter Bagge cartoon came up as my screen saver - Stinky and Buddy Bradley from the "Hate" comic jamming on drums and guitars. Seeing their goofy, distorted comical faces comforted me...comix (with an X, the underground ones) had a great way of centering me and helping me to see the comical in the mundane seriousness of life. Switching on my iPod, I began looking over some character sketches for my current novel in progress.

The most consistent things in my life had always been my love of music and writing, but since I hadn't become a rock star or writer, I'd had gone into hair styling. That didn't mean I'd given up on my original dreams. I had promised my mom and dad that I wouldn't give up on the music or writing when I started doing hair, and I didn't.

I was still working on a great American novel from a female perspective, and I still wanted to record a CD of original songs - even if was only done via my computer. I'd begun a novel back in Chicago, and really needed to get plugging away on it again. I'd written a couple self- published short story compilations, but I was really hoping I could bang out something that could bring in income. My grand plans of getting rich through writing were over, but a few royalty checks would make me a legitimate writer in my own eyes.

One of my clients back in Chicago had published mysteries and a few lesbian novels, and she'd given me the name of her agent. The current novel was supposed to be something in that vein, but I was honestly having trouble cooking up a good solid story. My hope was that Canada would provide a good backdrop for a novel. Maybe my uncle was thinking of this too, because apparently he had some kind of grand plan for me that he'd never let me in on.

I put on my headphones and started writing.

About 2am, I started to wilt. Out of the corner of my eye, I noticed a red blinking light in the reflection of the window in front of my desk. It seemed to be coming from the front desk behind me.

I walked through the office door and peered under the front desk, and sure enough, there was a red blinking button. It looked a lot like the panic button that banks used, the one tellers' pressed if someone was trying to rob them. Naturally, I wondered what would happen if I pressed the button. I tossed the idea around for a few minutes and decided to go for it. It wasn't likely to be a bomb or anything, after all. I pressed the red blinking button, and suddenly the most god-awful screeching/slamming noise echoed throughout the building.

Metal shutters closed up all the windows like some sci-fi spaceship. The lodge had turned into Fort Knox with the press of a button.

Combover was freaking out and ran to my side. I was shaken too!

"I think Uncle Tav was a little paranoid." I told the dog. I pressed the button again to try and turn it off and the noise stopped, but the windows and doors were still in Fort Knox mode.

I had found a packet of white powder wedged into the bible next to the nightstand in my room, but I'd never pegged my uncle as a druggie. Why was this place so well- protected?

Suddenly, there was a banging on the front door. Ned yelled, "Press the blue button by the front door behind the coat tree!"

I did as directed, and the shutters and door went from Fort Knox back to cozy cabin. Ned stood on the front porch panting, in a coat obviously tossed on over his pajamas.

"Ah, hi?" I said, confused. "What are you doing here?"

"The alarm went off a few minutes ago." Ned said. "And I'm a volunteer deputy, so I responded."

"How come you never mentioned this alarm thing?" I asked him.

"I forgot." Ned said evasively. "Sorry."

He was lying. I could tell.

"Well!" I said cheerfully, "I'm cool. Thanks. Come in," I said, ushering him inside. "Do I need to know about any other surprises that come with the lodge?" I asked warily, once Ned was in the front room and my ears had stopped ringing.

"Not that I can think of." he said, but I wasn't sure I believed him. "If everything is okay, I'm going to head back home. Good night." he said, patting my shoulder, and walked back to his truck. I stood in the front door and watched him go, realizing how tired I was.

I had to work at 11am, which wasn't early for most people, but I had a horse commute. That made me chuckle as I locked up the door. After my bath, before I turned out the light, I wondered suddenly what exactly Uncle Tavis had done for a living.

I stopped off at the post office before work to pick up an enticingly fat stack of mail.

It was mostly cards from my friends back home, plus a curious red envelope. I opened the envelope on the way out to grab a coffee, since it was from Mr. Functer. It had a little note enclosed. I stopped walking and read the note, standing in the middle of the post office.

Your Uncle knew you couldn't maintain the standard of living that you'd had in Chicago here, so each month you'll receive a $500 check from his estate. Do not share this information with other family members.

That came as a relief, especially after realizing yesterday just how little I was going to make doing hair in Fossil Creek. There was also a weird bill from McTrainer Assisted Living addressed to my uncle. I was going to stamp it "return to sender," but something made me forward the bill to Mr. Functer. I didn't open it - it wasn't addressed to me, and I have a long history of my own curiosity coming back to bite me in the ass.

Sophie was there as well, picking up her mail. "I love my hair, Lucy," she commented cheerfully.

"That just warms my heart. I was just headed over to the Diner to pick up a coffee." I replied, since she was the owner of the only real restaurant in town. She looked a lot cuter today in jeans, a baby blue wool sweater with a silver snowflake on the front, and a cream-colored turtleneck.

Since the snow had all but melted it felt like fall again, but Ned had warned me to always wear layers. The weather could change with a moment's notice up here.

"You look so adorable with those curly-qs, I think I'm going to bring my granddaughter Ellie in to see you. She needs some help - she brushes it and brushes it and it's just a MESS of frizz."

"Bring her in, I'd love to help." I assured Sophie. Sophie told me she'd be coming to the Halloween bash and was really looking forward to it. We parted with a wave and I was back on my way to get a fresh coffee.

I turned Tao over to his stall in the barn and walked a few blocks to the Hair Hut.

Randy let me in.

The salon looked very autumnal today.

"What do you think?" Randy asked. "I got here early to decorate. The basket full of gourds only cost a dollar, and I carved the pumpkins myself.

There's scented candles in the pumpkins, since I've got a perm to do today."

"I love it." I told him. "Especially the colored fake leaves - those are great."

"I didn't want to do too much Halloween," Randy said, "because then I'd have to decorate all over again for Thanksgiving."

"Joelle's lucky to have you."

"I agree!" he said, smiling. We sipped our coffee in the break room, sitting on bright pink plastic chairs. "These chairs use to be in the waiting area twenty years ago, when this place was Pepto-Bismol pink." Randy told me.

"When did you move here?" I asked.

"Oh, I'm from here," Randy said, surprising me. "I spent time in New York, LA and San Francisco - but Fossil Creek is home, you know?"

"Randy, I'll just come right out and ask." I said, because this question had been bugging me since my decision to leave Chicago. "Is it hard to be gay around here?"

"Are you asking for yourself?" he asked, with a quirky smile.

"Yes, actually." I replied.

"You're not alone." Randy said. "I'm having a little soirée this Friday, if you want to come by. Bring a drink and a plate of something. You can meet the other nellies, and the butchies too."

"Sounds great." I said. I was so excited I wanted to break into a routine from Riverdance!

A gay community in rural Canada... The odds against it were astronomical. *Quelle surprise!*

"Do you want me to keep it on the down-low?" Randy asked.

"I guess," I said, thinking it over. "I don't really care as long as I don't get a cross burned on my lawn."

"People are pretty cool here," Randy assured me, "as long as you're not too in their face."

I nodded, thinking that Randy's jet-black pompadour didn't really blend right in with the rest of the town's outdoorsy style.

We finished our coffee and he fired up the candles as the first clients began to arrive.

Randy had a lot of teenage girl clients. Most of them seemed awed by his travels, and anyone could tell they had crushes on him. From what I could gather, there were a lot of people living in Fossil Creek who rarely - if ever - left the town. If they did, it was for business, or to visit relatives.

I was busy doing highlights for a lady from Mountain Ridge, who was deep into her latest issue of US Weekly, when I overheard one of the girls chatting away excitedly.

"I'm going to take off Saturday. I've just got to get out of this hell-hole. My fucking father is being a total ass about Andy and me, so we're going to do it. We're just going to leave." Her comments were peppered with Quebecois slang, which I didn't exactly understand, but I got the general gist.

The girl speaking was a teenager with short black hair and long bangs that swept below her jaw line. She and her boyfriend were apparently planning on leaving for Los Angeles.

I remembered back to when I'd been that girl in Northwest Indiana. I used to call Hohman "the armpit of the nation." It had been a nice enough town, but to a teenager reading about Andy Warhol, David Bowie, and Candy Darling, and CBGB in New York City, a small town in Indiana was the last place I wanted to be.

Joelle was having problems with her boiler at home, so she wasn't coming in. Pasha had a hot date planned for that night with her boyfriend, who lived in Montréal, so she was quiet and in her own zone. Candy was doing a french braid on a girl who was attending a dance.

We had a fun music mix that I'd brought in, and everyone seemed to like it. It included Stevie Nicks, Justin Timberlake, Meredith Brooks, Stones, Siouxie and the Banshees and another two hours of songs I had burned off my enormous collection of CDs.

Pasha loved the "I'm A Bitch" song by Meredith Brooks. "Oh yeah," she said, winking at me, "this is MY song."

Then "Fool To Cry" came on. "Who sings this?" Candy asked. "I like it."

"This is the Rolling Stones," I told her, "off the Black and Blue album, my personal favorite of all their records."

"Records?" Candy asked curiously.

"God, Candy, how old are you?" I groaned, laying in the last foil and walking my client over to the dryer.

"Twenty." Candy answered, tying a pink ribbon around the end of the girl's braid.

"Records are like CDs, but bigger." the teenager in Randy's chair explained. "My boyfriend is totally into vintage vinyl." The girl winked at me. I wasn't sure if that was a compliment or a slam.

I did love working in a salon!

My cousin Jeff had called, and was going to be at the lodge Saturday morning. I was pleasantly surprised that he was so hot to trot on getting here to visit me. I was just starting to feel a little like I needed a familiar face. Even with Jeff's new snoopy routine.

I was going to be tired on Jeff's first day here, though. Randy's party was Friday after work but I needed some fun. Going home alone every night and getting up every day to repeat the daily motions of life up here was getting monotonous.

I thought about inviting Amanda to the party as a good-will gesture, but I hadn't seen her since the sleigh purchase and I didn't want to make things awkward between us. For all I know she had a boyfriend. Not that I was scoping her out - or maybe I was.

At any rate, I was slowly but surely getting to know people in Fossil Creek. Thursdays were cool - I was getting to know all the non-drinkers in town at the weekly meeting at the Houndstooth. Boozing runs rampant in cold, remote areas without a lot of social outlets other than the local bar, but I was pretty good at finding non-drinking fun no matter where I was. So far, I knew at least twenty people and kids were coming to my Halloween party.

"Expect more people," Bob had said when he came in to the salon for a trim. "I told Hank and Bridget you were showing Bride of the Monster."

"I've never seen it," I said, "but my dear friend and comic book pal Larry sent it to me."

I was glad to be going to Randy's shindig before my gathering. Meeting a bunch of people at a party would make me feel a lot less like the new girl at school.

Randy's party was a real shocker, though not in an unpleasant way. It was *not* just a gay affair. First of all, the kitchen was taken over by a hot Dungeons and Dragons game - two of the guys were dressed as wizards or something, and a man with a beard smoking a fat cigar was the Dungeon Master. "When you live in a tiny town like this, you can't afford to be exclusive." Randy told me, onion dip in hand. "You invite ALL the freaks, not just your particular kind." He asked me to grab the chips on the counter, which I did, and then I explored the rest of the party.

His front room was taken over by a game of Twister, and the CD player was cranking "Baby Got Back" at full volume. A card table was set up, in the dining room with guys and gals doing shots and playing dice.

"Bob told me you were into comics," a skinny, trendy- looking girl said, pouring me a soda.

"I'm Straight Edge," she explained when I asked if she wanted some rum in hers. No booze for her either. Bob had been talking about me?

This town was really blowing my mind. I felt guilty for assuming Fossil Creek was a small town full of small-minded people. As it turned out, it was a thriving community that seemed to really get along and work together.

"Um, yes, I'm into alternative comics," I explained. "I'm having Fantagraphics Press send me comics so I don't go crazy out here, I'm addicted."

"We do sell comics up here," said the girl, "but they're more mainstream - Spiderman, Fantastic Four, Green Lantern. I like the Vertigo stuff, like Transmetropolitan. We should take a road trip to Montreal, the Drawn and Quarterly publishers are there!"

I was so excited to hear this I could've birthed a bulldog. "Love Vertigo stuff! Very Neo-Futuristic, great drawing styles. But I'm more Peter Bagge's *Hate* and Harvey Pekar's *American Splendor.*" I never had any-one to talk alternative comics with back in Chicago, and now here I was at a party in Fossil Creek chatting easily about them with a girl I'd just met.

"You like Daniel Clownes, Ghost World?" she asked.

"Of course!" I said excitedly. Never get comic book geeks talking about comics - unless you're looking for a long chat about small presses, comics and comic book conventions.

"Comics saved me from a serious depression, helped me get out of my head and learn to laugh at life's flaws and daily soap opera's." I explained while we watched the Twister game. A lanky kid was dropping and stretching, but he was also looking down a buxom girl's shirt. This game cracked me up.

The song, "Move It "came on and a bunch of people started dancing... badly. It was awesome! Pony tails were swinging and the "white man's shuffle" was the hot dance, complete with the bizarre facial expressions.

Not a lot of rhythm in this crowd, but I was going to help that along. I was shaking some serious ass. The black guys use to call me "Soul Barbie".

At college, my roommate was half Swedish, half black. She took me to step shows, most notably the yearly show that Alpha Phi Alpha, a black frat, put on. It was one of the most amazing dance shows I had ever seen. These guys were like gymnasts mixed with hip-hop steps.

Combover was having a great time at the party. Everyone was pet-ting and loving on him. I sort of felt bad for Tao, back home in the lonely old barn. I'd walked over here and figured someone could give me a ride home.

"So you gonna give the kids sleigh rides when it snows again?" Bob asked me a little while later. He and his wife were putting on coats and getting ready to leave, and I hadn't even had a chance to talk to them. I assured them that sleigh rides were a definite plan. Bob's wife Trudy asked me if I wanted a ride home.

I felt I had been at the party long enough to get a lay of the land and do my meet and greet.

"That would be great, thanks," I said. Randy had offered me a ride, but he'd had one too many margaritas for my liking.

I waved goodbye, still not really knowing who the gays were. Where was Kathy Griffin when I needed her?

In the car, Trudy asked, "Do parties make you uncomfortable, since you don't drink anymore?"

"Trudy!" Bob scolded.

"No, I don't mind answering. It doesn't bug me because if I drank, I would've stayed too long and probably made an ass of myself, not gotten home to feed the horse and been late to work. None of those options appeal to me anymore."

"Randy is going to be hurting tomorrow morning." Trudy shook her head, smiling. Her voice was husky but she didn't smoke. She had the whole biker-chick mystique thing going on, a sort of dangerous femme fatale-with the big heart type. Bob and Trudy seemed really in sync. They had what I'd always dreamed about - a best friend and lover all in one.

It was still early when I got back from the party, only about eleven, so I decided to take the horse out for a bit. For a big horse, he moved very quietly. The snow had melted and the night was all crisp autumn moonlight and earthy breezes. I decided to ride past Amanda's cottage and down to the lakeshore. I stopped the horse about fifteen feet from her cabin, and I could hear Amanda sobbing.

"Oh, how sad." I whispered to Tao. It was heartbreaking, and I felt like I was eavesdropping. I petted Tao's neck and he seemed to understand it was time to move on. We turned away and followed the path to the lake' edge.

As I sat atop my big baby, loose multicolored leaves swept past my head like nature's confetti. A couple of yellow dots, almost like fireflies, speckled the darkness around the lake. There were other homes, full of people getting ready for bed. I didn't feel lonely tonight as much as I felt different. It seemed that the more I followed my true path in life, the more

removed I felt from other people. Getting along with others was no problem my Uncle used to call me "The Charmer", finding a group of which
to belong had always been an illusive quest. Maybe that would change,
maybe it wouldn't, but at least here in Fossil Creek I felt at peace about it.

Jeff arrived at noon the next day, considerably later than he'd planned.
"Sorry I'm late!" he said. "Can you believe I got lost? Damn MapQuest!"

"That's why I wanted to pick you up!" I told him. "Joelle gave me the
day off," a last minute blessing.

"Yeah, I know, but..." he trailed off, lost in his own thoughts as he got
out of the car. He set his rolling suitcase against the front porch. "This
place is incredible. I wish I was related to Uncle Tavis." Jeff said, survey-
ing the lodge.

"You make a good buck working for Spitzer Labs." I reminded him. "I
think you should become a neighbor!"

"Oh, yea...it's good pay. Boring work. But hell, we can't all be you!"

Smack. That little quip kind of hurt.

"Jeff," I said, "that sounded a little bitter."

"You just always follow your dreams," he replied, "and everything seems
to work out in this perfect little package. You're just blessed, I guess."

I didn't know how to respond to that, so I didn't. "Let's go in and get
you settled." I said instead.

We stuck to discussing family and jobs, which was nice. "I want to
give that car of yours a proper tune up." Jeff said after lunch.

"Um, okay." I replied. "We can get car stuff from Bob."

"Who's Bob?"

"He has the general store...it sells everything from snow boots to face
cream and motor oil."

"Dandy." Jeff said. He looked very dashing in his J. Crew outdoor
attire.

We walked to his car. He had brought his Lexus SUV but a truck would
have been a better choice for up here. Once we got to town, I introduced
him to everyone I knew.

"Want to see where I work?" I asked.

"You got a job?" Jeff said, amazed. I nodded reminding him that Joelle was the lady who had given me the day off, so obviously I had a job. It was like he'd lost whole chunks of information I'd given him. Jeff seemed preoccupied.

"Hello!" I said, "I gotta pay my bills. I got a lodge from Tavis, not a free ride."

"I just thought..." Jeff started.

"That Uncle Tav was covering all the bills." I finished for him. "Well, he's helping from beyond the grave but I still have to do my part. These hands have done a lot of manual labor." As I showed him my calloused fingers, I noted his nicely manicured ones.

"I remember when you and your dad built the sixty five steps down to your old lake home." Jeff said. "It was sad when he sold it. I loved that place." Jeff and Lauren had spent some fun times with us at our family lake home on Klinger Lake in Michigan. I'd even fantasized about getting rich and buying the place back, but it wasn't like buying a house would buy back my childhood. I nodded. "Yeah," I sighed, "but Dad and Irene wanted a country club retirement."

"Yup. I wouldn't mind that." Jeff agreed, taking in the quaintness of Fossil Creek's main drag. He commented about the French/English signs on the windows of the shops, and I waved at Sophie, who was talking to one of the Diner's patrons from the porch of the restaurant.

Jeff would have that country club retirement too. My stepmother had sort of adopted Jeff as her special favorite and Neil as runner up...it went back and fourth depending on her mood...she and dad were leaving all their money to the twosome. I knew it, but Jeff didn't realize that I was aware of the contents of Irene's and my father's will.

Bottom line it was their money and they had worked for it...the situation just hurt my feelings; to be so discarded inexplicably.

That's why all this talk of Uncle Tavis being so good to me and how lucky I was kind of pissed me off. That's why I worked like a horse building my savings and stocks so I wouldn't end up too old to work as a hairdresser with no savings and no ability to retire.

When we returned to the lodge, our spirits were back up. I couldn't let family secrets and conflict get in the way of a nice visit. He'd come all this way to see me, and that's what mattered.

"I'm going to go work on the car." Jeff said, pulling his toolbox out of the Lexus' trunk.

"Do you want to eat at the diner tonight, or have steaks here?" I asked. "We can grill out."

"Steaks are good," Jeff replied. "If you don't mind, I may want to take a walk later."

"Sure."

About three o'clock, I peeked outside the front window to find that Jeff was gone. His car was still parked out front, and the tools were strewn about on a mat behind my car. I guess he'd decided to take the walk alone.

I finished folding the laundry and setting up for dinner. Comby needed a walk and I took my coffee with me as we strolled. Amanda was chopping wood when I walked past. She waved me over.

"Who's that man at your place?" she demanded.

"My cousin." I said. "Why?"

"He's been nosing around at all the sheds, like he's looking for something," Amanda explained. "He even went up towards the chapel. No one's supposed to go in there, Ned made that clear years ago."

"I know." I agreed with her, and then asked, "what's up with that place?"

"I don't know," she admitted. "Your uncle just said it was private, and I didn't question him. Once in awhile, these shady-looking guys would show up there."

"Probably just friends," I said, half to myself.

"No." Amanda said. "These weren't his hunting buddies. They came at night, just two of them, and they always left a few hours later."

"What did they look like?" I asked.

"Long coats and hats. The skinny short one had a limp or something - the other guy was always helping him walk."

"Oh..." I scratched my head, puzzled. "I have no idea, but I'll go up and get Jeff."

"Watch yourself." Amanda warned me. "Money does strange things to people."

"Money?" I said dumbly, looking towards the chapel. It was one of the buildings Lauren and I had never made it into, since the keys for the place weren't on my ring.

"I gotta go." Amanda said hurriedly. "The phone is ringing."

How convenient, I thought.

As Amanda had predicted, Jeff was sniffing around the chapel.

"Hey Jeff!" I called out.

"Oh, hi!" Jeff replied, looking very surprised to see me. "Um, check this place out. It's really pretty."

"It is, but for some reason Ned told me to stay away from it. I haven't really poked around it much."

Jeff snorted, "It's your land! Why does he have any say about what buildings you're allowed to investigate?"

"Sometimes," I said, "it's better to go with the flow, you know? I'm new up here. There must be a good reason, if Ned felt he had to warn me away."

"Lucy, that's crazy." Jeff said condescendingly. "He probably didn't want you in here because there's something to find. People used to say your uncle was connected to the mob, after all."

"Oh, please," I said, rolling my eyes. "People say a lot of crap. Especially about their own families."

Jeff looked bemused. "You of all people," he said, "you always wanted to know the scoop, and you're not even curious about something as juicy as mob connections?"

"I was curious years ago, when I was a little kid. Then I grew up." I replied. "I knew Uncle Tavis pretty well. He was way too good hearted to be a gangster."

"I guess you're right." Jeff said, but he sounded unconvinced. He reminded me of a hungry dog that had just gotten a whiff of food. I noticed he'd changed into his North Face jacket and expensive hiking gear, like he was going off in search of the lost tomb of King Tut... *in the woods*.

He was even carrying an ancient shovel, but he put down as he walked towards me.

"Maybe you're right." he said, shrugging. "Maybe he was just a sporting goods mogul."

Now it was my turn to shock him. "He did own a strip joint off of Rue Ste-Catherine's in Montreal." I mentioned casually.

Jeff looked at me, wide-eyed.

"His girlfriend told me, I think that's how they met." I explained. His eyes got even wider for a few seconds.

We walked back to the house, discussing theories of how Tavis had ended up with the lodge and his money. *I had my own theory about Jeff -* my suspicion was that he was up here because he needed money.

Years ago, he'd been banned from a number of casinos for card counting and had run up some serious debts in the process. Then, as far as I knew, he'd straightened out, paid up, and settled down. Except his current attitude and behavior reminded me of the old Jeff, the one who owed a lot of money to a lot of unsavory people and was nervous as hell because of it.

The sun was starting to go down and it smelled like snow was coming. I heated up some chili and cornbread for us to nibble on, while we waited for the steaks and asparagus to grill. Jeff and I ate dinner on TV trays next to the fire. We didn't talk too much, and I kept examining him out of the corner of my eye. He'd been the family rebel, as a teenager. Jeff had turned me on to the scandalous *National Lampoon*, and off color humor of *Mad* magazine. He'd read over the top and sometimes-offensive Robert Crumb comics and knew all about the cool counter-culture things that I so adored.

It was so strange to me to see how he'd turned out, an archetype of conformity and conventionalism. He sat there talking about the merits of a conservative life, and that just added to my suspicions that he was back to gambling. I tried to get him talking about the old days, to remember the good times. But he was stuck on something that he was not sharing with me. By the time I was sipping decaf and he was downing some 12-year old scotch, he seemed to be calming down, acting more like the Jeff I knew and loved.

Jeff was getting tired, so we called it a night. I went into my room to take my nightly bath and read the latest novel from the used bookstore in town.

I awoke with a start about three a.m., which wasn't anything new. My family used to call me Hawk Ears or Hawk Eyes, because I heard and saw everything. Currently, "everything" included the front door clicking shut behind Jeff as he tip-toed out the lodge. I knew exactly where he was going - up to the chapel, to see if Uncle Tavis had mob money stashed somewhere.

Son of a bitch, I grumbled to myself, getting suited up to go outside. Then I stopped. Why bother? There wasn't anything up there, as far as I knew - Jeff could just go wear himself out in the cold and dark. There was no reason for me to go after him.

I stripped off what outdoor clothes I'd put on, and got back into bed. If Jeff needed cash so badly that he was willing to dig around in the Canadian wilderness for the faint possibility of some money, he might as well take it. That was assuming there was any money hidden at the chapel, which I highly doubted.

While I'd found small amounts of cash hidden around the lodge in various odd places, I didn't think my uncle was likely to have buried a pot of gold somewhere.

When I got up in the morning, Jeff was making omelets. He didn't look any the worse for wear for his late night trip.

"Smells good," I said pouring a cup of joe and sitting down at the kitchen table.

"I got bacon and sausage, and made some hash browns, too." he replied.

"How'd you sleep?" I asked, genuinely curious about what he was going to say.

"Oh, pretty good," Jeff told me, "All this cold Canadian air, you know."

He was so full of crap!

"Find anything good up at the chapel?" I said casually, after another sip of coffee.

He took the omelet pan off the stove and turned the burner off.

"You always did have eyes in back of your head." Jeff mumbled.

"Listen, we haven't been close in a long time." I told him. "I didn't think you were coming up just for the scenery."

"I'm sure you'll be glad to know that the chapel is a shrine to your aunt, the one who died. Pictures of she and your Uncle, a bed with a quilt that has her name on it, right down to what looks like her clothes in the closet. Kind of a shrine to Greta...it was fuckin creepy, Luc."

"Any embalmed bodies?"

"No, *smartass*," Jeff said, "but I have to say I kept waiting for something to jump out at me. There was weird feeling to the place. It was pretty goddamned clean for an abandoned chapel, too."

"I'm gonna be straight with you, Jeff." I said, and then asked him flat out. "Are you hurting for cash?"

"Well, not really hurting, but the baby and, well, the fact is, I have some gambling debts." he admitted.

"Not bad enough to get you killed?" I asked.

"Jesus, no!" Jeff said, startled. "I just don't want my wife finding out that I went back to the casinos. I didn't want to ask your dad for cash, because he'd be sure to tell her."

"How much do you owe?"

"I'm paying it, it's just going really slow, because I owe...um, about fifty thousand. Or so."

I almost fell over with shock - that was a whole lot of money, American or Canadian, and it'd take him years to pay that off if he was doing it in increments - but pulled myself together and played it cool.

"I can help, Jeff," I told him, "but I have to keep this place afloat. I don't have a husband, and my job will never make me rich."

"Any help would be great," he replied, clearly relieved. "I'll pay you back."

"Call Functer, the attorney." I told him, drinking more of my coffee. "You can say you're rehabbing the barn for me."

"How about you call him?" Jeff asked, smiling nervously.

"Fine," I grumbled. "But you have to know, I can't help you out after this. This is the last time you can ask me for money." I didn't want to sound like a jerk, but addicts and gamblers always need more. I should know. There was never enough booze for me back in the day...and there would never be enough dough to keep him rolling in the gambler's life.

"Don't worry," Jeff assured me, "I don't want to go through this shit again."

He seemed sincere about it, and actually spent the rest of the day working on the barn's heating system. He used to build helicopters for the military, so his engineering skills were saving me a big chunk of change.

Next morning, he was out fixing the dock when I went to work. That night, we ate at the Diner in town, and things seemed much more at ease.

Lucky for both of us, Functer didn't question me as to what I was doing giving that much money to someone to rehab my barn, and the cash was wired to Jeff's account almost immediately.

I gave Jeff a bear hug before he left. "Seriously, if you need more help, I'll come up," he said, and he seemed to genuinely mean it.

"I know you will." I told him. "You've always been a stand-up guy." When I was an immature twenty-something, he'd been there for me, so now we were even.

"Thanks Lucy," Jeff said seriously. "You're really saving my ass, and I'll never forget this."

All my life I'd felt like the odd one out in my family, the one who never quite lived up to expectations. Lauren was a surgeon, Jeff had an impressive job at Spitzer Electronics and Labs, my brother Neil was a stockbroker, my father had his own business and me? I was a hair stylist. It felt strange to be the one someone had come to in distress. I had always felt like my cousins and my brother were the adults, and I was the kid. It felt good to help. When the chips had been down in my life, they'd helped me. Lauren had given me a bed when I couldn't afford one, Jeff and Neil had always been my movers - Jeff even broke his hand moving my couch out of a fourth-floor apartment. Now I could help, but I didn't want to start throwing cash around, even to my relatives. I had a lot invested in keeping this place and trying to get my dreams unburied and back on track, so I couldn't afford to be Santa.

My co-worker Candy was disappointed when Jeff left. "He was so cute...too bad he's married. He looks like Kevin Costner."

"I'll be sure to tell him." I said.

Ned paid me an unexpected visit the next night. "I thought I told you to stay away from the chapel," he said abruptly. "Well, come in, take off your coat, stay awhile." I said jokingly, but Ned clearly wasn't in the mood. I got serious very quickly and explained the situation. "I wasn't up there, Ned. I took you seriously. My cousin Jeff was visiting and he went up there one night, mostly because he was convinced there was a pot of gold or something under the floorboards."

"Aw, shit." Ned muttered, and then seemed to make a mental decision. "Sit down," he ordered.

"You're going to find this out anyway, but you might as well hear it from me."

"Tell me it's not your love nest." I said. I was joking. Mostly.

"Hell, no." Ned snorted. "But - see, I don't know how to tell you this, I didn't expect to have to tell you about this."

"Spit it out." I said. Now I really wanted to know what was going on.

"Your aunt Greta." Ned said. "She isn't dead. She survived the plane crash, but she's got severe brain damage. She lives at the McTrainer Assisted Living facility."

"Oh my God!" I gasped. "Ned, why didn't you tell me about this sooner? I could've visited her!"

"Your uncle didn't want anyone to know." Ned said. "She's real messed up - the doctors didn't expect her to live. That's where he got the money to start his sporting goods business, from the settlement after the plane crash."

Now a lot of parts of my uncle's life made more sense to me. "I knew he wasn't a mobster!" I said, relieved.

"A mobster?" Ned said disbelievingly. "What would give you that idea?" He clearly thought I was off my rocker for even suggesting the idea.

"No one in the family ever knew where he got all his money from. Tavis was always traveling, he had lots of expensive toys - nice boats, nice cars, guns, and a Cadillac golf cart - and then there was the strip club that he owned. I think most of the family knew about that."

Ned nodded.

"The burlesque club was sold a few years back," Ned said, shaking a pack of cigarette's out and lighting one up. "The people who bought it were Russians and maybe not so...well, you know...on the up and up. But Tavis wasn't in the mob."

I thought for a few seconds, trying to process what I'd just heard. The next logical step for me was to go and visit this poor woman. So I broached the question with Ned.

"If you want to visit her, that's fine I guess." Ned said. "I bring her to the chapel for a little visit every so often." Then he paused for a minute, and scratched his head like he had something else to get off his chest. "Actually, the strip club was owned jointly by your dad and your uncle. Tavis just kept an eye on things when he came to town. Your dad was the silent partner."

The house of cards that was my mental image of my family was falling down. I wasn't too surprised about my dad, since I'd known for years that he loved porn. Neil and I had found his collection as teenagers. It had all been suspiciously labeled with totally unappealing titles like "Vatican Highlights", The Carter Years," "Cold War Confusion", "Dorf On Golf Part V." Nothing my dad would actually WATCH, aside from Dorf on Golf.

At east the mystery of the short skinny man who came to the chapel in the middle of the night was solved. It clearly had to be my aunt, not a mobster.

Amanda must've seen my aunt and uncle when they came up to the chapel. The whole thing was mind-boggling, but Ned was very sympathetic and let me talk. I was pretty shaken up, to be honest. Secrets were normal in my family, but this one was a doozy.

On my next day off from the salon, I had Ned take me to visit McTrainer. The halls of the facility were a bit ominous, but the live plants, flowers arrangements, oil paintings spread through the building made it seem more like a retreat house than a health care facility. My aunt was in a wheelchair in her room, with her long, curly, still-brown hair down and flowing over the shoulder of her cranberry velour dressing gown. It was very old Hollywood. I immediately felt a kinship towards her. She'd lost her Playboy Bunny good looks to age, but vestiges of beauty lingered in her bone structure and features. She was very pleasant, in a childlike way.

"She's had a traumatic brain injury, and she's elderly...so don't expect a lot." The nurse had explained before she allowed me into Greta's room.

I took my aunt to the solarium to get acquainted with her in friendlier surroundings. The hospital was located in a beautiful wooded area and the views were spectacular. It wasn't hard to see why my uncle had chosen this location, especially since it wasn't too far from Fossil Creek. Then again, it wasn't too close, either. McTrainer was just outside Quebec City.

The combination of the brain injury and age had clearly affected her seriously. "You have a nice face," she said, slurring her words. "Bring me candy?" Her eyes noted the box in my lap.

I turned over the sweets, which she seemed to really enjoy. I tried to tell her I was her niece, but that was beyond her level of understanding.

"You nice, you nice." she said, after I'd tried to explain.

"The nice niece!" I said. Maybe that would sink in.

I put on some classical music they had in a little CD player nearby, and I talked about moving to Canada. She listened attentively.

"You talk a lot," she laughed. "I'm a hairdresser," I said, "we do that." Greta just smiled. The nurse had explained that when the emergency workers had brought her in from the plane crash, she hadn't been expected to live. Somehow, she'd hung on. Her face was scarred on the left side, from burns sustained in the crash, but the rest of her face was fine. The nurse had told me, "Her face doesn't bother her. She'll tell you that she was a pretty girl a long time ago, though."

Talking to my aunt gave me a lot of mixed emotions. I was happy to have found her, sad that she'd been so damaged, angry that she'd been hidden away for so long, and not just a little annoyed that my family kept secrets so well. I could tell she was getting sleepy, and probably losing interest in the conversation, so I patted her knee and let her know I would be back soon.

As I signed out at the front desk, I told the nurse "I'll come once a month to visit from now on."

"That'll be nice," the nurse told me, smiling. "I think she's missed having visitors."

All the way home, I chatted with Ned. He told me little stories about my aunt and uncle, and it was good to finally see the pieces start to fit together.

When we got to the Lodge, I hugged Ned goodbye. Then I raced to Amanda's door, knocking as hard as I could before I'd even stopped to think about it. She answered the door, and I sat down at her kitchen table before she even had a chance to invite me in. Then I dumped the whole tale on her. It occurred to me, mid-story, that this could be a bad idea. After all, Amanda wasn't my best friend, or even someone I was particularly close to, but I had the feeling she'd listen to me.

"Well," Amanda said, after I'd spilled the whole story, "that's a pretty nice thing for you to do. Visiting, I mean."

"She's my aunt!" I said. "Actually, I think it's kind of shitty that my uncle hid her away."

"He was ashamed, I bet" Amanda said. "Men are different that way. They don't know how to deal with these things." Clearly, she was in a talkative mood. I hadn't heard this many words in a row from her since I'd moved into the lodge.

Suddenly, Amanda asked "What really made you move up here to the sticks, Lucy?"

"Many things," I said. "I'd considered relocating from Chicago to Canada a few years ago, but my partner at the time worked for the government and we had to stay in the states and the East Coast was too expensive."

"Your business partner?" Amanda asked.

"Personal partner." I replied. "Like a spouse."

"He..." she said, openly curious. "No." I said. "She."

"Ohhh..." Amanda said, looking at me keenly. There was a pause in the conversation.

It was bordering on uncomfortable, so I started talking again. "I was getting sick of the scent of open manholes and dumpsters, the rat race was wearing me out, and at a certain point, you just can't take overhearing people screaming at each other on their cell phones at three a.m. anymore."

"Believe it or not," Amanda said, "I miss that sometimes. I'm a city girl myself - from Manhattan."

"I thought you were from up here?" I asked, genuinely surprised.

"Oh no, I'm not a native." Amanda told me. "I moved up to Canada after a break up. Then some bad things happened, so I moved to Fossil Creek, rented this cabin from your uncle, and that's the end of it."

I noticed a photo of a woman on the mantel. "Is that a relative?" I said, pointing to the picture.

"*That's my former partner,*" Amanda said. "She ran off with a man. Like I'd said - bad breakup."

"Oh, God," I said, wincing. "I'm so sorry."

"It's a reminder not to trust your heart." Amanda told me. "It'll only let you down."

"I used to feel that way." I replied. "And I got cold and unbreakable, I became the ultimate ice queen. Then one night, I was watching my friend Joanie crying in a bar over a guy who dumped her and I realized I wasn't actually gaining anything by closing off my heart. I wasn't any happier - I was just numb. That's when I opened my heart back up."

"But you broke up with your partner." Amanda pointed out.

"Tears pass." I said. "We have to keep moving - I refuse to live in the past. I had seven years of therapy to teach me that."

"Good for you." She nodded, not sure if she agreed.

I decided I'd taken up enough of her time.

"Tomorrow is the Halloween party," I told her, "and you're still invited. If you decide to come, be sure to bring your appetite."

"I don't think so," Amanda said, "but thanks." She didn't sound as definitely negative as she had before, and I had the feeling she might actually show up at the party.

Joelle gave everyone a half-day off so we could all go to the party. It helped that it was a slow week and no one had any bookings for the day. Ned, Kathy, Bob and Trudy had gone over early to set up the buffet, which was incredibly nice of them. It was the sort of thing people did for each other in small towns.

I had set up a picnic table for the pumpkin carving contest, and the TV in the back room off the kitchen had The Great Pumpkin, Goosebumps and other scary kid fare. Oddly enough, the kids seemed to really enjoy my personal favorite, which was "Monster Squad." It was a great movie from the eighties where the kids save this little town from monsters.

The adults were mostly in the main area with the fire going, the beer was flowing and the horror movies howling. I had turned the reception desk into the bar, and one of Ned's friends from the VFW played bartender.

By ten, the moms and dad were starting to filter out, toting of goody bags for the kids and their prize pumpkins - everyone had won a ribbon for something. All of the guests were so polite and charming that it was making me worry that the other shoe would drop and someone would be revealed as a total jerk.

By eleven, the party was in full swing. Bob's son Todd, who now had steady work with me as a stable hand, and his band set up in the main room and played some great classic rock. His girlfriend did a great Grace Slick on "Don't You Want Somebody to Love."

"C'mon, Lucy, do a song," Todd requested, though the guys from his band looked a little leery of the idea.

"Nope." I replied. "This is your gig."

"Seriously, I know you know Neil Young's Heart of Gold, I've heard you sing it in the barn!" Todd said coaxingly.

"Ok," I said, "I'll do the one song."

So I sang, and it turned out great - except for a lady who had enjoyed one too many beers.

I had just finished singing when I heard the commotion from the bar.

"She thinks she's such hot shit," slurred an obviously impaired woman, "coming up here trying to buy everyone into liking her...what the fuck, she's just a goddamned..."

Before she could say another word, Big Bob was there, helping her to the door.

The woman waved him away and snarled "Fuck you, you old drunken has-been, I don't need this shit!" Her boyfriend hustled her out the front door at record speed.

People were looking at me, wondering what I was going to do.

"Hey, there's always one at every party..." I said lightly, swinging a hot dog in my hand.

Todd started playing his final number, and the party stayed in full swing until one thirty a.m. That's when I started flashing the lights and announcing "Last call..."

Candy, Randy and Kathy helped me to clean up the majority of the mess. "You guys have been great," I told them, "but I'll get the rest in the morning."

Ned and Bob had loaded up the buffet tables and chafing dishes, which had been provided by Sophie from the Diner. I'd promised her free haircuts, one for her and one for her granddaughter Ellie.

"Darlin'," Sophie had said, "you don't have to do that." "I know, but it's just my way of saying thank you."

It was two thirty in the morning by the time the last guest had left, and I couldn't believe I was still awake. Maybe it was all the coffee I'd consumed over the evening.

Just as I'd plunked down in my easy chair to relax, there was a knock on my front door. I got up to answer it, hoping that it wasn't the drunk woman with the apparent grudge against me, and that it was just someone who'd forgotten something and come back to get it. Much to my surprise, it was Amanda. "I figured you might need help cleaning up," she said, holding up a box of Hefty garbage bags.

"My God, that is so sweet." I said. "But we actually have the mess pretty much under control."

Amanda actually looked disappointed.

"But I do need some help," I said quickly. "When I play hostess, I can't eat. I've been dying to try Sophie's Pumpkin Cheesecake Pie - do you want a slice?"

"Ah, okay." Amanda said.

There still was coffee on, and I cut a couple of slices of pie for us. We ate them in front of the fire.

"It was a good time...you should've come earlier!" I told Amanda, around bites of pie. "You missed the drunken girl who was going to tell me off."

"Oh, no!"

"Oh yes!" I said, "But her boyfriend and Bob came to my rescue."

"Just the booze talking."

"Yeah," I said, "but I'm sure there are others who feel the same as her. I'm a big kiss-ass. I like people, I like people to like me, and sometimes that pisses other people off. I'm not from here, I'm new, so I expected sooner or later someone would get in my face."

"Long ago, I was a people person," Amanda said, staring into the fire.

"You can always get back to that person you were...if you want to." I replied.

"If I want to." Amanda said wryly. "That's the catch."

"Baby steps..." I prompted.

"I heard you singing," she said suddenly.

"Really?"

"I was going to come earlier, but I was listening to all the people. It seemed really overwhelming to me. But I was enjoying the music. Also, some one peed in your bushes."

I shrugged. "It's a party hazard."

My eyes were getting droopy, and I think Amanda could sense me falling asleep on her.

"Well," she said, "I better get moving, I'm glad the party was a success. You're a nice person, and I hope you stay."

"I think I will." I replied. Then I took a huge chance and gave her a hug. She hugged me back stiffly, but at least she was smiling.

Chapter 10

My alarm clock went off to "Keep On Rockin' In The Free World," and I lay in my bed under the warm covers and thought about what a great song Neil Young wrote.

At six a.m., I looked like a "hot mess," as we use to say in hair school. My hair was in a lovely Don King 'do, and I was wearing my super-soft faded South Park "Respect My Authority" T-shirt with long underwear I had tie-dyed with black zebra stripes about a million years ago. Out here in logger country, I figured no one was going to be bothering me this early, so who gave a shit what I looked like? There weren't any morning joggers or homeless folks waiting outside the lodge to critique my looks.

Don't ever think the homeless aren't fashion critics - I'd had run-ins with them in Chicago numerous times. My *favorite* memory was an early morning walk down by Loyola Beach.

"Are those parachute pants?" an androgynous looking gal said to me one very, very cold December morning when I was walking Combover.

I tried to muster up a chuckle and responded, "I just love these pants! They're so comfy you can sleep in them and then go out in public." My Pat Boone impersonation didn't endear me to her.

"Well, dear, it looks like you slept in them." Then she gave me a British style sniff, flaring her nostrils.

I'd wanted to shoot back "And it looks like someone used your face for a mattress!" but I held back and smiled, chuckling and kept walking - and she'd heckled me. "*The eighties are over, the eighties are over*" she'd kept bellowing.

I'd hotfooted it in the opposite direction.

Needless to say, it was something of a surprise to have Todd turn up while I was feeding Tao and letting Comby out.

I excused my super-sloppy look. "What's up?" I asked, pretty sure I hadn't asked him over for any chores or for an early morning chat.

"I'm in trouble, Lucy." Todd said, hanging his head. Looking like a forlorn Curt Cobain.

It was a week before Thanksgiving, work had been busy, and I wasn't really in the mood to listen to teenager having a crisis. But he was a sweet guy whom I'd come to count on so I put on my best counselor face and we chatted.

"Ok...give me the scoop." I said, finishing giving Tao his breakfast.

"Sheri is pregnant." Todd muttered.

Now I understood why he had that same exhausted, baggy-eyed look that I did.

"Do you guys want to have a baby?" I asked.

"I wouldn't mind, really," Todd told me, "but Sheri is a definite no."

"How far along?"

"Well, we can't do that morning after pill if that's what you mean."

"Let's go in the house and have some coffee...it's freezing out here." I said. I'd rather talk about huge, life-changing issues after I'd been caffeinated.

"Okay," he replied, moping along after me like a ten year old kid who'd just wrecked his bike.

We sat by the fire and stared into it, like it was going to give us all the answers.

"Do you think there's any way you can convince Sheri to not get an abortion?" I asked Todd.

"ABORTION! God!" Todd yelped. The reality of the situation seemed to sting him like a bee bite.

"That's the option that's not having a baby. Well, there's adoption, too."

"No fuckin' way." Todd said fiercely. "If she has the baby, I'll keep it myself. Adoption is completely out."

"Okay." I said, handing him a hot cup of my strongest coffee to warm his red, chapped hands. "Do you make enough money to support this kid and Sheri?"

"She's in school getting her art degree, and I work for my dad, I do chores for you, and I have a paper route, too." Todd replied.

"You make $500 a week?" I asked.

"Hell no," Todd told me. "More like $250 or less…except if I pick up odd jobs."

"Does Sheri have a part-time job?"

"At a clothing store. She gets paid minimum wage, and she'd be lucky to make what I make in a month. She's got a full schedule this year."

"I don't mean to be rude," I sighed, "but what happened to condoms or the pill?"

"She's on the pill," Todd said, "but she took a break and then started this new one. It must have happened in between, during the changeover."

"Well…did you talk to your mom or dad?"

"Hell fuckin' no." Todd exclaimed. He was huffing and cursing like a wounded Spanish bull.

"Really, you think your dad would be a jerk about it."

"He bought me my first pack of condoms when I was 12. I wasn't doing it, but he was making a point. Sooo, yeah, he's gonna be pissed."

"You and Sheri need to come to a decision." I told Todd seriously. "If she decides to have an abortion, you need to be there for her. There are people who think women take this decision lightly or something, but they don't. It's a very emotionally traumatic experience, and physically painful, too. Some men withdraw, and it's important that you not do that. That will make a big difference in her experience and how you feel about yourself.

I took another sip of coffee and starred into the swirling cup…"But I really think you should talk to your dad; he's had a lot of experiences in his life that you may not know about."

I couldn't break Bob's anonymity, but at the Twelve Step meetings, he'd shared some very powerful stuff. He didn't strike me as an uncaring asshole or a hard-ass, and might have been in this position himself as a kid.

"What do you think, Lucy?" Todd asked. "What would you do, if you were Sheri?"

"I'm not Sheri or you." I replied flatly, and then relented a bit. "I was in a situation where the condom slipped off, and I spent two horrible weeks wondering if my period would arrive or not. The guy I'd slept with was not going to be part of a baby's life, and I was in college and living in my grandma's attic with absolutely no money. Not a good situation to take total responsibility for a child."

"Yes!" said Todd, "Just like Sheri!"

"For those two weeks, I kept thinking that this maybe-baby could be such a smart little cutie pie, because the guy was on academic scholarship at Purdue...and yea, he was cute. I never wanted biological kids, but the more I thought about it, the more confused I got. I'm pro-choice all the way, but I'm telling you, that would have been a really hard decision to make. In the end, my period came and I breathed a sigh of relief."

"Lucky you." grumbled Todd.

"The best advice I can give you," I said, "is to talk to Sheri, and talk about it with your dad. Sorry I don't have more for you." I reached over and patted his knee. "I'm honored you came to me."

Todd stood up and began putting his jacket on, saying, "I'm really going to need to step it up. I need to start thinking about my future and getting a better job no matter what happens. Maybe I need to reconsider school - I used to want to build cars."

"Great idea." I told him, as he left to go. When he was in the drive, Todd looked back at me and grinned. "So you did sleep with dudes!" he said gleefully.

"Yes." I said, in a put-upon manner, rolling my eyes. Todd nodded, turning sober. "I'll let you know what happens," he promised, "and I think I'll talk with my dad."

"Good luck," I told him as he walked away, "and I think whichever decision you make will be the right one."

Todd walked down the drive and I went back inside to find that the house seemed suddenly big again.

As I looked around at the splendor of the lodge, it reminded me of the wealth of Malibu or Cape Cod. I couldn't imagine how a person could make enough money to support my aunt and I indefinitely. I'd worked ten hour days, five days a week back in Chicago and never seemed to get ahead financially. I recalled keeping tons of tips in my sock drawer, which always looked like a ton of cash. Then I'd count it, and spend it on books and makeup rather than saving for the new bed or condo I'd always promised myself. When I'd discussed this with my sponsor, she'd laughed and said, "Welcome to the real world!"

I was never good at saving money, but I used to cheat by taking money from my paychecks and putting it into my saving account automatically. That had helped me sock away a little something rather than fritter all my money away.

The thing was that eventually, I'd hit a point where I didn't want to live like a college student anymore. I wanted to be a grownup - have a condo, go on vacations, etc. My view of money had gradually changed as I got older, and I began to save more aggressively and invest my savings. All of that had come back to bite me in the ass when the market crashed, of course, sending seven years of saving and investing and careful planning right out the window. I'd been lucky to end up at square one, right where I'd been before I'd started being careful with money. There's no way I'd have had anything close to this level of lifestyle without Uncle Tavis and his legacy.

I'd had dreams of being a mogul of some kind, writing books, producing my own music, touring to screaming audiences, *c'mon I grew up in the Big 80's*, but at the end of the day I was just a hairdresser. Maybe that was okay. I had everything I needed and was beginning to think I might have most of what I wanted, too, just not in the package that I'd expected it to come in.

So much for my light relaxing morning.

Since I was all wound up and it wasn't even noon, I decided to work out some stress by cleaning. The front hall desperately needed vacuuming, so I hauled out the machine and got down to it. Combover's hair was starting to form little dustballs around the edges of the Native American statue in the hallway, so I muscled it out of place and shifted it a few inches. That's when I noticed the door built into the paneling of the hallway wall. There was a small push button door lock; hopefully it wouldn't set off any alarms.

The door popped right open when I pushed the button. I turned on the light and stood wide-eyed, taking in a full-sized hidden room.

It looked like a general storage locker for a pack rat. There were boxes full of old snow gear, horse blankets, fly-fishing poles, a jar full of old Cracker Jack prizes, a vintage pigskin football, tons of other random crap. There were even flags, probably for the pier. Maps and old art were hanging from hooks on the walls. It was a secret treasure room, the kind I'd always dreamed of finding when I was a kid, and digging through it was going to be a blast. Maybe when I got home from work each night, I'd go through all this cool booty.

I'd definitely have to dust before I started digging, because the spiders had set up a condo complex in this room. But the smell of year's gone past, old wax and aged wood was a momentary tonic to my somber thoughts.

I loved flea markets, resale shops, garage sales and this place was the mother lode! "Mrs. Zwich" was written on an old beer box, and inside were Christmas ornaments, precious intricately blown glass angels with tarnished faces, feathers that had been bent and discolored and glitter that was shedding and no longer sparkly. Maybe I'd bring these to my Aunt, in case they were hers. I'm sure Ned and Bob and Tavis hadn't bothered to decorate this place for the holidays.

At least I wasn't the only hoarder in the family.

I scooted out of work right at 6p.m. "Got a date with a pile of junk!" I told Candy.

It was already dark as a cave on Main Street. The thoroughfare was mostly closed for the evening, with drops of streetlights glowing yellow, the neon of multicolored beer signs, store front advertisements and closed signs lighting my way to the stable like an airport runway.

There was no one in the stable, other than Tao. There was, however, a red tin bucket hanging from his stable door that said "Put payment in here." Ah, the honesty of a small town. I smiled, feeling like I was a long way from Chicago in a lot of ways.

On the dark ride home, I decided to invite Amanda over to help me loot the treasure trove from the hidden closet. It was a good excuse to have company.

I focused on that during my ride home, instead of weird chills that were shivering up my spine tonight. I usually had my iPod to drown out the silence, but I'd forgotten it this morning in my rush to get to work. Without it, my ride seemed spooky and ominous.

When I saw Amanda's cabin lights like a lighthouse in the ocean of dark blue-black night, I rode a little faster. When I got to her door I knocked, along with crossing my fingers and hoping she'd be in a good mood. Amanda answered the door and I blurted out "You still want to help me clean up?"

"Sure," she replied. She was looking at Tao, who was peeking at her over my shoulder. "Let me get my coat. Oh, here's a bunch of carrots for Tao." The carrots still had the leaves attached, and Tao crunched his treat happily.

"Thanks," I said inanely. "We haven't been home yet." In my stomach, the butterflies chanted she was thinking of me, she was thinking of me. I tried to ignore them. She was thinking of my horse, which wasn't exactly the same thing.

We took Tao to the barn and took care of him - food, grooming, etc.

Inside the house, I popped in a Tombstone pizza and showed her the hidden room.

"This is amazing!" Amanda said. "It's like an archive of family treasures!"

"I want to use this stuff for decoration around the lodge," I told her. "I figure we can hang the snow shoes over the front desk, with this stuffed pheasant in the center. The best way to clean up this space is to get all of it out of here and use it - maybe I'll mount and frame the Cracker Jack prizes, and I'm definitely putting the fur coat on the Indian."

"These maps are amazing!" she said. "Look at this one." Amanda pointed to the framed map on the wall. "That's hand-drawn."

I goggled at the map. How anyone had the attention span for that kind of work was beyond me. Amanda suggested that I send the fur coats I'd found out to be cleaned by a trapper she knew. I was even gladder that I'd invited her. Who would have known that a reclusive mountain woman would be so knowledgeable about fur coats and fine art?

We chatted over the pizza. She filled me in on who was doing what and to whom in town, and talked about the money problems that had hit Fossil Creek when the two manufacturing plants had closed last year.

"Chicago got nailed too." I told her. "The worst part has been the housing bubble bursting, though. There's all these half-built 'condo-carcasses' that are never going to be finished. These things are all over the place and the newer subdivisions that shot up are like empty graveyards of homes with ratty-looking For Sale signs staked into the unkempt yards. These were really nice homes only a couple of years ago, but after being vacant for two years, they're eroding."

"That's an eerie way to describe it," she replied. Amanda's clear blue eyes sparkled like snowflakes in the moonlight on Christmas Eve. The more time I spent with her, the more attractive I thought she was. Who would've thought a cleaning project could be so wonderful!

We finished the pizza and went back to our task at hand.

Turning on my boom box for some background music, I began going through an old box of mementos. There were scads of matchbooks from exotic locations, little boxes with collectable coins from foreign countries Tavis had visited, kitschy cloth-covered figurines and bobble head dolls from Florida State University, Brown and Indiana University, and hula-girl dolls. The photos were fun. People had dressed so much better forty years ago. I was excited to find a photo of Aunt Greta in her Playboy heyday, complete with bunny ears and powder-puff tail. I flipped it over to check the date and noticed the inscription. "Dear Sweet Gibbon...For All the Good Times."

That was my dad's name, not my uncle's. *OK*, this was a cheesecake shot of my aunt, dedicated to my dad? I was starting to wonder if they had an affair, and then I wondered if Uncle Tavis had ever seen this. I concluded that he must have seen it, because it was here in the storage room. There was no one else who could have put it here.

I decided to get a second opinion and called Amanda over to show her the picture.

"Pretty lady." Amanda commented.

"She's my aunt." I said. "Greta. The one I thought was dead."

Amanda asked me if I wanted to hang the photo, which was unframed.

"That's not the thing." I explained. "Look at the back. It's inscribed to my dad, not my uncle."

"*For the good times*." Amanda read aloud, and then she put the photo down. "Sounds like they were...intimate," she said.

"It does." I replied, uneasily. "And this is some strange kind of family secret, I can tell. I guess it's just another case of Lucy being the last to know - my dad had a heart attack last year and I didn't find out until he was home from the hospital and my brother mentioned the hospital stay in passing in an email. The Zwich family isn't big on communication."

"I don't have any family anymore." Amanda said slowly. "Whatever secrets there were, I never found out about. Though my mother told me on her death bed that I was a blessed surprise for her and my dad."

"Not something you'd want to find out when your mom is dying." I sympathized.

"Exactly. And looking at their wedding photos, they were all taken from the front or from the chest up. I felt a little stupid, because I should have figured it out before then."

"Your mom probably didn't want to talk about it - memories of the scandal."

Thinking aloud, I wondered "But why does my uncle have all my DAD'S college stuff here?" I held up all the things I was excavating and showed them to an intrigued Amanda. There were whole boxes and old Navy trunks full of my dad's memorabilia, from his prized FSU football from when he played at Florida State, a well-worn high school letterman's jacket, tickets to plays in Florida and Chicago, and a few matchbooks from the Playboy Club in Chicago - which had my Aunt Greta's signature on them. That was weird. Then there were photo albums full of my dad's frat brothers and postcards, even a few textbooks - none of it belonging to Tavis. It was all my dad's stuff.

"Why was my dad using the lodge for his storage facility?" I asked, half curious and half annoyed. "And what's up with my aunt's name being all over this napkin, the playbill and this photo?"

"Have you ever thought maybe..." then Amanda stopped. "Maybe what?"

"Nothing..."

"Maybe they had an affair? Yeah, that's why I called you in, to get another opinion, but it's the only thing that seems possible." I sighed suggesting we take a break.

The butterflies in my stomach were turning to moths.

"Good idea." Amanda said. "It looks like you're having an allergic reaction to the dust."

"Oh great," I sighed, looking at my red hands and scratching at each one. "It's been years since this happened. What a time for it to reappear."

"I have some salve at home that should help," said Amanda. "I'll run and get it for you. It's stinky, but by tomorrow the rash will be gone. Plus, it stops the itching immediately."

"I won't argue." I replied gratefully. She disappeared out the door, and I grabbed a bottle of water and sat by the dying fire.

Amanda wasn't at all the unfriendly hermit that I'd pegged her for. She was nice, and I loved her long braided hair and her husky voice. Still, I didn't want to freak her out by developing an obvious crush.

"Here," Amanda said, shoving a tin into my hands and shocking me out of my dreamy daze. "Go get a towel and I'll put some on your hands."

"You don't have to." I said. She told me she wanted to do it, so I got an old towel from the pantry and sat still while she rubbed smelly goo into my itchy red hands while I gazed at her fondly. It was too late to fend off a crush. I was smitten.

"Are you American Indian?" I joked.

"I'm a quarter Chippewa."

"How'd you end up so fair haired?" I asked.

"From my mom. My dad was the one with the Native heritage, my mom was pure Scandinavian."

"Did your father teach you this kind of thing…

making salves, living in nature? You seem to know a lot about this."

"Oh, please," Amanda scoffed, shaking her head no.

"Don't forget I'm from New York City. My dad went there to work as iron-worker, most Native Americans aren't bothered by heights, or so the story goes. It was impossible for him to ever get around to actually fixing our roof, so the jury's still out on that one. My mom was German and Norwegian, to be specific."

"I'm part Norwegian!" I said. "From my mom."

Amanda stopped rubbing the salve in, but our hands were still touching. She looked down, not making eye contact. "Well," she said, "I'd better be getting home. I hope you like the way I hung the stuff - I can always fix it if it isn't right."

"I'm sure you did a great job." I reassured her. It was taking most of my concentration to avoid pulling her in and kissing her, but I knew it wasn't the right time. I didn't even know if she was interested. I was dying to just pull her close and lay a big lip lock on her but I knew it wasn't the right thing. I could never tell when girls liked me for more than friendship. Guys were easier, they got boners…women, you never knew. That's why I had always been thankful I liked butch women, because then at least you knew they liked girls. But Amanda wasn't that easy to read and I wasn't sure at all.

Amanda put on her Daniel Boone cap and shimmied into her coat. "Good night," she said. "Thanks for the pizza."

"Thanks for the help." I said apprehensively, wanting to say something far wittier, something memorable. Then Amanda disappeared into the night. I was left wondering if I should have made a move.

After some further consideration, I was glad I hadn't. I'd been the pursuer in every relationship I'd ever had, and it was time to sit back and see if anyone was going to go after me. I was tired of doing all the work. My conviction didn't stop me from thinking about her until I feel asleep, though, and it didn't keep me from listening to tortured romantic songs from David Grey at bedtime.

Hair Hut was slow the next day. It was just Randy and I, which was always a good time.

"Would you ever think of buying this place if it went up for sale?" he asked me, leafing through a dog-eared copy of Paris Match magazine. "Maybe." I said. "I mean, I don't know, I always wanted to be a rock star and a writer and went into hair since the other stuff wasn't producing a living wage."

"So, no?" he pressed.

"Maybe, like I said..." Randy nodded and proceeded to show me a photo of Lady Gaga wearing a meat dress. "The caption should be A1 with that," he said, changing the subject.

I went to the resale shop after work to get a couple of new books and see if they had a toaster. While I was poking around, I ran into Tippie, the comic book fan I'd met at Randy's party. "Looking for anything special?" I asked. "I don't know," Tippie replied. "I'm killing time till my girlfriend gets off work at the lumber yard - she's a secretary there." she had a slight challenging tone...like she was fishing for me to *come out*.

A sister! I did an internal dance of glee. "Does she like it there?" I asked casually.

"It's a job." Tippie said, smiling and twirling a ratty feather duster, as we strolled the isles.

"I'm in need of a toaster," I told her, "and some action/mystery type books."

We gabbed for a while, and she invited me over for dinner. We chatted nonstop until we got to the lumberyard. I was shocked when she told me she was in her thirties - I'd thought she was in her early twenties. "Good genes, I guess," Tippie snorted.

Her girlfriend Janis looked about fifty but was the exact same age as me. Hard living, maybe? That rough edge always appealed to me. Janis was tall and rawboned, with small blue eyes and a shocking red buzz cut. She had a Cheshire Cat grin that made her look twelve when she laughed.

"Cool, company." Janis said. "I'm sick of talking to this one night and day." She lit up a Camel, inhaling deeply.

We talked about Chicago. Janis had a brother there, but they weren't close, and Tippie had spent a summer there with a friend in Andersonville, a neighborhood that I had worked and lived in the majority of my years in Chicago.

"It's like the little gay Mecca now." I told her. "Super yuppie, too. All these specialty shops selling gourmet olive oil, vintage furniture and upscale clothing boutiques."

"It was a little Swedish neighborhood when I was there." Tippie said, and then asked "Is Simon's still there?"

"Absolutely." I told her. "We go there for glog at Christmas. I'd have the hot chocolate." Explaining I don't booze it up any more.

"Where did you work?" she asked.

"The hair salon across the street from Ann Sather's restaurant." I said. "A place called Blasé."

"That place was wicked expensive." Tippie said.

"I miss the money." I admitted. "I had the most amazingly cool clientele. Smart, eclectic group of people."

Janis jumped up and twirled, "Guess who did my crazy-ass hair color!"

I chuckled, and said "Tippie?"

"How'd you guess?" snickered Janis. "All the guys keep teasing me at work."

Janis was doing chef duty and we had an insanely great beef stroganoff with a dollop of sour cream. "I like comfort food," she told me, smiling. "Hope the green beans aren't over cooked."

It was nice just hang with the girls and have a real home cooked meal, as I was likely to just heat up a can of soup and make a sandwich when I was on my own.

One thing I loved about Fossil Creek was that everyone seemed to have a fireplace. They were the kind actually used for warmth, not just for looks, since the power went off a lot during the winter. Tippie and Janis' home didn't have a huge amount of space, but there home was filled with book nooks and china cabinets built into the plaster walls. The hissing of steam heat was music to my ears, reminding me of my apartment in the city. I was so cozy and comfortable that it was hard to get up and go. It was beyond cold out, and I was not looking forward to taking the horse home.

After dinner I explained to the girls, "Tao's stabled by the salon, so I should get going."

We were still around the kitchen table, on the second cup of coffee. "Not till you've had some hot apple pie," Janis said, "it's only seven."

I checked my watch and sighed with fake exasperation. "Ok," I said. "You really twisted my arm."

We all enjoyed the Dutch apple pie with big sugar chunks.

Maybe it was the food coma or the balmy kitchen heat that made me blurt out a confession. "Girl to girl." I said, "I think I've got a crush on some one. Actually, I know I have a crush on someone, but I don't know if it would ever work. She's got some baggage."

They leaned in like I had just told them the hottest scoop of the century. Gossip was a popular way to spend time in Fossil Creek. Anything new was pounced on hungrily.

"Who?" Tippie asked. "Do I know her?"

"Amanda." I said.

Both Janis and Tippie exclaimed "AMANDA?!?" In voices more appropriate for some kind of deeply dramatic revelation.

"Is that bad?" I asked feeling embarrassed.

"I don't know." Janis said. "It might be a bad idea. She's a hard nut to crack."

"Yeah," Tippie said, nodding agreement. "We tried to befriend her, believe me. There's not many of us up here, but she totally blew us off. She was dating this girl for awhile."

"The one who ran off with a guy," I said.

"I guess, though she didn't tell us anything about it. Randy knew the girl. She was cute, but a real game player." "She struck me as a gold digger." Janis said, pouring me another cup of decaf.

"Well," I said, "Amanda doesn't seem to have any money for the lux life."

"Who knows?" Janis said. "All I know is that Amanda bought the girl a car, which she then proceeded to take off with, guy in tow, or so Randy says. The guy worked at the lumber yard, just for the summer, he was one of those free spirit guys who had rich folks back in Newport."

"So you think I'd be Amanda's type?" I asked pathetically.

"I think Amanda is a lost cause." Tippie said, clearing the dishes. My heart sank.

Now it was officially later and I was thoroughly full. "Ladies, this gal has a horse to pick up." I said.

"The stable does do overnights," Janis told me. "In case it gets too cold or whatever. You can always stay with us in town if the snow gets too bad; we've got a pull out bed."

"Thanks." I said. "I'm sure I'll end up camping on your couch. I have to make it if I can, though, to get back to my dog."

Tippie helped get me bundled up. "I am so glad we hooked up," she said pulling my hat over my ears.

"Makes me feel a little less lonely." I said. "I just may take you up on the overnight offer in the future, but tonight I need some sleep!"

"We do a game night once a month, if you want you can come meet the other lesbos." Janis smirked.

Tippie gave me a mug of coffee to go and a bag with some cool comics then drove me to the stable.

Tao was snorting and ready to go when I got to the stable. I gave the guy a tip for the late night pick up, then put in my iPod and rode home. I smiled to myself, thinking about the lovely evening. It made me forget about the weird inscription on the photograph. I didn't forget for long.

Monday was my day off, and I decided to make my phone calls, and maybe even work on some writing. Dad was always in the office Monday through Thursday, so I decided to check in with him. If I worked up the courage, maybe I'd even ask about Greta.

"Hi, Loretta." I said to my dad's secretary, who not- really-secretly ran the entire office.

"Hi Lucy! Your dad is here - you want me to get him?" "That'd be great." I said, "Thanks!" "Hi, darlin'." Dad said, in his usual upbeat growl.

We made small talk, and he told me he was glad to hear I was settling in well. He had warmed to the idea of me up here, I guess.

"But I miss our lunches." he complained.

"Me too." I said sadly. But an hour once a month for lunch was not enough of a commitment to keep me in Chicago.

I decided to be brave and ask him about the photo. "Dad," I started hesitantly. "I found a weird thing in one of the clutter boxes in the storage bin."

"Okay..." he said, already too quiet. My dad is never quiet. He's always the loudest one at any party. It's a Zwich trait.

"It was an inscribed photograph of Aunt Greta in her Playboy Bunny outfit. But it wasn't inscribed to Uncle Tavis. It was inscribed to you, and it said something that seemed really personal."

"Oh, yeah," said my dad. "It was something to show the guys. You know."

"For the good times?" I said skeptically.

"Lucy," he said. He was getting that exasperated tone with me that I had heard a lot when I was a teenager. "When you come home to visit next time, we'll talk about it. It wasn't a time in my life I'm proud of, but it lead to good things. After all, if it weren't for me, Tavis never would have met Greta."

"Did you guys have a romantic thing?" I asked straight on, dreading the answer.

"I don't want to talk about this on the phone," my dad said, the irritation in his voice mounting.

"It's not like we can talk when you're home." I said. "Not with Irene there."

My stepmother had a nasty habit of listening in on any conversations my dad was having.

"Just," he stammered, "we'll talk about it after Christmas. When are you coming home?"

"I wasn't planning on it." I said. "But I could."

"Get the tickets now, it'll be cheaper," he said, clearly trying to change the topic.

"Okay." I said, resigned.

There's times I love my dad so much it makes me want to cry - sometimes with joy, and many times in frustration. I never wanted him to be unhappy, but sometimes a secret can really sour the sweetness of any relationship. I could smell the bullshit over the phone line.

Next call on the family list was my mom. She and Gus were doing really well, which was amazing. I'd never heard her so happy. It had been a few years since "joyful" and "my mom" could be mentioned in the same sentence!

"Neil called," she said excitedly. My younger brother was still her baby, even at 33. "He and his wife are going to visit!"

My brother and my mom did not get along at all, when Neil had been younger. They'd gone years without speaking, but little by little, though emails and postcards they'd been breaking the ice.

"That's great!" I said.

"Oh, honey," my mom wailed, "I wish you could come! It would be so perfect!"

"I will, at some point." I reassured her. "With the move and everything, there's just no way I can finance a trip to Greece." I didn't point out that she didn't work and had a bunch of extra cash and was totally capable of visiting me. I knew from experience that it would only end in drama.

"We bought a boat," she told me, trying to make conversation. "It's not real expensive," she assured me. "Things are cheaper in Greece. I bought you a few little surprises and mailed them, so be on the lookout.

Have you made friends? Are you staying busy? Is it snowing?"

After answering the laundry list of questions I managed to get off the phone when my front doorbell rang. Saved by the bell!

It was Amanda! "Hi, I made some cookies," she said when I opened the door. "I'm afraid that if I don't get rid of some, I'll eat them all myself."

"Oh, fatten up the neighbor." I said cheerfully, inviting her in.

I poured some coffee, and we sat comfortably at the kitchen table.

"I met two new buddies!" I said, mouth full of cookie.

"Really." Amanda replied. She sounded... jealous?

"Tippie, this girl from Randy's party who digs the same kind of comic books I do, and her girlfriend Janis. They even made me dinner. I could have sworn Tippie was about twenty, but I was wrong."

"Ha," Amanda laughed humorlessly. "She's a bit older, just dresses like a kid."

"You know her?" I inquired slyly. "They invited me over a couple of times...but..."

"You weren't in the mood to socialize?" I winked.

"Exactly." Amanda said sheepishly.

The clouds outside were beginning to darken, and there was snow in the forecast. I lit a candle that smelled like balsam and cedar. Combover cuddled up to Amanda, and laid his head on her knee.

"I think people should be more like dogs." Amanda said suddenly. "They just act from their hearts."

"He's such a good boy," I said fondly. "He sits up with me while I write. The poor thing gets so sleepy, but he won't leave my side."

"You're a good person." Amanda said into her coffee cup. "They know those things."

"I'm glad you think I'm a good person." I said. "Sometimes I feel like I'm an asshole trying to cover up my bad side."

She smirked and replied, "I don't think there's a malicious bone in your body."

This time I laughed outright. "You should talk to my ex's. They'd disagree."

"I just think you're very guarded," Amanda said. "Comedy is a good way of keeping people at arm's length."

She was on to me.

"I hope I didn't hurt your feeling," she said, putting her hand on mine.

I didn't know what to do. This was my chance, and I was terrified of blowing it. Amanda got up, like she was going to leave, so I got up too. Instead of leaving, she took me in her arms and held me.

"Calm down, you're tied in knots," she whispered, holding me in a gentle embrace. For a woman who had trouble making eye contact, she sure was in control now.

Amanda rubbed my back a bit, then leaned down, nestling her head into my neck and began to kiss me up the side of my cheek till she found my lips. Her kiss was enveloping and deep and I couldn't form thoughts. I just felt. Her strong hands were in my hair, pulling me closer into her...I felt like we were liquid being, poured into one another. Amanda pulled slowly away and looked at me. Her eyes were so clear blue that it seemed like they were made of smoke or fog, encircling me. I was mesmerized.

"I've wanted to do that since you came to my window that day and asked about the sleigh." she said.

"Oh...um." I muttered. "You know, I have a really big crush on you." God, I sound like a total idiot.

"Honey, I have a fierce crush on you, too," she said, her smirk sexy and full of trouble. She took my hand and put it to her heart. "You feel that? It's because of you." Her heart was racing just as fast as mine. I could feel my knees going week and rubbery and desperately wanted to sit down by myself and process what just happened.

"Quit thinking." Amanda whispered in her hoarse, sexy midnight DJ voice. "I can hear those wheels turning from here."

"I don't know what to do." I said quietly.

She touched one of the curls that had fallen into my face. Her stare made me feel childish and uncomfortable. The light had faded and the room was lit only by the glow of the candle. This was what I had dreamed of, and now I didn't know what to do. It was suddenly real, and reality is so un-reassuring.

"I love watching you struggle to deal with this." Amanda said. "I watch you in crowds, so sure of yourself. You say all the right things and you have them all captivated, but you're standing here like a young girl. You're not jaded, you just haven't lived yet."

Gulp. "Now you're angry at me," she said sadly. I couldn't tell what expression was on my face. "I'm not mad, just in shock." I said. "I didn't even know if you liked me, let alone were interested in me."

She began to walk out of the kitchen then we just drifted to the sofa in front of the fireplace. She sat down smoothly, putting her arm across the back of the couch. I didn't sit with her, and stood there staring, unable to talk. I didn't know if I liked this or not. I had no control over the situation; all the cards were just tossed up.

"It's OK," said Amanda, trying to draw me in to sit beside her. I resisted.

"Let me guess." she sighed. "You want me to leave so you can call one of your friends to discuss all of this and see how you should proceed."

"Jesus, Amanda," I spluttered, "Have you been studying me or something?"

She was quiet for a moment, the firelight flickering across her face. Then she said, "You're easy to study, and it's not exactly difficult."

"I'll be honest," I said. "You've planned all this out and I like it, but I'm freaked out by it, too."

"Well," she said. "You could've pushed me away, but I didn't think you would. I just had to get over my own shit before I did anything. I'm sure Janis and Tippie told you about my history. It's not a secret."

"Most people don't seem to know much about what happened - only that something did." I said.

She chuckled, moving closer and putting her lips to my ear. "You've been studying me too..." Amanda whispered then began to kiss my ear, tracing it with her tongue and tracing it feather light over my neck to my mouth. This kiss was strong, but less sure, needier. "I want you to want me like this..." she continued. Amanda's lips went to my neck as she pushed me down on the couch gently, almost protectively. "Sweet girl," she sighed. She let out a soft moan, lost in the moment with me. Amanda was the warmth on my skin, as she kissed my chest bone, unbuttoning my sweater. Her body pressed against me as she pulled my shirt off. "Do you feel me, Lucy?" she asked, pulling my hands to her chest. Her words were hypnotic and calming.

"Oh, Amanda..." I sighed, and brushed her hair away from her face. "Honey." She looked so sad and beautiful.

"Just kiss me." Her eyes were closed, voice hoarse with passion and I kissed the tear away.

"I'm sorry someone hurt you, they were a fool to..." I said.

"Shhh..."

I unfastened the buttons on her shirt and unhooked her bra, she deftly shed her shirt and bra onto the floor. I kissed her softness as she arched over me, tracing my fingertips over the curves of her beautiful belly and the round fullness of each breast. It was like we had all the time in the world and I was the teardrop traveling over her body, healing each curve, replacing pain with love and tenderness.

I tried to unbuckle her belt. She gently removed my hands. "No, not yet." she murmured, "I want to, but not too soon."

I pulled her back to me and drowned her in endless kisses. She leaned on her elbow, stroking my face. "What a surprise you are," she said, "that you came into my life." She smiled, kissing me on the forehead and told me "Mmmm, you even smell good; I just want to crawl inside you."

"I never knew you'd have such a way with words." I told Amanda. Her hair was like a gauzy curtain, and I stroked it, pulling her head to my chest. "Now you can feel my heart beat for you."

She nestled into to me and we held each other. Oh, man, I thought, *I've been bitten by the love bug.* Lauren was going to kill me.

Chapter 11

The grandfather clock chiming in the front room sounded like the far-away call of some forgotten voice. I lie there stroking Amanda's hair, so glad she was here and sad because I knew she'd leave soon.

We had fallen asleep on the couch, and I woke up feeling unusually relaxed. I watched Amanda sleep, and thoughts of my past relationships ran through my head. Passion burns hot in the beginning, and then romance becomes sharing your free time and life with someone else, working around schedules and idiosyncrasies. Not a particularly romantic thought, but I had to be practical. I had made a new start here, and I was really going to try and do things right.

I stroked her hair and whispered "Amanda."

Did she have to get up early for work in the morning, I wondered. Most people didn't have Mondays and Tuesdays off. I had a hard time believing this was even happening, and a million thoughts ran through my head like an electronic billboard in Times Square.

The sound of her breathing in the evening silence was making my heartbeat sound like something out of *The Telltale Heart*, and I finally had to say something.

"Amanda, I hate to wake you," I whispered as I smiled down at her. "Are you going to have to work tomorrow? Do you want to stay tonight?" Actually saying that gave me a lump in my throat, suddenly terrifying me that she was going to wake up and run off, turning this beautiful thing into just a passing moment, God that would be crushing.

"I'm an editor." she replied groggily. "I work when I want as long as I make my deadlines."

"That's fantastic!" I replied a little too loudly. I had a pillow propped behind my head, and Amanda was snuggled in with her face on my belly, looking towards the fire. She made no move to get up.

"I edit mostly textbooks, so it's really not that exciting. I used to work at a university a long time ago, but I wasn't really into the whole scholarly atmosphere."

"It's funny," I said, digging around in my memory, "when we first met, you sounded different. More...rural."

She laughed and said "That keeps me from standing out - and keeps people away."

"Haven't you been lonely?" I asked. "Being up here...not associating with people much?"

"I'm not like you." Amanda replied. "You need people - you're a born communicator, an extrovert. You inhale people and they exhale you, but I like distance."

"I guess it's weird for me to both write and sing." I said. "One hobby is so hermit-ty, the other is so out front, so I do understand the need for solitude."

"They both keep people at arm's length, don't they? That's where I think we are alike."

"Makes us sound like control freaks."

"Us? Never." Amanda replied. She rolled off me and stood up, completely comfortable in her partial nudity.

It made me want to touch her and get dressed at the same time. I wanted to stare, but I didn't want to be rude.

"You can look at me." Amanda said, when she noticed my gaze. "I like looking at you. That's why I didn't make eye contact when I met you...I thought you'd know I was smitten."

She had that Cheshire Cat grin on her face again.

"I think that's the same word I used to describe how I felt about you..." I said.

She broke the little bit of tension by reaching over and pulling me into her arms.

"You're so proper...it's cute." Amanda said, then switched topics completely and asked, "When did you quit drinking?"

My head rested on her shoulder, and I felt like I should face her, but I didn't. I was trying to be comfortable, and when I talk I'm an 'edge of the seat' kind of person. So we stood in a motionless waltz. It occurred to me how awkward I was in this setting.

"How did you know?" I asked quietly.

"The Houndstooth, every Thursday night. Plus, when I watched you at the party, you only had soda."

"You are such a voyeur." I said, amused.

"I have a lot of time on my hands."

"I quit when I was twenty nine," I told her. "My best friend told me that if I didn't get help, she couldn't be my friend. She said she couldn't watch me committing slow suicide."

"For all your laughter...you carry some sadness." Amanda told me. "I think that's why people trust you."

"Maybe. It's a long story, but in a nutshell my folks had a bad divorce, my stepmother has this weird love/hate relationship with me, so growing up, I was either her confidant or she hated me. I was always a reminder of the "other woman" and she's a very jealous person. My birth mom has had a lot of husbands and I think she's suffered from emotional issues, on and off. Yet she just loves me to pieces. My mother ended up married to one of my ex-boyfriends - how's that for complicated family relationships?"

Amanda arched her eyebrows. Incredulous was a good look on her. "I don't even know where to start," she said. "You dated men?"

I laughed. "The last guy I slept with was this Russian, resembled Rudolph Nureyev. I kept thinking 'maybe if I'm with a super-hot guy, I won't be gay!' But, well, here I am. He was crazy, almost drove me to a nervous breakdown. It was a totally dysfunctional relationship. We'd get drunk, smoke pot and fuck with each other's heads. It didn't actually last that long, and afterwards I did some serious soul searching. He was the first person I came out to and get this - he came out to me too. What about you?"

"I was the other way around," Amanda told me. "I always liked the girls. This made my relationship with my father stranger. He didn't rape me, or touch me, or anything, but he loved to have me dress sexy for him. This made my mother jealous of me. She'd rage at me, and then apologize, but it was an unbearable living situation.

I ran away at sixteen - my mother cried, but she didn't divorce him. I moved to Greenwich Village with a much older woman, then we lived on a commune upstate for a while, it was all free love and bullshit. By the time I was twenty-five, I'd been a big girl slut and I thought maybe the reason I was so miserable was I wasn't living a proper lifestyle. I dated this guy who ended up having serious, serious issues. So I left him, moved up to Mountain Ridge and never intended to stay, got raped, got pregnant, lost the baby, and then met your uncle."

The way she said 'met your uncle' kind of bothered me. "God," I groaned, "did you sleep with my uncle?" I was dreading the answer.

"Nooo!" Amanda howled, looking aghast at the very idea. I sagged with relief. "He took pity on me," she explained "he loved to rescue girls in trouble. I was so depressed, drinking heavily, going to the Houndstooth and getting shitfaced every night. Tavis was in there one night, I must've told him my whole sad story and he set me up here. I can't say I was real nice to him at first, and for a long time I just didn't trust anyone. Especially men. Most especially nice guys with money, which seemed to be an oxymoron."

"Then you met Carey?" I asked.

"Yes, then I met Carey. She seemed so sweet, like the perfect housewife, and at the time I just loved that. I made the money, she took care of the house. Over time, though, those roles started to wear thin on both of us. She had quit her job and intended to enroll at the University, but that never happened. I think she became bored with the monotony of our relationship. She eventually met this guy who was here for the summer, and figured he was a better deal financially.

She left me in a blaze of drama. After her, I was just numb. I threw myself into work and projects, like the sleigh. Your uncle, God bless him, kept trying to befriend me, but I was over friends and people in general, so I just pretty much ignored him."

"He was an amazing guy." I said wistfully. "You're right about lost souls...he just loves them. He met my aunt at the Playboy Club in Chicago; she was the little lost German girl. After she *supposedly* died, his other girlfriends were all very much the same, Little Girl Lost types. The last one was an ex-working girl, I think. My dad on the other hand loves the blondes; he had a big crush on Cybil Shepherd. I use to look at her on that show 'Moonlighting' and think, he'll never think I'm as pretty as her, I'll always be the goofy looking daughter."

"Goofy...you're beautiful!"

"Bette Davis style, and this wild curly hair...it looks good now, but let me tell you, growing up, it was ugly. I tried to straighten it, which made me look older. The high school guys didn't find me very attractive, but I think the teachers did. I stuck out like a sore thumb in my hometown."

"Honey," said Amanda, "You blossomed."

I blushed, but the room was dark, and off in the distance the wind howled.

Time had passed like ripple in a river. When I looked at the clock, it was already coming on to morning.

"Will you stay over?" I asked again hopefully. Amanda hugged me to her, and I could feel her face in my hair. "Mmmm, I love your curls," she said offhandedly. She was quiet, and I could almost hear the wheels turning in her head.

"I want to," she said, "but we haven't even had a proper date..."

"Lesbians are notorious for moving fast, aren't we?" I answered nervously, staring into the dying embers of the molten bits and pieces of charred log.

"How about we meet for breakfast at my place?" Amanda suggested then kissed my head.

Right on cue, my heart fluttered. I was a total dork when it came to romance. "Okay!" I said, smiling with an obvious eagerness. My brain was chanting she likes you, she likes you, she likes you at me endlessly.

She put back on her shirt and said, "Don't get me wrong, I want to stay - I just don't want this to be a fling. If we move too fast, that's what it might turn into, and I don't want that."

"Now who's over thinking things?" I commented, tossing the dog's chew toy at her playfully.

Amanda took me into her arms, holding me so dearly, as if she were capturing the moment. She kissed me with such force it took my breath away. I loved the way her hands searched me, as if she were memorizing my body through her fingertips, in case our tryst was just a fluke. It occurred to me that she was afraid I would change my mind.

Before she left I asked, "Do you have a CD player?"

"Of course..." she said, almost offended. "I'm not a technophobe just because I like living in a rural town - and you moved here!"

I laughed and jogged into my office to grab my little gift to her. I returned with the CD which I'd unconsciously/consciously burned as a romantic "set" for my iPod, but I'd liked it so much I thought I'd make a copy for Amanda. I had burned of all my favorite love songs, all the ones that reminded me of her back when I was just wishing and hoping. Yeah, I had thought about all of this right from the beginning.

"Here," I said, handing the CD to her, "listen to this while you go to sleep tonight. I made the compilation with you in mind."

She smirked in that cute, shy way and reached out to touch my arm. Again, I felt her eyes taking a picture of me. "Good night, sweetheart, sleep tight." She kind of swirled out the door, in a very Chaplin-esque style. Amanda was such a character, and it hurt me to think she'd been in self-imposed exile all this time.

I was wide awake with joy at 6 a.m., the way you are when you're in love or lust and everything is going perfectly. Comby was snoring loudly and occasionally farting next to my bed. Bulldogs have the worst gas!

The phone rang. Who the hell would be calling me this early? I answered, torn between happiness at the world in general and annoyance at an early-morning call. "Hi, honey." said my dad. Without any more social chit-chat, he said "I'm flying up there tomorrow. We need to talk."

I was suddenly terrified. "Are you okay? Are you sick?" I asked, apprehensive.

"No," he replied, "I'm fine, but that conversation we had bothered me. I want to straighten some things out. I'll be there at noon and catch a cab, I know you've got to work."

"Um, ok," I said, "is this bad news?"

"No, not really, it's just not something we can talk about on the phone. I'll see you tomorrow." And with that, he hung up on me. My dad! Hung up on me! What the fuck?

Now I was really awake. I took a shower and got ready to go to Amanda's place - we weren't meeting till nine, but I was up and might as well get started.

I walked Comby, all bundled up in his sweater and puppy snow boots. Tao needed some exercise, so I rode him down to the lake and watched the fishermen float. It didn't take long to feed both animals, unfortunately, so I went out to burn some garbage and finally, finally it was nine. God, I hoped she hadn't reconsidered.

I knocked and there was no answer.

Ah, crap. My heart sank. Then I heard her snow mobile in the distance. The way the weather changed around here was going to take some getting used to.

I turned around and saw Amanda waving. She came around and parked. "Forgot eggs!" she shouted, turning the loud motor off.

"You could've had me bring them," I said, still slightly cranky from my scare. "I have some."

"I didn't want to interrupt your beauty rest." Amanda said, winking at me.

"Oh, please," I scoffed, "my dad called and woke me up at six."

We went into the house and while she cooked, I told her my early-morning drama.

"So what do you think is the big news?" she asked, placing my plate of hot cheesy scrambled eggs in front of me with some turkey sausage. "I think it has to do with my Aunt Greta." I said through a mouthful of food. "But I guess he could've just told me over the phone that he did the nasty with her. It's not like it would be that big of a deal."

She eyed me and said nothing, just nodded.

"Lucy," she said finally, sipping her coffee thoughtfully, "have you really looked at that picture of your Aunt Greta?"

"Yes" I said. "Well. Um. Yes."

"Okay, I'm not sure I should mention this, or even how to bring it up, but did you notice anything specific about your aunt's appearance?" Amanda asked. I thought about it for a minute. The picture of Greta showed a woman with lovely big eyes, big boobs, and a riot of curly brown hair.

"Oh." I said stupidly. "She looks a lot like me. Kind of exactly like me." My stomach felt like it had dropped into the basement.

My mom was absolutely stunning - a hot blond in the Loni Anderson tradition. Greta was more of an Ava Gardner type, and although darker in complexion and hair than me, very similar. We had the same big eyes, facial bone structure, and above-average height. There was no mistaking the similarity. On the other hand, my mom Tanya was 5'1" and build along more delicate lines. I could have passed for my aunt's blond twin. Greta was related to me by marriage, I'd assumed, not by blood.

I had always just figured my appearance was due to some kind of recessive genes, that I'd gotten my height and riot of blond curls from some distant relative on my dad's side. It had never even occurred to me to wonder why I didn't look anything like my mom.

"Amanda," I said slowly, "what if......what if Greta IS related to me? What if she's my MOM?" All of a sudden, I couldn't shut up about "what if" and "that would explain" scenarios, and I barraged poor Amanda with my theories.

Amanda just sat there patiently listening. I was pacing, "You know what I thought was really weird, growing up? When Greta's name would get brought up - which sure wasn't often - my mom would give my dad the stink-eye and say...I don't want to hear about that woman."

Amanda nodded, wisely not interrupting my flurry of verbal puzzle-piecing. "One time my dad replied, 'you should thank that woman.' Being nosey, as a kid, I jumped up from behind the sofa and asked 'Why, Daddy? Why should we thank Aunt Greta?' My mom hit the roof!"

I felt an almost overwhelming excitement at the thought, at the very idea of Greta being my biological mother, but it felt like I was watching this on television, not experiencing it in real life. Then I dropped into the chair because it hit me...it suddenly felt like I'd belonged to no one, because if a basic fact of my life - the identity of my parents - turned out to be false, what else about my life was a lie? "I wonder if my dad...is even my dad?" I asked meekly.

"Lucy," Amanda finally spoke up, "you look unequivocally like your father."

I lit up a smoke, and nodded, we sat in Amanda's kitchen with our coffee, staring at my family photos. For the first time, they all looked like strangers to me.

Finally, we switched subjects, to a much more upbeat topic. "How do you feel about things this morning?" Amanda asked. She tried to be smooth and even- keeled, but I could tell she was nervous. She tilted her head, and looked at me sideways. "You know...about last night," she said.

"The same way I felt when I burned the CD." I assured her then grinned. "But better!"

Amanda returned the smile and put her hand on my knee. I loved how she reached out to me. I'd never been good at casual affection; I was always too stiff. I didn't want to be standoffish, but when your culture frowns on two women showing more than friendly affection, you learn to be discreet. The result is that when you're in a place where you can finally physically express your feelings, it can be incredibly awkward.

"Amanda," I said, "I know I'm really laying all my cards on the table here, but I really hope this works out because I'm crazy about you! I'm no game player and I hope to God you don't find me too intense. I'm just at this point where I just feel like being honest."

"Suits me just fine." Amanda told me firmly, the poured me another cup of coffee. "I think we need to lighten up - how about a boat ride!"

Lac de Lune was the small lake the lodge was situated on, and it was a jewel. The icy blue waters warmed up enough in the summer for swimming, but right now, they were cold and exhilarating!

She explained the history of the boat as we walked down to the pier, which was soon to be taken in for the season. "I bought this 1938 Chris Craft at a yard sale, it was a total mess. Termite damage to the wood, dry rot from sitting in an old garage...just dinosaur bones." She had obviously changed all that, because the boat now looked like a vintage classic!

She helped me into the docked boat, then untied it and pushed us off. The motor started with a rumble and cloud of diesel poof. The smell of boat fuel brought back wonderful memories of childhood - freedom and endless summers of day dreams and sun bathing with my cousins and my friends, with our Walkmans over our ears listening to the hot bands of our era - Styx, Iggy Pop and Asia. Life on the lake in the summer was all swimming, and baby oil sunburns, late night whispers about the romantic futures Crystal, Lauren, and I all intended to have with our dream guys. I thought I wanted a dream guy too…it was all about the fantasies we read out in books and watched in movies…we didn't focus on reality, because we hadn't experienced any yet…or at least *verrrry little*! And now I had my dream girl!

Amanda had definitely downplayed her rehab of the boat. This baby was like a gleaming red wood rocket! The boat coasted beautifully through the water, cutting through the icy autumn waves like a shark fin. The contrast of shiny silver chrome against polished red brown wood reminded me of cedar wood chips and smelled like the Smithsonian... mmm, museum scented.

The sun had come out, and though it was colder than the Chicago autumn I was used to, the temperature didn't even register. I was just so happy to be right here, next to Amanda with her long hair whipping in the wind like a flag, guiding this beautiful relic through the waves...it couldn't have been a more romantic experience!

She cut the engine, and we drifted onto the banks of Little Noah Island. The tiny tuft of land sat like a lone cupcake in the center of our icy lake. Covered in a sky- scraping confection of evergreen trees, the scent of pine oil mixed with the scent of the water and the rocky soil into a unique perfume. Amanda jumped out of the water to pull the boat up on the shore.

"Your boots!" I cried. "Waterproof." She said, busy with guiding the boat.

"You need to get a pair like these, if you stay up here." I hopped off the roof of the cabin and into her arms. She kissed me right on the sandy shores in the bright sunlight. I felt lit up from the inside and unbelievably happy. We walked around the island and Amanda showed me a marmots' den, telling me about the endangered animals that had been captured by a town resident and set free on the island to breed.

"Isn't that illegal?" I asked curiously.

"Probably." Amanda admitted, laughing. We tried to find a fox den that she'd seen before, but the only additional wildlife to be found was a beaver swimming past and some ducks dipping their heads beneath the water for food.

We walked around the island, sharing stories of outdoor adventures, until the sun began setting and the temperature grew colder. It was time to get back to the mainland, and prepare for my father's visit.

As we docked the boat and snapped on its cover, a thought occurred to me. It was strange to be in such a stable, untroubled frame of mind when a family storm would soon be coming my way. I tried not to focus on the negatives of the situation, telling myself firmly that I was no longer a child and that I could hold my own against my father and force the truth out of him, if necessary.

Part of me felt like I should call my mom, but she was so melodramatic about the smallest things that I cringed at the thought of raising such a major question with her. Besides, over the last few years, my dad and I had become closer. He was a lot more emotionally stable than my mom, and probably a better person to withstand the kind of inquisition I had planned.

Amanda helped me clean a bit around the lodge, and we put together dinner together. By the time Amanda left, I was exhausted and ready for bed. I tried to read, but was just too zonked. I passed out to the sounds of Combover snoring like a pirate with inflamed nasal cavities.

My dad arrived in a cab from the airport in Montreal early the next morning full of distraction and energy, talking a mile a minute about the flight, about Canada, and about what I'd done to the lodge.

"Amazing, what you've done to this old boys' club!" my dad told me, grinning with pride, and a look of awe sharing space with the smile. He looked thinner and balder, but still fit and confident.

He walked around behind the front desk and opened my office door to look inside, then came back to the living room. "You really turned this old place into a home. I'm glad to see you're using the fireplace!" he said I'd started the fire about an hour before he'd arrived, when I realized the temperature had dipped from autumn to arctic I took his bags to the room I was using to display all Tavis' college sports memorabilia, with the assumption that he'd be interested in the décor, or at the very least, impressed at the collection.

After the obligatory tour and chit-chat, we finally sat down by the big picture window. My dad started talking right after I provided us with mugs and a carafe of black coffee.

He cleared his throat as we settled in for the big talk. "I'm not going to beat around the bush here, Lucy," my dad said ominously. "I came here to tell you something that's really going to impact your life - and I hope you don't hate me after I tell you." He sounded like a politician trying to confess some awful sin, and I hated to see my Daddy like this. He looked nervous, scared, and ashamed. Nothing like the positive, confident man I knew my father to be.

"Greta's my birth mother, isn't she?" I asked abruptly.

"You figured it out." my dad replied, once he'd recovered from the shock of having his big secret guessed in less than half a second.

"Just yesterday." I said. I didn't want him thinking that I'd walked around with this knowledge for a long time.

It must have been a relief to be able to talk about it, and my dad went off at a mile a minute to fill me in on the whole story. "The story is actually pretty short - I met Greta at the Playboy Club in Chicago during my senior year of college, we had a "one-nighter" when I was home from college for Christmas break. Then a few months later, I got postcard from Greta letting me know that you were on the way. She didn't want a baby, had no interest in being a parent, but believe me, Lucy, I did. I loved you already, as soon as I heard about your existence. Tavis loaned me some money and took care of the financial details...she stayed with him during the pregnancy, since it was impossible for her to work as a cocktail waitress while pregnant.

Dad took a another sip of coffee and went on, "Anyway, your mom Tanya and I had met at a dance a few months earlier - my fling with Greta was a sort of last chance thing, since I knew that when I went back to school I was going to propose to your mom and that would be it. You weren't something I could keep from her, so I had to explain the whole sordid situation. I expected the worst - she'd dump me. To my surprise and *after a few choice words* of less than exemplary behavior, she explained she really wanted a baby. She'd known for years that her chances of actually getting pregnant and having a baby were pretty slim. Believe me, your mom was right on board with being your mom. She was downright thrilled about it, in fact, aside from knowing that I'd been with Greta. It seemed to work out perfectly for everyone, but it was something of a surprise when Tavis fell for Greta.

"Really dad," I raised my eyebrows, in disbelief, "she was a Playboy bunny."

He cleared his throat. Nodding in agreement. "Your mom was really not happy about Greta and Tavis. As far as she was concerned, as soon as you were born, Greta could just cease to exist. Tanya hated that Tavis married Greta and tried to involve her in the family. As it turned out, Tanya got her wish - in the worst possible way." Dad took a deep sip of his extra strong coffee and continued.

"The thing was that Tavis only met Greta because she was pregnant with you. As soon as you were born, he whisked her off to Vegas and they got married. Greta always said it was love at first sight. They were together for a few months, mostly living up here, so we didn't see them much. That suited your mom just fine. Then Greta took a trip back to Germany to see her family and tell them about the marriage - and maybe about you, I don't know. Tavis got held up at work, since he was just starting that sporting goods store, so he didn't go with her. And you know what happened - on the way back from Germany, Greta's plane crashed. She was so badly injured that no one thought she'd live through it, and then it was clear that she'd live, but she'd never function independently.

Tavis just about lost his mind. He went on a complete bender, almost lost his sporting goods business. He even got drunk and went scuba diving, of all things. Nearly killed another diver due to negligence, but that's what sobered him up. He buckled down, worked at his business, and paid for Greta's care. He wouldn't divorce her - that's why he never married again."

Dad cracked his knuckles, watching for my response with wide, worried eyes.

"But why keep Greta's survival a secret, Dad?" I asked. He shook his head. "You're from an Oprah- influenced, divulge-all generation, so I'm not surprised you don't get it. We just thought it would be best, since she was brain damaged and didn't know anyone in the States, to just not discuss this situation anymore. Greta's family came to see her, they were fine with the decision to move her to assisted living with full-time nursing care. She's a paraplegic with a traumatic brain injury, so McTrainer seemed like the best option. Plus, your uncle was in Canada at least once a month on business, so he could visit regularly."

"Wait," I said, "rewind a bit." I shook my head in disbelief, trying to comprehend. "So you came back to Hohman, Indiana from Florida State with a wife and a baby, and no one in your hometown questioned this?"

"I was gone for 4 1/2 years at FSU. We said we got married in Tallahassee and I wanted to finish my education before we moved back, and that was that."

Dad paused for a minute. "Well," he amended, "for the most part. Back then, people didn't ask all that many questions."

"Why did Mom think that she couldn't have kids?" I asked.

"She was in an accident as a kid that broke her pelvis. Your brother was a definite surprise, that's for sure - I guess the doctors were wrong after all."

"Can you tell me more about Greta?" I asked. I didn't really know anything about her, other than that she was German.

"Her family was circus horse trainers." Dad said, and smiled. He knew I'd love the idea of coming from a theatrical bloodline. "Her mother died in childbirth, and her father raised her. In addition to the horse-training, her family owned a tavern in Bern. Her father died a few years back. She had some cousins, but no siblings."

"I met her, you know." I said, watching my father closely for a reaction.

"Functer told me," my dad said, sipping his now cold coffee.

"Does Neil know?" I asked. I was pretty sure my brother had been kept in the dark, but I wanted to be sure.

"Of course not," my dad said, horrified.

"Irene doesn't know, either. I called Tanya yesterday to let her know that I'd be telling you about your origins. She's really broken up, thinks you won't love her anymore if you know she's not your biological mother. Would you give her a call, let her know that it doesn't matter? It doesn't matter to you, does it? Tanya thinks you'll disappear from her life."

"How could she think that?" I asked, shocked.

"You know Tanya," my dad sighed. Yes, I knew her. And her sensitive tendency, along with her talent for overreacting to the smallest thing - and this was no small thing. I use to jokingly describe my family as "a real soap opera," but the way things were turning out, it absolutely was exactly that!

My dad got up and walked to the bar, asking "Got any Bailey's or Frangelico for the coffee?"

"Actually, I do." My uncle had left a pretty hearty stash, so I kept it for company. I opened the Bailey's and poured a heavy shot in his coffee.

"How is Greta?" Dad asked, his eyes reminding me of a sad looking hound dog.

"Greta is pretty bad." I said. "Like, I kept saying I was her niece, and she kept saying nice."

"Talk to her," my dad advised. "See what happens. With that kind of injury, you never know what they remember..." he looked down at the floor. "You must hate me," he said quietly.

"I could never hate you." I told my father. "But the secret-keeping has got to stop. It's always made me feel like I'm not truly a member of the family - I always knew there were all kinds of things I didn't know and that no one was willing to tell me, and that put an invisible wedge between us."

That only applied to my dad's side of the family, of course. This was probably the only secret my mom had ever kept!

In my mind, my father was eternally forty, as I looked at him, though, he seemed old and stooped, and I reminded myself that my dad was sixty-three and in poor health.

It just wasn't possible for me to end or damage our relationship because of a mistake he'd made in his youth. The longer it took him to tell me about the circumstances of my birth, the harder it was, and I wasn't surprised that he hadn't told me until he absolutely had to do so.

"Dad." I said to him, taking his hand. "I'm glad you wanted me." I reached over and hugged him, feeling his stubbled face press into mine.

"Oh, darlin'," he said, slightly choked up, "the first time I saw your face, I knew I'd never love anything as much as I loved you. You were so fragile, but so strong."

Just like you, I wanted to say, but I didn't know if he would take it as the compliment I meant it to be.

"There are no mistakes, Lucy." he said, wiping his eyes and letting me go. "God has his ways."

Dad was exhausted after the long trip. While he was taking a nap, I went over to Amanda's cabin.

"Okay, here it is." I said as I burst into her front room. "You were right, Greta is my birth mother.

My dad's only going to be here for a short visit and he probably won't be back up here soon, that's just the way he because of his wife Irene, who hates me, so I know it's really early but I want you guys to meet. I know this is all hugely presumptuous, but I'm not keeping any more secrets."

Amanda looked very uneasy. "Can I get some time on this?" she asked.

"He's leaving tomorrow." I said then assured her, "If you don't want to meet him, that's fine. I won't hold it against you."

"We've never even gone on a date." Amanda pointed out.

"I know," I said hurriedly, "but I've kissed your tits and slept next to you, is that close enough to a date to count?"

She burst out laughing. "So this is the straight talk I'm in for?" she giggled.

"Yup, pretty much." I said.

"God, what have I got myself into?" Amanda groaned. "I guess, well, I guess I'm meeting your dad. Can we at least do dinner? I hate small talk in the morning."

"Dinner it is." I said, relieved. "I'll talk to him when he's up from his nap."

A worried look crossed her face. "Is he going to go crazy on me?" she said, wincing at the thought.

"I'd say no. "I told her. "But I will warn you that he didn't like my last partner, so I can't promise you warm and fuzzy. He's a polite guy, though; he won't cuss you out or anything."

"How reassuring." she replied.

I came over to her and put my arms around her. "I'm never like this." I confessed. "I'm a really private person, I've been accused of being too closed off and unwilling to let people into my life, but here I am introducing you to my family. I don't know, maybe it's the Canadian air." Then I leaned my face into her shoulder and took a deep breath. The scent of Amanda's hair reminded me laundered spring sheets and home, my idea of what a home should smell like. She rubbed my back as I held her and she murmured, "I think I got a nutty one." into my neck.

"Nutty for you, baby." I said, and smacked her on the ass gently. She laughed easily, and I hoped it was a new trend.

I told my dad about Amanda over lunch. He didn't seem precisely thrilled, but I could tell he was willing to give Amanda a fair shake.

"This is so hard for me, my beautiful baby." Dad sighed. "I can't lie. I was hoping you'd meet some lumberjack and fall in love, forget about this whole lesbian thing."

"I know." I said, patting him on the back. There wasn't much else to say, so I guided him to the easy chair and flipped on ESPN.

I made the family favorite blue cheese dip, got Dad a Beefeater martini, and started cooking. Growing up, spaghetti and French bread was a family favorite, so I attempted to reproduce Mom's recipe. I was so nervous that I was shaking, though, and thought longingly of a meeting at the Houndstooth. I could really use one about now. There wasn't any way to get to one at the moment, so I made do by calling Bradley. He was speechless upon hearing all my news, but not for long.

"I leave you up there for three months - and you find your long lost birth mom, whose existence you never even suspected, and a fabulous new lover. You work FAST, girlfriend."

"I've got to call my mom." I told him, distracted by drama and meatballs. "She left a voice message, crying so hard she could barely talk. It was awful, but I'm just not ready for the emotional typhoon tonight. I'll call her back tomorrow."

"You'll do no such thing to the poor woman!" Bradley scolded me. "Call her tonight, even if you have to cut it short or put a time limit on her, because she's not going to sleep until she talks to you."

"Okay." I said meekly. Brad knew a lot about crazy, and was very fond of my mom. She'd met him several times in the past, and both felt a real connection. He was really good with my mom, and I know she kept holding out hope we'd "change" and marry each other. Unfortunately for my mother, neither Bradley nor I were likely to complete her fantasy.

The sauce was too thick, the garlic bread burned, and the noodles were sticky, but my dad was smiling all through the meal. My dad was a big talker, and Amanda was a good listener.

"You've been living out here all by yourself?" he asked, stuffing more spaghetti into his mouth.

"I did grow up in New York City." she pointed out, sipping some of the surprisingly good red wine I'd dug out of the wine cellar.

"I use to dream about living in the big city." Dad said, surprising me. "I had big dreams of moving to the Big Apple and becoming a poet. Never made it. I got to New York and I hated it - felt like a little fish in a big, hostile pond and I couldn't wait to leave and go home."

"You wanted to be a poet?" Amanda asked.

"Ha!" snorted my dad. "We'll just say that I realized very quickly I wasn't going to be the next Bob Dylan. I wanted to write music like his, but I couldn't sing. I couldn't even write all-that well. I can bullshit - that's where my storytelling skills come in handy."

She laughed and listened closely, which were Dad's two favorite qualities in dinner companions actually, his favorite qualities in other people, period.

We had coffeecake for dessert, and I could tell my dad was just about tired out. "I'm going to call it a night, girls," he told us, and winked cheerfully.

The alert on his phone explained his plane had been delayed due to storms. The rain was turning to sleet so he'd be stuck here the next night, too. Honestly, I don't think he really cared much. It was Irene, my stepmother, who didn't like Dad spending too much time with me.

I gave him a bear hug, and he shook Amanda's hand. She whispered something in his ear, and he gave her an affectionate pat on the shoulder before he ambled down the hall. The man was full of surprises.

After he left, I turned to Amanda, who was cleaning up from dinner. "So what'd you whisper to my dad?"

"It's between us." she said. I almost argued, and then I thought better of it.

I walked Amanda home and noted that sleet was now wet slick snow, which had accumulated during our dinner. We crunched-slipped through about four inches of new slush on the path leading up to her front door.

"I'd ask you in," she told me, "but your dad might notice that you were missing."

"He could sleep through a bomb dropping on the lodge." I said.

"Is that a hint?" Amanda asked.

I scratched my head, unsure. "I'm supposed to call my mom, but I don't think I can do it tonight. My world just got turned upside down – and I'm doing OK, so I don't feel like fucking it up by having Tanya go Joan Crawford on me."

As we stood at her door, she kissed me as the snow fell silently. Her lips moved over mine with rich warmth, her body so close I felt the heat rise from her collar. Amanda walked me backwards into her home, towards the bed, laying me down on the quilts. The weight of her body immersed me in the feathery softness that surrounded me.

I could feel her grind slowly on my leg, her hands fumbling to unbutton my coat, pulling off her own clothes and my sweater. "I want to feel you against me," she whispered, hurriedly stripping off her own jeans and helping me with mine. It was a shock to realize that she wasn't wearing underwear. "Feel this." she said, putting my hand to the wetness between her legs. "This is what you do to me – it just hurts me to even look at you, sometimes." I loved the way she spoke, dirty and passionate words murmured in her husky voice. She was gliding her body up and down on me, back and forth, and I wrapped my legs around her waist. I clung to her, so smooth and velvety, as her arms pulled me to her and embraced my whole body. Amanda pulled away and kissed me along every line and curve. Then she made her way slowly, almost painfully slowly, down my belly.

Amanda teasing every inch of my body's hidden angles...all fingers, lips and softness, flicking and circling until I was a shuddering wave of convulsion in her arms.

She crawled slowly back up to me and I nibbled and flicked her ear with my tongue. "My turn, baby." I growled softly. She rolled over nervously, covering her breasts with her hands. "Oh no, honey," I breathed into her ear. "I want it all." I pressed my lips to her neck, sucking in little kisses, luxuriating in her soft heat. I let my tongue roam over her shoulders, down her arms and to her fingers, sucking each one slowly as the wind rattled the glass panes on the windows. I circled the palm of her hand with my tongue and traced back up her arm. Her moan was low and soft, like she was trying to hold it back.

Her back arched and I caressed her belly in soft strokes with my fingertips, circling around her navel, my lips roaming over the side of her body. I made my way down to her hips, sucking and kissing until her legs trembled.

"Let me love you." I massaged her back, kissing the back of her neck and her head, and then I straddled her body, running my fingertips up and down her spine. Amanda was so easy to love, her body long and full, with so many rises and valleys to explore. I wanted to rip into her like an animal, but I kept myself under control. This was worth savoring. I kissed my way down her tailbone. She was quivering with goose flesh. I teased her with my tongue, using my fingers to explore more deeply. Finally, she was ready to explode, and I buried my face in her until she collapsed, face down on the bed. I followed her down, sliding up to bury my face in her unbound waterfall of hair.

We didn't speak for a while, recovering. Finally, she turned over and embraced me. I felt embarrassed and excited at the same time as we lay in one another's arms, quietly looking at each other. "I've never had that done to me before." she said shyly. "My God, it was wonderful."

You just needed a city chick!" I laughed. Then I turned to her, more serious.

"You were wonderful...it was perfect...God, you're beautiful," I said, stroking her cheek with the back of my hand.

She brought my head to her lips and kissed my forehead. "I hope we didn't move too fast – we fall into bed a day after I say I want to take it slow. I just lost my head, I wanted you so badly." Amanda said.

It was nice to be wanted, I smiled to myself slyly. She smiled at me, eyes heavy.

"No one has ever been as warm and loving to me."

"Like I said, you just needed a strong, confident gal *who was really turned on*!" She gave me a good smack on the ass for that one.

"You'd better get home," she sighed. "It's late, and your dad will need entertaining tomorrow."

We talked idly as we got dressed, sneaking kisses between pieces of clothing. "Couldn't your dad come down for a proper vacation?"

I sighed. "My dad can't be away from Irene for that long," I explained, there's a protocol.

"Wow," Amanda marveled, "they love each other that much?"

"They are very devoted to each other. It's unbreakable routine of commitment. I think they both find comfort in their discomfort. Everyone's idea of love is different, different strokes," I added.

"That's very sweet?" She said, lifting an eyebrow in disbelief.

"Love is many things...a mystery with lots of interpretations, that's for sure."

Chapter 12

Dad was going nowhere. There was two feet of snow and ice storms predicted. He was going to be stuck here for a while. So much for his whirlwind visit.

He'd definitely switched into what I privately thought of as the AARP lifestyle. For one thing, he was up at the crack of dawn. My dad. Who'd always been the last one out of bed when I was growing up? When I came into the kitchen, I found him drinking coffee and eating a piece of toast, watching the stock reports on the tiny portable black and white TV.

"Damn," he muttered. I sat down next to him with my own cup of coffee. "Lose some money?" I asked.

"Hell no," he replied, "but I bet your brother and Jeff did." He went on, but I didn't really understand what he was talking about. Not that he cared very much – his financial discussions were always more rhetorical than anything else. When he got into his Daddy Warbucks Zone, it was always best to just nod and look interested.

As I listened, there was a nervous ache in the pit of my stomach. Was this how Jeff was losing the money I'd loaned him? Trading is just another form of gambling, and you can lose just as big on the trading floor as you can in Vegas. It's just more socially acceptable to lose all your money in the stock markets than it is to go broke playing poker. When my father was finished pontificating, I asked him why he'd never given Jeff or Neil the benefit of his advice.

"They wouldn't listen." he grumbled. Then he grinned, mischievously. "Plus, what fun would that be?"

"It just seems like it might be a nice thing to do, especially if they're losing money – you never know, they might listen." I said, hoping that it was true.

Dad changed the subject. Typical.

"You got this in the mail at my house," he said, tossing me a pale pink envelope. I nodded, looking at what seemed to be an invitation. I opened it with a butter knife. As expected, it was a wedding invitation. It was from Nancy, our old nextdoor neighbor. We'd been friends when I was a little kid, and I'd dated her brother briefly when I was fourteen. It had gone about as well as most early teenage relationships – lots of horny fumbling set to the music of Journey, lots of adolescent dreams dashed. Prince Charming never had braces, and part of growing up is the realization that what you see in movies and read in romance novels are highly embellished.

"We got one too." My dad said finishing off his last bit of toast.

"Are you going to go?" I asked.

Nancy and I use to trade old Harlequin romance novels, and it looked like her dream of becoming royalty was coming true. She was marrying a baron from some small principality - not quite a prince, but still pretty impressive. The wedding would be in Harrisburg, Brussels.

"Hell, yes, we're going." Dad said, then snorted. "Irene wouldn't miss it. Not every day you get to attend the wedding of a baron and rub elbows with royalty. If you want to come with us, we can all room at the same hotel. My treat." He still was facing the television when he said this.

"I don't know." I said hesitantly.

"Last time, Irene was really...unpleasant." What she'd done was verbally rip me to shreds, tearing into me about my lack of class due to my crass sense of humor and 'the foul people you associate with' and telling me I was no longer part of the family. It had been devastating and painful and didn't leave me with a lot of warm, fuzzy feelings towards Irene or towards the idea of spending time with her in a foreign country. She was just mean. I wasn't going to say that to my dad. The most he'd admit to was Irene's difficult nature?

"I'll talk to her," my dad said. "If you want to go, it's the chance of a lifetime. There are some very important people who are going to be there – it might be your only chance to meet royalty."

"And that's going to do what for a hairdresser in Fossil Creek, Quebec?"

"Oh Lucy," my dad sighed, "when did you get so down- to-earth? You and Irene used to eat up all this royalty stuff." He picked up the remote and switched the channel to the BBC news.

"I'll let you know." I said. I wasn't even going to touch the comment about Irene. "I'll have to talk to my boss, see if I can get the time off."

"Please," my dad sneered, "how much do you even make at that rinky dink place?"

"Any job worth doing is worth doing well." I said primly. "You taught me that. Besides, the people here are the ones that are my friends.

Nancy might be marrying royalty, but I haven't heard from her in twenty years."

My dad was still on the topic of my attending the wedding. "I really like Amanda but you just met her, and ah...she can't come with you." he told me. "It wouldn't be proper." I was really tempted to tell him that as far as I was concerned, bringing my girlfriend to a wedding was a whole lot more proper than knocking up a Playboy Bunny and marry-ing another woman while the Bunny married your brother. I restrained myself. Getting snide wasn't going to accomplish anything, so I changed the subject.

"You're not going home today, right?" I confirmed.

"The airport is still closed, not that I could even get there from here." Dad said.

Then he waved a hand at my answering machine and told me I had messages.

"Right." I said, picking up his coffee cup. "Let me get you a refill, and I have to go call Mom." He nodded at me, staring at the television. "You should do that." Dad said absently. "I'm kind of glad the weather is bad," he said, smirking at me as I left the kitchen. "More time with my Best Girl." He winked. Such a schmoozer! I chuckled to myself.

I hit the red LISTEN button on the old answering machine. It was just such a different feel than dialing into voicemail that I was never going to give it up. I couldn't pretend to be Jim Rockford without an answering machine, after all.

There were seven messages waiting for me. Six of them were from my mom, sounding increasingly hysterical. One was Joelle from work, calling telling me that the salon was closed for the day due to snow. Not exactly surprising, but kind of a pity, since going to work would have gotten me out of the house for the day to rebalance myself. I wasn't used to hanging around my family members for extended periods of time. Although I was glad to have Dad visiting me, we both liked our independent routines.

I called Mom back, holding the receiver a little away from my ear in case of a shill scream. When Gus answered on the second ring, I only got out a "hi" before he was telling me that Mom was a wreck, that one of his sisters had spent the night consoling her, that he was worried about her. I tried not to notice that he didn't ask how I was, or how I was handling the news that my parentage had changed overnight but he did put Mom on the phone almost immediately.

She was howling in my ear immediately. It was absolutely deafening.

"Mom, calm down," I said loudly. "I love you, I love you, you're still my mom, you've always been my mom nothing has changed."

"I was so worried," she gasped out between sobs, "I was so scared you wouldn't want me for your mother anymore!" Her cries went through my head like a cheese grater scraping down a chalkboard.

"Mom," I said tiredly, "it's me who ought to be worried. You could always just decide I'm not your kid."

That probably wasn't the best thing to say, because the volume of the wails ramped up to banshee levels.

"You will ALWAYS be my baby, always, that woman didn't want you, she didn't love you, and NO ONE loves you like I do!" my mom screeched.

"I know, I know," I reassured her, "please stop crying, you're my mom and my only mom, I know that, I love you." I guess it's good to be loved.

Gus was in the background, offering similar reassurances. Despite his recent rudeness, I felt bad for him. He'd married the emotional equivalent of a tornado, and I knew from experience how hard it was to live with her.

"It's bad enough that I have to share you with Irene," my mom sniffled, "but you know about Greta now, too."

I assured her some more that she was the mom who'd raised me, the mom who mattered, that it didn't matter how many birth moms or step moms I had because she was my MOM. Eventually, I tried to move on from the topic of my mother's emotional state, and invited her and Gus for a visit my new hometown "I can't come to see you now," she told me, like I'd asked her to fly to the moon on a moment's notice, "it's all snowy and dangerous, I'll come in the spring, or maybe the summer. Maybe I should come...I don't know." She always had to do things her way. "Can I bring Gus?" she asked plaintively. Had I not just invited him? "Sure, Mom." I replied. There was no use pointing it out.

"I just don't want to meet her, Lucy." Mom said suddenly. "I don't want to be anywhere near Greta."

"I don't expect you to fly down and spend time with her, Mom." I replied, "But she's a paraplegic with a traumatic brain injury. She doesn't even know who I am."

Mom's tears paused, and she blew her nose loudly. "I suppose it's terrible of me," she said, "but I'm glad."

She might be my mom, and emotionally fragile, but what a terrible thing to say. I said so, as gently as I could, and added "Greta's been shut away in a mental institution for decades – have some compassion for the woman."

She began wailing again, naturally. "See, you're defending her, you always defend everyone but me!" she sobbed.

I scratched my head and sighed. Conversations with my mom on emotional topics were always rife with meltdowns and irrational explosions, but I couldn't avoid this one.

"I love you a ton." I said. "You'll just have to believe that."

"Okay," she whimpered. "I do believe you. I sent you some emails. Write back."

"I will." I promised, rolling my eyes. It's nice to know I'm loved, but my mother is very overwhelming. Especially when she feels threatened.

I smiled in spite of myself, staring at the silver- framed photo on the little table in front of me. The picture was one of those family portraits from 70's Olan Mills Photo Studio; my dad, my mom, Neil, and the twelve year old me, complete with a fake library background... now, more than ever, I felt like her kid.

We finally ended our conversation on a positive note and she explained she would look into a visit for herself in the spring.

Comby was at my feet like a little Buddha, giving me a compassion- ate look. I patted his wrinkled bulldog brow and answered the phone as it immediately rang, praying it wasn't my mother, again.

Luckily, it was Todd. Regardless of the state of his life, he wasn't likely to sob at high volume into my ear.

"I'm in your barn." Todd told me, as soon as I said hello. "It's so nice to talk to someone I'm not related to." I told him honestly. He laughed. "I'm coming in to pee," he said. "Just didn't want to surprise you."

When he came in, he was totally covered in snow. "It's really coming down out there," he said. "My dad sent me over to check on things, and I think Ned will be by later to check the propane tanks."

My father instantly liked Todd, who could barely break away from the barrage of questions to get to the bathroom. "That's a fine young man." Dad told me. As if I didn't know. "You could have a kid like him," my father added helpfully. "I think you'd make a great mom."

I pointed to the Amish-made hope chest in the corner, which he'd bought me years ago at a county fair. "Keep hoping, dad." I said wryly.

He grinned at me and said, "Well, you definitely inherited my sense of humor."

Todd came back into the main room, and we sat down for a few min- utes to chat. "The band and I are supposed to play the Houndstooth tonight," he told me, "Sheri usually sings, and she's stuck at school. Want to sing a few with us? It'll be a short set, but I don't want to cancel on the bar – in weather like this, everyone needs whatever entertainment they can get."

"This is really short notice." I said, conflicted.

My dad was behind the idea. "Come on!" he said cheerfully, "I never get to hear you sing anymore!"

I agreed, a bit reluctantly, and Todd told me to come by about six for a run-through. The show was at eight.

"How'd it go with your dad?" I whispered to Todd, as I walked him to the door. "It was awful and good too," he said, and pulled me onto the porch after him. "You were right, my dad was great, my mom cried, but then she was happy, it was going okay, but then Sheri started bleeding. She lost the baby. But I was there; I went to the doctor with her, held her hand through the whole thing. I love Sheri, and I've decided to start mechanic's school in the spring. That way, wherever her art takes her, I'll be able to follow." I felt like crying, for some reason. So I did. I hugged him tearfully, and he cried too. "Sorry!" I said, sniffling. "I'm really sorry!"

Todd was crying with me. "I really wanted to be a father. I wanted us to be a family," he said, like it had surprised him.

"I know," I said, "I really do know." We bear hugged and I wished I had some better words of wisdom for him.

When I got back in the house, I realized I looked like a wreck. "Jesus, Mary and Joseph, what was that all about?" My dad demanded.

"It's personal." I said. I wasn't going to discuss Todd's secrets with my dad. "Oh, you kids," my dad said, and I didn't reply.

"So, Dad, what do you want to do today?" I asked. "I want some real breakfast," said my father. "Then maybe you can show me the horse." I was shocked - my dad wanted to see the horse?

Not only did Dad want to see him, he even rode Tao, singing the horse's praises afterwards.

He even complimented me on my barn's housekeeping. "Todd is my stable hand - you can thank him for the housekeeping." I told Dad.

"He's a good kid." Dad said. I nodded. "You see why I love it here?" I prodded.

Dad sighed. "It's not the life I would have chosen for you, but it's the right thing, I can see that. Tavis said you'd always been looking for a home. He was afraid that you'd never feel loved. Isn't that strange?"

As we walked into the house and were hanging up our wet things on the chairs by the fire, I asked Dad, "Did you know he was going to give this place to me in his will?" "He was very vague," my dad said. "I suggested just leaving you the money but he made some comment about that not being the point. He felt very paternal about you, and he thought giving you the lodge would be best." Dad stood facing me, red cheeked and smiling, "I guess he was right."

Chapter 13

It turned out that Tavis knew me better than I had imagined. It quietly occurred to me that there were a lot of people who loved me, but I had been so full of self loathing and so busy fixating on what was bad in my life that I'd never noticed all the good stuff.

Dad and I changed clothes and he helped me do some "handyman" stuff around the lodge. Then we snacked and decided to walk the grounds.

"Are you making it financially?" Dad asked me.

I walked next to him as he rode Tao down to the lake. He really liked the horse action!

"Feel like John Wayne on this beast," my dad said, smiling heartily. "Sooo, are you ok?" he asked again.

The scene reminded me of a Vermont postcard I had received as a kid. I had it framed over my desk and when I would get frustrated with my math homework I would look at it and sigh...it made me smile every time.

Now I lived in that world, it seemed.

"I am Ok dad," I replied, "it's a lot cheaper to live here than it is to live in the city." I'd decided not to tell him about the extra money that Tavis had left me with for the lodge. Functer's words echoed in my head, telling no one included not telling my father, but it felt weird. Just as I'd demanded that my family stop keeping secrets, I started keeping one.

"Jeff and his family, they're having a really hard time of it out in California." Dad told me, halting the horse and gazing out onto Lac de Lune. Ice was starting to form around the edges of the lake, but there was still waves crashing against the buoys. A few boats still lingered, like floating ducks in the distance.

"He really got into a financial pickle," said my dad.

"But don't worry, Irene and I took care of it."

Oh, really, I thought. My dad took care of it, and then Jeff came to me with what was likely the same story and I took care of it, too. I just shook my head, looking out onto the glittering icy lake and realizing how blessed I was by my good fortune.

"He'll be fine, got a trust fund set up for his kid." Dad said, off-handedly.

Jeff was chasing self-esteem, which was something that bookies don't payout. The chase to find validation from something – or someone - outside yourself was a road I had run before… straight into alcoholism, and I was glad that race was over.

Dismounting Tao, Dad patted his neck. Tao snuffed, blowing a plume of warm air out of his quivering velvety nostrils.

"Neil and his wife are switching islands." Dad told me, continuing the family gossip. "To Kauai, probably."

"Very cool." I said dreamily.

My brother's life seemed so spectacular to me. As kids we were obsessed with Magnum p.i. The camaraderie of the friendship the characters had on the TV show, the cool car, *Robin's Nest* (the estate) and the idea of working for yourself. Neil and I kind of saw an idealized version of my dad in Magnum. Our dad was like a superhero to us.

My brother and his wife Jenny had lived in Hawaii for seven years, on Oahu. It seemed that both of them had acclimated to island life enough to move to the more remote Kauai. I often daydreamed about my little brother and his daily life in paradise, but he'd never shared too much with me. I never knew if it was intentional, or he just didn't see how cool his life was to an outside observer.

"Jenny got a better job there with a farm of some sort, growing plants for pharmaceutical testing. She's a smart girl, just a bit of a workaholic. They may keep their house on Oahu and rent it out, because the company she's working for is renting a home for them!"

Dad said proudly.

"Very good." I replied, wishing I didn't get the tingle of sibling comparison I was feeling.

We started walking back up to the house after I noticed my dad's nose was running and that he was having a hard time walking in the snow. Dad didn't want to get back up on the horse, though. There was a good foot of powder, which posed no problem for Tao, but it was a bit harder for humans with shorter legs.

"Dad why don't you get back up on Tao?"

"Riding a horse is crushing the family jewels," he chuckled.

I winced with imaginary pain. My dad and I always joked around...and it was good to be with him.

The last time my dad had been active was when he was playing college football. So, as soon as we were back inside, Dad conked out in the armchair.

I decided to visit Amanda. As I knocked at her door, I could see her through the window, pounding away at her computer's keyboard. She seemed happy enough to abandon it and answer the door.

"What a morning," I told her as I came inside. "I'm ready for my dad to leave, I'm worried because things are going so good...what if something happens."

"But he's not going anywhere until the snow subsides." Amanda added, with a confident nod.

I sat at her table and told her about my parents, my dad's comments about my life, my inferiority complex when it came to my brother. Then there was the Todd situation. I explained our little weep-fest as completely as I could without breaking his confidence.

"I have to say," I concluded, "God has a funny way of giving the Zwich family a spoon full of sugar to make our medicine go down more smoothly." I smiled weakly patting Amanda's arm. Amanda was more like a cup of sugar but she smiled at the compliment.

"I could barely compose a sentence this morning, thinking about last night." Amanda said, then leaned over and kissed me, stroking my arm.

I blushed. "Well," I said reluctantly, "I have another bomb to drop. Just a little one, though."

"Oh God," Amanda groaned. "What now?"

"My dad wants me to go to a wedding." I said.

"That's no big deal." Amanda replied, clearly relieved.

"Bigger than it sounds." I said. "My childhood friend Nancy is marrying some freakin' baron in Brussels...and I hate, hate, hate weddings. Dad wants me to come, and he wants the whole family to stay in the same hotel."

"This is bad?" She leaned back in the kitchen chair, with her arms crossed across her Irish wool cardigan, a bemused look in those Bacall-blue eyes.

"From my perspective." I sighed. "The last time I saw my stepmother Irene, she went on a total rampage. My dad had left the room, and she started in on me – told me not to call her 'Mom' any more, said I was an awful daughter, a bunch of other really hostile shit that came out of nowhere. Among other things, she said I'm not a part of the family anymore."

"Your photos have been taken down," Irene had added with rancor.

"*Real nice*." Amanda said. "Isn't she kind of out of line?"

"It would seem like that to anyone outside the family, but she's got this voodoo-like stranglehold over all the Zwich's. Half the men in my family used to play college football, tough jocks… but they're scared to death of Irene. She just has a way of slicing right through people in this really degrading, cruel way."

"God, she sounds like a nightmare." Amanda was no longer leaning back in the wooden chair, but instead scooted closer to me, at full attention.

"I just don't want to be stranded in a foreign country with Irene, you know? We were in Michigan on vacation the last time I saw her, and that was bad enough. Being in another country, surrounded by foreign glitterati and no friends at a high profile wedding it's going to bring out the absolute worst in her."

"Yes, but you're prepared now," Amanda reminded me, "and a different woman then you were all those years ago."

She had a point.

Amanda's work phone was going off and she went to take a call. My mind was reeling, was I strong enough to not be so crushed by Irene. My gosh, she was just a woman...but some how the people that loom largest in your childhood have the most power over you in adulthood. *It was time to put on the big girl pants and get over the mythology of Irene.*

I was hoping Amanda would say she'd go to the wedding with me, but she didn't. I didn't out and out ask her to come, either. It wasn't her family, and this relationship was too new.

Pissing off my Dad wasn't such a great idea, either.

Still – I didn't want to attend this wedding alone. Honestly, I just plain didn't want to attend it at all.

Amanda and I chatted about inconsequential things a bit longer and then I totally reversed my thinking and blurted out "I'll go if you go," in the middle of talking about something totally unrelated.

Amanda said incredulously, "To the wedding?"

"No, to the bathroom." I snarked rolling my eyes, "Yes, the wedding, I'll go if you come with me."

"No." Amanda said, very definitely. "I can't."

"You could wear a nice suit," I coaxed. "I'll buy it for you. It'll be a great trip."

"Honey, I've got to draw the line somewhere." Amanda said, crossing her arms. "There are certain things you just can't depend on me for, and attending a royal wedding is one of them."

"Come on, the bride was my best friend in grade school. Nancy and I use to read trashy romance novels and trade stickers, her brother always had a boner and was trying to hump me all the time, you'll be able to hear all about my past and my childhood. C'mon, please?"

"No. I mean that *sounds enticing* but no." Amanda replied facetiously. "Case closed."

I sighed. It had been worth a try.

"I'll be there when it's important." She added kindly.

"I have another proposition!"

Amanda, dropped her shoulders…shaking her head.

"Will you come to the Houndstooth tonight and keep my dad company? I'm singing with Todd's band."

"You keep asking me to do all the really choice jobs."

Amanda said.

"I think he does like you." I told her.

"I will come to hear you and yes, I'll gab with your dad."

I got up from the table and tried not to knock the piles of edited papers off the table while I gave her a big hug.

"Thanks! It'll only be a few songs, Todd and I haven't had a ton of time to practice with his band. They're really good, though!"

"Go wake your dad up and I'll meet you by the sleigh. I'll hook Tao up and we'll all ride together for dinner at The Diner. They're having a fried chicken special tonight, I think."

I gave her the thumbs up and jogged back to the lodge. Shockingly, Dad was still napping and Combover was on his lap, both of them snoring like gorillas. When Dad awoke a few minutes later, I explained our night's events and he seemed excited.

When Dad saw the sleigh, he was delighted. Seeing him sitting next to Amanda under the big woolly blanket was hysterical.

I let Amanda drive, and even my slightly macho father knew when to "turn the reins over" to an expert, I chuckled to myself.

I watched the snow fall on my dad's Stetson and Amanda's Daniel Boone cap. The wind was whistling in my ears, and I couldn't hear a word they said. Tao was full of energy, and we kept up a quick pace to town.

We all ordered the fried chicken and mashed potatoes at the Diner I scarfed it down quickly and then left them to enjoy their dessert and coffee while I went next door to the Houndstooth. The boys and I needed a run-through of my songs and some practice before we performed.

By eight, the room was packed. The body heat and roaring fireplace smoke were a little overwhelming, considering the bitter cold outside. The guys and I tuned up and ran through a few bits of the songs. I paper clipped the handwritten lyric sheets to the music stand so they wouldn't blow away mid performance. The few bar flies nodded with approval and the sound check was set...showtime!

Bob, Ned and Dad were whooping it up, beers all around, and Amanda was smiling and nodding, obviously glad Ned was there. I watched them thinking that once Dad was out of Irene's self-consciously posh environment, he was a lot happier.

Ned's wife Kathy came up to me to chat before we went on. She was giggling as usual, but it was a sweet giggle. "I can't believe you got Amanda out to the bar! Ned used to call her 'The Shadow' since she'd come and go like a ghost. She's even smiling!" Kathy said, winking at me obviously. "Kindness can go a long way." I said evasively.

"I'm prying, right?" Kathy asked cheerfully.

"Nooo!" I said, winking back.

"What can I say?" Kathy sighed. "Fossil Creek is really small, and there's nothing to do but gossip on these long cold nights."

Tippie and Janis arrived, and immediately pulled up chairs next to my dad's table.

"We're the reinforcements." Janis announced, sipping from her bottle of Coke.

Finally, we were ready to go on. I was ready to throw up. My stage fright was coming over me in waves. Luckily, Todd and the rest of the band understood about cold feet and kept me busy.

We started off with Roy Orbison's "Blue Bayou." Which honestly, I sounded a little shaky on, but no one seemed to care, and then we went right into an 80's power rock, "Your Love Is Driving Me Crazy" by Sammy Hagar. Todd was rocking, and the boys really backed me up on the harmonies - it helped that I sang in the same key as Sheri. I was singing directly to Amanda, and my dad noticed, but didn't seem to care. The boys came right up and we were singing into the microphone together. Mid-song, I noticed the bass player checking out my tits. It was kind of funny.

I had to admit that I did look pretty hot in my black riding pants and low cut black tight shirt - you've got to give the crowd what they want, and a little "tits and sass" is part of the package for a female singer.

I walked the little stage and sang to a chubby guy in an impeccably cut white business shirt, who looked completely out of place. His eyes were like saucers, and he was nodding his head to the beat, I nodded to his girlfriend to bring her in so she wouldn't get pissed. I'd learned years ago; never alienate the girls. She was way too pretty for him, anyway. She had long, blond, straight hair and looked like Stevie Nicks, with pouty lips and big blue-green eyes.

I pulled away from the front of the stage so Todd could do his short solo. The sweat was starting to pour off me in waves and I was riding high on adrenaline and the crowd's energy.

The next number was just Todd and I doing my original song "Good As It Gets", a soul/slow rock song. When I wrote it I was listening to a lot of Adele and Anita Baker. As the dance floor switched to the slow grooves, even older couple began waltzing and I felt tears come to my eyes. There was something in this song that spoke to people about appreciating "the now". Todd looked a little worried but kept strumming as a tear ran down my cheek. The crowd went crazy with applause and it was a golden moment.

Then we did a medium tempo song called, "Rudi Nappi's Girl," which was very Stray Cat's with that 50's upright bass grooving in the background. I wrote it when I was reading a lot of pulp fiction and noticing all the best lurid book covers were done by an artist named Rudi Nappi. His portrayal of the bad girls was the theme of the song!

We switched abruptly to "A Strong and Fading Sun", not a dance song at all and yet people kept dancing. It was strange, but cool. A few eyebrows went up encouragingly when the folks who were listening to the words realized it was about a guy who was selling his house to save his boat, to keep his livelihood and his family alive. I always had a soft spot for sailors and this was kind of a love letter to them.

Why had I never been able to find a band that fit me this well in Chicago?

We did one more quick dance number, and then moved on to our final song, which was just Mick on the keyboards and my vocals. I announced the song, which I had learned back when I was doing cabaret back in Chicago. I was lucky that Mick's dad had been a pianist and had taught him this rare Jaques Brel, gem years ago. "This is for you French-Canadians... be kind, my French is pas mal, pas bonne." I said into the microphone.

The audience laughed, and someone shouted something in French that I couldn't understand.

My forehead was clammy and the expectant faces in the audience made me suddenly self-conscious. "The song is called If You Go Away," or "Ne Me Quitte A Pas," I announced, and Mick began to play slowly. In my opinion, this was one of the saddest and most beautiful love songs ever written. I'd written the French vocals down phonically in case I forgot the words, and kept my eye on my index card if I looked at Amanda right now...it would have been a disaster.

When I looked up after a few measures, the crowd was rapt. Amanda looked stricken, but I kept singing...because that's music, the unexplainable magic of it, it reaches into the soul like the voice of God and touches even the coldest of hearts. The crowd went nuts when we ended, the French crowd hooting like crazy. When I learned this song many years ago, in my heart it was dedicated to the loss I always felt towards my parents...not a lover. My greatest heartbrake's always had to do with my family.

We did an encore. "Do you guys know Layla?" I asked, and the band nodded at me like I was stupid. "Ok, I'm gonna do the Weird Al version, but you just play it regular." They laughed, but they had no idea I'd be singing about *Yoda*. I'd always found it's good to end a set in a happy up-tempo song, classic rock preferable.

Todd loved this tune and I'd heard him playing it before. God knew I was familiar with it, as I'd used to perform it with my old band back in Chicago.

The entire audience cracked up, once they figured out what I was singing about. Dad, Ned, Bob and Amanda were swaying and clapping to the beat. Tippie flicked her lighter, and suddenly the flames all went up. It was awesome!

I sort of screwed up the words at the end, but no one noticed. They were having too much fun.

The band descended from the stage, and the reaction of the crowd made me feel like a superstar. When the compliments and pats on the back had died down and the band was clearing their stuff, the jukebox came on with some Johnny Paycheck. Amanda ordered me a coffee, and we sat close. I could tell this evening was really overwhelming for her, and suddenly felt a wave of gratitude that she'd come out with me tonight.

The guy in the white shirt came over with his girlfriend. "This was a big surprise, young lady," he said, shaking my hand.

"You were great!" the woman said brightly. "That was so much fun!"

I looked at them appreciatively – it was nice to be complimented. They kept looking at me like I should know them. I ran down a quick mental list, but couldn't place them - I'd have remembered either of them, so we hadn't met before. Then the man spoke, "I'm Morrow, from K-Top Music out of Montreal," said the man, answering my unspoken question.

"Our car broke down here, and we're staying over at the Cedar Wood Motel. Here's my card, I think we should talk."

Naturally, my dad was standing next to the couple and overheard what the guy said. He reacted like a lightning bolt had struck him right in the pants – pumping the music guy's hand, singing my praises, even talking about his own poetic struggle.

Mr. Morrow was as nice as he could be, and listened patiently, but finally cut my dad off. "We have to go," he said, still polite. "Please call me, though. Our company doesn't pay like the big international ones, but we're hooked into Pandora, Spotify... we've got artists in Pitchfork, SXSW... contacts at the radio stations, we can get you exposure."

"I will." I said, wide eyed. "I'll call you. Thank you."

"Who would've thunk it?" Dad said, plopping back down in his chair. "Out here in the middle of nowhere, someone from a recording company. What a goddamned coincidence."

Part of me was unbelievably excited at the prospect of a recording contract, but a larger part just wanted everything to calm down. I wanted to go home with Amanda and my dad and just be peaceful. Musical disappointment had caused me a lot of misery in my life and to be pulled back into...chasing the dragon, as I used to call it...made me nervous.

I was immediately worried that things with Amanda would go south. In the past, when I'd been buckling down and really trying to make music, any hint of notoriety or popularity had become a bone of contention between me and whomever I was with at the time.

Eventually, I'd lost my confidence and given up my dreams of succeeding in the music business. I wanted *peace* of mind more than I wanted to be a professional singer at this point. On the other hand...maybe I wanted both. Professional and personal success?

People love the idea of loving an artist, but real life with one is far less appealing. Writers demand a lot of alone time, and singers are even at rehearsal or on the road... in a studio. It's hard to keep a relationship going under those conditions.

I'd actually stopped telling people that I was a singer, which was much easier than telling them that the brilliant music career I'd envisioned had never materialized.

For some reason, I didn't mind identifying myself as a writer.

People asked fewer questions about unpublished writers than failed musicians, it seemed. The real problem was that most of my answers had just felt like excuses.

I'd never figured out why my music career hadn't worked out, my 12-Step sponsor was fond of saying, "In God's time." Was it time?

Turning my ear to the end of one of my dad's stories, I watched Ned and Kathy belly-laugh and Amanda look thoroughly absorbed...it was cool.

We finally called it a night and piled into the sleigh. My dad was talking Amanda's ear off and she was nodding thoughtfully. The snow had stopped, and it actually felt warmer outside. The beer hit my dad about halfway back to the lodge, and we ended up walking him in and getting him settled before we unhitched Tao and got him into the barn.

The sweet smell of fresh hay from Todd hard work and the soft glow from the over hanging light made the barn seem enchanted. "Did you have a good time? I know my dad talks a mile a minute," I asked.

Amanda walked back around the horse. "The apple doesn't fall far from the tree!" she said, chuckling. She tackled me into the hay.

"You were great up there," she said into my ear. "You were born to perform and now I know who you get it from!"

"I just don't want this chance to detract from my new life. I like where things are going." I said quietly, looking up at the barn's vaulted ceiling, smelling the cedar from the wet wood.

"This is a God-given talent you have, you can't ignore it." Amanda responded firmly.

She kissed me fully on the mouth and tried to get her hands under my coat. "This really would be easier on the beach," she said, clearly frustrated. We both cracked up.

My dad and Combover were shaking the walls with their snoring by the time we came back in the house. We crept down the hall, careful not to wake him, and I felt about sixteen. How did I manage to get into this situation – sex on the sly with my dad down the hall, at my age?

We got into the shower in my bathroom, warm jets of water slicking up our bodies. I soaped up my gorgeous long haired mare, sliding soapy hands all over her body as she braced herself on the wall. I kissed her neck, using my body like creamy soap, all over hers, getting on my knees slick and warm, slippery. Her hands in my wet curls trying to hold back as I caressed her. Amanda was a tangle of movement and sighs and I pulled myself up in front of her, straddling her body. The friction was perfect as I slid up and down, finally convulsing with my lips on hers, her hair covering me like a mermaid's song. We got out of the shower and I watched her dry off.

"Just wait until this summer when I get you in the lake at midnight." I said, grinning.

"The always ice- cold lake? We'll have to see how you feel about that in July." Amanda replied, pulling on her clothes.

"I really want to spend the night with you." I said, sighing.

"Your DAD is here. I don't think so."

"I know. Bad idea" I agreed.

"He won't be here forever." She winked.

I gave her the a-ok sign and pulled on my yoga pants and long buttery soft blue cotton night-shirt.

"Besides," said Amanda, "we still haven't been on a real date."

"You plan it and I'm there." I promised, kissing her forehead, then eyes, then her thin, perfect lips.

She disappeared, and I fell asleep as soon as my head hit the pillow.

When I got up, I dressed for work leisurely. I expected Dad to be up, drinking coffee and watching the news, but the kitchen was empty. I found a note in his chicken-scratch handwriting next to the coffeemaker, telling me that he and Ned were going for a ride around town, and that his plane was leaving later in the day. Ned would give him a ride to the airport, and Dad would stop by the salon to say good-bye. Sometimes I forgot that dad had known Ned longer then me!

Later, when Ned and Dad arrived at The Hair Hut, I was just putting one of my clients under the hooded dryer. I made introductions. Everyone was extremely nice and Joelle flirted sweetly and harmlessly with Dad, which I could tell made him feel good.

Walking my father to Ned's car, I bear-hugged him, and he reminded me, "Don't worry, Lucy, everything will be okay." He patted my head like a poodle's, and they were gone in an instant.

Chapter 14

It was only four in the afternoon, but the November sun was almost gone, its weak silvery light fading into a gray suede sky. I had been working all day in the lodge on my book, and hadn't seen hide nor hair of Amanda.

The retro digital clock on the mantel bleeped every so often, like a slumbering R2D2 from above the stone fireplace. At one time, I'm sure it was cutting-edge chic, but now it was a relic from another era; the odd noises were probably why I found it hidden in my bedroom closet. That made it more valuable to me…I'm just a sentimental sort of gal.

I stared out the window and thought about all the men who'd stayed here on vacation, sipping their scotch *neat*, smoking hand rolled cigars, arguing about politics that ranged from Roosevelt all the way to Bush, Jr. I was probably the least likely of the family to inherit this bastion of male privilege, but oddly, the one who appreciated it the most.

I liked being alone with my writing. It gave me sanctuary, a space where I could retreat – despite the fact that elements of my real life always crept into the fiction I wrote. It wasn't much of a retreat today, as a visit to Greta tomorrow loomed, like a echo in my already distracted mind.

I decided to take a break and sit by the fire with my new comic book.

The "Hate Annual" lay glossy and bright in my hands with its trademark fun-house-mirror-appearing characters on the cover. My heart beat with childlike anticipation. Cartoonist/satirist Peter Bagge produced work that was sort of a Simpsons-meets-Portlandia. Low paying jobs, sibling rivliry, alcoholism, social commentary and general distress due to modern living, a psychotic soap opera that was thoroughly engrossing…and easy to relate to! It's characters slanted toward the members of Generation X, over educated and under-employed.

The type of graphic novel I read took a look at ordinary life and brought out extraordinary circumstances of the human condition. With Joe Sacco's graphic novels the theme was the human epilogue of wars (The Fixer and Soba) discussed in the most intimate ways; with Harvey Pekar it was a jazz lover/frustrated writer (American Splendor and Cleveland) and his Studs Terkel way of getting to know people wherever he went. I loved people and their stories and that's what comix with an X was all about for me. The only superhero's here were literary/music agents and art gallery owners…willing to give our *hero's* a brake.

When difficult situations with my family or work life arose, artists like Bagge, Bob Fingermann (Minimum Wage) let me imagine that I was a director (Harold Ramis, preferably), filming a screwball comedy, and that gave me the conviction to go on with my illusive dreams. Better to imagine your family as a zany cast of characters in a movie than retreat to bottomless pit of booze.

So I welcomed the butterflies in my stomach that the simple pleasure of a new issue brought. Putting on an old jazz record album that was a thrift store find I snuggled into my big over stuffed lounge chair and sipping my tea and enjoying my stories. While the sleeve of the record might have smelled like moldy basement, the record inside wove a smoky musical spell that was instant relaxation for me. This was the heart of my life.

Records and comics were simple enjoyment, and I longed for that feeling more and more in my life. I hummed Art Brut's "D.C. Comics and Chocolate Milkshakes" to the tune of Count Basie while I reveled in the peaceful feelings.

My dad had left yet another message about the wedding, reminding me that I was supposed to let them know if I was coming by early November. I still couldn't decide, and I wasn't really sure I actually wanted to leave Fossil Creek. I might have only been in residence for a short time, but I felt pretty rooted in this little town.

The music rep from K-Top, Morrow, had finally called me back, after I left him four messages. His phone manner hadn't matched his in-person enthusiasm, but strangely, that didn't bother me. I had a feeling in my bones that something good was going to come out of working with this company. Morrow had then dropped me an email to say that he would be calling on December 1st to chat, and I felt pretty good about it.

Considering I was usually not always an optimist, it felt a little weird to not be tied up in knots about all the possible things that could go wrong. Laying my comic on my chest, I noticed absently that the record needle had lifted and the front room was quiet again. I closed my eyes as the chair embraced me into dreamland.

On Sunday night, Janis took me to a new Twelve Step meeting out by the lumberyard that was a great change from our usual meeting at the Houndstooth. There were five women out of twenty attendees, and it was nice to not be the only female face in the crowd. The energy was different, with more women in the room. On the way home, I suggested a Fossil Creek spin-off women's Twelve-Step group to Janis. She nodded and asked, "Where would we have it?"

"My place." I said. "It's not like I haven't got the room."

"Ok...how about I'll bring it up at the next meeting." I gave her the thumbs up.

"Hey," Janis said, "how's Amanda?" Her eyebrows went up, Groucho Marx style.

"Good," I replied, then told her, "Things are going so well that it makes me a little nervous."

"Ah, young romance," Janis sighed. "Just wait till you're going on seven years, like us."

"Are you having issues?" I asked nervously. "Oh, no. It's real good. Its married life - you know, you've been in long term relationships," she reminded me, and lit up the butt of an old cigarette from her ashtray. When we got to the lodge, I gave Janis a hug and thanked her for the ride. Just outside the driveway, Amanda was out walking Comby. "Hi," I said, and waved like an idiot. "How was the meeting?" Amanda asked.

"Good. One poor guy was in his first twenty-four hours, he looked pretty rough."

"When I quit drinking, I just never looked back. Never even missed it." Amanda said casually. I wasn't sure if she was being condescending, or just stating facts.

"Lucky you," I answered. "People tell me that sometimes. All I can say is the last place I wanted to be was in a Twelve Step program, it just seemed so...uncool. I'm an artiste," I said dramatically, "but no matter how much I tried to curb my substance habits, they took up most of my life, and my music and writing played second fiddle."

She nodded, clearly trying to understand. "I'll take your word for it," she said. We walked towards the lodge, our feet scrunching the snow and icy leaves beneath our boots.

I squeezed the back of her neck playfully, inhaling the night scents of the outdoors.

"Let's go for a ride together." Amanda suggested.

"Sure, that sounds great." I agreed. We stopped by the lodge to drop Comby off, but my phone was ringing and I felt obliged to answer it.

"Lucy," said Ned, "glad I caught you. We can't go see Greta tomorrow – it'll have to be next week. Kathy's in the hospital with female trouble."

"Oh God, is she gonna be ok?" I asked.

"Eventually." Ned said. "They have to do a D&C."

"Ok, next week then." I sighed and hung up the phone gently.

"Everything all right?" Amanda asked. She was fishing a dog bone out of the ceramic "cookie" jar by the door.

"I guess we're not going to see Greta - Ned has to be with Kathy for some surgery. In a way, I'm relieved." Amanda nodded almost joyfully. "Great!" The response was a little weird. "I mean, it's bad, of course, but good for me...and I'll tell you the whole story later." Amanda said.

The grass, snow and icy patches crunched under our feet as we made our way to the barn. We saddled up Tao and rode double – *very romantic*. Amanda leaned her chin on my shoulder and we just let Tao lead. He walked up to the chapel.

"I still can't figure out the purpose of this place." I said, watching my breath cloud into a stream of steam. "It's not like Tavis was religious, so why would he want to bring my aunt – I mean, my mother – here?" The word "mother" stuck in my throat. I still wasn't used to the idea that my mom wasn't actually my mother, in the biological sense.

"Maybe it's a sort of a monument to love....sacred love," Amanda mused.

We were quiet, each contemplating our personal thoughts.

"It's more like the Love Shack." I said, trying to wrap my head around the fact that the aunt I'd never known was the woman who'd given birth to me.

"I don't think you should get hung up on labels. Just call Greta, Greta...mom, at least to me signifies someone who participates in your up bringing."

I breathed a sigh of relief, "Thanks! That makes me feel a whole lot better, actually."

She gave me a squeeze around the middle and Tao snorted into the cold air.

"What time do you work tomorrow?" Amanda asked. I thought a moment. "Well, it's Monday, so I'm off...remember I was going to see Greta!" She snickered and said "Save the date. We're going to Glen Maple. They have a little lesbian B&B there with a hot tub!"

"Ohhh," I said, "so that's my mystery-surprise!" Glen Maple was a scenic little town on the river. I had only been though it once, when Janis needed help picking up a shipment for the lumberyard. I had driven her car and she brought the lumber truck back. I had noted little rainbow flags in some of the businesses and Janis had explained that the town had become a little gay oasis.

"Sooner or later, it'll end up like Provincetown," Janis had sighed, "It's too beautiful to stay this charming and quaint."

Tao took us around a little path where he seemed to like to go. He knew these woods better than I did. It felt a little sneaky, riding in the twilight, around the farms up the road and watching the blue light of televisions flicker as we made our way around the lake. When we finally got home, my hands were numb and red with cold and my lips were in need of some Rose Lip Balm. I hoped Amanda would stay, but she gave me a deep, warm kiss and promised that tomorrow night was worth waiting for. I grinned...seemed I was smiling a lot these days. Would this good patch end I wondered, as I feel asleep that night.

Amanda came and got me bright and early the next morning. It had been hard to get going, when my warm bed was so cozy. Comby had a way of becoming a furry sack of potatoes molded to my feet. But the "to go" cup of coffee she had waiting for me helped as I tucked myself into my red down jacket and grabbed my night bag, locking up. Todd was going to pet sit for the night and I had left keys under the empty barrel by the barn door.

It was so lovely that we lived close, but not claustrophobically so - our homes were far enough apart we were more like neighbors. We'd spoken early on about living with lovers, and how we'd both had mistakes in our past, moving in with a lover for the wrong reasons. I didn't want to be the stereotypical lesbian couple who meet, have one date, and move in together after the second date.

Lauren had advised me to take it slow, and said very wisely that every relationship has only one chance to be new. For now, Amanda and I were perfectly happy in our separate residences.

"Did you check your mail?" Amanda inquired, as we walked to the car.

"No," I said. "Do I need to?" Then it occurred to me I had to go into town to get my mail, since all I had was a post office box. There was no mail delivery at the lodge.

"There's a letter from Chicago – someone named Brandy. It was in my mail by mistake." She sounded a little suspicious.

"Oh, that's my ex – Diana - her youngest daughter," I said. "She's a real doll. We write back and forth. You may get to meet her this summer, if she doesn't do summer school."

"How old is she?" "Now, she's nineteen. When I first met her, she was eleven."

"You were there for a big chunk of her life."

"I miss our special days." I admitted. "We'd go to all the music and comic stores and to all the funky vintage and resale shops on Belmont, like Hollywood Mirror, for kitschy jewelry and rock and roll shirts, then upstairs to Ragstock, for retro pantyhose, clothes, patches, and Doc Marten boots - it was always the best kind of treasure hunt." It bothered me that I'd heard very little from Brandy as time had passed, after Diana and I had separated. Brandy was in college, of course, but I suspected it was something more – maybe a sense of loyalty to her mom, which was understandable, and probably some anger at me for leaving. The thing was, you couldn't tell kids everything, when a relationship ends.

Amanda looked at me sideways. "There's so much I have yet to learn about you, Miss Lucy."

"So, were you jealous?" I joked, nudging her. "A little." Amanda said contemplatively. "It was strange that she wrote today – I got a letter from Cary, too, so it got my mind working about people from the past."

Now it was my turn to feel a little green. It wasn't that Amanda had left Cary – Cary left Amanda. It left a question open to me that maybe Amanda was still longing for Cary.

"So," I said, trying to hide my unease with the topic, "what did Cary have to say?"

"I guess things aren't going so well in fancy old Newport. She thinks this guy's family is judging her. Stuff like that."

"Stuff like that?" I pried. "Oh, you want to know if Cary's writing because she wants me back?" Amanda asked. Her blue eyes were unreadable, and she didn't say anything as we loaded our stuff into her truck. She took my bag from me and hoisted it into the back seat.

Amanda had a F150 fully loaded Harley Davidson edition truck, not exactly what I would have expected from the simplicity of her home. I noticed how cute she was dressed today, in a surfer-style Baja hoodie. The earth tones of the Baja suited her pink cheeks and fair skin, and her long, limestone-colored hair that I'd grown to love so much, and was now pulled back in a cloth head band. "Hey," I said breaking the silence.

I pointed to the bandana headband, which I recognized from a high- end catalog. "Did you get that from Sahalie?"

She laughed out loud. "It's the Buff color," she said, grinning from ear to ear, "I have about ten of them, all from Sahalie."

We got into her truck and she finally addressed the unanswered question hanging between us. "Lucy, Cary is old news," she said flatly, with a slight hint of annoyance.

A mental image of the cute little Skipper-doll face in the picture on Amanda's mantelpiece flashed before me, Cary was no slouch in the looks department. She was also younger than me, probably no cellulite. I sighed.

"Lucy," Amanda said, taking my hand before we pulled out. "You've got no competition. She could be naked and begging and I'd turn her away. Good enough?"

"I guess..." I said, still feeling insecure and unattractive.

We laughed and talked some more, but the fear still lingered inside me. I guess it was good to be a little jealous, it meant you valued what you had. I was in deep with Amanda – I'd never fallen so quick or so hard for someone in my life, and it scared me.

Glen Maple was a vision of quaint loveliness - cobbled streets, gas lamps, ship wheel signs, and nets decorating the windows of the rustic-looking shops.

"I feel like I'm in New England," I said gawking at the harbor town splendor.

"Ah, they learned everything they know about fishing villages from the Canadians!" Amanda said with pride.

The bed-and-breakfast was adorable. It was an old cottage that had been rehabbed with cedar shingles, tiny spruce trees in old fishing buckets, with fishing nets tacked up artfully on the front of the cottage. The whole building was rimmed with tiny white lights, and beat-up fishing rods and reels leaning against either side of the front door like guardsmen. We parked in the small gravel lot next to the cottage and carried our luggage inside. A cute old butch gal was behind a captains' desk talking on her cell, and she motioned for us to hang on.

"Sorry ladies," she said, when she hung up, "It was the missus."

"We have a reservation." Amanda said, retrieving the papers from her backpack.

"You two are our only guests - November is quiet as a mouse in off season. Here's the listing of winter hours for the shops, restaurants and the ferry," she said, handing Amanda a pink sheet of paper with a rainbow lobster hugging a goofy looking crab.

The proprietor's name was Henrietta, and she gave us the breakfast hours, then showed us to the "Siren Suite." "It's our nicest room," Henrietta told us, "and I think you'll enjoy the hot tub, there are bubbles in the cabinet."

There was a full entertainment setup, and even movies. Lots of lesbian flicks, obviously, but also the latest blockbusters, and cable. "Due to bad weather we like to keep DVD's incase the cable goes out," Henrietta explained. Big, cuddly, white bathrobes hung on the back of the bathroom door, and the bed was plush and firm at the same time. The bedspread was a gorgeous quilt with two mermaids holding each other.

"So lesbo-themed!" I chuckled, falling back onto the bed as soon as Henrietta was out of ear-shot.

Amanda laughed. Putting the luggage on the rack.

We decide to go for a stroll and do some window-shopping. There was a sexy adult toy store called Tickle Me Pink that looked like it would be fun to explore. When we walked in it, the store smelled of lavender candles and essential oils and had a weirdly cozy atmosphere for a sex shop. I was a little disappointed – when I go to a sex shop, I want the full-on tacky, triple-X experience. Teddy bears and lace really don't do it for me.

"How do you feel about strap-ons?" Amanda whispered.

"I have mixed feelings about them." I admitted. "They always seem to get in the way – but if you're into them, I won't stop you."

She was so nervous in the store. It was cute.

I bought some feathers, massage oil - the good stuff as opposed to upscale baby oil.

Usually, I bee-lined for the porn, but it didn't seem like I should bother with that. I had plenty of ideas about what to do with Amanda without outside input.

Amanda didn't let me see what she bought. It was fun getting to know one another. Being new we were getting more honest and less inhibited.

The girl behind the counter looked kind of stoned but seemed nice. Her head bobbed, and she kept brushing her long, razor-cut bangs out of her eyes. She wore heavy black eyeliner and reminded me quite a bit of Joan Jett. She was very informative and regaled us with the history of some toys and what they did, which cracked me up. This was her job, and she took her smut seriously!

"I remember ordering this kind of thing from Good Vibrations, back when I lived in Indiana." I said, pointing to one of the vibrators that was on sale. "My first vibrator was the Green Hornet. $30, and I thought that was way too expensive at the time. Little did I know the big price for a little kink!" I told our Joan Jett look-alike. Let me tell you, sex toys ain't cheap!

We had lunch at The Mariner, an upscale diner with lobster and chowder. It was exactly what we were looking for."

"When I first met you," Amanda confessed, "I thought you were going to be more pillow princess and less tiger."

I laughed. "Appearances are deceiving. One of my first girlfriends said two tops don't make a bottom – so I dumped her."

"Harsh." Amanda giggled.

"Not really," I explained. "I was just coming out, and I was upfront about not wanting to get involved in anything too intense. My first sexual experience with a woman was when I was twenty-three. She was a stone butch who made KD Lang look femme."

"Interesting." Amanda replied, warily.

"She was a bouncer at this dyke bar out in the Chicago suburbs. She'd been in jail - a really rough girl on the outside, but warm and slightly insecure on the inside. I did her wrong, and ended up feeling just awful. I was just so fucked up on Southern Comfort when we got together that

I hardly knew up from down, but it gave me the courage to really go to town on her. So we had a great tryst."

"You didn't call her back?" asked Amanda.

"No." I said, still ashamed after all this time. "Not for, like, six months. I had my roommate put her off. It was so immature and awful. Then I tried to get her interested again, but by then she was over me."

"I can't imagine you would've been happy with her long term."

"Probably not. But I had always looked at everyone I had dated and their resume…so to speak, for once I just wanted to be with someone I thought was sexy." I admitted. "She had vocal cord problems and could barely speak." I added.

"Perfect first time." sighed Amanda. "All sex, no conversation."

"*Hey*, what was yours like?" I asked.

"I was the one who got fucked over. I really loved this girl, we were in high school, she was a cheerleader. I should've known it would end badly." Amanda stirred the sugar into her tea with a bit too much focus.

"So you liked cheerleaders?" I asked, nervously.

"Well, she was very preppy and sexy as hell in this athletic-Farrah Faucett way. She pursued me like she had to have me." Amanda explained. "I mean, all she wanted to do was have sex, and I wanted to love her, but she had this wall up, you know? Then one day, she wrote me a note and said it was over. She would make eye contact with me when she was with her new boyfriend in this really longing way and it just tore me apart."

"Oh, man." I said sympathetically.

"It was bad enough when I saw her with the guy…but she didn't dump me for him…she moved on… Can you believe she dumped me for another cheerleader? Go figure." Now Amanda just shook her head, like a grown up…able to laugh all these years later. First loves, oye!

"What about the commune?" I asked. It seemed a pretty big jump from a cheerleader to a free-love commune. "I was so stoned and confused. Francine was around 40, and I was 17, but I'd lied and told her I was 18. We lived in this big old converted warehouse. It wasn't really sexy, there was just a lot of sex - it was the 70s, it was all about experiences and experimenting with everyone. We were more interested in escaping reality then dealing with it."

"I tried so hard with guys." I confessed. "But they just tore me up emotionally, and the sex was missing something. It felt unnatural."

"I've never heard it described like that, but yeah, that's exactly it." Amanda agreed. "I had some great times after I left the commune, traveling, painting, working at different universities, but it was lonely."

We stopped exchanging stories long enough for lunch, which was worth our full attention. Our food was fantastic, and we ate and shared more war stories.

"After I came out a few of my old friends asked if I ever thought of them 'that way' and I was emphatic, no, because for me my friends were like my family…"

"Lets hope you are not having *relations* with family," Amanda nodded.

Afterwards, there was nothing we wanted more than a long nap. The walk back to the bed-and-breakfast was just long enough to settle everything.

"I really want you to visit my hometown," I said, as we walked past the local school.

"Really?" Amanda asked skeptically.

"I had the best of times, and the worst of times there but Hohman made me who I am. There are really good people there, and my childhood friend Crystal still lives there. She and her husband have two adorable little boys. Her husband's a great guy, High School Principal in Gary, God bless him."

"Isn't Gary like, the murder capital of the world or something?" Amanda enquired. The sun was setting as we gazed into the harbor, now relatively quiet in these autumn months.

"I still don't get that, but I've heard that too. It's a heartbreaker, that city. If you drive around, you can see the vestiges of what was once a thriving city. There are old homes with beveled glass windows and beautiful architecture that people have just covered in graffiti and totally trashed." Amanda skipped a rock as we stood by the shore, it skidded over lumps of solid water floating like ice cube's in the bay. A shiver ran up my spine and Amanda reached over to rub my back. "Lets get going," she said.

As we walked back to the B&B, I noticed most of the stores were closed. I couldn't imagine how a business could afford to be entirely seasonal.

We watched a set of parents plop their toddler on a mechanical horse in front of a gift shop, and the conversation topic shifted to the parental.

"So your parents are divorced, and your dad and mom are both remarried?" Amanda asked.

"I was three when my parents split up, and Neil was a year old. My dad had primary custody, but I saw my mom every weekend. We lived with her for a while, in a sort of joint custody arrangement, and that was working out all right for us. Then she remarried, and her new husband wanted us out of the way. His suggestion was boarding school. My dad hit the roof and we went to live back with him again."

My mom was taking all these tranquilizers at the time, and wasn't in really good shape."

"Why didn't you stay with your dad in the first place?"

"He remarried right after the divorce - Irene liked us at first, but then that changed. She couldn't demand all of Dad's attention with us around, and we were a constant reminder that he'd been married before. Irene made things really difficult for him. Still does - for all of us."

"God," said Amanda, "that sounds pretty terrible."

"The thing is that when you're a kid, you don't know any better. However crazy your life is, you just accept it as normal. I didn't have to change schools, so from my perspective, it wasn't as awful as it could have been. Plus, when we came back to Dad's house as older kids, Irene was different. Not a whole lot better, but she tried. Mom and Irene just hated each other, and I got caught in the middle of that."

Amanda nodded, unlocking the door to the hotel room. I'd talked her ear off all the way back to where we were staying.

"Lauren helped a lot." I said. "She lived close enough that we saw each other often, we were the same age, and she was my best friend and confidant. She didn't care that I was this gawky nerd with learning disabilities, thick glasses, and even an eye-patch, for a while. I was her cousin and her friend and none of it mattered to her."

"Well, Lucy, the ugly duckling turned into a beautiful swan." Amanda said, putting her arms around my waist.

"Oh, I don't have any regrets." I said. "The anger I had about my parents and how Neil and I got shuffled around has dissipated. We all just do the best we can, you know? Parents are people and they make mistakes. Growing up in an environment like that made me strong, self-sufficient, and even spiritual."

I had blathered on far too long. Amanda just smiled an impish grin. "I hope I didn't over-talk." I said nervously. "I tend to do that."

"Not at all," said Amanda, "It's giving me real insight into you - I'd always figured you'd led a charmed life that you were a spoiled rich kid with a heart of gold."

"I was! HA! *But then I got a real life education*..." I said, "I just gave you the nuts and bolts. But I'd like to know more about you, too."

"It'll come," Amanda said.

We only had one night, so I hoped my incessant talking hadn't totally put a damper on the evening.

"I'm freezing." Amanda said putting a log in the fireplace. She lit it on the first try - her easy competence was one of the things I found so attractive about her.

We lay on the bed together and popped in a film. My choice, so it was The Hunger, one of my favorite sexy movies. We'd brought a bunch of tea lights and lit them as we settled in.

"God, I wanted to be both Catherine Deneuve and David Bowie." I said, snuggling into the crook of her arm. "Like you wanted to be Joel Gray and Liza Minnelli in Cabaret?" Amanda asked.

"Them too." I replied. We'd watched Cabaret a few nights before. "Yes, I'd like to be male and female - but I love looking like a girl." I giggled.

"Well, I feel like I'm in the mood for the woman in you tonight."

"Ohhh, I like the sound of that." I said.

We turned off the movie at the part where Bowie gets carried to Catherine's vault of coffins of ex-lovers.

Amanda and I were both lying on our sides facing each other, and her long hair was pulled back in a loose braid, "I could just look at you all day," I said quietly, as she pulled me closer.

She just smiled and slipped off the bed.

I undressed and added another log to the fire. There was a classical CD in the stereo, a trio playing something slow, maybe Debussy.

Amanda came back in a blue satin kimono, her hair down over her shoulders. I was lying with pillows propped up behind my head. She straddled me pulling my face to hers with a deep, long kiss - the kind of kiss that rolls you right out of time and space. The room was dark except for the fire, and her embrace surrounded me as the light outlined her body from behind.

Her fingertips massaged the front of my collarbone and her hair enveloped me like a cape as she hovered like an apparition from above. I was helpless under her weight... Reaching out for her, I slid my arms inside the robe to feel the curves of her back. I felt a little nervous, since she seemed so sure of herself. In the fire-lit darkness of the room, my neck and jawbone felt the power of her searching lips and deft hands as they wove endless caresses around me. Her raspy groans were like an aphrodisiac, and she followed the line of my body with her lips, using her hands as well; a metronome of firm, long strokes that sought refuge in the core of my body. My hands were in her hair, their corn silk tendrils weaving over my hands, a web I couldn't break. Her open robe covered my shivering body, and she moved like strong, sure animal. I tried to touch her, to pull her closer, but she arched away, untamed. Her hands stroked me, long and smooth, as I wrapped my legs around her. "I love feeling you beside me, Amanda....Oh, Amanda." I sighed, and my lips covered hers as we crushed our mouths together. She pulled me even closer with startling strength. Her rhythm was faster now, more urgent, in total harmony with me and I gripped the sheets, pushing myself to her. She tore the sheet, drawing me in, until our passionate duet ended in a white-hot sudden shudder of release. We were fever and fire as we collapsed in a speech-less embrace. The music had long since faded, replaced with the crackle of glowing embers, our breathing, and our heartbeats.

"Amanda," I said, "I love you." I was almost surprised to hear the words come out of my mouth.

"I loved you the moment I met you," she whispered next to my cheek.

Chapter 15

After the weekend away, things changed between Amanda and I. We became more of a couple – the change was unspoken, but it was there. Little things, like giving me a ride to work, repairing a loose step on the lodges porch, making sure the light on the porch was on when I came home late. In turn, I'd put a load of laundry in for her or make a casserole in microwavable portions for her late-night snacks.

Better yet, we were discovering that we both had pretty healthy boundaries. We called ahead before we stopped by each other's homes, and she didn't run out to say hello every time I walked Comby by the cabin.

In very little time, the perspective on my whole world had changed. The slower pace of Fossil Creek made my former urban life seem completely unreal. When I'd left Chicago, I was unable to see its romance because it was part of my daily landscape…but now as I worked on my book, I was reimaging the city I loved. These days, I walked around the main streets of Fossil Creek and could almost forget how tough the economic times were back home – but home is such a funny word, I had trouble really defining it as it applied to my life…I never felt safe enough to call any place home.

Big Bob, who'd spent some time in Chicago and the outlying suburbs, had one thing to say about the American economy. "It's time you entitled Americans started living like real people instead of pretending you're all Donald Trump because you've got a credit card," was how he put it. Big Bob's opinion was largely shared by the Canadians I had gotten to know, cutting hair…ya talk a lot. But they had their own share of issues. I couldn't help but wonder what they thought of me. Maybe I didn't want to know.

My dad had sent me an email that morning, "last call for Brussels, let me know."

I'd make the decision...tonight but for now it was time to scoot to work.

The windowpanes shook with each gale of wind, like nature's icy hands tossing wet sleet in angry pelts. I ran to my car, thankful I had chains on my tires. My travel mug was full of hot coffee, and I'd brought a copy of "Out of Africa" in my backpack, as well as my journal. I had a feeling clients would be canceling due to weather, and I wanted to be prepared.

Plugging my iPod into the car's stereo system, I selected "TV Themes of the 70s and 80s," and began my icy drive into town to the tune of Rockford Files, which always put a smile on my face. Before I could say "Charlie's Angels," I heard a dull thud and felt my car rock. Shifting into park and hopping out of the driver's seat, I ran around to the passenger side of the car.

There lay a dead goose. I felt terrible- I hadn't seen the little guy in the crap weather, and now he was mashed. Shaking my head in disgust, I ran back into the car for shelter, as the sleety snow was getting worse by the minute. Halfway to town I noticed a bad smell in the car. Why did the car smell like dogshit? I couldn't fathom where it was coming from – and then I parked and realized I had stepped in one of Comby's turds. This day was getting off to a rousing start.

Inside Hair Hut was total chaos. Instead of the bad weather blues, we were in full swing. Running back to the break room I changed my poopy boots to a pair of loafers I had stashed there and dumped my backpack in a nearby chair.

It was a week before Thanksgiving and festivities were in full swing.

Olga, the social center of Fossil Creek, had been in everyday for blow-dry and curling iron sets for all her holiday festivities. She was kicking off the Christmas season with Fête des lumières, and hers would be the first house in town to light candles in the windows, paying homage to the Virgin Mary. Olga and her daughters were having a bake-off, organized by their church, where they made almost a hundred Buche de Noël cakes to sell for a fundraiser. Then she'd be off to New York, visiting her her eldest daughter and son-in-law.

Olga's elaborate plans made me feel a little guilty about the fact that I still had no idea what my Christmas plans would entail. Bradley had mentioned coming to visit in passing, but I suspected that the charm of a small, cold, Canadian town in mid-winter wouldn't hold the same appeal as South Beach, which was his usual destination at this time of year.

I put Olga under the hooded dryer with her rollers and we chatted. While she'd started out as one of my most demanding clients, we'd reached a level of détente that was almost a friendship. Her father had been a diplomat, and her mother a noted psychologist. All other issues aside, Olga gave excellent advice and had some truly penetrating insights into other people. Of all the residents in Fossil Creek, she was probably the best person to give me advice on how to handle my current family drama. I told her about the pressure to attend the *Royal Wedding*, as I was calling it. "I'm in a quandary, Olga." I sighed. "My dad is set on me going to this event, but I really don't want to go, which he knows, but he booked me a room anyway."

"Why in God's name would you turn down a trip to Brussels?" Olga asked incredulously. Her pretty chiseled face gaped at me; her Bacall-blue eyes squinted in disapproval.

"I moved out here for a reason - to get away from the posturing, pretense and politics of city life. I feel comfortable here, I can just be me."

She smiled kindly at me, with a hint of vexation in her grin. "The previous part of your life is a part of who you are, and the more you run from it, the more it looms large in your mind. How often have you thought 'what if' or 'I'm not as good as'? You need to clear your mind move through the mist of your previous experiences and relationships so you can truly get on with your life. Enjoy the lavish event so you can enjoy the little blessings here more fully."

Shazam, she'd hit me with some of her real life jewels. "Thank you, Olga," I said, "that really helped." It had – I felt both relieved and inspired.

She nodded smugly at me. "Glad to be of service. If only other people appreciated me as much as you." She rolled her eyes meaningfully towards Sophie, the queen of the Diner. Sophie returned the eye-roll with a facial expression usually seen on people who've just changed a dirty diaper.

Fossil Creek might be a lot smaller than Brussels, but we didn't lack for drama.

The Hair Hut was so good for me. Working with hair kept me focused on others, it kept my creative juices flowing, and it helped people look and feel good.

Wild Jimmy, the town's crazy-man who had proclaimed he'd never step foot into "Beauty Parlor," ended up being one of my most regular clients since I had shaved his head. "Now, Lucy you have to keep the peach fuzz off," I nodded and book him in for every two weeks.

"He only had about six hairs left anyway." Pasha had joked when Jimmy finally let me cut off his scraggly ponytail and trim his beard.

Pasha had turned out to be a real pal, surprisingly. Ever since we had the "tutorial" where she showed me how to do roller sets and the old- fashioned updos that the town ladies wanted, we were all good. She just needed to be the big cheese, and I was perfectly happy being the baby Gouda. Pasha was also something of a magician with herbal concoctions, and had mixed me up a special Russian remedy for my aching hand. My right hand's index finger had really been bugging me, waking me up at night with throbbing pain. Pasha's mysterious mixture improved it immensely.

Candy turned out to be quite a little fashion princess. We did a class on a dull Wednesday for the teenagers and twenty-somethings in town, teaching them how to use their existing makeup in new ways. The chardonnay and soda flowed freely, and Candy was in her element, showing off all her tricks with eyeliner and foundation. I learned later that Candy was one of eight sisters, who'd all spent their teenage years practicing hair and makeup on one another. She blew everyone at that class away with her skills. It was great for business, and people lined up at the end of the evening to book haircuts and color.

Joelle was very pleased with me, as the class had been my idea.

Church Lady Marilyn had brought me all her friends. Even though my wash-and-set skills were still in the "junior stylist" zone, they came for the celeb gossip I could provide. God bless the Internet, and Bradley's chatty emails, which kept me up to date on who was sleeping with whom and who was cheating and who was pregnant. When I was a kid I read Vanity Fair, W, People and every gossipy mag I could find, because the stars were so dazzling. They knew artists, philosophers, great minds, writers, royalty living in exile; they traveled to exotic places, hopped from Kenya to Milan on a whim. Now it all seemed so cheap – reality TV and prepackaged fame had ruined the cult of celebrity for me, generating people who were only famous because they were famous. Yawn.

The snow/sleet onslaught wasn't subsiding at all and the roof of the Hair Hut sounded like someone was tap dancing with golf shoes by our chimney.

"What are you doing for Turkey Day?" Bob asked, during his monthly trim.

"Tippie invited me over." I replied. "That's real nice - is Amanda going to join you?"

Who says men don't gossip? Bob was just as bad as Olga, Sophie, or Marilyn.

"Yes, Bob." I confirmed. "Janis and Randy are going to make a turkey, Tippie and I are doing the potatoes, and Amanda's baking a couple of pies."

"Sounds peachy!" he said, and winked. I changed the subject.

The church ladies were all atwitter over Todd and me going to Montreal with the rest of the band for a meeting with K-Top. They were convinced that a meeting meant a recording contract, and that a recording contract automatically came with fame, fortune, and instant success. People watch too many *Behind the Music* documentaries on the 70's and 80's. In the 2000's things have radically changed. People don't buy CD's anymore so that revenue is gone, its about YouTube, packaging an artist to see stuff… the music can almost be secondary. But out with the old and in with the new can also mean new frontiers to forge…so it was the beginning of something new in the music business but nobody knew quite what that meant.

"Mary," I told one of them, as I curled her hair, "don't get so excited about this. Its not like Fleetwood Mac where millions accompany a record contract." It was pointless to try to put the brakes on her speculation, because she just went on and on about our inevitable fame.

"We're just going in to talk to K-Top. It's a meeting." I protested.

Mary, a widow with a lot of time on her hands, frowned. "Don't downplay the blessings of God, young lady, this is a great opportunity! Not just for you, either. This could give Todd a very nice nest egg, so that he can marry his young lady."

Everyone knew everything in this town, I thought to myself, shaking my head in awe.

"You're right." I said, and sent her to the dryer to let her grey locks get their curl back.

She was right. If the K-Top meeting went well, if we got a contract and recorded an album, it wouldn't just be good for me. It would be good for all the members in the band, most of whom could really use a little extra cash. I had a day job – most of them were still living at home.

It wasn't about just about money for me…it was about being a professional. I was so sick of the years of repeating the same old hope and dreams…I was getting too old to play the hopeful artiste…I was starting to look delusional! Todd wanted the security and status that came with being a proper musician. I wondered if I'd be up to the task if we got the chance.

That night I emailed my dad and said yes to Brussel's and said yes to my future. *Get out of your head and into your life Lucy*! I said to no one but the dog. If he had a tail he would've wagged it.

Thanksgiving went really well, other than Tippie burning her hand on the stove rack. We all enjoyed a great meal, and a hot game of Balderdash. As we hugged everyone good-bye and made our way to the sleigh, we noticed Tao acting skittish. I thought he was just happy to see us, until we threw off the blanket and a raccoon popped out, hissed at us, and ran into the woods. We screamed like the girls we were, and then settled into the sleigh for our magical ride beneath the stars…home.

One hot topic over dinner was the fact that I'd ordered a dress for the wedding. Olga's words of wisdom had convinced me to just go with my dad's plans and not worry about it. The dress was a lovely second-hand Carol Henny Ascot, a designer I'd always loved for the class and style of her clothes – plus the ability of her dresses take off about ten pounds. Even "vintage," the dress strained my budget. But if I was going to this wedding, I was going to do it right.

The wedding was December fifteenth, and if the band got a contract, I'd have something to brag about. Still, I didn't hold out a huge amount of hope. I prayed my dad hadn't said anything to anyone.

The Monday after Thanksgiving, I went to go get my mail at the post office and my dress had arrived from Chicago! It was in a huge box I had to sign for and I eagerly scurried back to my car to get home and bedazzle Amanda.

"Amanda," I said, rushing into the Lodge kitchen, where she was making dinner, "I'm going to try on this dress and you tell me honestly what you think, I can always send it back." I hadn't even taken off my coat, and my face was still cold from the wind outside.

I went into the bedroom to change while she worked on the pot of soup simmering in the kitchen, and then I called her out into the living room to deliver a verdict on my dress. "Okay…." I said, and did my best supermodel stroll in front of the fireplace. Amanda grinned at me lasciviously.

"You're going to knock them dead, Miss Lucy." she growled.

"I'd wanted something more flamboyant, but the store owner said this was my dress and refused to send anything else." I explained, the dress shops owner was a former client of mine from Chicago. Nothing like buying clothes from people who have definite opinions on what you ought to be wearing.

"Love the buttons that go all the way down the décolletage. And I've always found black velvet very mysterious," she said, staring at me intensely. "Very John Sargent, Madame X... You're going to have to be careful to not get seduced away from me by some filthy rich European."

"Oh, please." I said. "I'm going to be so out of my element that it's not even funny. All the hoopla and Neil isn't going, and then I have to deal with Irene." I sighed, already annoyed, "I'm staying away from her talons if possible." I stroked the long black lace sleeves, adjusting the little black, gold, and pearl buttons.

Maybe this would be a good dress to perform in at a special event in the future. A dress that could serve more than one purpose would go pretty far in justifying the bill at the bottom of the box.

"I have a feeling you'll be just fine." Amanda reassured me. I nodded, unconvinced, and retreated to my room. The dress went back on a hanger, and I and changed back into my usual jeans and added a sweater with Day-Glo lettering that announced "ROCK THE MULLET." It was obnoxious and I loved it – the sweater was the only thing I'd ever knitted successfully, and I ignored the fact that one sleeve was considerably longer than the other.

The soup was full of veggies from Amanda's cellar, and she'd used my frozen chicken and turkey for the base. "How does it taste?" Amanda asked, buttering her crusty bread.

"It's super fowl!" I responded enthusiastically. She looked at me, obviously shocked.

"You know what I mean - F.O.W.L, because of the two bird mix!"

Then she laughed, and we started chatting about town gossip.

The sound of my cell phone ringing interrupted dinner, which meant I had to leave the table to go hunt it down. By the time I located it, the call had been switched to voicemail. The Caller ID showed that it was my brother, calling from his home in Hawaii, and I tried to call him back. Naturally, my call went straight into his voicemail. "Tag," I said, "you're it!" I told him.

When I returned to the kitchen to finish my soup, Amanda scooped us out some ice cream and asked "Ever thought of living in Hawaii?"

"I thought about it." I said. I could tell that surprised her. "I wanted to be around my brother," I explained, "we have a great time together, he's funny.

Plus, he's got great perspectives when I've got a problem or an issue. Realistically, though, I wouldn't want to do 365 days a year on an island the size of Chicago. It's a very mellow and slow-paced out there, especially out in the remote areas, which is where my brother lives. But vacationing and living there are two different things." I took another bite of my butter-pecan.

I kept explaining. "It's been a while since I last considered moving to Hawaii, and now that the internet connects everything, it could be a cool retirement option."

"So," Amanda responded, "I guess Hawaii is more of a possibility than I'd thought."

"It would take record contracts, books getting published...a lot of miracles."

"Would you take me with you?" Amanda asked, almost shyly. I reached over and hugged her. "I think that could be arranged." I said, stroking her beautiful hair.

It turned out that Neil had called to fill me in with the actual, true details of the wedding I'd be attending. Irene was prone to embellishment, Dad tended to play things down, and between them, it was easy to get a totally inaccurate picture of a situation.

Nancy was marrying into a family connected to nobility – but the groom-to-be had to work, even though he had a title. He wasn't landed gentry. She wasn't getting married in Brussels, either – the wedding would be in Chimay, a city about 45 minutes outside of Brussels, known for its Trappist beer. "I'm so pissed I can't come," my brother griped, "but my sister-in-law is coming that whole week and we can't ask her to reschedule." He told me that the cool thing was that the actual wedding was taking place at the Castle of Chimay, which hosts an annual music festival. My brother, who's almost as big of a music fan as I am, was really enthusiastic about the castle. "They have this big kick ass Rococo-style theater, *impressive as hell*. You should look it up online. It's where the ceremony is actually taking place – pretty kickass for Nancy. You're lucky to be able to go." Neil told me. I was lucky, come to think of it. Why had I ever not wanted to go on this trip?

After Neil's message, I was really geared up to go.

Amanda dropped me off at the airport with a kiss. As I exited the car it occurred to me how much louder things in the city are compared to Fossil Creek. People running around catching flights and loud speakers going off in French and English, were almost dizzy making. I was becoming used to the more laid back ways of small town life.

I discovered at the airport that my dad had booked me on the cheapest flight possible. I spent the trip to Belgium crammed in the back of a double decker plane next to a sleeping guy who kept drooling on my shoulder and a little girl who kept running up and down the aisles.

I was almost relieved to get off the plane and immediately board the bus that would take us to Chimay. Amanda had stocked up my carry-on bag with travel food – granola bars, peanut M&Ms, dried fruit – so I slept in between snacks on the plane, and the bus, and arrived in Chimay feeling pretty rested, despite the jet lag.

My dad had arranged for a cab to pick me up, once I got off the bus. The young cab driver chatted merrily about all the merits of his beautiful country as we drove down winding cobblestone streets, where Christmas markets were gearing up for the impending holidays.

The world's finest chocolate was calling to me from each boutique and stand! Dad had booked us rooms at the Abbey du Gris. The resplendent old fortress was built in 1863 and reminded me delightfully of a set for a black and white horror movie, the ones where everyone is supposed to be asleep and sneak around dressed in their robes and someone always ends up murdered. Tapestries hung on the walls, coats of arms and thick draperies decorated the long winding halls, and there were working fireplaces in each of our rooms. My bed even had a canopy. The only drawback was that my room was located right next door to Irene and my dad.

Irene was getting the full spa treatment when I arrived, so Dad and I went out to explore. If I wasn't feeling the Christmas spirit before, I sure was after walking around Chimay. Europeans know how to do Noël! The light snow falling enhanced the holiday atmosphere, and when Dad and I stopped at a coffee house, the desserts could have put a diabetic into a coma. I've met friendlier people than the people in Chimay, but no one was nasty, just a little more reserved than outgoing Americans.

After the cafe, we browsed the shops. I bought some perfume, and Dad found a beer stein that was a foot tall featuring little Red Riding Hood being chased by a wolf. "Your brother is going to love this!" my dad proclaimed loudly. A man nearby observed, "That's not Belgian, it's German," he sniffed. My dad just winked at him and took the stein to the register.

After we left the store, Dad whispered, "Don't let the turkeys get you down".

That was some serious foreshadowing into the rest of our evening. Dad insisted on one last stop before going back to the Abbey - the jewelry store, to look for a gift for Irene. In the store, I came face to face with the most gorgeous ring that I'd ever seen. It was perfect for Amanda. I made the decision to leave the ring where it was; it was too soon to start thinking about rings.

As we made our way back to the hotel, a man walked by with a cello case. "I was really hoping you'd find out about that music contact by now." Dad commented.

"I know." I said in agreement, "It would have been great to know."

Dad was so excited about the night's events that I had the feeling he and Irene weren't getting out much anymore. He started a rapid-fire monologue at me on the topic of the wedding – the money spent, the guest list, the press coverage, the venue, the food, and the flowers. This was a society wedding, and although my parents could be some big spenders...this was far more expensive and upscale than anything we'd ever experienced. I think Dad was nervous. At home in Hohman, he was a fairly big fish in a small pond, but here, he was just another old American guy.

We eventually made our way back to our respective hotel rooms. "I'm going to take a little nap before dinner, honey," my dad said, getting out his room key. "Meet us out in the hall in about two hours."

"Sounds good." I said, and gave him a big bear hug. "Thanks for talking me into this trip, Dad. I'll never forget it." Before I took a nap myself, I wanted another cup of coffee. I followed my nose to the end of the hall. After listening at the door and hearing someone laugh inside, I knocked.

A woman who looked to be about my age answered the door, and I explained my search for a before-bed cup of coffee. She invited me into the little sitting room-kitchen that the housekeepers used, and said "My English is very good!" proudly. Another woman was there, supervising an industrial grade coffeemaker. I gratefully accepted a cup of coffee from an already-brewed pot, and she indicated that the new pot was for the woman in the room next to mine. Ah. Irene wanted coffee, apparently.

"I'll warn you ahead of time." I said. "That woman? She's difficult."

"We know." said the girl who'd answered the door, and the other woman nodded. Apparently, Irene had already made a name for herself with the hotel staff. I wasn't surprised.

Stopping into the service room on my floor was the best idea I'd had all night. I got the entire scoop on Nancy's groom Bernard from the Abbey employees – essentially, the big money in his family had dried up long ago, but guys like Bernard are never really poor. He was the descendant of some Flemish aristocrats named Bonnaert, had some nice real estate assets, a lot of powerful friends, and a collection of priceless art. He owned a company, too, but the housekeepers couldn't tell me exactly what he did.

They did know that one of his best friends owned Fiat, the car company. From what I'd read about the Fiat stud, he was a party-hearty guy, with above average looks and a decent head for business.

The girls had to get Irene's late afternoon treat to her, so I took another cup of the perfectly delicious coffee and went back to my room for a nap. The jet lag was catching up with me, and I had to be at least conscious enough to get on the dress and make it down to the lobby for the ride to the wedding. I fell asleep as soon as my head hit the pillow, and woke up feeling totally refreshed. Maybe a delayed reaction to the two cups of amazing coffee, or maybe the Belgian air, or the perfectly beautiful surroundings, but I felt pretty terrific. I felt even better when I got dressed and surveyed myself in a full-length mirror. My former client had been right – this dress was everything I wanted.

A black Mercedes limo picked us up – me, Dad, Irene, and Anita and her husband. Anita was an old neighbor from Hohman, a buxom brunette who was a dead ringer for Catherine-Zeta Jones. She was known for her positive, chatty nature and her husband was equally good looking in that J. Crew-All-American type way.

"I'm really glad you're here," I told Anita, as we got into the car. "I don't know a soul other than Nancy and you!"

"Can you believe Nancy?" Anita enthused. "My God, she's done well for herself! Who would have thought?"

Anita's husband was playing the tall, dark and bored role. He didn't even attempt to interact with anyone else – just stared out the window and kept adjusting his cufflinks. "So!" said Anita cheerfully. "You're not married?"

There was a pause. I had lied so many times, made excuses at my parent's Christmas parties, been evasive around strangers, tiptoed around the topic with clients, and I just wasn't in the mood to pretend. Wasn't I a little old to be worried about what my parents would say?

"They don't allow my kind of marriage in the States…but they're working on it." I chuckled.

This got Anita's husband attention and Irene's as well. "Oh, my God!" Irene squealed.

I ignored her. "What do you mean?" Anita questioned, cluelessly.

"My partner – my significant other – she's back in Canada. She wasn't able to attend." I said. Irene squawked wordlessly, her jewelry jingling like a broken glass slipper.

The car went silent for a minute, broken only by a soft snicker from the driver. Anita began to babble about all the gays she knew, and her husband was eyeing me in an unsettling way. Usually, when a guy looks at me like that, he's wondering if he can convince his wife to try a threesome.

My dad said nothing, and Irene huffed and puffed. It was quite a way to get the evening rolling.

It was a short ride to the castle, which was a blessing, and we got out of the car and gasped. The castle was beautiful. Inside, the hall was incredible, reminding me of an ornate stone and marble cathedral. We were guided to our seats, and the ceremony began. It went on forever, and it wasn't in English, so there wasn't much for me to do but admire the architecture and the gowns on the guests.

The sparkling candles lit up the place like Notre Dame Cathedral and I was blown away by the beauty of it all. Everything is so new in America, compared with these castles built in the 1600s, a constant reminder of tradition and history. It's grounding for the Europeans, a reminder of their past and where they came from. In the US, we tear down and rebuild constantly, never allowing any sense of permanence.

Nancy looked amazing in a hand-embroidered lace dress, which wasn't surprising, given that Brussels lace is so famous. It had long sleeves and a high neck, with a train that seemed a mile long. Her veil that sparkled like it had been sprinkled with diamond dust, and the tiara would have been the envy of any princess.

Just as I snapped a picture, I noticed a goofy- looking guy waving to me. I groaned internally. It was Nancy's brother Mitch, who we'd nick-named in high school 'King of the Boners.' He shot me a thumbs up, and I didn't know whether to feel complimented or grossed out. There were way too many teenage hand jobs that I didn't need to recall. Seeing him made me recall the girl I'd been back then, young and naive, a romantic - who would've thought I needed to live all this life to get here?

Finally, after the ceremony half the ordeal was over, and we exited the castle to a flurry of flashbulbs and rice, the European paparazzi and all the guests like thoroughbreds heaving through the gates of Balmoral.

The reception was at the American embassy. The colors were white, silver, and gold, and the reception was absolutely sumptuous – elaborate cages full of doves, ice sculptures, and champagne all around. I was lucky to encounter a kind waiter who took pity on me and got me a glass of Pellegrino.

As usual, Irene and Dad had taken off, leaving me to fend for myself in a crowd of strangers. I mingled as best I could, and put on my game face.

Those years of reading Town and Country turned out to not have been wasted after all, as I was able to hold my own with the Toledos, a famous artist/designer couple. Julie Andrews, of all people, was standing next to me at one point, and I managed to not make too much of an idiot out of myself gushing over her oeuvre. She was gracious and friendly, and turned out to know Bernard's family from work they'd done for the American Cancer Association. I tried not to act too dazzled by meeting her, but I'm not sure I managed to pull off nonchalant.

Besides internationally famous stars of stage and screen, there were plenty of less immediately recognizable people, members of the society elite. While I was busy trying to find someone I knew, a lovely older woman tapped me on the shoulder. I turned around and she smiled at me. "Love your dress," she complimented me, and I realized with a shock that this was Carol Henny Ascot – the woman who'd designed my dress.

"A real artist designed it." I said, trying my best to be charming.

She took my arm and we were off into the crowd. "The bride is an old friend." I mentioned, before she could ask. "How lovely!" she said. "I designed her dress – such a sweet girl, such fun to work with."

"I thought the dress was very Grace Kelly." Ms. Ascot clapped her hands with glee. "That was our main inspiration!" she said, taking my arm again. For some reason, I was saying all the right things to this lady, and I was grateful the Universe had decided to provide me with someone to talk to at this thing.

Irene, my dad, Anita, and her dud of a husband had completely vanished. I had a choice between hanging out with Carol, who seemed taken with me, or go find Mitch, who'd probably be hoping for some action just for old time's sake. I was going to stick with Carol.

"Let's go somewhere with a little less noise, shall we?" said Carol, and I agreed. The hall was gorgeous, but the volume was incredible. She led the way to a darling little sitting room with a huge fireplace and lovely brocade sofas. Books lined the walls on either side of the hearth, from floor to ceiling, and astonishing art decorated the walls.

"You have no idea how stressful this all is for me." I admitted, while we walked up to a bar that had been set up in the corner.

"What will you have?" Carol asked. "Pellegrino? Something nonalcoholic."

"Ah." she said, and nodded. She fixed our drinks in two crystal tumblers and sat down close to me on an overstuffed sofa. "So," she said, "where are you located now? I'm assuming not Indiana – that's where Nancy said she grew up."

I loved the way Carol said Indiana; it sounded like some kind of languid tropical escape.

"It's not the big city – I went from small town to smaller town. Ever heard of Fossil Creek?"

"Where in God's name is that?" Carol asked. "The closet city you'd know is Montreal." I said.

"Great furs there." Carol commented, "But I've spent more time in Toronto." She touched my arm, sliding down to my hand and taking it firmly. "I was like you once, just a babe in the woods. I'm from a small town in Spain originally."

"Oh." I said stupidly. "That's where your accent comes from."

"You like it?" she asked coquettishly.

This was...uncomfortable. I was starting to feel less like I'd made a friend, and more like I was the target of an attempt at seduction "Um."I said intelligently. "It's lovely."

That, apparently, was the cue, and she pounced on me. She was a hell of a kisser, but I pulled away as swiftly as I could without actually throwing her off and running away. "I have someone at home." I said, not really regretfully.

"Well," said Carol, smirking, "I do too. But they're not here, and we are." I stood up and tried to get out of the situation gracefully.

"I suppose that gaydar thing really does work!" I said humorously.

"I'm not gay, darling." Carol said flirtatiously. "I'm married to a man."

I didn't know what to say. A stunning, glamorous woman who'd pursued me, pulled me into an out-of-the-way spot, and attempted to seduce me, and I was turning her down flat. WHY HADN'T THIS EVER HAPPENED WHEN I WAS SINGLE?

I should have just walked away, walked right out of this overly-opulent room and back into the noise and fuss of the wedding reception, but I was still standing there. Partially because I couldn't believe this was actually happening to me – it was like Elvis putting his hand on your leg, if you were a straight girl thirty years ago. It was a BIG DEAL.

Carol took my lack of movement as encouragement, and stood up to kiss me again. "I know you like it," she whispered, looking into my eyes with that promised an unbelievable experience, for one night.

"It's not that I don't like kissing you, it's that I don't cheat." I tried to explain. Carol cackled and threw her head back, laughing. "How very plebeian, how Midwestern, you're such a good little girl, aren't you?" she mocked. This was now officially weird, and I was more freaked out than turned on.

"You're going to turn this down? Turn me down? This must be why you live in a place called Fossil Creek," said Carol haughtily.

I looked at her silently, annoyed. I didn't need any of it – not the fancy hotel, not the limo, not the gorgeous wedding, the designer dresses, the embassy reception, none of it, because it came with too many jerks like Carol.

This was the kind of event my parents dreamed of, because they played this game. I'd spent most of my adolescence desperately trying to be popular, famous, beautiful, and knowing that I'd never make it because it wasn't who I really was. I didn't want to be a stereotype, or a plus-one if I could ever be a star it would have to be on my own terms.

This was a game I had no interest in playing, because there was nothing for me to win that I actually wanted. What I hadn't understood in high school was that eventually, I'd be really glad that I never managed to reach my goal of becoming one of the glitterati. I was Lucy Zwich, reader of underground comics, singer and writer and hair stylist, I had cool friends, and I loved my family. I had a girlfriend who took my breath away, and I didn't cheat.

"You're really hot, but no matter how plebeian you think this is, I've got to live with myself after the party's over." I explained moving myself toward the door.

"That's all really sweet, but complete bullshit," she said, with a new, slightly threatening quality to her voice.

I turned the doorknob and left - out the door, down the hall I flew into another hall, and another hall, finally making my way out of the maze of the embassy. I felt bad that I hadn't had a chance to say congratulations to Nancy or sit down to dinner... but it's not like she'd even have noticed. This was her scene, and more power to her, she saw me taking her picture, I rationalized.

The limo driver waiting outside looked surprised to see me, but took me back to the hotel with no questions asked. I explained to him that the rest of my party was still there, and he shot me a knowing look.

Back at the hotel, I ordered room service and checked the front desk for messages, but Amanda hadn't called. My cell phone wasn't getting any reception, and so I walked sullenly back up to my big, beautiful room and tried to call Amanda from the landline. No answer. She should have been home – it was morning in Fossil Creek. In this big, gothic space, the desktop computer looked extremely out of place, but I found myself very grateful for modern technology. I paid the nominal fee for Internet access with my debit card, and wrote Amanda a quick email. If she was working, she might have turned off the phone, but she'd be online. I waited, pacing the room, stressed out. An hour later, there'd been no reply to my phone message or my email to Amanda, so I called Lauren.

Her voice was like a tonic. She knew what Dad and Irene were like, and completely understood my situation. "You really said that in the limo?" Lauren gasped admiringly.

"I did." I said. "Now let me tell you the best part – but you have to swear on your child's head you won't tell a soul."

"Swear, swear, swear!" Lauren loved a scoop. "Do you know who Carol Henny Ascot is?" I asked.

"Yes, the designer. I have one of her suits," she answered, confused.

"She was at the wedding reception, and she totally made a move on me." I squealed like a teenager.

Lauren started coughing violently. "I think I just got coffee up my nose!" she gasped. I waited for her to recover.

"Holy shit!" Lauren finally said. "She's a lesbian?"

"She said she's married to a man, which means she's not a lesbian or some shit, but let me tell you – the way she kissed me said otherwise. I think she was looking for a good time and didn't really care about who it was with."

"Was she a good kisser?" Lauren asked. She always was nosy, but I didn't mind.

"Hello!" I said sarcastically. "Yes! But I put a stop to it – I can't do that to Amanda."

"What did she say when you stopped her?"

"She wasn't very nice. Said it was 'bull-sheet,' or at least that's how it sounds when she says it."

"Wow." said Lauren. "A famous designer hits on you, and you don't go for it – she wasn't hot?"

"I'm with Amanda!" I said exasperated.

"I know, I know, it's just...she's Carol-Fucking-Ascot."

"Believe me, I am well aware of who she is. I could've rocked her world or she mine and maybe it would have helped my music or writing career, since she knows everyone who's anyone, but if that's the way I have to make it, then I guess I won't!" I said, disgusted. "This is why I hadn't wanted to come to this wedding, it put my integrity to the test."

"Then I think you survived...and I can't even tell Bill," pouted Lauren. I knew she would tell her husband the minute she got off the phone with me, and that he wouldn't care about it at all. I had to tell her "NO! NO ONE!" to drive the point home.

"Okay, okay," Lauren sighed, "You know I can keep a secret. But this is JUICY."

"I really wish you were here." I said feeling overwhelmed.

"When are you meeting back up with the folks?" Lauren asked.

"Breakfast," I said, "but I'll bet you twenty bucks that Irene won't be speaking to me."

"Imagine if she knew about the Carol stuff." Lauren said.

"She'd be drooling. Irene would be thrilled to have a lesbian step-daughter if her lover was someone famous."

"I know." I sighed, "And you know what's sad? I actually considered letting the Carol thing go on because it would make Irene and Dad so excited to have me hook up with someone like that. Even now, I want their approval."

"You've always just wanted Irene to love you." Lauren told me.

"But she doesn't love anyone." Not even herself, I thought sadly.

We talked a little about some drama she was having at the hospital, and when we ended the conversation, I felt a lot better. Lauren saved the day. Again.

My room service was delish but I went to bed with no call or email from Amanda, and woke up to no reply from her, either. It hurt more than I thought it would. Thankfully, the next morning Irene had a headache from too much champagne, so it was just Dad and I for breakfast. He wasn't at all pleased about my coming out so casually to Anita.

"You know she's going to be on the phone with everyone from your high school graduating class." he grumbled at me.

"Dad," I said patiently, "so what?"

"We have to live in Hohman. These people are our friends and neighbors," he said gravely.

"About half my graduating class is gay." I said, and ran down the list of names, taking a perverse thrill in the stunned look on my dad's face. For all of Irene's love of gossip and her social-climbing ways, there was a lot she didn't know about Hohman.

"I don't want to fight," Dad sighed, and took a gigantic bite of crepe. We ate, and chatted about the wedding. My dad could be just as gossipy as any hairdresser, given the right opportunity.

"That groom may be from some kind of famously influential family, but let me tell you, I think there's been some inbreeding going on there," he said, and I giggled. He was right – Bernard was not exactly a looker. I kept thinking of that 30 Rock episode with the Baron, played by Pee Wee Herman, who looked like a broken tuxedoed marionette.

Nancy got the wedding of her childhood dreams, and the Robin Leach lifestyle, but George Clooney he wasn't.

Our tired-looking waiter exited with Dad's credit card while we hugged. "You go get that ring you were ogling at the store, and call me when you make it back to the frozen tundra." We bear-hugged one more time, and I watched him walk away. He looked lonely. An hour and a half later, I was on a plane to Montreal, full of mixed feelings.

I was dead tired by the time the cab dropped me off. The front porch light was not on, and inside the lodge was very chilly; thankfully, Comby was curled up by the dying fire, trying to stay warm. There was a message from Ned on my voicemail saying the heat should be back on by tomorrow, but that he had to pick up a part that had been back-ordered. At least someone was keeping an eye on the place – one of the benefits of a small town.

I desperately wanted to run over to Amanda's and see what the heck was going on! When I stepped outside to make my way to her cabin, I saw an unfamiliar Jeep parked next to her house. Weird – Amanda wasn't much for visitors. Maybe something to do with her job? I didn't want to be nosy, but I also didn't want to interrupt anything, so I peered in the window carefully. Much to my shock, there was Carey, asleep on the bed.

It felt like a kick in the gut. I'd turned down Carol Henny Ascot, and Amanda was back here screwing around with her ex. Without really knowing even what to think, I went back to the lodge and almost ran to my room. I just wanted to scream. I flipped on the light and almost shrieked – Amanda was lying in my bed, snoring soundly. I'd been doing pretty well with controlling myself up to that point, but I just lost it.

"What the HELL is going on here?" I said, angrily, almost frothing at the mouth from rage. Amanda shot up in bed like I'd just doused her with cold water.

"Welcome home!" she said, almost cheerfully.

Getting to the point I asked, "Why is your ex-girlfriend in your bed?"

"I take it that you didn't notice that I'm here, in your bed." Amanda pointed out.

"I was only gone three days – and I come back to your ex in your bed? I don't believe this shit!" I fumed.

"You need to calm down." Amanda said firmly. She got up from the bed and walked over to me. "You had a bad trip?" she sighed.

"Let's see – yes, and no. You really want to hear the laundry list of what went okay and what was royally fucked up? *Then go open your email*, or were you too busy? And you were also too busy to call me back? How the hell am I supposed to feel like I can count on you," I huffed, "I need to walk the dog," I cut off my tirade, and turned around and left the room.

"The dog has been walked," she said, following me down the hall.

"I'm always screwing myself." I muttered, making my way to the kitchen for a cup of Pasha's special herbal "Nite- Nite" tea.

"What are you talking about?" Amanda asked.

"What's going on?" I replied, trying to calm down, filling the kettle.

"Carey came back. She's all full of regret for the way she acted, but it's too little and way too late. I told her so. We've had rolling power blackouts due to the snow, so I wasn't able to call and the computer wasn't work-ing. Internet has been down, too. I've been running the propane heaters in here. Did you notice how it's not completely freezing?"

"Oh." I said. "So, what, Carey just stays with you until she finds some-where to go?"

"No." Amanda replied. "She's leaving tomorrow night, going to live with her sister on Prince Edward Island."

The tea kettle was starting to whistle. I sighed, shaking my head and feeling as if I was suffering from what director John Waters' has called "assholism."

"The trip was...dramatic." I told Amanda, while making my tea. "I saw this girl from my home town, came out to her in a limo, and this rich, well-connected supposedly straight woman hit on me like you wouldn't believe." I told Amanda the whole story. "Beyond the intrigue," I told her, "it was an enchanting village. I wish you could've been there with me."

"It sounds like you got some soul resolution, so aren't you glad you went?" Amanda asked.

"Yes." I said sheepishly. I was, too. I was glad I'd gone, even with all the weirdness and tension.

"What a way to come out!" Amanda said, laughing. We made our way out to the living room and she put a log on the fire and stoked it up. "Yeah." I said, sipping my tea, Comby warming my feet. We sat on the rug by the fire, and I let the flames welcoming heat roll over my cold face. Amanda put her arm around me. "Honey, when I said I loved you, I meant it. I'm not messing this up for myself. I'm too damn old to play the field."

"You're only in your forties." I pointed out.

"And there's not much of a field in Fossil Creek." We laughed together, and decided it was too cold for the front room.

Amanda slept over and we huddled for warmth in the cocoon of my bed. I relaxed in her strong, tender arms. This was better than any palace with a famous lesbian designer - I wasn't a one nighter-type of girl and never had been.

A sound awoke me. The clock told me it was five in the morning, but I could hear movement outside my window. This early rising was for the birds, not for humans. Amanda was still sound asleep, looking so graceful and peaceful that I stroked her cheek. She smiled in her sleep, rolling over with a little groan.

I threw on the fur coat I'd found in the storage room, since it was the warmest thing I owned, and shoved my feet into the waterproof winter boots.

Coffee, I decided, was the next step. Amanda already had the pot set up, so I hit the button and watched the coffee brew. Thank God for back up generators. I really felt like writing, so maybe I'd go do that today. Only after walking Comby, though, who was frisking around my feet and clearly desperate to go outside.

Outside, the chill was brutal. We took a quick walk over to the barn and while Comby did his business, I popped my head in to check on Tao. *Carey was there* petting him and I felt like my territory had been slightly violated.

"Hello," I said, smiling and faking friendliness.

"Oh, hi!" Carey said. "Is this your horse? He's really pretty."

"Sure is. He's a good old guy."

We started with the small talk and being the sucker that I am, I invited Carey in for coffee. She turned out to be a fontain of never-ending Amanda information. I couldn't figure out if she was trying to make me jealous or just inform me, or maybe a little of both.

We were in the Great Room, facing the impending dawn on the lake. The fire was still going, but I added a few logs to try to raise the temperature in the room. "She's really different now." Carey said wistfully. "Whatever you guys have together, it's really warmed her up."

"I'll take that as a compliment."

"You know she used to be a real player, had a lot of girlfriends. Most of them short-term, till she met me."

Jab. Ouch.

"I was an idiot to run off with Christopher." Carey sighed. "But what can I say? I've never had good judgment."

"So you came back to reignite things?" I asked, trying not to sound threatened. She shifted uncomfortably in the armchair, sipping the coffee I'd made.

"Um. Yeah. I have to admit that I thought you might just be one of her flings, so she'd be willing to...you know."

"Is she a cheater?" I asked. No way around it, I was invading Amanda's privacy, but how could I not? Her ex was drinking coffee in my living room.

"I don't really know if you'd call it that. We had a sort of open relationship where we didn't ask and didn't tell."

"That never worked for me." I said.

"You're really pretty." Carey said, looking at me.

"I'd hoped you'd be a dog, honestly." She smiled weakly, looking down at the floor as tucked her blond straight hair behind her tiny ear...I realized who she looked like…to my chagrin…my dad's ideal beauty, Sybil Shepherd.

"I guess that's sort of a compliment."

"Yeah. Well, Amanda likes them young and pretty, what can I say. How old are you – late twenties?"

I laughed. "More like thirty-something, coming up on forty." I said. And all this time, I'd thought Amanda was some stoic hermit. I looked at Carey critically. "So do I have something to be concerned about, with her and monogamy?" I asked. She snorted, "I guess not," she said, looking put out and annoyed. "Honestly, I really tried to sway her, and she wouldn't budge. I even did the down-on-the-knees thing she likes. Nothing."

Fascinating. I wanted to know more, but I felt like Pandora's Box was opening just a little too much. I just nodded to Carey and gave up on the third degree. I'd found out what I'd needed to know, anyway.

Amanda appeared in the room with no warning. "Morning." she said, and immediately sat on the arm of my chair. Which made me feel better than a thousand stories from Carey about how firmly she'd been turned down.

The three of us talked for a little while longer, but I could tell Amanda really wanted Carey out of there. Carey could tell too, I guess, because after a few polite exchanges, she said, "I'm going to go finish packing," and left the room. Not without a certain sexy swagger to her walk, though.

"I saw that," she whispered in my ear. "Her sashay?"

"No, you and your eye-rolling." Amanda said.

Carey left not long after and I hoped that was the last of her.

Amanda surprised me by being willing to come with Ned and me to see Greta. I'd finally decided to drop the bomb and see if Greta had any memory of giving birth to a baby – it didn't seem likely that such a major life event could be lost completely, but traumatic brain injuries were tricky.

When we got in to see her, Greta was sitting in the solarium in her wheelchair, facing the snow covered pine trees. Her gray curls hung loosely around her face and her eyes looked tired.

"Hi Greta," I said cheerfully. "Remember me?" She nodded, and said "Nice niece." I gave her the box of the chocolates she loved so much and we made small talk. I could tell she was lost.

"Do you remember Tavis?" I asked.

"He's dead." Greta said sadly.

"Yes, he is. Do you remember Gibbon?"

She frowned. "No." she said firmly. But her eyes became alert. I had the feeling she did remember my dad.

"Greta, do you remember having a baby?" She frowned again, and this time a shadow came over her face. She didn't answer. I didn't know what to do. This clearly wasn't something Greta wanted to talk about, but I needed to know. Should I keep going, or just give it up? It wasn't like there was a manual or guide for this kind of situation. "I'm sorry if I'm upsetting you, Greta." I said softly.

She didn't answer. That wasn't very helpful, and it didn't seem likely she was going to answer more questions, especially ones having to do with my dad, or having a baby.

"Greta, do you want me to go?" I asked.

She looked at me and smiled. "Nice niece."

I ran over the facts in my head. I was the baby she didn't want and maybe didn't even remember having, and telling her that I was actually her daughter could really cause a lot of emotional damage to her. She was damaged enough already, but I wanted to know – did she remember me? Her pregnancy? Any of it?

I didn't know if I should be selfish and push forward with the questions. The real thing I needed to know was if she wanted me as a daughter now. That was the bottom line. Could I handle if it I came clean about who I was and my relationship to her and she denied it, or didn't remember it, or worse, said horrible things to me? I was still kind of raw from all the emotional stuff going on in my life lately. Whatever the answer would be today, it wasn't going to make my life any less stressful.

"Oh Greta," I said tearfully, "I have a very hard question to ask and I'm really afraid to ask it – do you understand what I'm saying?"

She just smiled like a child, "Nice niece." I sat there and shook my head. Reaching for her hand, I looked deep into her eyes, trying to find the answer in there. Are you peaceful?" I asked her. "Is this life happy, are you happy here?"

"Good food," she said, nodding. "Nice Betty, nice Jessie..." she named off some of the nurses, "Tavis nice man, love Tavis...dead, no visit, sad, so sad."

Something in my gut told me to let it be. Greta had suffered enough in her life and from what I could see, she was well cared for and she did seem content. What would be gained from making an old, sick woman deal with something she might not remember and in any case, happened 36 years ago? I might satisfy my curiosity, but at what price? It wasn't worth it. "Okay, Greta, I'm going to go." I told her. "I'll be back soon and I'll bring you some more goodies."

"Nice..." Greta said happily, and opened her arms for me. This was the first time she had tried to embrace me! My eyes welled with happy tears while we hugged.

I sighed, walking away from the solarium, and Nurse Jessie passed by. "You didn't ask her, did you?" Jessie asked.

"Didn't have the heart..." I said.

"I think you're making a good decision - that's not a medical opinion, just a feeling." I walked down the long, antiseptic hall and warm, fat tears rolled down my cheeks. I had prayed so hard for the courage, but my gut had stopped me from asking. There was nothing to be gained by it, and a whole lot to be lost. When I got into the car, Ned was on his cell and Amanda had run to the gas station for a drink. The sun was coming out through the trees, and a hard breeze shook the truck. Neil Diamond was on the radio singing, "Hello Again," and it made me want to cry again. I held it back and lit up a smoke.

Amanda came back and Ned put the car into drive. No one asked me any questions. Maybe it was my red eyes, or the stiff way I was holding myself.

"It's so sunny today, you'd think it would warm things up." I blathered, trying to fill up the silence. Ned talked about the weather report for the week.

"Hope it doesn't unload too bad tomorrow night, I've got a hot poker game with the guys in the backroom of the Houndstooth. I'm already getting that cabin fever, and let me tell you, it won't be warm until mid-April, if we're lucky."

The ride home was comforting, and the light conversation eased my mind a bit. When Ned dropped us off, Amanda and I walked into the lodge in silence.

"Thanks for not asking me anything." I said, taking off my coat. "Just so you know, I didn't have the heart to ask her."

Amanda cupped my head in her hands and kissed me tenderly, just holding me in her love. She had the art of silence and affection down pat.

It was getting dark, and I wanted to go for a little ride on Tao.

"I'll get dinner started." Amanda said. I thanked her and suited up, then walked out to the stable. Tao was a little skittish tonight. I hugged his big neck and spoke some soft words into his furry ear, which seemed to calm him down.

We had just crossed in front of the house and were headed towards the path when out of nowhere I heard a huge crash directly in front of us. Tao reared up, making an unearthly noise that set my hair on end. I almost made the same noise when I saw the massive bear in front of us on the path. It was all I could do to cling to the saddle and reins, but not for long. Tao threw me off as he bucked and turned in terror, and I flew into the air, landing on my back with the wind knocked out of me. This bear was pissed off and probably pretty scared himself, but not as scared as I was. It reared up in front of me, towering like a six-foot-tall statue, teeth bared and growling. I was staring death in the face, I realized, and I lay as still as I could. I was desperate to scream, to run away, but I'd always heard that the best way out of this situation was to play dead. Tao was long gone, and I was the only thing the bear was interested in. It came right for me, and time seemed to stand still. A sudden shot rang out, and the bear collapsed, claws mere inches from my body. It was still snarling, still alive, and I rolled away quickly and got to my feet. There was one more shot, this one directly to the skull, and I watched the bear's blood and brains explode onto the white snow.

Amanda was at my side in a flash. "Are you okay?" she asked frantically, patting me, looking for injuries.

"Yeah. Yeah, I'm okay." I said, and then I couldn't speak anymore, shaking from residual terror. "I heard Tao," Amanda explained, "he came straight back to house. And I know that sound - they've been doing work around the lake and there's been talk about them disturbing the bears."

"I thought they hibernated or something, during the winter," I huffed, trying to regain my breath.

"Not if you rile 'em up." Amanda said. I was shaking uncontrollably. It was an awful feeling, like I wasn't in control of my own body. Amanda got me in the house and sat me down in one of the easy chairs.

"His paws were the size of my face – I could feel his spit. I could've died out there if you had come one second later." I said.

"I'd give you some whisky...but I don't know if that would be a good idea." Amanda said. That made me laugh even though I was still shaking.

"Let me go turn off the stove," she said, leaving the room for a minute, and then coming back in with a mug of hot tea. She handed it to me. "Drink this." she directed. "It should help."

I took a long sip. "Is Tao ok?" I asked anxiously.

"I'll go see, you stay right here," she said, getting up. "Oh, God, I'm not going out there again tonight – the dog can poop in the house, I don't even care." I muttered.

A few minutes later she was back inside. "The poor thing was in the stable. He was scared, too."

"Thank you, thank you, Amanda." I said. "You...you saved my life!" I got up and ran to her, hugging her tightly. I loved this woman so much it hurt – even when she wasn't literally slaying wild animals to save me.

Chapter 16

Amanda was working on editing two Christmas coffee table books for the publishing house she worked for in New York City. Since it was a business trip, they'd be putting her up at QT Hotel in the heart of Times Square. I was so in the mood for some cosmopolitan flavor, I bashfully asked Joelle if I could take a little time off. But, as with most salons, she explained December was peak season and no one was to take off or it would cause a commotion between the other stylists.

"We close the salon for three weeks in January," she explained, trying to cheer me up. I had an odd feeling Amanda was kind of relieved I wasn't going, when I regretfully told her I wouldn't be able to join her.

Fossil Creek really looked enchanting during the holidays - colored lights dotted the window frames of the shops, and fresh green spruce wreaths decorated with paper flowers, metallic ribbons, and apples dominated everyone's decor, along with and the ever-present sapin de Noël, or what I would have called a Christmas Tree back in Chicago.

There was a public crèche in the center of town, and I was amazed no one had vandalized it or was complaining about religious symbols in a public space. The US had become so conflicted about religion that the entire issue seemed to be broken up into the religious zealots and the militantly secular. These days, many times, "Merry Christmas" was said as an effort to jam religion down someone's throat, or you specifically avoided saying it to prevent offending another person – there wasn't any middle ground, it seemed. It made no sense to me this constant tug of war over positive traditions when there was the ability to bring more holiday cheer to the table; I wasn't strictly religious or secular, but I sure enjoyed the holiday season and the reminder of good will to all mankind.

I think it's ironic that the commercialism survived over the sentiment. SO what really got accomplished?

I always felt that it was harder to be prejudiced when people share their celebrations. That being said, I was missing city life and its cornucopia of diversity.

"I'm a little homesick for Chicago." I said to Tippie over comics and coffee at her house. "Christmas always makes me nostalgic." she replied, and looking around her Christmas wonderland house, I wasn't surprised. From the garlands around the mirrors, to the mistletoe in the door ways, to the stuffed-felt Frosty the Snowman sitting on the couch - not to mention the genuine pine tree decorated in blue lights and with its silver and white flocked branches, heavy with homemade ornaments in the foyer - you couldn't miss Tippie's love for the season.

"The first winter was hard here," Tippie told me. "I cried a lot. The endless cold, the darkness, the snow... I'm sure it's been more extreme this week for you."

"It's been really quiet, with Amanda in New York." I said. "I've had too much time in my head. Thank God for the Twelve Step meetings."

"There's a reason people get drunk and screw around a lot up here - the cold and boredom can be mind numbing." Tippie handed me a thin book and smiled, telling me "This will keep you busy." It was titled Love Is A Mix Tape: Life and Loss, One Song at a Time.

"Not only is the story good," she said, "but you'll be burning up your credit card with your iTunes account, downloading songs."

As I was flipping through the book, she asked if I'd heard anything from the music company. "Yes, they emailed me and it looks good. Strictly between you and me, we're going to go into the studio in Montreal and record in the spring. They've assigned us a manager, some young guy named Guy Savior. He's interested in my original songs, you make more money off originals because you don't have to pay for rights. "Appointment at the End of the World," "Rapa Nui," and the Halloween favorite, "Why is There A Casket In Front of Your Front Door." He's stuck on those."

Tippie put out a big bag of lo-cal popcorn, some cookies and poured me a soda. Then she sat down, "Ok, enquiring minds want to know...Are you and Amanda still going hot and heavy?"

I snickered like a high school student. "We are. It's a little freaky, because I usually can get a little bored with routine. What can I say? *It's a Gemini thing.*"

"Oh my God!" Tippie gasped. "Me too! May 30!"

"I'm May 31st!!!" I squealed.

We gossiped a bit more, and I said, "It's so nice to have a close lesbian friend. In Chicago, I had a lot of gay guy pals, and straight friends, but I never had anyone I could talk to like this. Just talking about Amanda and stuff..." I explained.

"That sucks. But I guess it's the case...moms like to talk with moms and gay gals like to talk with gay gals," Tippie said with a smirk. "You and I don't have a huge generation gap but even five years made a big difference in the scheme of acceptance. Remember, Lucy, your generation was the first to be even slightly gay- friendly."

I agreed. "*There was still a lot of prejudice.* I would wake up in a cold sweat, worrying that my parents were so disgusted with me...there was so much shame. Did you read Stone Butch Blues?" I asked. "I mean, the butch gal was put through hell. It's worse for the butchies, they can't hide so easily. They are not safe."

"I almost got raped in my hometown by a gang of men, just because they knew I was gay." Tippie said so offhand about it that I was shocked.

"Jesus!" I spluttered. "A couple of girlfriends and I went to play pool at the local bar, and these drunk guys started in on my butch friend Melanie. We thought they'd calmed down after she told them off, but they were waiting for us in the parking lot when we left the bar. One guy had his dick out and everything, but the bartender came out with a baseball bat and told them to fuck off and go home."

"Oh my God!" I breathed. "We thought it was over then, but they started following us when we left the parking lot. It wasn't like we could go to the police - this was Nebraska, and for all we knew, they could have been cops."

"What'd you do?" I asked.

"I called my dad on the cell - this was only ten years ago, not the stone ages or anything, and we drove to his house – and he came out of the house with my brothers, and they had words with the gang of drunk guys. The assholes got scared and drove away in a flurry of screeching tires and beer bottles."

"That was really cool of your family."

"My dad is incredible." Tippie agreed. "But get this - somehow, those guys figured out where Melanie worked and vandalized her car. Wrote Cunt Dyke Bitch on the hood."

"Oh shit..." I said.

"She had balls...well, ovaries." Tippie corrected herself, laughing. "Melanie drove that Yugo around with that shit painted on it for a week."

"Then what?" I asked, fascinated. "Then she left town. Those assholes threatened her mom's job at the plant, and Melanie felt so bad that she packed up her shit and took off in the middle of the night."

"Did you ever hear from her again?"

"Actually, just last year. She lives in San Francisco and runs a rape crisis hot line and publishes a bunch of lesbian 'zines."

"Did those guys ever come after you?"

"Not physically, but I used to hear the one guy muttering under his breath about how if I'd get fucked by a real man, I wouldn't be a dyke. He worked at the hardware store my dad and I used to go to, so it wasn't like I could avoid him. Small town, you know? I just keep my head low, didn't respond. It may not sound brave, but I had to live there."

I nodded. "I didn't get too much shit, but I didn't come out until I moved to the city." I told Tippie. "Plus, I was engaged to a man for a while, when I lived back in Indiana."

"Really?" Tippie asked curiously. "Were you gay then?" "I hung out with a lot of gay guys, but I wasn't sure until, after Gus and I broke up. I was going to church a lot and I fell in love with a female minister, and then I realized that I could love a woman, that it wasn't just a kinky fantasy...I adored her."

"Did you guys smooch?" she asked, wide eyed.

"No way! Minister! *And celibate!*" I said. "I gave her a bunch of love poems and asked her to *critique them for a class* I was taking. Then I told her, once she'd she returned them, that they were about her. That's when she told me she was gay, but had taken a vow of celibacy. I was devastated!"

"How sad." Tippie sympathized.

"It was like teen romance drama," I sighed, "but after I moved, I'd get wasted and prank call her. I was living in Chicago, but I'd drive back to see her sermons every Sunday. Finally I stopped - I just couldn't take it anymore. She ended up leaving the ministry for the administration side of the church, and I never saw her again."

"What about the fiancé?"

"Oh, he was a great guy in a lot of ways," I said. I paused to finish off my frosted Christmas tree cookie. "I felt bad when he found out I was gay. It sounds superficial, but I didn't want him to think it was because he wasn't good in bed or anything. Actually, he was a great lover, but there was something missing," I smiled, *"he wasn't a woman."*

Tippie cracked up, tossing the stuffed snowman at me.

"He's married to my mom now." I paused again for effect.

"OH MY GOD...seriously?" Tippie's face was a mask of shock.

I had learned to have a sense of humor about the...situation. "Way after I *dated* Gus my mom was at his restaurant, he didn't know she was my mom and she didn't know he was my *for-a-minute-fiancé.* He and I were together during a time she and I weren't speaking."

"That is so weird." She was eating popcorn, listening with rapt attention. It was making me kind of nervous.

"*Weird*, not anymore. They are really happy and she is as centered as she's ever been. I attribute that to Gus. My mom and I have always been more like really close best friend/sister's...that's probably why I'm not grossed out."

I paused for a moment to contemplate if that statement was really true. It was...I was just so happy my mom was being taken care of by a good man. I wanted the best for her.

"There are times when my mom is regaling me about her life, Greece, the boats and islands… I thought, maybe she was right… I was just making it so hard for myself…that I should have just stuck to guys, married a man. It's not like I find men repulsive…but I get the butterflies with my macho ladies."

Tippie agreed and went on, "I used to like really effeminate men…later I found out most of them were gay or bi-sexual." Tippie nodded. "I mean I was in L.U.V with Boy George!"

"Me too!!" We both cracked up.

"My parents weren't happy, to say the least, and they never liked anyone I dated. But I think I had some internalized homophobia, too, because I kind of kept my parents and my lovers apart. I occasionally tried to integrate my lovers with my family, but I don't know if I really had courage of my convictions. Christmas was especially hard."

"God," Tippie said, "do I know."

I took a swig of soda, and went on, "I just couldn't do it, I couldn't live a lie. It would hurt too many people, including me. My parents are finally calming down about it."

"Parents and kids have dreams for each other…no one ever lives up to the fantasy…but its loving each other in our reality that really defines what a family is," Tippie said, as she sealed up the bag of popcorn.

Now it was my turn to be awestruck by such a deep statement. "Tippie, you said a mouthful!"

The conversation ended when Janis came clunking into the house, rosy-cheeked and obviously exhausted. "Getting nippy out there." Janis told us, pulling off her ski cap and polishing her steamed-up glasses.

That was my cue to exit, so I said my goodbyes to both of them. The walk to the stable was icy and dark, even with the neon bar signs and holiday lights, it felt ghostly. I listened to Bob Seger's "Main Street" on my iPod, and the song warmed me up while I saddled Tao at the stable.

I thought about how lucky I was not to have to live in the closet, like so many gay people are forced to do… and the damage they do to their straight spouses who can't figure out what they're doing wrong. "It Isn't

Gonna Be That Way," a great song by Steve Forbert came on my iPod, and sentimentally it kind of felt right. No plan is ever perfect, but I felt like all my struggles had meaning, and I hadn't struggled for nothing. The ride home turned out to be very winter-postcard perfect. It was always surreal, riding down a deserted street, and then turning off onto the gravel road home.

The moon was so full that the night was illuminated, leading me home. I really felt that the lodge was my home, and that I had created a life for myself here in Fossil Creek. I might have left the big city, but I'd gained love, friendship, a career and a future. Uncle Tavis had been absolutely right about my needing a place to belong, a place to find out who I really was, and I thanked him in my prayers as I rode Tao home.

I was looking forward to a hot bath and the new Michelle Tea novel that had arrived that morning, but I was also tempted to skip the novel and start on the book Tippie had given me. My life was just full of difficult decisions these days. I smiled to myself, as I approached my driveway. It started to snow in earnest and I saw an SUV parked in my driveway that I didn't recognize.

I sighed. A strange vehicle in my driveway was unlikely to lead to a long bath and a good book, regardless of who was inside. Staying on Tao's back, I tapped on the fogged-up window with my foot. The person inside the car rolled down the window and I nearly fell off the horse into the snow. What was my MOM doing here?

"Mom!" I yelped, "How long have you been out here?" *Tonight of all nights!* I thought to myself.

"Too long." she slurred. She was clearly drunk, and her makeup was smeared from crying. The women in my family were ugly criers, and she was no exception.

"Let me get Tao hooked up and we'll go inside." I said. She nodded, got out of the SUV, and followed me into the barn. My mother was uncharacteristically silent as I unsaddled Tao and settled him into his stall.

"Mom, what's going on?" I asked, once we'd gotten inside the house and taken our coats and boots off.

"I need a drink." my mother replied, so I fixed her a scotch and soda with booze left over from the Halloween party.

I could tell this would be a long night already. I thought wistfully of throwing on my pj's and brewing a pot of dark roast.

Dramatically, like a star of the sliver screen she blurted out, "I think that goddamed Gus is cheating on me," my mom snarled, after a long gulp of her drink.

Even after tears and a long ride, my mom still looked strong and beautiful, I thought. Her voice was bitter.

"Then on top of that, my brother is being such a jerk. He won't let me stay with his family, and I didn't know where to go and I just had to leave and...I came here, Lucy," she said pathetically, perched like a lioness in the big wing back chair by the unlit hearth.

My mother's beauty never failed to amaze me. She had movie star good looks, her white blond, expensively coiffed hair a little below her shoulder, striking blue-green eyes and fair unblemished skin. Slight wrinkles at her forehead gave away her age but she would have been a hot date in Cougar Town. Men literally had pushed me out of the way to talk to her wherever we went. Most of them not the kind of men I trusted with my mom. I loved her and I didn't want anyone to hurt her. Most of the guys were pervy...and creeped my brother and I out.

"Did you talk to Gus?" I asked.

"Read this." she said, and tossed a letter at me as she pulled a quilt off from the back of the couch to cover herself.

"This" was a letter from Gus' ex-wife, saying that he owed her alimony... not that she wanted to get back together with him. There were some odd, affectionate references but only a paranoid person would see this as a threat. It occurred to me, maybe that was why I was so suspicious with Amanda.

"Mom," I said patiently, "this is just a letter. Has he even read it?" "Read the last fucking line." she growled, pounding her drink like a thirsty sailor and going back over to the counter to help herself to another cocktail.

"I'll see you at our special place like before? If you want to." I read aloud. I put the letter on the table in front of me.

"Mom, this doesn't mean he's cheating. It could be their special place from way back when they were together. Gus always hated his ex- wife, she was always more interested in politics then romance, according to him." The only reason I knew this was because Gus would complain about her back when we were together.

"Whatever," grumbled my mother. "I just know. He hasn't been real attentive in the sack, that's for sure." Then she started giving me details.

"Mom," I begged, "STOP, please." She looked at me and it was like she'd just realized whom she was talking to.

"Oh," she said, "*sorry.*"

"I think you should take a hot bath and get some sleep." I said firmly. "It's late. We'll talk more in the morning."

"Are you giving me the brush off?" my mother demanded. "Do you want to talk about Greta or...oh, God, I'm such an awful person..." she wailed suddenly, her hands crossed over her face like Joan Crawford after a bad night.

"No, I'm not brushing you off, and I don't want to talk about Greta right now." I assured her. "I worked all day, it's late, and I'm tired. I think things will be clearer in the morning."

"Fine." My mother snapped at me, she was angry, but she'd get over it.

I got her stuff unpacked in a guest room and she fell asleep before the bath was finished filling. I decided not to wake her. I skipped the bath and climbed into bed myself, eyeing the Michele Tea novel, feeling bone-tired and not looking forward to the conversations I'd be having with my mother the next day.

I woke to the sound of the vacuum cleaner. It was only seven in the morning, and my head hurt. Although my mom had passed out quickly, I had been up reading my Michele Tea book till the wee hours. The first thought that popped into my head was that I couldn't believe my mother was so functional after the load of booze she consumed last night.

Then I listened to the telephone messages from last night. There were a million from Gus, increasingly frantic about reaching my mother. Poor guy, I thought putting the phone back in the cradle and laying my head back on the pillow.

My mom popped her head in my bedroom. "You need to keep this place a little cleaner," she said affectionately.

"What time did you get up?" I asked, bleary eyed.

"You know me!" my mother chirped. "Always the early riser." She seemed almost chipper.

"Mom, Gus called a bunch of times. You'll want to hear the messages - *he's coming up here*." I got up and put on my slippers and contemplated breakfast. I wasn't really in the mood for coffee, but juice sounded good.

"Oh, God," she groaned. She was feigning annoyance but I could tell she was delighted.

"He's not going back to the ex. In one of the messages he left, he called her a shriveled up old witch." I told my mother. I knew she wanted to hear that. She smiled and kept vacuuming. After juice and Advil I flew back to my room to get ready to face a day of my mother, and probably Gus as well.

"Can we watch some TV?" My mother asked, looking around for the TV remote.

"How about a conversation instead?" I said. "Gus is going to be here in a few hours. He called from the plane."

"Did he really call her a shriveled up old bitch?" Mom asked.

"Yes, and some other words I'm not repeating."

She laughed like a schoolgirl.

By the time Gus arrived, I was about to leave for work. My mother and I had not exchanged one word on the topic of Greta, or the fact that my parents had kept me in the dark about my adoption for so long. With such self-absorbed mother figures, it was a miracle I'd turned out as relatively functional as I had, really. Mom and Irene weren't exactly the models of maternal devotion, but they were independent thinkers…in their own way. If it wasn't for them, I probably wouldn't have turned out as driven or hard-headed.

Gus, who still resembled Telly Savalas with a full head of hair, turned up just before I left for work. I was glad to see him.

"Make this right," I whispered as I left. He nodded in response, and I had no doubt that he would.

I was running late for work, so after feeding Tao, I took Amanda's snowmobile to town. I'd never been so grateful to be going to work in my whole adult life. At the salon, Joelle was in a crappy mood, and even Candy was not her usual bubbly self. We were overbooked, and Pasha was at the front desk arguing with a lady about the cost of a haircut. "Fifteen dollars is highway robbery!" the woman yelled. "You were only with me for ten minutes!" She took her cat out of her bag - the poor thing must have been suffocating in there - and shook it in Pasha's stunned face. The cat meowed pitifully, and its owner stuffed it back in her purse.

I slipped into the back and smiled as I plunked my stuff in the break room. Reality was as warped as anything else, these days.

After work, I scooted over to Bob's and picked up something special for dinner, plus food for the animals. I took the long way home on the snow-mobile, enjoying the speed and power of the machine, but I did have to get back to the lodge eventually. When I walked in, I could hear Mom and Gus talking and laughing. This was a good sign - a sign that eventually, my mom would be departing with Gus back to Greece. I walked into the living room, and Gus said, "It's colder than hell up here," to me. He was drinking a beer and had his feet up on the footstool, totally at home. He and Mom had even had pulled my lounge chairs closer to the fire. She was wearing a new neck-lace, so I assumed whatever Gus had done (or not done) had been forgiven.

"I like it." I said, smiling. Mom smiled and stroked the "bejewl-er'y" around her neck.

"We're leaving tomorrow." Mom informed me, patting my knee. "What, you're not going to stay and meet the town folk?" I asked dryly.

"Seriously," I added, "you should stay for Christmas."

Gus shook his head at me. "I guess your mom didn't tell you - I've opened up a cafe on the beach, I can't stay away for more than a day or two. We've got to get back."

A cafe? That's probably why he hadn't been so frisky towards my mom.

"No rest for the wicked." I said, trying to lighten the mood. They didn't respond.

Maybe it was me being overly sensitive, as Irene always claimed, but every so often it would've been nice to just not be swimming in theatrics.

We had a nice dinner and talked about inconsequential things. "Who's the lady in the photo on your fridge?" Gus asked. "She's cute, in that earthy way."

"That's my...partner." I said, trying to keep my tone casual.

"You work fast," he said, looking down at his empty plate. It was hard work to not mention the two waitresses he was "drilling" a week after we'd broken up, but I managed.

"I don't know how to reply to that." I said.

My mom added "See? That's why Gus and I are made for each other, always sticking our feet in our mouths," she rolled her eyes, and began clearing the plates.

"Mom," I said, "you don't have to do that."

"No, you two go relax," she said cheerfully, "this won't take me but a few minutes." I'd have felt bad if it were anyone else clearing my table, but my mom had always seemed to genuinely love housework. Note to self, make mom a mix CD and include "Cigarettes and Housework" by Rachel Fuller, a great singer.

Gus and I took Mom at her word, and settled ourselves before the fire in the living room. "You've done pretty well for yourself." Gus said, waving his arm around.

"Thanks to my uncle." I replied.

"Did you ever talk with that Greta lady?" he asked.

That Greta-lady. My biological mother, I thought silently. "Yes."

"Does she know who you are now?"

"No." I said. "I never said anything to her. She had a traumatic brain injury - it wouldn't be right to drop that on her, even if she did understand what I was saying."

"Oh..." Gus said, nodding. He looked away from me, into the fire.

"Your mom was really torn up about that Greta revelation," Gus told me. "So was I."

"You're so strong. I always admired that about you. Like when you told me I needed to stop babysitting my father's business and start my own - I really owe you some thanks for that. You were only nineteen, but you had a good head on your shoulders. And I think it's great you don't drink anymore."

"I've got to ask." I said suddenly. "You're not fucking around on my mom, are you?"

"Please." he said with a snort of annoyed conviction. "I'd never bang my ex-wife. No way."

"You have such a way with words." I said, but for what it was worth, I believed him.

I had been a very heavy drinker when I'd been with him. I felt awful about it - but then again, I'd been nineteen when Gus and I were together. He'd been thirty-six. Someone choosing to date a teenager couldn't be all that surprised when the teenager acted like one.

"Thanks." I said, since I couldn't think of anything else. We sat and stared off in opposite directions, avoiding any further discussion. This was what Gus and I tended to do, when we were alone together. How else were you supposed to deal with your ex- boyfriend who'd become your stepfather? It wasn't like there was a manual for this relationship.

"Your mom and I are good together." Gus said to the air. "The necklace was a nice touch." I commented. Mom's new jewelry looked to be made of emeralds and diamonds.

"They're your birthstone, you know." Gus said, surprising me. He usually wasn't this talkative. "Lucy, your mom really loves you. Neil may have come from her body, but you're just as much her child. She raised you. You're Tanya's baby, and you always will be. I'm glad things are working out for you. Are you happy with the girlfriend?"

"With Amanda?" I said, surprised by the question. "Yes, very."

He nodded and lit up a smoke, still not really looking at me. "You may not believe this," he said quietly, "but I'm happy for you."

I didn't reply. What could I say? We sat there for a while, listening to my mom clank around in the kitchen.

There was a knock at the door, and I got up with a certain amount of gratitude to answer it. I reflected for a minute on the fact that I lived in a remote town in rural Quebec, and still wasn't free of unexpected guests two nights in a row.

It was Amanda. "Hi, hon." she said, and gave me a smooch on the cheek, pulling up short when she spied Gus looking at her curiously from his chair by the fire. I smiled as Amanda raised her eyebrows at me expectantly, waiting for me to explain the presence of a middle-aged Greek guy wearing sweatpants in my living room.

"Come on in." I said, and stood aside to let her into the room.

"This is Gus Oreolous, my mom's husband. Gus this is Amanda."

He got up from his chair and shook her hand. His smile was a little creepy and he was obviously checking her out. Amanda knew it, too. She didn't take off her coat, and didn't get more than two steps into the room.

"I can't stay." she said stiffly. "I have calls to make."

"Come meet my mom." I coaxed. "She's in the kitchen." Amanda hissed "Is that your old boyfriend?" as we walked down the hall.

"Um." I said awkwardly. "You mean the ex-boyfriend who became my stepfather? Yup."

"Oh...wow." Amanda breathed. I could feel her loosen up and relax beside me.

"I told you." I said. "My family is a little eccentric." "With your mom marrying your ex-boyfriend? Yes, I'd say so."

I introduced my mom to Amanda, and was completely shocked at how nice my mother was to her. In previous years, she'd been coldly polite, if that, to anyone she even suspected of being my lover. She'd been completely dismissive to Diana.

And here she was, shaking hands with Amanda and telling her warmly how nice it was to meet someone her daughter cared so much about. I was tempted to check the back of the lodge for pods...was this the *Invasion of the Body Snatchers*? This couldn't be my mom!

"She's very striking," my mom whispered, when she called me into the pantry, faking a search for coffee.

"Thanks, Mom. I think." I sighed. "She's got good vibes."

"Mom, that's straight out of the seventies." I said, amused.

"Is this the one?" Mom asked quietly. "Like, for life?" "I hope so." I told her. She nodded befuddled with my mom's new attitude.

"Found the coffee!" she announced loudly. This was my mom, the real one she seemed to hide...not the selfish, weepy, drunken stranger of the previous night.

The rest of the night went smoothly, with the exception of a slip on Gus' part.

"Lucy is such a loving person - she always calls to make sure I get to my hotel safely when I travel." Amanda said, just making small talk.

Gus nodded. "She was awesome like that, with the little notes and phone calls," he agreed. Then he stopped dead, mentally reviewing what he'd just said. Not a step-father type thing. That was an ex- boyfriend comment.

Thank God, my mom wasn't in the room. She always got weird about the fact that Gus had dated me before he'd married her but that was just *tough.*

A few hours later, Amanda called it a night. My mom and Gus actually gave her goodbye hugs, which was a welcome surprise. They left early the next morning, and I was glad to be back to what passed for normal in Fossil Creek.

Seeing my mother go was bittersweet – there was always this hope, in the back of my head, that we could go back to a time when the two of us were close. In the summer of 1988, she'd paint my nails at the kitchen table and we'd talk about boys and dreams and plans while we drank wine. She'd been so positive and hopeful, without that cynical edge she developed later. She was so supportive of me, and I'd felt very protected for that short little window of time.

All that ended after I "came out," and although things felt much cozier now, we'd never get back to the relationship that we'd had that summer.

Losing the close bond my mother had been a deep loss, but we'd worked through it to a point where we were at least comfortable with one another.

Then I'd found out about Greta, and we were back to walking on egg-shells around one another. So much hard stuff, but it couldn't have come at a better time in my adult life. I could handle a lot of things now, which would have sent me over the edge when I was younger. I was a grown woman, and I could protect the little girl inside me. Though now that I thought about it, I'd been protecting myself for a long time.

Amanda was surprised that they didn't stay longer, but it didn't surprise me at all. My mom was queen of the whirlwind trips. Deep down, she was like a queen that needed to get back to her castle.

Amanda being away so much lately was lonely, in a way, but it was also forcing me to get into my own groove. With band practice, work, and writing, my time was nicely scheduled.

Amanda had another short overnight trip to Montreal. So she, my mom and Gus disappeared as dramatically as they'd come! Amanda had a meeting at McGill University, one of Canada's most prestigious universities. We had strolled around there a few weeks back and had heard an impromptu concert of beautiful opera singers from the front steps of one of the halls off Rue Sherbrooke. Standing on the frozen steps listening to enchanting music was a wonderful memory. I was getting to know the city, little by little.

In July, my friend David from Chicago was going to be one of the comedians in the Just For Laughs festival in Montreal and I was excited to see him and be at his show, maybe show him around.

The phone rang just as I was running back inside from putting Tao away in the barn. I made a mad dash for the phone and slid on the rug straight into the end table. I let out a bloodcurdling scream, but grabbed the phone just in time. It was Amanda, calling from Montreal.

"It's warmer here in the city, but I can't wait to get home. There's a protest in the park and it's been chaos here. I'll be glad to get home," she said.

"I have a surprise for you!" I laughed, rubbing my bruised leg. She'd told me previously that she hadn't had a Christmas tree for years, so I'd taken it upon myself to make sure this Christmas was different. I told her that when she came home tomorrow, we had a "decorating" project.

"The other line is beeping, so I've got to let you go, but I can't wait to see you tomorrow!" I told her. "Love you," she said quickly. "Love you, too." I said, smiling, and switched over to the other line. Whoever was calling had a blocked number, according to caller ID.

"I miss you so much!" squealed Bradley, directly into my ear. I winced. "When are you coming back to Chicago?" he asked. "We're getting a week's paid vacation as a Christmas bonus, I hope you don't hate me, but I'm going to South Beach."

"I already told Amanda that you were fickle," I told him, "and that you'd ditch us this winter."

"I just really need some sunshine," he sighed. "I swear I have Seasonal Affective Disorder! Are you in heaven up there, little Miss Snowbird?"

"Honestly, I am! But there are days when the sun isn't shining and I'm riding my horse home from work and it's so bitter cold I have to wear a face mask and I wonder if I might be happier in Hawaii after all. But I've made the suffering into a facial regime - I take off all my make-up, slather on the Neroli oil and facial cream and put on the silk face mask to keep in the heat, so really it's like a treatment."

He burst out laughing. "Only you, femme-girl, only you." Bing Crosby and David Bowie were singing "Little Drummer Boy" in the background, and I was digging through boxes and realizing that a lot of my ornaments had been broken in the move. "Do you have me on speaker phone?" Bradley barked at me. "I'm multi-tasking. Getting all the tree trimmings set up for tomorrow." I explained.

"I'm assuming you and Amanda are still together? You'd have said, otherwise."

"So far, so good. Are you still having your yearly tree trimming party?" I asked. Back in our drinking days, Brad and I and forty of his closest friends would cram into his one bedroom apartment and pretend we were having a tree trimming party. The tree was an excuse for a complete bacchanalia.

"Last Saturday it was," he said. "Only a few people this year. People just don't whoop it up like they used to. I packed away the ornaments pretty haphazardly last year, so it was a surprise to see what I still had left."

"Tell me about it." I sighed, examining another crushed box. "With the move, I've got a lot of really pretty broken shards of multicolored glass."

"Mitch got so drunk at the party he puked all his eggnog into a plant in my bedroom." Bradley whined. Mitch was one of our old co-workers. "And what was he doing in your bedroom?" I asked archly.

"Passing out." Bradley said matter-of-factly. "Oh, I didn't tell you who stopped by to get her hair done! Guess!"

"I'm bad at guessing." I groaned. "Mary, the trannie poet?"

"No, from your hometown. The wedding..." he prompted.

"Oh God, don't tell me it was Anita."

"Yup, you guessed it! She dropped a cool seven hundred for Japanese straightening, and was at the salon all damned day."

"Wow! How did you guys hook up?"

"She called looking for you, than started to fake laugh and said oh-I-forgot-she-mooooved. Since I've been taking all your clients, thank-you-very-much, she came to me."

"Oh, boy,"

"After she found out you and me were pals she proceeded to tell me about you and your big confession in the limo. She wanted your email."

"Did you give it to her?"

"No way - what do you think?"

"Thank you." I said relieved, walking over to pet Combover on the couch.

"Her diarrhea of her mouth took over. God, can that woman just talk and talk and talk. She thinks her husband is gay, because they're not doing it much lately."

"I told her to check his computer for porn, but I really don't think he's gay. I told her to get a couples counselor."

"Good boy." I said approvingly.

"Never get involved in that beehive of problems. Was she a big ol' hussy in high school?"

"I barely even remember her, except for the fact that she had a crush on this guy in my Sunday school class and I heard she gave him a blow job at Great America."

"No shit!" he giggled. "Scandalous, back in the day." I said. "I've got to go, the doorbell is ringing. Send me a postcard from Florida!"

"Will do," he promised.

Chapter 17

"Merry Christmas!" announced my brother Neil, standing on my front porch next to his wife. I gawked at him, speechless. They lived in Hawaii, and neither of them had called to say they were coming.

"Come in, come in guys." I stammered.

"Are you surprised?" Neil asked cheerfully, dumping a humongous duffel bag on my carpet by the door. His wife, Jenny, looked like an Emperor penguin, with a huge black and white down jacket that came all the way down to her feet, and a knitted hippie-style pointed wool cap that came down over her ears and tied under her chin.

Jenny was from Jamaica; my brother had met her in college at Indiana University in a chemistry class. She took off her hat and her gorgeous braids fell down her back. "How do you live with this cold?" she asked, shivering and giving me a hug.

"How do you live in that tropical heat?" I asked back. "Do you mind?" my brother said rhetorically, lighting up his bowl and plunking on the sofa. My brother is a huge lover of the wacky tobaccy, which for some reason I've always found endearing.

"Go for it." I said, guiding Jenny into the house. "Want a tour? Something to drink? I can't believe you guys are here!"

I was excited beyond belief, but a little nervous due to previously made plans. It was going to be tricky rescheduling everything. Thank God my Twelve Step meeting was going back to The Diner for the rest of December and January, it was too difficult in the snow to get down my drive way, so we'd decided somewhere in town would be a better choice. The overwhelming smell of weed wouldn't have gone over well at a recovery meeting.

Neil and Jenny's arrival was as good as Santa coming to town! I'd been missing my brother something awful so their presence was the present!

I lit a "Christmas-scented" candle, and helped Jenny cart everything to their room. She apologized for not warning me about their visit, but explained that Neil really wanted it to be a holiday surprise. I'd given them everyone's favorite room, which was decorated in sports paraphernalia and all things vintage. It was a scene right out of Boy's Life magazine, and had seen more guests than the other rooms put together since I'd moved in. Gus had described the bed as "like sleeping in a cushy baseball glove." They should be cozy.

"So," I said, "You guys just wanted to come visit for Christmas?" We tossed the luggage on their bed, making our way back to Neil.

Her voice dropped, "Yeah, but I think Neil is kind of depressed. Business had not been great, the market stinks, and I'm working all the time at the greenhouse. We're working on a cancer-fighting drug that also acts as an anti-nausea medication, to go along with the chemo treatments for people with cancer. It should help a lot of people."

"Amazing," I said, and I meant it. I really admired Jenny. "Are you going to visit Dad and Irene?" I asked.

"Neil's fighting with your dad," Jenny explained. "He won't talk about it...another reason I think he's depressed."

When my brother is depressed, he gets really agitated, not mopey like most people. I think that's why he's always loved marijuana.

"He's been so down that he rebuilt the back bedroom and the attic into a loft." Jenny explained. I blinked. "I thought you were renting?" I said weakly.

"We are, rent to own," she replied. "But you know him, when he gets into a mood. Our landlord couldn't be happier with the free renovations."

He'd lost a really big trade of some sort and decided to build a carport to vent his frustration. but then he got so exhausted the chain saw slipped and cut up his hand. During his recovery, he'd sent me a series of twelve photos of his hand in various stages of healing. There had been so many stitches in his hand that it looked like his fingers were fused together with barbed wire!

"Are you guys ok financially?" I asked.

"Oh, sure," said Jenny. "I just got a raise. But it hurts his ego, when the market is down." Jenny hung up her mattress of a coat by the door. She was in cords, a thick sweater and turtleneck.

"Where did you get all these great winter clothes?" I asked, amazed since Hawaiian parka's weren't so popular.

"On line," she replied.

I walked her around and showed her the place. She'd been a devout animal activist since she was a kid, so I wondered if all the dead animal heads on the wall and the elk horns she'd hung her coat on were pissing her off. If so, she didn't say anything, Jenny was very centered. Her easy acceptance of life on life's terms was probably very attractive to my worrywart brother.

"We better get back in there." I said, and pointed to the great room. Neil had made himself at home. He'd filled up his wine glass, and switched the CD player to the Johnny Mathis Christmas album.

"So," he said, "you going to show your only brother around this place?"

I gave them the fifty-cent *grand* tour - he loved the hidden room behind the Indian. "Is this where you found out about Dad and Greta?" Neil asked, as he put his big arm around me and gave me a squeeze of love and understanding.

"So you know." I sighed. "You know Dad - he can't keep his mouth shut," he snorted.

"I know." I replied. "I'm going to visit Greta over Christmas. She still feels like a stranger to me."

"What's she like?" My brother asked taking another hit off his mock cigarette.

"Very pretty, though she's in her late sixties. Very brain-damaged."

"Does she know who you are?"

"No. I couldn't just tell her like that - I think it could have really freaked her out."

"That stinks." Neil sympathized. "What about Mom, was she nuts?"

"She was awful, crying like crazy. Then she just showed up here a few weeks ago and involved me in a bunch of Gus drama. Wouldn't you know it, she didn't really even mention Greta."

"It's pretty awful that you had to go through all this shit, which must've been hard on you. Dad said your girlfriend was really helping."

"Amanda has been a Godsend. Really, this whole town has been a prayer answered. The people here, they're like long lost family."

"Now I know why Uncle Tav was always so sweet on you. He really loved Greta." Neil said, and gave me a wink as we walked out of the "secret room".

"I wonder what happened to Uncle Tavis' girlfriend - the one I met awhile back on his boat?"

"I remember her," said Neil. "Didn't Dad tell you? She killed herself. Took a bottle of pills, shot herself up with junk and took the boat out...she drowned. They think it was planned. The Coast Guard found a note taped to the captain's wheel."

"Jesus." I said. I was shocked and saddened. She'd really deserved better than that.

"Bummer in a big way." Neil said, inhaling a big puff of blue smoke that smelled like armpits and chili. We walked back into the great room, chattering like a couple of chipmunks. "This view has got to be spectacular at day break." Neil said, looking out the window.

"It's amazing." I agreed. Just then, we heard Amanda's voice from the front room. "Hello? Anyone home?"

We went back out to the sitting area and there was Amanda, looking regal and official in her long wool navy pea coat, with her hair up.

"Hi, hon," I said, giving her a big hug. "This is my brother and his wife." Jenny had just come in from the bathroom. My brother shook Amanda's hand, and Jenny waved.

My sister-in-law wasn't much of a hugger, I use to take it personally, think it was the gay thing - until I met her parents, who were almost British in their standoffish manner. Jenny just wasn't the effusive type.

Everyone sat down together, and I went into the kitchen to make tea. When I came back to the great room, Amanda was looking a little uncomfortable, but Neil was chatting her ear off about construction. "I saw that sleigh outside," Neil said, "We've got to take a ride; Amanda said she totally rebuilt it!" He sounded like an excited little kid. "You have no idea how much I miss snow!"

Amanda smiled at me as she took the mug of tea. Her eyes sparkled, and for a split second, my heart just jumped. She had such a great effect on me, like a priceless treasure that you couldn't resist gawking at. There were times I couldn't believe she loved me. Jenny wanted to go see the horse, so we bundled up and went out to the stable.

"Oh Lucy," raved Jenny, "she's beautiful."

"She's a he." I said, "And his name is Tao. He's very sensitive. Although we discovered he has a good sense of self-preservation, since the bear incident. We were lucky that Amanda got him with her first shot."

"You killed a bear!" Neil said in awe.

"You do what you have to out here." Amanda said. "This is the wild."

Jenny chimed in "It's the same where we live. It maybe the Hawaiian Islands, but we're still living in a jungle. We have very dangerous wild boars that tried to kill one of the dogs last year; Neil scared them off with the flare gun."

I looked up at my tall, strapping brother and felt a wave of love rush over me. I was so glad he was here, and he seemed to really like Amanda. He'd always been polite with my "dates," but never really enthusiastic about any of them, whether male or female.

Patting Amanda on the shoulder, he said, "Thanks for taking care of my sister out here. I was kind of worried when Lucy said she was moving to Fossil Creek – she's always been a city girl, even when we were growing up." I nodded in agreement. "Any of your friends come up here for a visit?" Neil asked me.

"Well, Brad was supposed to come," I said, "but he chose South Beach over me."

My brother rolled his eyes. Neil had known Brad from when I was in high school, where we'd been friends since freshman year, and they'd never been friendly.

My brother had always been a huge kid, who eventually topped out at 6'8". Brad walked home the same way Neil and I did, and when they crossed paths, Brad always teased him about his height. Needless to say, Neil never really took to Brad.

During Neil's "puberty-blues" years, Brad would always ask him if he had grown any new hairs, referring to his pits and crotch. My brother was sensitive and would turn ten shades of red. I thought it was funny, but Neil had always been one to hold a grudge.

We walked back to the house together, after admiring Tao some more. "You look great," my brother told me quietly. "You've lost a lot of weight, and I know that means you're happy."

Amanda and Jenny were trailing behind us, talking about the different types of fir trees that surrounded the property. "She's pretty...Amanda," my brother said. "For a granola girl." He snickered.

"I'll take that as a compliment." I replied.

"You guys going to, like, get married or have a commitment ceremony or something?" he asked.

"Neil," I said, "we've only been together since October."

"You just seem, like, really together-ish. Plus, I heard all you lesbians hook up the U- Haul on, like, the first date."

I smacked him in the shoulder playfully. "I know we busted into your Christmas...We won't be in your hair all the time. Jenny's got to go up to Manitoba, which is a hike, so we'll be in and out. I got GPS; this area's a real bitch to drive around."

"I'm glad you came to see me." I emphasized the word me, thinking about Mom, my cousin Jeff, and Dad, who'd all come up for their own reasons.

"It's nice to have a relative just visit for the joy of it," I snickered.

Later, Jenny and I went online to pick out Christmas gifts for the family, while Amanda and Neil sat around and gabbed over tea. It was weird, hearing him talk about me to her. And, of course, Neil was over-sharing.

"Our stepmom Irene really had it out for Lucy, I think because she was a reminder of the other woman. Like if only Lucy didn't exist, Irene could pretend that my dad had never been married to our mom Tanya. I was the boy, and a baby, pretty much, so it was different."

Just what I needed, Neil telling her all about our childhood. It was a topic I wasn't too excited about revisiting, though maybe it was good that Neil was the one sharing this information with Amanda. It meant I didn't have to talk about it. Neil was now singing my praises. "Oh, Lucy used to bartend at Chicago's most prestigious jazz venue, Jazz Showcase and she knew everyone. She's got a great way with people, but she can get really quiet, too, have you noticed that? Quiet means she's being creative, or you're in the doghouse," he said, and I could hear him laughing.

I was trying not to listen, but here and there I overheard things. Neil told Amanda about my car accident (neck brace for a summer), my old high school boyfriend Butch (I always liked them butch, was Crystal and Lauren's joke), my singing, and then Neil started talking about my self destructive period. "It used to scare me," he said seriously, "once, Lucy was building an album holder. She put a nail right through her hand and didn't shed a tear, though she did cuss a lot. At the time, she was going through this whole Ice Queen phase, and thank God she got over that. She's never gotten over being funny!" A lot of people found it hard to believe that I suffered from serious depression at one time simply because I was so together now. Going into recovery and quitting drinking helped the depression big time – the Twelve Step program gave structure to my life, and that made me want to have a life.

Neil talking about the nail through my hand incident made me wonder about his chain saw accident and whether or not it was really an accident – we'd both always had the ability to turn our emotions on or off. At this point in my life, I realized this was unhealthy...did he?

I was always looking at my behavior on a scale of healthy or unhealthy, trying to keep things on the "healthy" end.

One of the reasons I was reluctant to pursue singing again was that it reminded me of my drinking days – the fear, the anxiety, the pressure to perform, the inevitable crash after performances. I'd also had a lot of near misses, where fame knocked at my door but I just didn't get there fast enough. Like a drafted football player who keeps getting cut, it's awful to keep chasing a dream you can't catch. I was still dealing with it...and secretly, I dreaded April, the month I'd have to go to K- Top and prove myself musically.

When I'd mentioned my fears to Todd, he'd suggested I go with him to a couple of clubs in Montreal to "remember" why I loved music. The new, healthy me said yes!

Todd said, "create new memories," and that's what I was doing...with my brother and with this next phase of my life.

I decided to spend the night at Amanda's and give Neil and Jenny some privacy. Besides, it had been a long week without her. There were a lot of fantasies in my head, fantasies just waiting for the right person to share them with. I had a surprise for her that night, and I was pretty sure she didn't suspect a thing.

I got my brother acclimated to the house, and I could tell he and Jenny were really happy I was going next door. Neil loves his privacy...they live on an island for a reason.

Before Amanda and I left, I donned my floor-length coat and she knew something was up. I had dressed up in one of my old singing getups. One of my friends had been a great seamstress who'd worked in the costume shop at the Lyric Opera and various theaters around Chicago. She had a side business, making fetish wear, which probably paid more than all her costuming jobs put together.

I'd had a singing gig at a vaguely skanky-but- cool bar on Halloween, so I decided to dress up as a sort of dominatrix – but of a very specific kind. We'd taken our inspiration from the slinky, sexy suit Catherine Deneuve wore in "The Hunger," and my friend had created a suit of body-hugging black mesh that clung to me like liquid latex, and added thigh high black leather boots.

It was a completely macho-femme outfit, and I was grateful I'd never gotten rid of it in my many moves. I wore my black leg warmers over the boots so Amanda couldn't see what I was wearing, and had the added benefit of hiding the boots from Neil and Jenny. I was close to my brother, but there were some things I didn't want to share with him.

When we got inside Amanda's place, she took off her coat and kicked off her boots when we were barely in the door. I just stood there for a moment, not sure of my timing now that it came down to the critical moment. "Are you going to wear that coat all night?" Amanda asked. "I missed you...I kept seeing all these great things in New York and thinking how you should be there with me."

I smirked at her and said "Well, I've got something I want to show you - but you have to go put on your kimono, and sit in the chair by the bed. Pull the curtains around the bed; I want this to be a surprise."

"Okayyy." Amanda said suspiciously, but moved into the sleeping area and pulled the curtains behind her.

I popped in a CD mix I'd made for us with really sexy songs, and hung up my coat, putting on my dark sunglasses. I started doing a snaky little dance to get myself in character, then threw open the curtains. Then I did my best sexy stripper moves and pulled out the riding crop, which I'd tucked into my boot. "No touching," I said, as she reached for me.

"Tonight it's all about you, baby."

I did a back bend, using the pole that supported the curtain, then flipped around and slowly shook my ass in her face while I slid the riding crop up the length of my leg, and then up the length of my body.

While she starred, I flipped back around and put my boot between her legs, leaning into her, sliding my riding crop up the front of her kimono. I pushed the opening a little bit apart, just enough, and slowly slid the tip of the crop up between her breasts, following the line of her neck, her chin, and then trailing the crop down her shoulder as the music got slower.

Amanda's head was back, her burnished gold and silver hair strewn like ribbons on the back of the head rest. Her eyes held mine, and again she tried to reach for me. "Not yet." I scolded. I untied her kimono, tracing the velvet tip of my riding crop in little circular motions over the exposed skin. Putting down the riding crop, I got on my knees and put my hands on her waist. My hands slid gently up and down over her torso, gently stroking my finger-tips creating goose-flesh on her warm skin. Her fragrance was intoxicating like a warm morning bed. Amanda's hands dug into my hair, knocking off the sunglasses that I'd flipped up on my head. Then I glided up the front of her body to give her a deep full kiss, crushing her lips to mine, finally straddling the chair, kissing her so deeply I felt I was part of her. We were connected as one, riding together, her arms around me as I steadied myself on the back of the chair. She was obviously shocked, because she didn't say anything. Instead, she just took my face in her hands and gave me a dreamy kiss. That led to bed. We didn't actually fall asleep until early morning, when I could hear the birds chirping cheerfully.

Chapter 18

Christmas had been lovely. My brother cooked a big ham with cheesy mashed potatoes, peapods, salad with bleu cheese dressing, and a sweet potato pie with whipped cream. He'd really outdone himself. For a family that had been so crippled by situational dissection, it was amazing how close and loving I felt towards all of them. Most of the time.

Neil had brought me a new portable stereo, complete with turntable, cassette player, CD player, and iPod hookup. I could even record different formats onto my iPod, or just to CDs. I was so thrilled! Neil explained "I made sure it was easy, Sis, so you could make compilations and stuff, like you did when we were kids...I expect to see some in my mailbox!"

I actually had made him cool comedy song compilation-CDs with rare 45s that I'd bought at a garage sale. There was a disco parody from Steve Dahl, a famous Chicago DJ who'd really nailed the "tacky/fickleness" of the disco era, Grace Jones singing a cool Studio 54 disco song, "Nipple to The Bottle," Steve Martin's classic "King Tut," Cheech and Chong's "Wink Dinkerson" and "Sister Mary Elephant," a bunch of kick-ass Ian Drury, "Superman's Big Sister" and "Everybody Wash" by Burt and Ernie of Sesame Street. In between the comedy songs, I'd put some really cool soul grooves that I'd picked up when this bar on the South Side of Chicago closed - a friend of mine bought their jukebox and sold me most of the 45s. There was "Get Off" by Foxy, Apollonia 6 singing "Sex Shooter," and Diana Ross doing, "Muscles". It wasn't anything Neil would hear on the radio, that's for sure.

Jenny had picked out a fantastic all-weather coat from Orvis for Amanda, with a label that said it was good for boating in extreme weather. An amazingly appropriate gift, considering that Jenny had never even met Amanda!

Since Neil and Jenny liked to travel, I'd gotten them two airline tickets that could be redeemed for a domestic location of their choice, or they could add to the tickets if they wanted to go to Europe or Fiji or somewhere else international. I figured I could use some of Uncle Tavis' money for a snazzy gift for my baby brother.

When they left, Neil bear-hugged Amanda and said, "I still have the fantasy of going to England...all of us. To Strathmore, the most haunted place on earth." He'd been talking about this trip forever. I was amazed that such a scaredy-cat wanted to stay in a haunted castle on vacation.

Amanda spoke before I did. "We'll do it," she said firmly. "Maybe in the coming year?"

Jenny had gotten over any issues she may have had and gave big, sweet hugs goodbye to both of us. After Neil and Jenny departed, Amanda and I went to sit by the Christmas tree, with only the glow of the little twinkling lights illuminating the room.

Honey, this is the best Christmas I've ever had." Amanda said, leaning her head on my shoulder.

"I'm so glad, sweetie, and I couldn't agree more." She got a misty, far-away look in her eyes.

"I didn't realize how lonely my life was without you, without other people around. I was living with so much mistrust and fear..." She sighed. "When you tell me that you're afraid of how much you love me, Lucy...let me tell you, I understand."

Squeezing her shoulder tightly and putting my head next to hers, I agreed in silence. Anything worth keeping usually involves some risk, especially where love is concerned. I was dead tired, so we decided to turn in early and sleep until noon.

Amanda had also adopted a rescue horse, so our new thing was riding around the lake and practicing our French. I had ordered the Rosetta Stone CDs, and we were trying to become bilingual. There was still a good six inches of snow, but the weather had been in the upper twenties. "Lauren will be coming soon, I'm so excited," I said in broken French.

She replied, in similarly awkward French, "Your cousin is your best friend; *I think I will like her better the second time around*. You have a lot of friends and people who love you."

I switched back to English. "I've realized that it's God's greatest gift to me." I said seriously. "Talent, luck, fame…love…everything is starting to feel differently for me. Music and writing used to be unreal expectations… I obsessed about getting famous now I just want to be legit. I've done the work…I don't know a life without these endeavors."

"And you'd do it even if there was no chance for fame?"

I thought about it. "Yes. It's part of who I am…with modern technology…hell, I'll just put it all on a website or something. Amanda, I'm used to things not working out. I'm the MacGuyver of life!" I laughed inhaling heavy cold air as my lungs felt the icy pressure. The horses kept in stride.

"Have you thought about what you'll do if you get that recording contract?" Amanda asked.

Shaking my head, looking into the darkness of the wild Canadian forests… "I can't feel the dream anymore, it will be or it won't."

"Just focus on the pleasure of the music. When I saw you sing that first time, Lucy, it was clear. You were right where you were supposed to be."

"What would you do if I had to tour?" I blurted out. My stomach was doing flip-flops. Amanda wouldn't go to Brussels with me, she loved the silence of the woods, and I seriously doubted her ability to adapt to life on the road with a touring band. No privacy, farts, long days and nights, stinky laundry.

"If I have my laptop, I can work." Amanda said hesitantly. "I'd go with you sometimes, if you wanted me to go. I can always come back here if it gets too overwhelming, or if we just need a little break."

"I just want you to know that touring with a band can be a real boy's club - *rude language and poor hygiene*." I warned her, as we started back home.

"You're really selling it Lucy! *I think I can handle it*," she replied. Did you forget I lived on a commune?"

I just wanted my life to keep going the way it was going. Did I need legitimacy so badly? Music was the best part of me, music had saved me...options were scary.

We stabled the horses and stopped talking about the impending unknown. Amanda had work stuff to do early so we went back to our separate residences. The house was soft silent. The fire wasn't crackling anymore and had burned down while we were gone. I changed into my pajama's and sat on the couch with the dog starring into fierce dying orange molten embers. They lit up the room with quiet power, not needing to burn to prove they had heat. For some reason, thinking about the embers made me smile and fall into a deep and restful sleep.

I went to see Greta both before Christmas and afterwards as well. My brother had elected not to meet her, and I couldn't blame him for it. I went alone to McTrainers these days, since poor Ned didn't need to be dragged along for each visit. Visiting with her alone, without feeling rushed because there was someone waiting, allowed me to just be with Greta in a way I hadn't before. The last time I'd visited, I'd sung her a few Christmas songs, which she enjoyed. I couldn't tell if she realized it was almost Christmas, but I knew she enjoyed music.

After the holidays, I drove up with a photo album to show Greta. I was curious to see if the pictures would spark any memories, if they'd encourage her to divulge information, just to see if any secrets might emerge from her damaged brain. The basic truth was that I wanted to connect to Greta, even if she didn't realize I was her daughter, and have something in common to talk to her about - even if our conversations were mostly me talking and her listening in a distracted way.

When I got to the nursing home, the nurses thanked me for the sandwich tray I'd sent over on Christmas Eve. A client at the salon in Chicago had always done that for us, and I'd thought it was a sweet gesture. Having worked on Christmas Eve myself, I knew just how much it meant to know that someone was thinking about you. I wanted to carry on that tradition of goodwill.

"Hi, Greta!" I said, seating myself next to her wheelchair in the solarium. "You look so festive in your Christmas robe and fur slippers, like a film star." Greta smiled shyly and nodded.

"I brought you some pictures, thought you might like to see them." I'd put the album together myself. There were photos I'd found of her laughing with Uncle Tavis, another of her as a little girl in a cute frilly dress, and many of her posing for goofy G-rated bathing suit cheesecake photos taken with an old Polaroid. She'd flipped the pages of the photo album carefully, hands gnarled with arthritis and residual paralysis. She turned the pages slowly, using her index fingernail to separate them carefully, like they were priceless relics from a museum. I guess in a way, they were. This was Greta's archive. I watched her face as a plethora of emotions moved over it, watching her haunted eyes.

Sometimes she would smile. "Good!" she said, and pointed to a picture of herself and Uncle Tavis sitting on Santa's lap at my Grandma's house. She'd tilt her head, sigh, and smile at some pictures, but when she came to the one of my dad, she frowned and flipped the page quickly.

The last page had a baby picture of me lying on an orange shag rug in my Great Grandma's living room. She stared at the photo, and her face twisted with fear, disgust, and anger. "No baby!" she said strongly. "No want baby....baby bad. Ruin, ruin, ruin!" She pushed the photo album off her lap. I walked over and picked it up. I felt a lump in my throat, and swallowed hard to keep from crying.

Sitting back by her side, I put my hand over hers, and she let me. "I'm sorry that made you mad." I said quietly. Greta was looking down at the floor, and then she looked up at me.

"Nice niece...sorry, sorry." she said sadly.

"No," I said, "I'm the one that's sorry, I didn't mean to cause you pain." I pulled out a box of Godiva chocolates. I smiled with tears in my eyes, but I didn't let them fall. If you want to ask a hard question, you have to be prepared for a difficult answer. I had my answer. Even after all these years, she didn't want a child. Greta didn't want me as a daughter, but she liked me just fine as a niece.

I had a mom already...and it wasn't Greta, except in the biological sense. The stars had worked in my favor, and I had the love I needed. I even had Greta's affection and love, even if it wasn't in the fairytale package. I put on some Ella Fitzgerald, Greta's favorite, and we watched the sun go down together. I didn't stay for dinner. "Will you be back to visit?" asked one of the nurses, who'd been watching us.

"Of course." I said. I put on my ear muffs and walked out into the night.

The drive home seemed painfully long. My cell phone kept beeping to let me know I had messages, but I left it in my purse. Instead of dealing with the phone, I turned up "Harvest Moon," a great Neil Young song. It reminded me of coming down off acid in my toasty apartment with all my roommates on a snowy winters day. We'd all piled in my little car and gone out for breakfast at the Golden Platter, a 24 hour Greek diner. We'd all been so young, and we had such grand plans for our lives. Greta had probably had big plans too, at that age. I thought of the people I had known when I first moved to Chicago and now here I was in Fossil Creek.

When I finally pulled into my driveway, I felt a wave of relief come over me. I went inside and let Comby out, and watched him jump into snowdrifts and pounce on imaginary foes.

Being true to your self can be really lonely sometimes. No one can soothe you out of what you must confront in life's grand scheme.

I blew my nose on an old napkin I'd found in my pocket. "C'mon, baby boy." I said, slapping my leg. Comby came running and we walked to the house. Looking into the bathroom mirror at my red eyes, I knew I'd be all right, but for tonight I would sleep alone with my thoughts.

Chapter 19

Late one night soon after the "Greta Epiphany" I was settling in with some extra strong Earl Gray tea. A breeze that felt something like spring rustled the window panes as Combover and I sat in the big plaid over stuffed chair by the picture window.

Miles Davis was on the stereo and I was feeling contemplative.

On the car ride home from Greta's when I accepted things between she and I would stay the same some mysterious weight had been lifted from my life.

From that moment on I didn't feel the need to be anxious about every little detail. This acceptance of "life on life's terms"…as they say, changed everything.

When the package from my friend Rick (he owned a used book and Music store called Shake, Rattle and Read) in Chicago arrived a wonderful feeling of completeness came over me. I feared when I left Chicago I would lose what I had created in my life…but as I leafed through this wonderful treasure trove of books, music and collectables, I realized life was acquired. We kept filling it up with new experiences…friends, losses, acquaintances, dreams and goals. Life kept developing and expanding. When I feared the loss of the old Lucy little did I realize I was simply adding onto my creation.

Bradley came for a visit and we began unpacking things and getting him set up in the farthest guest bedroom down the hall from mine. Brad was a terrible sleeper and this way he could wander around and be close to the front room and not wake me up with the TV.

"This place is like Orvis, I mean just darling!" Brad said genuinely impressed. He looked great in his spring city boy best but he would stick out like a soar thumb in town...looking more like a Kennedy then Fossil Creek.

Thanks Bradley, I knew if you gave it a chance you'd dig it!"

He regaled me with stories of urban life and as much as I enjoyed it I didn't feel a sad yearning like I would've just a few months before.

"Oh, you're not going to believe who came sniffing around the salon looking for you ?" He said salaciously.

"Who?" I was baffled.

"Betti Lou...the girl you had the terrible crush on!"

"Her parents were either sadistic or hillbillies," I groaned. *That name on that fine woman."*

"She asked about you, of course. She's single again, renting the art studio in the back from Susan."

Susan owned an art gallery two doors down from the salon and had rehabbed a huge coach house in back of the salon that she rented to various artists. "So..." I prompted Bradley.

"Well, Betti Lou, *she breezed in to the salon twice*, and I could tell she was looking for something, so I asked her if I could help. I have to admit I was thinking what's a no-frills dyke like her interested in a bottle of thirty-dollar shampoo. She admitted that she was wondering what was up with you, so I told her about your big move up here."

"I was so googly-eyed for her." I lamented. "Whenever she was single, I wasn't, and vice versa. Except the last time I was chatting with Lee, he named some of the women she'd dated – I was like damn, that girl is the Hugh Hefner of lesbian Twelve Steppers!"

"She's never single for long." Bradley agreed.

"My heart was broken when I found out she was with another girl and I was finally single."

"Well, I told her about Amanda."

"Was she disappointed?" I asked.

"She played it off, but yes, *she was*. Speaking of love interests, where's Amanda?"

"Oh, she'll be over, she's just finishing up an edit on a cookbook."

"She's a book editor? *How convenient*. You know, Lucy, I find it absolutely...how do I put it..." Brad sighed and stared at the stuffed boar mounted on the wall, "a sign from the universe, *you were meant to be here*! Book editor, music connections, love of your life, all in this little completely out of the way town!"

"I know...I moved to the city to make it big, and I've gotten more opportunities here than I ever did in Chicago. Oh, yeah, speaking of connections, Randy's coming for dinner tonight. He's the gay guy at my salon I told you about."

"Oh, the one with the pompadour." he said snottily, snorting like a brat. It was false blustering because I could tell he was excited.

"Yes, and Candy, the other stylist, is coming over too, so it won't be too couple-y."

"Is she the big slut?"

"Bradley! No, she's just super sexy and all the guys want her. But she's a very good girl. In fact, we had a photo day at work; I had everyone bring snapshots from when they were growing up. Here I am, thinking that young Candy is going to be the spitting image of Britney Spears or something, and she was this gangly kid, with thick glasses and scabby knees."

"I've only known one other Candy." Bradley said, and we both smiled, recalling the girl with her trademark thick black eye liner. "The one from my Girl Scout troop who hid the condom under the rock?" I said.

The memories flooded back. Candy was a bad girl in the best sense of the word. She feared nothing and was a complete sneak and prankster – any parent's worst nightmare. She was madly in love with Rick James, and played his cassette "Wonderful" over and over. It's still my favorite Rick James album.

"Yeah, well, you were the instigator!" Bradley said. "Didn't you guys take the condom from her dad's dresser?"

"We sure did, and we hid it and then showed it to the whole Girl Scout troop."

What we hadn't shown the rest of the troop was the Polaroid snapshot we'd found with the condom, the one of Candy's mom and dad naked.

Brad didn't waste time making himself at home, brewing up a mocha with ingredients he'd brought from home. He immediately plunked down on the sofa in the great room, ready for more reminiscing and gossip. "Didn't Candy's family have a heated Olympic-size indoor pool?" he asked.

"Yep. One time, I thought her little brother had pooped in it when I stepped on a brown squishy log in the bottom. It ended up being a drowned mouse!" We both cracked up. Candy and I were only friends for one year and then, for obvious reasons, my folks dissuaded me from hanging around with her.

Years later I was talking with a friend, who had no connection to my home town, and she knew *The Candy Weiner* - turned out that Candy had been shipped off to Catholic school, while her mom got addicted to cocaine and her dad did time for fraud. It was like the Simpson's TV cartoon family on PCP, all grown up, with added tragedy and pathos.

Amanda came over about an hour later, followed by Candy and Randy with some twice baked potatoes. We had a nice old-fashioned chicken dinner with steamed carrots, salad and crescent rolls. Everyone was gabbing and enjoying each others company...it felt so normal. Finally Randy suggested Candy and Amanda go out and see his new car. Which gave Brad and I some time to finish the *dish*(es).

"You did a shine treatment on her hair, didn't you?" Brad asked, when Amanda left to go to the bathroom.

"Nope," I replied, "that's her lemon rinse magic. She learned to do it at the commune – it got the pot smell out of her hair and detangled it, too."

"She lived in a commune?" Brad groaned, rolling his eyes.

"I know, I know, but it was the late sixties, and she was a 15 year old runaway...and I recall you living in the bath house for two weeks when you got evicted."

"Oh, God," he said, "that was when I started to consider joining a Twelve Step program. I still can't stand the smell of bleach or Pine sol."

"I still can't believe you didn't call me," I scolded him, "you could've lived with me."

"You and your crazy ex, Natalie? No way." Bradley scoffed. He knew all my exes. Natalie had put me through the wringer. She had a temper problem and was on all these meds that didn't help. Growing up, her live-in cousin would beat the crap out of her constantly, and her entire family had looked the other way. The thing was, though, that Natalie let her past trauma destroy her adult life by holding onto the resentment, which made her constantly angry and depressed. God bless her, I was such a drunken mess, I was no dream to live with, either. We'd been quite the dysfunction junction pair.

"Brandy stopped by the salon and said she was going to come visit you on summer break from college." Bradley said.

I was slightly surprised because I hadn't heard anything after I invited her up to visit on Facebook.

"I really miss her." I said sadly. Brandy had been the best thing about my relationship with Diana – I'd loved her so much but me leaving had put an obvious wedge between us.

"I hope she doesn't end up taking care of everyone but herself. Every so often she contacted me on Facebook and updated me on what was going on, mentioned that Diana finally met someone. Brandy hasn't said whether she likes her or not."

Brad asked, "how's she doing in college?"

"Good! And she seems happy. She's going into geriatric medicine. Anyway, she said she thinks her mom finally found her soul mate. The woman sounds like a soft butch; likes camping and sky diving, even got Diana to start eating vegetarian!"

Randy, Amanda and Candy came back in talking about cars they had owned. We finished dessert in the Great Room by the open windows.

"guys I hate to be a party pooper but I still have edits to do," Amanda apologized.

Randy got a devlish look in his eyes, "if you don't mind, I thought I'd take Brad over to *Boy's Night*, over at Cy's Bar in Mt. Ridge, ya know… show him where the boys are."

Candy chimed in, "can I go too?"

Randy nodded, "sure sweetie…how about you Lucy?"

"I worked today and so I'm going to bed with a book."

Hugs and kisses were exchanged by the door. Brad whispered, "are you ok with this...me leaving on my first night?"

"You'll be here awhile longer, have fun!"

Amanda explained, "I'll be over to start breakfast around 10 a.m.?"

"Yes, later better since Sleeping Beauty will be exhausted," I said nodding over to a sheepish looking Bradley, who smiled and made a hasty exit.

Amanda gave me a smooch and was off into the night. Bedtime called and I smiled to myself feeling good all over.

Chapter 20

Amanda was scrambling eggs, and I was pounding back the day's first cup of coffee, spellchecking my blossoming novel. The book I'd been working on since before I moved up here was kind of like therapy for me. When you read about your life in black and white, it helps you to keep things in perspective - and in my case, helped me to be more appreciative of what I had! "Lucy," asked Bradley, "what's with the pennies I keep finding in the corners of all the rooms?"

I snickered. "Oh, yeah, I'd forgotten about those. I was watching Michael Chiklis, you know, the guy from 'The Commish,' on Leno one night, and he was talking about some old Jewish tradition. They put pennies in the corners of the rooms and it's supposed to bring financial stability or wealth. So I figured, who am I to argue with tradition? I put pennies in the corners."

"Is it working?" Bradley asked, standing in the hall in his robe with a towel turban around his head, striking quite the pose.

"Yes, Sultan, it is, actually." I replied. "Since I've moved here, I've had no financial worries."

"God, remember the Ramen and peanut butter days?" Bradley groaned, and lumbered over to the coffee pot. He filled a coffee cup that read "Lady of the House" to the brim and topped off Amanda's. I could tell she was a little nervous with him strutting around in his skivvies.

"And you with your onion and beer," I reminded him. It was our standing joke. Back when we were both still drinking, I came over one time and asked him if he had anything to eat. He told me to check the fridge, where I found three cases of cheap-o beer, and one lonely onion. During that time Brad had decided to forego food, he'd gotten so skinny people kept asking me if he had AIDS. Those were not our best years, health- wise.

"Remember when I picked you up at the police station by that one leather bar, Touchès?" I asked.

"Oh hell yes." Amanda craned her neck our way and arched her eyebrows.

Brad had been "rolled," coming out of one of the gay bars, stone drunk. They'd beaten him up in the alley, taken his backpack, which had contained all the new headshots for an acting gig, and all his money. At the time, he was waiting tables and carried a lot of cash. The muggers wiped him out. When Brad finally woke up from the beating and the alcohol in an alley on the north side, he had to pee. Naturally, he relieved himself behind a dumpster. At that point, he got arrested for indecent exposure and hauled off to the Rogers Park police station to sober up and recover. The charges were dropped, and the officer I talked to was actually very sweet. "Lady, your friend here needs serious help," said the cop, when I came to pick up the beaten, bedraggled, and hung-over Bradley.

"Can you believe I wanted to be an actor? I was the worst."

"No, you weren't, as my friend Holly says...*I've been a victim of theater*...and Brad you weren't the culprit." I said definitively."

"I don't miss those days...although we had stories for miles, didn't we."

I said wistfully, "We did...I have no regrets! I just don't miss the shame, anxiety and cotton mouth of the next morning." Bradley nodded in agreement as we sipped our java. Amanda just shook her head.

It was important to me to remember what a sad lush I'd been. I never wanted to sugarcoat the past and run the risk of going back to being *that Lucy*. I'd finally gotten to the point where waking up in the back of a funeral home with my clothes on backwards didn't seem funny anymore.

After we finished breakfast Amanda offered to give us a ride to Montreal where she had business. Bradley and I went to a morning Twelve Step meeting, and then we all piled into Amanda's car for a drive to Montreal for shopping. We hit the art stores and boutiques and I got new pair of work shoes at *Boutique Le Marcheur*, cute and comfie. Got a bag full of local newspapers to check on up coming events and last but not least *Disques Beatnick* for used vinyl.

We had lunch at a great place called *Fondue Mentale*, which had a relaxing, artsy vibe to it. After lunch, we strolled around the St. Denis Street area, where there were music and comedy clubs. Our feet were numb little stubs by the time we returned to meet Amanda at a unique little coffee shop. We both bought too much crap, and had a great time doing it. We were exhausted but happy on the drive home. Amanda dropped us off at the lodge; she was heading over to Big Bob's for a poker game, so it gave Brad and I some more special time.

Bradley was settling in by the fire in the great room by the time I got there, after ducking into my bedroom to change into my Harley-Davidson sweats, a gift from Big Bob and his wife for Christmas.

We'd each brewed up a mug of Pasha's special 'nite- nite' tea. "This tea rocks, it tastes really good," Brad said, sipping the hot elixir and we got cozy in The Great Room.

For all the years I had known Bradley we had never spent this much time *really talking*.

"It's funny; I always had a sneaking suspicion you might be a lesbian."

"Well, that shit with Kerri was a real trauma, so no way I was coming out after that." Kerri had been one of my best pals in the sixth grade. We were just learning about our bodies, partially from reading "The Whole Earth Catalogue," which had lots of sex stuff in it. Plus, my dad had piles of porn in his workshop – stuff like Oui, Cheri, Hustler and Playboy.

We'd read all this stuff and get turned on, so it seemed to me that we might want to try some of this stuff out. I sent her a note in class one day, very obviously asking her if she wanted to try some of what we were reading. Our star quarterback got a hold of the note and immediately told everyone who'd listen that Kerri and I were lezzies. I was harassed daily and immediately lost most of my girlfriends. One day, while sitting alone in the lunchroom, the well-known middle school bully Leeza decided to take the harassment up a notch. She got the whole lunchroom chanting stuff about "girls go with boys and boys go with girls," over and over.

The lunchroom went deathly quiet as Leeza walked up to me and flicked my headband off. Then she cackled in my face. I stood there with no idea what to do. I finally just left the lunchroom, walked down to the nurse's office and said I was sick. Which I was, since I started vomiting as soon as I made it to the bathroom. The nurse took one look at me and called my Grams, who was on the school's emergency pick-up list.

I didn't report the bullying to the school authorities or to my family because I was too ashamed of what had prompted it. I lie in my Grams' bed for the rest of the day, praying that I'd just have a heart attack or something and die.

Grams knew something was seriously wrong, and tried to get me to talk. But I'd heard her make a bigoted, hateful comment about Lily Tomlin earlier that year, so I was not about to share what had happened.

The next day, Leeza was waiting for me with "Thick Lips Moran," (she was famous with the boys for those lips) another bully. This time, the plan was to beat me up behind the library. "You, me behind the library and I'm gonna kick your ass." She said with one hand on her designer jeaned hip and the other pointing at me. "Yea," Thick Lips, echoed...like the dumb ass she was.

I had guts. I showed up at the appointed time ready to get the shit kicked out of me in the rain. But no one showed up. I rode my bike home sopping wet, only to meet my stepmom Irene at the front door. She demanded an explanation for my lateness, and I tried to explain. I thought I was being very brave!

Instead I got grounded!

I could still hear her lecture, like she was standing in front of me.

"Ladies do not fight, Lucy. I am so disappointed in you. Here I am, trying to raise you to be a lady, and you get into a fistfight. You're grounded. Take this book to your room." The book was Amy Vanderbilt's Book of Etiquette. Sure to solve all my problems.

About a week later, everyone had moved on to bully another girl, who was getting molested by her dad, or so they said. The worst was that the new victim went after me in the lunchroom, saying some shit about lezzies. I shot back "At least I'm not fucking my DAD," and immediately felt awful the minute it came out of my mouth. All the kids in the lunchroom cheered as she stormed off in tears.

I got sent to the office for saying fuck. Years later, I was at a party at Crystal's house, and the same girl showed up. My heart sank. We were much older now, eighteen or so, and I hoped she'd forgotten. She hadn't. She made some quip, so I stood up, went over to her, and apologized.

"I'm so completely sorry about what I said all those years back." I said. "I know, Lucy," she said kindly. "They were bullying you, too. It was a crappy time for us both, hun."

"Yeah." I mumbled.

We shared a couple of beers, and had a great talk about the group of jackasses who'd made our young lives hell. At the end of the evening, it felt like a weight had been lifted off my heart. Kerri, my former Whole Earth Catalogue friend, and I had never spoken again, after the middle school incident. I started reading a gay male porn magazine called *Inches* to try to *change myself* – I was going to learn to love the penis, and know everything there was to know about it! And I did, in a way...but you can't change Mother Nature.

Bradley looked shocked. He'd never heard the whole story. "Hey, I've got dirt on Miss Leeza... did you know that she's a lesbian now...ironic, huh?"

"Are you fucking kidding me?" I yelped, and for some reason, I was suddenly seriously pissed off.

"God, I wish you would have told me this story a long time ago! She and Thick Lips, and Linda..."

"Linda, the big slut?" I gasped. Wow!

Years later, I was at my friend Adele's house. She was a really tough Latina chick I'd met at the greenhouse where I'd worked that summer.

Adele and I were hanging out, and who showed up at the house but Leeza! I told Adele the basics of Leeza's bullying behavior in school, and Adele had wanted to kick her ass. I'd said no. Leeza, by this time, looked like death warmed over - her hair all ratted, bags under her eyes, and bruises all over her skinny legs. It was pitiful. She'd gotten her comeuppance, and she didn't need any more grief. My generosity of spirit wasn't rewarded. Leeza was a bitch to me all night.

Bradley and I reminisced into the wee hours. It was about 4 a.m. by the time we called it a night. The next morning, Amanda came over with a coffee cake she'd made and a broccoli, bacon, and cheese quiche. "I can feel my cholesterol levels going up by the second," Bradley said, drooling. He loved bacon.

After puttering around for a while, cleaning up after brunch, the three of us decided to go for a ride. Amanda and I rode double on Tao, and Bradley rode Amanda's horse, Hope.

"God, this is a beautiful place." Brad said as we got to the other side of the lake. We stood there and looked at the view for a few minutes, and then something caught my eye.

"What's that over there?" I asked, pointing to a red rowboat in the center of the lake, with what looked like a large blanket inside, just floating.

We all squinted at the spot. Brad spoke up first. "It looks like a guy, passed out in his boat."

"Oh, shit." said Amanda, and we galloped the horses to the dock and jumped into Amanda's boat.

A little old man was hunched over, just lying face forward over his cooler. Amanda jumped off our boat and into his, checking for signs of life. "He's still breathing," she said, relieved.

We called the hospital on my cell phone and they sent an ambulance. Eventually, they had the poor soul wrapped up in warming blankets and on a stretcher. The EMTs told us that he'd probably had a stroke.

We followed the ambulance and sat for a while in the ER waiting room, waiting for word on the patient. The word turned out to be pretty good. "His name is Fredrick Calhoun," the doctor told us, when he came out to let us know what was going on. "It's a good thing you found him when you did. He had a stroke, but we expect he'll make a full recovery." I couldn't help thinking that in America, we wouldn't have been told anything about the guy – it wasn't like we were family.

"Adventure in the outback," Bradley said, on our ride home.

"Why do you call it the outback? This is Canada, not Australia," Amanda said, laughing.

"It's all the same to me." Brad said.

When Bradley was ready to leave Randy stopped by with a souviner… his phone number and email and a pound of Tim Horton's coffee.

Amanda, Randy and I waved good-bye and the tears were rolling down my smiling cheeks.

Chapter 21

Ned came by bright and early for coffee, and to sneak a smoke. "Kathy would kill me if she saw me puffing," he said, inhaling a Marlboro Menthol.

"So, Amanda's back down to New York?" "I guess so...she never invites me! I'm starting to get city-jealous!" I said, only half joking.

Todd and the band had been over three nights a week practicing for our big gig, the one that would determine if K-Top music was going to sign us. And then I'd face a whole different set of questions, if they did sign us. Would we cut a CD? Would they spend money to publicize us? Would we tour? I wasn't a total novice in the music business, and I knew exactly what record companies could do to musicians.

A guy I sang with years ago had been signed by Sony and felt he was on top of the world, until it turned out that they just held his contract and did nothing. He never got the success he'd dreamed about, and had become bitter and jaded by the time I met him.

How big was I willing to dream? Was I willing to get excited about something that had a pretty good chance of not happening? That's when I wrote the song *Echo In A Silent Town*. Fear can be productive!

When Amanda came back from New York a few days later, she looked like death warmed over. "Honey," I said hugging her, letting her lay her head on my shoulder, "what are they doing up there to you in the Big Apple?"

"I just...it really exhausts me." Amanda said, looking blanched.

"Maybe next time I'll come with you, if you want..." I suggested. She sighed, and hugged me tighter, but didn't reply.

We joked around during lunch, and she told me some funny stories of things that happened during her trip. The best/worst story was that a bum had peed on her suitcase while she was standing on a street corner, so she had to buy all new clothes. Not to mention a new suitcase.

"My poor girl!" I emphasized, pouring her some more Devil's Lettuce coffee from Dark Matter coffee house in Chicago. Some people are wine snobs...I am a coffee connoisseur.

"When I get back from Montreal - after I meet with the music people," I said, "I'm going to go home to Hohman for a week. I'd like you to come. Change of scenery from New York and from Fossil Creek."

"Let me think about it." Amanda said.

"I like my solitude." Her response was deflating.

"Oh, come on," I said. "If you can deal with New York, Hohman is nothing!"

"Going to New York is different – I don't have a choice about that," Amanda snapped.

"Can I ask you why you don't want me to come with you?" I asked, feeling hurt. "Is that like...your special time? I mean, you always come home so sad and worn looking."

Amanda stood up and began pacing the kitchen. "I've got reasons..." she said then shook her head, her hair falling out of its loose ponytail.

"Ok." I said. "So what's the big deal?"

"The big deal," she said, then took a deep breath. "The big deal is Francine."

"Oh my God, your EX-LOVER Francine?" I choked. Suddenly very worried. "Your commune girlfriend? Are you...are you with her again? Or still?"

"No!" Amanda said defensively. "It's just, she's an old woman now, in poor health, and there's no one in her life to care for her. She's not a nice person. The reason I help her isn't so nice, either."

I sat back down at the kitchen table and lit up a smoke. If any discussion demanded a cigarette, this one did. "Go on." I prompted.

"I'm Francine's sole heir. She owns a building worth millions in Greenwich Village. Back when she bought it, the place was a flea-bag flop house piece of shit, but now with the area's real estate prices it's

– well, it's my retirement, let's say. The thing is, she knows what she's got, she knows that I know I'm her heir, and she holds it over my head so I'll take care of her. If she ever found out I had a lover, she'd freak out. She's old, but she's still crafty. She wants to have her fantasy of me being with her because I want to, not because I feel obligated."

"Have you seen the paper work?" I asked. "The actual will that names you as heir?"

"What?" Amanda said, giving me a blank look. "She says she's going to give you this golden egg, but do you have it in writing?"

"No." Amanda admitted. "She's got all the papers."

"You need to see them, especially if you're to do all this...service work for her. People say a lot of things when they're sick and alone – especially manipulative one's."

"Oh...God, I never thought about that," Amanda said. She looked stupefied. I sighed.

"Money is God in my family," I explained "and certain promises were made in my family. Promises that never got fulfilled, for one reason or another, but I took a lot of abuse with the understanding that those promises would be realized. So as much as I'm a pretty sweet person and I'd never screw anyone over...well, you need to know the rules of the game, if you're going to play it. My family made a hell of a lot of promises to me, and Uncle Tav was the only one who came through... the one person who never promised me anything." I stopped and looked at her huddled, like a child...so unlike the woman I knew.

Amanda, I learned it the hard way – no document, no ink, no deal. Like Samuel Goldwyn said, an oral contract isn't worth the paper it's written on. If you do nice things for her...do them because you care, that's really the bottom line.

Amanda still had said nothing. Was it that disease where the abused feels empathy for her captor?

"Francine won't know if I come up there with you," I said to Amanda.

"Well," she replied hesitantly, "I sort of...um, I stay with her when I visit."

"In her bed?" I asked, stunned.

"No!" Amanda assured me. "But she likes to believe we're still together, so..."

My mind was racing, trying to take in all this information, trying to figure out what this all meant, to me, to our relationship, to the trust between us, and all I could do was breathe deeply and try to stay calm. Freaking out wasn't going to help anything.

"Do you kiss her?" I asked. I wasn't sure I wanted to know the answer.

"We don't have sex, or make out...she's in a wheelchair, she's almost seventy." Amanda said evasively.

"That doesn't answer my question." I said quietly. "Don't judge me, Lucy, you've got it made. You've got no big financial worries, you own a big property outright, your life is set financially. I make a humble living, no retirement in sight - this is my only hope of having the financial freedom you take for granted."

"Oh no," I replied, stung. "Do NOT go there. You have no idea how broke I have been. My folks are good to me now, and Uncle Tav sure saved my ass, but I have lived in my car, I have lived on other people's couches so I could afford tuition at college, and my life has not always been pretty or even stable."

"It's not a good situation," Amanda backpedaled. "But if I...well, I'm, I'll get the paperwork I'll see what it says." Something just felt wrong about the whole deal, and I couldn't ignore it.

"Amanda," I said, "you've got to do what you've got to do. But let me tell you, it's not a good, warm feeling I'm getting here about our relationship."

"Don't leave me over this." Amanda begged. "Please, Lucy."

I sighed. "I've got enough of my own baggage. But you can't expect me to be thrilled about the situation."

"I love you. I don't want to lose you." Amanda said, suddenly serious and vulnerable. "It isn't a perfect world...and I wouldn't just throw away a chance to own a building in NYC." Judging a situation you had never been in was just stupid, but Amanda had always seemed so noble, living out here like a hermit, she suddenly seemed a lot more human. We had a quiet weekend together, not discussing any intense subjects, just being together. She went home on Sunday night, and we spent the night apart as we occasionally did. Was this the beginning of the end?

Monday morning, I glanced outside my office window when I heard a car on the gravel drive. An unfamiliar car was parked in our driveway, and the door to Amanda's cabin was open. I could see someone standing there, and hear her yelling pretty clearly.

"I knew something was going on!" the woman howled, the sound carrying all the way from Amanda's cabin to my house.

"What the hell are you talking about?" I heard Amanda shout back. I ran to my front porch to witness a showdown. This had to be Francine – it couldn't be anyone else, but she certainly wasn't the person I'd envisioned. My mental image of Amanda's ex was a sort of chubby hippy chick in a tie-dyed muumuu. But this woman was athletic-looking, wearing jeans and an expensive off-white Irish fisherman's sweater with a red turtleneck, her brown hair in a bun. Her face was chiseled and objectively attractive, especially for someone in her seventies, but the expression in her eyes reminded me of evil Nurse Rachet from One Flew Over the Cuckoo's Nest.

"All I had to do was go to the local shit-hole diner and drop a few hints - people talk, sister! What did you think, that you'd have your cake and eat it too?" Francine snarled.

It's not like I made a habit of watching people fight, normally, I tried to smooth over any unpleasantness as soon as it occurred. In this case, though, I had a strong feeling they needed to yell it out before I intervened.

I got a little closer to Amanda's house without either of them noticing.

"Listen, Mandy" said Francine meanly, "you're nothing but a two-bit dyke, without a pot to piss in. I've given you everything you've got that's worth anything, and you pay me back by hooking up with some big city lesbian who just moved to this God-forsaken shitty little town!"

What a bitch, I thought as I called Ned on my cell and told him there might be trouble coming, filling him in on the situation as quickly as I could.

He told me he'd pick up Todd and his pals on the way for backup, just in case.

Then Francine turned and saw me. She certainly wasn't wheelchair-bound and seemed pretty energetic, for an invalid, as she moved quickly towards me.

"You," she snapped at me, "get over here!" I walked down the stairs to the bottom of my front porch. I stood there, struck dumb by this crazy woman approaching me. But I'd at least had enough sense to grab the pepper spray before I'd left the house. Fossil Creek might be my home now, but I'd lived in Chicago too long to think that dealing with an explosive situation involving a nut job didn't require something in the way of protection.

"Hey, you're the cause of this shit, you little home-wrecker, so you face up to me!" Francine shouted, inches from my face.

I didn't flinch. "Home wrecker?" I snorted, crossing my arms and standing my ground. "I don't think so."

"You look like you've got some class - you want to be with that?" she sneered, pointing at a frazzled and distressed-looking Amanda.

"You claim to love her." I said calmly. "Why would you talk about her like that?

"Fuck you!" Francine shouted, and to my shock, went straight for my hair like an angry toddler. Comby, who had never attacked a creature larger than an ant, leaped between us and growled fiercely. Francine paused long enough to say "Hah, your little dog is going to attack me? This is rich."

"Francine," I said, "this is your shit. You and Amanda can deal with it the way you want. But let me tell you, I don't think you're going to warm her heart by insulting her and attacking me."

She screamed a stream of obscenities at me while I stood there, trying to figure out my next move. Comby was growling fiercely, and I held the pepper spray ready at my side.

I looked in the distance for Ned and the boys. My cell phone rang while Francine and I were staring one another down, startling both of us.

Then, over her head, I saw Big Bob, Ned, and the boys approaching in their trucks. The cavalry was arriving.

"I'm sorry." Amanda said. Francine turned around. Amanda had been talking to me, but then I realized it was a ploy to calm Francine down.

The guys quietly exited their vehicles and surrounded Francine as if she was a dangerous wild animal. Bob walked up to her and said something I couldn't overhear.

"Fine," Francine said loud enough for us all to hear. "But you haven't heard the end of this, Amanda." Then she got in her car and peeled out, Burt Reynolds style.

Ned told us that a waitress at the Diner had told him that Francine had rented a room at the B&B just off Main Street, so it looked like we weren't totally rid of her. Amanda nodded and said "I'll go talk to her. I think she may have been drunk."

Ned shook his head. "I don't know if that's such a good idea."

But Amanda had made up her mind. A few hours later, I was pacing the house. It had gotten dark, and my state of mind was equally gloomy. Comby was following me, concern in his eyes. Amanda called about eight to tell me that Francine had finally passed out.

"I wondered if she was drunk." I said. "Her breath could've straightened my hair," I said trying to lighten the mood.

"She was drunk." Amanda confirmed. "And she's leaving." "And..." I prompted, knowing there had to be more. "She cried, she spit in my face, and then she told me the truth. There's no building. You were right. It was all a way to manipulate me and keep me around."

"Oh, honey, that sucks," was all I could think to say.

"No." she said. "This lets me off the hook. It frees me. You have no idea how long this has been going on." Amanda was in my front room petting Comby by nine, and I felt relieved, but not secure. There was something a little dangerous about Francine, and I wouldn't be happy until she was on her way back to New York City.

We talked, and the mood was somber. "I've been such a fool. But she was like a mother to me...and it's true, she saved me when I was just a kid. She used to say it was only a matter of time before my dad crossed the line."

"That may have been the case but you left. She didn't brake down the door and beat him up."

She nodded, "Lucy I know the logic but it's like lloving any sick relative…you just can't let go."

That I could understand completely.

About ten, I was walking to my bedroom to get into my pajamas when I heard Amanda answer the front door, and talk to whoever was there. I detoured to see who it was and unsurprisingly it was our unwelcome guest.

Francine seemed a little calmer than she'd been this morning, but that wasn't saying much. "Sorry about this afternoon," she slurred, coming into the entryway when Amanda stood aside. She was walking in a funny way that gave me the creeps, holding her arm to her side. I was starting to wonder if she'd had a stroke until I saw the glint of steel.

"Oh, shit!" I gasped, as Amanda and I registered the knife at the same time. We both jumped back like lightning. Francine took a good long swipe at Amanda, leaping to grab onto her and letting out a blood-curdling scream. I yanked Francine back off Amanda by her hair with all the force I could muster and tripped her backwards with my foot. She landed hard on her back, and when she rolled onto her stomach, I slammed my knee into her neck, grabbing her hand and trying to knock the knife loose. It was no use – she had a death grip on that thing.

"Amanda, call the cops!" I yelled. She just stood there, holding her side, staring at Francine, blood dripping down over her fingers.

"Amanda!" I howled, "Now, Goddamit!" I kept slamming Francine's hand down, over and over, until she finally released her grip on the knife.

"If you fucking move, I will break your neck." I snarled. Where was my pepper spray when I needed it? Amanda finally managed to make the call, her hands shaking so badly she could barely dial her cell. Francine was gurgling and growling.

"Let her up," Amanda said, in an almost childlike way. I looked at her in disbelief. "No way." I said firmly. "Not until the cops get here. She just attacked you with a knife."

I didn't intend to take a knife to the gut or watch Amanda get murdered in front of me, so I was staying right where I was, pinning her down.

Lucky for us, one of the forestry guys was on duty close by. Henry and Big Bob were both deputized and heard the call over the radio. Henry came first, and Bob arrived almost immediately afterwards.

"Goddamnit," growled Bob, "I knew she was gonna go for round two." He was pissed, to say the least, and Amanda and I gave a short version of what had happened as Henry cuffed Francine. The Fossil Creek police chief finally showed up with the town's only squad car, and Francine was escorted out, cuffed and docile.

Amanda was not only terrified, she was emotionally confused, Francine had manipulated and twisted her emotionally for many years, which I could understand, to a certain extent. Irene's behavior with me over the years had certainly qualified me for an advanced degree in dealing with emotionally damaging people. I knew what it was like to hate someone who had a hold over you still.

When we finally got home, I held Amanda and let her cry, knowing only love and time could heal wounds this old and this deep.

I collected Francine's belongings and took them down to the station the next day. "Here, for when she gets released." I told the deputy. "It's not going to be for a while – we've found multiple restraining orders on her, plus a few outstanding warrants," he replied. The police chief explained that Amanda had not been the only victim of Francine's con. There was another, younger woman who had also been going through the same hell. Francine was extradited back to New York to be prosecuted for a whole laundry list of offenses. The young woman who's been Francine's latest victim was an underage runaway, so Francine was looking at some serious time in prison.

After the caustic effect Francine had put on Amanda's life it was a blessing when Amanda started seeing a therapist in Grover's Cove, one of the neighboring towns. Considering we'd only been together since October, I felt like we'd already been through enough traumas to fill up one lifetime.

March brought an early and much appreciated spring. Amanda started to build a storage shed for us, behind her cabin. It was more of a healing project then a necessary one.

"I painted a little sign for your new architectural endeavor." I told her, handing her the prize I'd created. The sign read "Outhouse," naturally. Amanda cracked up and grabbed me, swinging me around and planting a big kiss on my lips.

Later in the week, we raced our horses down by the beach. There were still patches of snow, even with the thaw, and the bunnies were out doing their bunny thing, nibbling on the new green buds.

"I have to admit, I'm ready for spring. This has been one damn long winter." I sighed, watching the ducks walk on the slowly melting ice of the lake.

"Get used to it, honey;" Amanda advised me. "We're facing long winters for the rest of our lives."

I liked the way she said that – the rest of our lives. It sounded good. I walked Tao over to her and we held hands, both mounted on our horses, and watched the sunset. I had a good feeling about what was to come, and for some reason, the worry about outcome of the band's foray into the big-time music business had all but disappeared.

Chapter 22

I dressed for success - well, what passed for it in the music business, at least. I wore a form-fitting black dress that made me look curvy and sexy, with black tights and black boots that came up over my knees. I'd chosen a pale foundation with smoky eyes and a pink nude lip-gloss, with my favorite black leather biker jacket (in the spirit of Lou Reed).

In my own humble opinion, I looked bad-ass pretty without trying to look like a teenager. The guys wore their "alternative" best - tight black pants, long sleeved t-shirts. Bradley had been nice enough to pick up the clothes at a high-end hipster boutique in Wicker Park, mailing them at his personal expense to Fossil Creek.

"I want pictures," Brad had reminded me.

Guy Savior, who was to be our new agent, was lucky if he was 5'1". I shook his hand and smiled as confidently as I could, towering over him in my high-heeled boots. We sat down in his office, which was decorated in gold albums, rock star concert posters and oddly enough, a ton of Cirque Du Soleil stuff. Turned out he'd been an investor, back with the troop was just launching.

The band talked with Savior about everything but business for the first hour, just having fun and getting to know one another. He managed a lot of Québécois acts like Raven, an old-school metal band; Paul Nello, who sounded a lot like a French version of Jack Johnson; and a sort of hip-hop group called Trois Fou Gatineau. In the states, he managed a band called La Bouche aux Deux. I'd looked them up online - they were a sort of gothic/pop rock kind of band that sounded a bit like the Cure.

Finally, we made our way into the rehearsal studio. Our first set was original song called *Sick As Your Worst Secrets*, and was inspired by the sound of an Irish punk band called Rudi. I had written it after being screwed over by two of my former co-workers back in Chicago. Guy nodded along and seemed to enjoy it. "Fun and snarky, I can see myself listening to it while I drive in a fast sports car down the highway," he said hopefully.

We moved on to our second tune, written by our keyboardist, Mick, called *Arrogant Bastard*. And who hasn't known a few of those in their lives! "A crowd pleaser," Guy nodded. Plus, it was a lot of fun to sing.

The refrain from *Drunk Lady* was a call and response comedy song that I wrote as a joke but then everyone liked it, (so did Guy).

Something Needs to Be Sacred was a little bit reggae/pop and our last tow had been co-written by Todd and me.We wanted to make sure our band didn't get pigeon holed as comedy-rock…or a novelty band so Good As It Get's and No Greater Love, were our big show stoppers…think Adele meets the Beatles.

Guy applauded when we were done, looking very excited, "the last two are your hits." He told us there were a couple other songs that he wanted to add, *Rapa Nui*, *How One Sided Have I Been* and *Spit In My Hair*. "I like your originals," Guy told us. "Honestly, I'm very surprised to hear them, since Bill made it sound like you were strictly a cover band." He kept talking as we held our collective breath. "I think we can work with you guys, I'm excited, Spit In Your Hair would be great for a movie soundtrack I'm working on," he guided us back down the hallway to his office, "let's go over the paper work and see what happens."

We were signing the contract with Presto Records, the "alternative" division of K-Top Music. The company was small and independent, so we weren't going to get rich. It was a good place to start, though, because Presto had strong connections in the music market.

The papers were signed, and the work began. I thought I'd be stressed and nervous in a professional studio, but actually it felt like home.

The boys in the band felt like family. Todd may have looked like Kurt Cobain but music was his drug…lead guitar, singer, songwriter and you know the rest. Mick doing keyboards and sax was the impish playful one who shared my love of comics and art, and Sims looked like Joey Ramone with his long hair obscuring his face but he played bass like Walter Becker of Steely Dan. Chibbs was our drummer and resident wild man. He idolized Ginger Baker from Cream...a little too much at times. He kept his emotions bottled up and then let loose on the drums but don't piss him off or a pint glass could be flying at your forehead.

It occurred to me that even though I'd been singing most of my life, I'd never had an opportunity to just hang out with a bunch of musicians and experience being with people who spoke the same language as I did. It helped that we all had similar musical influences - Neil Young, Squeeze, Stones, Concrete Blond, Lindsey Buckingham, Peter Gabriel, Van Halen, along with lesser-known acts like Steve Forbert, Millie Jackson, The Fatback Band, Roy Ayers, and Lemmy from Motorhead. We all loved soundtracks from movies like Times Square and Jackie Brown, along with the Troma Films horror punk compilation "Terror Firmer." It was a CD of little known punk bands, good for the raging-puberty crowd. I had become obsessed with classic soul and funk...and I was getting the guys addicted too. It was great to have a group of music nerds as obsessed as I was!

By the third full day of recording, I was really missing Amanda. The guys in the band were going out drinking. Sims, the bass player knew a bartender in town, a music fan who'd let the band drink for free. The whole crew disappeared as soon as rehearsal ended.

My best option, other than finding a meeting, was taking in a movie. I sat in the back of the theatre just as the lights went down. I settled in, Robert DeNiro was looking sexy (never loses that appeal) and some cheesy seventies music was playing when I noticed a shadow slowly advancing towards me. Before I could move away, the shadow put its arm around my shoulder and I knew exactly who it was. By this time, I could recognize Amanda's scent from across the room, and she was right here next to me. Amanda had come to me; she pulled me to her and kissed me deeply. No one was in the back row with us, so I just relaxed and let her make me weak in the knees.

"I'm so glad you're here," I said, coming up for air. "You being here makes it real somehow." I asked her how she found me.

Amanda confessed. "I was pitiful enough that the concierge told me you were here." Lucky for me, I'd asked the concierge for a movie recommendation, so he'd been able to tell Amanda where I was likely to be. Human GPS!

Amanda was being a very, very bad girl in the back row of the theatre, and I surrendered to her obvious plans with no protests. I didn't even notice most of the movie. We left not long after it ended, and grabbed a cab to the hotel. Amanda threw me on the bed like a wild woman, ravishing me with deep, longing kisses. The bed creaked like it would fall apart any moment. "Wow," I said, "I've got to go out of town more often!"

There was a CD player in the hotel room, and I put on a great WXRT mix compilation called "Live from The Archives." I'd picked it up at Starbucks before I left Chicago. It was one of the few 'unplugged' rock CD's I liked. It was pouring rain outside the window, and I stared out at the lights of Montreal, wrapped in a long robe. Amanda was taking a bath, and for one quick flash, I thought that my life couldn't get much better than this. Even if the music venture failed, it wouldn't matter, because my life was so beautiful. The last few months passed before me, each chord on Melissa Etheridge's guitar taking me down the winding paths of days...meeting Ned, singing karaoke at The Houndstooth, meeting Todd and sharing his life, my dad, my mom, learning about Greta and my own secret history. I thought about the cleansing, serene snowfalls and warm fires, moments with Amanda and the lodge, our horses, our friendships with Tippie, Janis, Bob, my job at The Hair Hut and my wonderful co-workers, even the awful confrontation with Francine that resulted in her incarceration and Amanda's freedom.

For once in my life, I didn't feel one step away from losing everything. No more living out of my car, in backpacks, waiting tables, no more bill collectors clogging up my voice mail, no more fear that a damaged hand would leave me out on the street with no way to make a living. No longer fearing Irene or feeling less than, because I was more than I ever thought I could be.

Nothing I had planned for my life had turned out the way I'd expected, but God had heard my prayers and had done a better job answering them then I'd thought. This, all from a girl who'd left Chicago to let go...

The next day at the studio, a woman came over to me, she was older, with an English accent and obviously knew the ropes. We struck up a conversation while I was on my break and she was on hers.

We started talking about songwriters, and how the reality of the music business was very different from the adolescent fantasies, she was very confident about her skills, unlike myself. She was a good listener and talker, telling me about the old days.

I felt a certain amount of jealousy, it sounded so amazing, so many great musicians. There was talent in every atom of the industry it seemed, back in the sixties, seventies and even the eighties. I longed for that kind of attention to detail the amazing pool of creativity. "Oh, it was full of shyster's and the industry was really sexist and racist, so it wasn't perfect. There's always challenges," She explained.

"Once the managers and money men took over it all became packaged, by the nineties, music was just another product. Only the independent labels really let people try anything risky...and risky is how rock and roll started," she said with conviction.

Amanda came over and proceeded to gush like a schoolgirl over my companion. "Oh," said Amanda, wide-eyed, "Miss Armatrading, I'm a huge fan of yours."

That's when it hit me, like being slapped with a side of beef: I'd been talking to a folk legend! I'd never been a huge fan of folk music, but I knew Joan Armatrading's name simply because I'd been part of the folk, jazz and women's music community. I felt like a fool, not knowing this woman I was talking to was Joan Armatrading, a hugely famous lesbian folksinger. She was on the XRT compilation I'd been listening to the night before. Another almost surreal coincidence, it seemed like I was right where I was supposed to be, doing just what I was supposed to be doing. The day turned into the night, then another day of recording, and the excitement mounted as each day passed.

Guy was extremely talented, and our producer Phil added special touches that made our music go from sounding like just another good bar band to a polished, professional group, adding sax (which I sorely missed in modern pop music), strings, and brass on some of the songs.

Todd and I had been playing around with a couple of new songs. Mick heard our rough demo of a song called "Algren", about writer Nelson Algren and Chicago's gritty city and told us he loved it. Guy was impressed that after the long days at the studio, we were still plugging away at night writing songs. But somehow, the band's commitment and passion, being in the studio, singing for an appreciative audience, had brought me back to my original love of the craft of music.

Our last day, I was beat, and glad I wasn't needed much. My voice was starting to sound rough, and I needed a break.

I kept thinking back to when I had met Etta Jones, (not to be confused with Etta James, had given me some wise vocal advice). Jones was a famous singer who had appeared at The Jazz Showcase where I was bartending many years ago. I had asked her the key to keeping the beautiful clarity and tone of her voice and she had said, "Baby, keep your sets short and great, and don't let the band drown you out."

I had broken all these rules over my years of singing, but I promised to myself not to forget those pearls of wisdom out on the road.

Amanda had blown me away. For an antisocial hermit, she was turning out to be a supportive, cheerful, and upbeat presence in our sessions. While we worked, she tapped away on her laptop in the background. She had a great way of being present, but not intrusive. She had even run out to grab us food and smokes late night!

We headed back to Fossil Creek high on joy, and with grand hopes for our future in the music business. There was still some mixing to be done, but Guy would call us as soon as the tracks were complete. Then we'd be setting up a touring schedule. The whole group of us stopped at a truck stop half way home and ate, excitedly talking a mile a minute. We'd gotten a small advance on our recording, and it seemed as if all things were possible. *Blinded By the Light* came on the radio and it was an absolutely magical moment. Also an omen, as it turned out.

We waited for word from Guy for weeks - there were pictures to take, and a kit had to be set up for promotion, requested by Presto.

Bradley had called me to let me know he'd found some great clothes for our low-budget shoot. "Girl," he told me, "I'm listening to Streisand's Superman and thinking of you! You're as close as I'll ever get to stardom... if you make it, you gotta get me in to meet her."

"Hold your horses, cowboy; things aren't even out of the gate yet." I replied.

"God, *you're so negative.*" He said dramatically.

"No," I sighed, "I'm just a realist."

He was getting exasperated with me, I could tell. He was huffing and puffing over his cell.

"You've never been this close before...it's gonna happen, I know it," he told me.

The bad news came at night. Amanda and I were painting the inside of her cottage when I heard my phone ringing through the open windows of our houses.

I was breathless when I answered the phone, grabbing it just before the answering machine kicked in. It was Guy.

"I figured it would be you," I said, panting. "I just had a feeling."

He was his normal cheerful self, but something was different. "Sweetie, I'll just tell you straight, Presto Records just went belly up."

"Oh, shit!" I gasped, stunned. "What about our tapes...the recordings, can we get them?"

"No...ah, they're going to be tied up in court. I can and will do my best to get them, but the owner, Bill, he's in big trouble financially, plus he's broken a few laws as well. Everything is locked up tight. I can't even get into my office," he said, and laughed uneasily. "I mean, right now, I don't have a job, I'm not getting paid, my salary is going to be tied up in court for the foreseeable future. I'm calling you from home to give you the heads-up because I like you guys, and we're all getting screwed on this one."

"Do the guys know?" I asked, in a fog of shock.

"I figured you could tell them."

"This really sucks."

"Tell me about it," Guy said miserably. "But don't give up hope. I hired an attorney and I'll do my best."

My next call was to Mr. Functer to see if he knew someone who could help us maybe a Canadian attorney could at least investigate and find out what was going on with Presto and the owner's multiple legal problems, and what we could do.

It didn't take long. A few days later, Mr. Functer gave me a call and explained what we were dealing with. "That Bill guy is bad news, Lucy. He's in more trouble than bankruptcy – he owned other companies, and all of them are being investigated for fraud, embezzlement, money laundering...really bad stuff."

The band had decided we'd go after the recordings that we'd made, but all Presto recordings were considered Bill's legal property – we'd signed a contract with Presto and received an advance in return for the music. There was going to be a LOT of red tape to get through before we could claim even copies, let alone the originals.

The guys took it as well as could be expected. I broke the news at the Houndstooth, as kindly as I could. Mick broke a beer bottle against the bar wall, Sims walked out of the bar entirely, and Todd stared at the floor. "Well," he sighed, "There's always mechanic school." Owen, the bartender, overheard the whole meeting and sent over some drinks on the condition that Mick didn't break any more bottles. By the end of the night, we'd pledged that we'd keep playing as a band simply for the joy of creating music, that we wouldn't let this experience sour our love of music and performing. Since we owned the copyright to our original songs, we could go record them somewhere else. Right now, though, we needed to rest and heal from our experience in professional music. For a moment, success had seemed so close, like when I'd heard the sax playing on our song *Funky Side of Life*. If we couldn't get those takes, if *Funky Side of Life* with the added sax was lost forever... we gave him *all* our songs!

I just cried, right then and there. The sound on those recordings was so professional and intimate, I didn't know if we could ever get that again. I was mad, at myself and at sleazy Bill and his legal troubles. I'd allowed myself to believe in the possibility of success and it hadn't happened. It hurt, worse than I'd thought it would.

Amanda seemed even more upset than I was – she was definitely more outraged, probably because she hadn't been involved in the bipolar nature of the music business before.

"After all that work you guys did, and all the hope they gave you, everything they talked about, digital distribution, CDs, touring – it's just fucking terrible! Lucy, you need to find another company."

"I thought the same thing, at first," I replied. "I have a feeling, though, that we need to let it ride. In a month, around my birthday, I'll give it some more thought. I'll have some more distance from the situation then. For now, we'll be playing every Saturday night at the Houndstooth, though we need to find a new bass player. Sims quit; he's done with the band."

Amanda hugged me until I felt like my guts would pop out, and it felt so good that I couldn't get myself all that worked up and upset. My music couldn't be killed or snuffed out. You can't kill spirit and that was one thing I had in this town, in my lover, and in my heart.

The internet was the new highway to the stars. We would put our music and maybe even my book (when it was done) on a website, connect it to YouTube and itunes and see how it rolled. I'm very scrappy... Lucy Zwich was if nothing else a survivor! The next adventure was just on the horizon!

Epilogue

It was such a beautiful day, Big Bob thought to himself. Good day to clean and polish his Ultra Glide Harley and go for a ride!

He got up from his desk by the window and that's when his heart stopped, his stomach dropped and he backed up into the shadows of his store.

His son Todd was pumping gas for one of the worst excuses for human filth that had ever walked into Bob's life. The reason he'd left the city and moved back to the safety of this small town.

"Red," Bob whispered, under his breath, "I thought you were dead."

Bob had been in a biker gang when he was young and full of whoop-ass. But after he'd seen Red kill a guy in a bar for bumping into him, he knew things would only get worse. Bob left, disappeared like smoke. But one thing Red knew is Bob could finger him for murder and bank robbery.

Red wasn't in town for a vacation, he was here to tie up some loose ends, permanently.

Suddenly Amanda's voice shocked him out of his silence. And for some reason he confided in her.

They would take care of the problem…together.

www.ingramcontent.com/pod-product-compliance
Lightning Source LLC
Chambersburg PA
CBHW051422170626
46809CB00006B/2282